THE
CLUB

THE CLUB

Empire, Power and the Governance
of World Cricket

ROD LYALL

First published by Pitch Publishing, 2025

1

Pitch Publishing
9 Donnington Park,
85 Birdham Road,
Chichester, West Sussex,
PO20 7AJ

www.pitchpublishing.co.uk
info@pitchpublishing.co.uk

© 2025, Rod Lyall

Every effort has been made to trace the copyright.
Any oversight will be rectified in future editions at the
earliest opportunity by the publisher.

All rights reserved. No part of this book may be reproduced,
sold or utilised in any form or transmitted in any form or by
any means, electronic or mechanical, including photocopying,
recording or by any information storage and retrieval system,
without prior permission in writing from the publisher.

A CIP catalogue record is available for this book
from the British Library.

ISBN 978 1 80150 950 3

Typesetting and origination by Pitch Publishing

Printed and bound on FSC® certified paper in line with
our continuing commitment to ethical business practices,
sustainability and the environment.

Printed and bound in India by Thomson Press

Contents

Abbreviations 9

1. Introduction: Two Worlds, One Game 11

PART I: Colonial Governance, 1907–1989 19
2. The Imperial Dream 21
3. Widening the Circle, 1926–1939 41
4. From Empire to Commonwealth, 1945–1961 58
5. The South Africa Crisis and Beyond, 1961–1968 . . 73
6. The Tectonic Plates Begin to Shift, 1968–1978 . . . 88
7. Platitudes and Procrastinations, 1979–1989 108

PART II: The Global Game, 1989–present 129
8. A Governing Body Fit for Purpose? 131
9. Lord Woolf, the Gang of Three and Beyond . . . 150
10. Events, Dear Boy, Events 169
11. The Future Tours Programme 192
12. Global Development 212
13. Women's Cricket 230
14. Umpires, Referees and Technology 248
15. Cricket's Dirty Secret: Match Fixing and Corruption 269
16. The Olympic Question 285
17. Franchises and an Uncertain Future 299

Acknowledgements 309
Notes on Sources 311
Index 314

For my father,

who introduced me to cricket,

and Ron Halcombe,

who helped me to understand it.

Abbreviations

ACB	Australian Cricket Board (1973–2003)
ACB	Afghanistan Cricket Board
ACC	Asian Cricket Council
ACU	Anti-Corruption Unit
BCB	Bangladesh Cricket Board
BCCI	Board of Control for Cricket in India
BCCP	Board of Control for Cricket in Pakistan (1949–1994)
CA	Cricket Australia (since 2003)
CEC	Chief Executives' Committee (since 2015)
CSA	Cricket South Africa (since 2002)
CWI	Cricket West Indies (since 2015)
DLS	Duckworth-Lewis-Stern system
DRS	Decision Review System
EAP	East Asia Pacific Region (ICC)
ECB	England and Wales Cricket Board (since 1997)
F&CA	Finance and Commercial Affairs Committee
FICA	Federation of International Cricketers' Associations
FTP	Future Tours Programme
GDP	Global Development Programme
HPP	High Performance Programme
ICC	Imperial Cricket Conference (1909–1965); International Cricket Conference (1965–); International Cricket Council
ICL	Indian Cricket League
IOC	International Olympic Committee
IPL	Indian Premier League
IWCC	International Women's Cricket Council
MCC	Marylebone Cricket Club

MOU	Memorandum of Understanding
MPA	Members' Participation Agreement
ODI	One-Day International
PCB	Pakistan Cricket Board (since 1994)
RDO	Regional Development Officer
SAACB	South African African African Cricket Board
SACA	South African Cricket Association
SACBOC	South African Cricket Board of Control
SACU	South African Cricket Union (1976–1991)
SANROC	South African Non-Racial Olympic Committee
TAPP	Targeted Assistance and Performance Programme
TCCB	Test and County Cricket Board (1966–1997)
UAE	United Arab Emirates
UCB	United Cricket Board of South Africa (1991–2008)
WADA	World Anti-Doping Agency
WICB	West Indies Cricket Board (before 2015)
WTC	World Test Championship
ZC	Zimbabwe Cricket (since 2004)
ZCU	Zimbabwe Cricket Union (1992–2004)

Chapter 1

Introduction: Two Worlds, One Game

ON 1 February 2012 the governing body of world cricket, the International Cricket Council, received a report which it had commissioned less than four months previously, entitled 'An independent governance review'. Its authors were Lord Woolf of Barnes, a former Lord Chief Justice in the UK, and a team from PricewaterhouseCoopers, the respected international professional services company, assisted by Mukul Mudgal, a former Chief Justice of Punjab. Charged with ensuring 'that the ICC is a recognised leader in the field of the governance of sports organisations', the review team conducted 60 interviews and received submissions from governing bodies, cricketers' associations, journalists and other interested parties in 38 countries. Its report was damning from the very outset: 'Cricket is a great game. It deserves to have governance, including management and ethics, worthy of the sport. This is not the position at the present time.

'The game is too big and globally important,' it went on to declare, 'to permit continuation of full Member boards using the ICC as a "club".' Its 65 recommendations amounted to nothing less than a complete overhaul of what the team evidently saw as a radically dysfunctional organisation, one of the greatest weaknesses of which was the fact that its current directors tended to see their 'fiduciary duty' as being to the national boards they represented, rather than to the ICC and the game it existed to administer and promote.

While it was careful not to name names, the Woolf report left little doubt that its authors saw the principal culprits as the representatives of the Board of Control for Cricket in India (BCCI). Over the previous two decades it had become by far the most powerful of the ICC's 105 members, ten of which had the status of full members, giving them an automatic place on the board. Unsurprisingly perhaps, the BCCI secretary categorically rejected the report within a fortnight of its release. Although a few of the recommendations were implemented, on points where the first steps had already been taken, the core principles of the proposed restructuring were rejected, especially those which related to the abolition of a resource distribution model which strongly favoured the full members. Worse still, in 2014 the BCCI, together with its new allies England and Australia, instigated a different series of changes, which reinforced the power of what became known as 'the Gang of Three', making the situation even worse than it had been before the review was commissioned. Lord Woolf was outraged, describing these new proposals as 'a retrograde step' which seemed to be 'entirely motivated by money'. If they were implemented, the ICC would become 'a members' club – with a very small number of members'.

But that was precisely what the ICC had always been, from its inception in 1909. The number of club members had varied, and so, to a degree, had the conditions for membership, but there is no question that from the formation of the Imperial Cricket Conference and throughout its history, the central objective had remained the same: to concentrate power in a small number of hands, and to protect the interests of that small group at the expense of anyone else who might venture to play the game. For all their high-flown talk about cricket being 'a gentlemen's game' and their invocation of 'the Spirit of Cricket' (since 2000 incorporated as a Preamble to the Laws), the sport's administrators had been consistent in their exploitation of race and class to maintain their grasp on power. The imperial regime presided over by MCC has given way to a corporatist regime presided over by the BCCI, but the underlying defects in governance remain. How this unhappy situation was created and then allowed to persist is the story we have to tell.

The changes proposed by the BCCI and its allies in 2014 were duly implemented, although three years later a coalition of other members was able to claw back some of the most obvious injustices arising from that coup, not least an absurdly unbalanced revenue distribution formula. Even under the distribution which was agreed in 2018 for the five years up to 2023, the BCCI took 22.8% of the money distributed to the members, while the top nine full members between them received 81% of the total. Zimbabwe, Afghanistan and Ireland were given about 10% between them, leaving just 9% for the remaining 94 members, an average per associate of 0.096% of the whole. And this, it must be remembered, was 'fairer' than the allocation which had prevailed between 2014 and 2018. The new formula was insufficient for the BCCI, and in 2023 another new model shifted the balance back their way. The root-and-branch reforms proposed by the Woolf review have never had the remotest chance of being put into effect.

It would be hard to imagine a greater contrast than that between the modern complex in Dubai's Sports City which houses the International Cricket Council, a green oasis in a desert landscape, and Lord's Cricket Ground in leafy, busy St John's Wood in London, where, over a century ago, the ICC was created. It was called the Imperial Cricket Conference back then, and those two changes of wording, from 'Imperial' to 'International' and from 'Conference' to

'Council', encapsulate the essence of the story. Born at the high-water mark of British imperialism, with the King-Emperor Edward VII on the throne and the Second South African War of 1899–1902 a recent memory, the Imperial Cricket Conference set out to harness the power of sport to bind together the scattered elements of Empire. For nearly 80 years, through the tumult of two world wars, the painful upheaval of partition in India, the transition from Empire to Commonwealth and the challenge of South Africa's brutal apartheid regime, it continued to do so. Throughout that period the Conference was managed, and largely controlled, by Marylebone Cricket Club from its offices at Lord's, and indeed it was described by one keen observer as 'MCC's Foreign Desk'.

But by the late 1980s the world had changed, and cricket had changed with it. The Conference's central task had always been to decide which countries would be recognised as entitled to play Test matches, the multi-day international games which were the sport's gold standard, initially restricted to England, Australia and South Africa. In 1926 the magic circle had been extended to include India, New Zealand and the West Indies, and in 1952, after some hesitation, the newly created state of Pakistan had been admitted as well. The rules still specified that only members of the Commonwealth could join, and after South Africa's abrupt departure in 1961 the six remaining governing bodies of cricket split into two factions: England, Australia and their ally New Zealand, who continued to play against the all-white South Africans, were generally ranged against India, Pakistan and the West Indies. The polarisation was not universal; there were issues, such as the limitation of short-pitched intimidatory bowling, on which Australia and the West Indies, with their fearsome batteries of fast bowlers, held out against the rest. But in general, the division was unmistakably along racial lines, with the white nations of the 'Old' Commonwealth opposed by the representatives of countries which had won their independence from the Empire.

Two other big changes had also transformed cricket's landscape. One was the creation, initiated by Pakistan, of a new category of associate membership, linked to the abolition of the old requirement that ICC members had to be from Commonwealth countries. The first associates accordingly included the United States, which might conceivably have been invited to join in 1909 but had been kept out by that unfortunate War of Independence back in the 1770s, as well as Denmark and the Netherlands. By 1987 the number of associates had grown to 19, far outnumbering the seven full members, now augmented by the inclusion of Sri Lanka, even though the full members had two votes each to the associates' one. The other great change was the emergence of limited-overs cricket, an alternative international playing format which greatly increased the game's attractiveness and which had opened the way to a World Cup, in which the leading countries could battle out a world championship in matches which lasted a single day; this brought cricket into line with other global sports where winning a world title was the unquestioned pinnacle of endeavour.

One-day cricket, moreover, had brought with it commercial opportunities of which the ICC's founders could not have dreamed. In 1977 the Australian media magnate Kerry Packer had set up a breakaway international series which challenged the sport's traditional authorities, subjecting them in the process to a humiliating legal defeat. Order had eventually been restored, but Packer's money had shown the players that they were entitled to demand fair remuneration for their skills and efforts, while Packer's radical approach had brought significant changes to the game itself: improved television coverage, evening cricket under floodlights, coloured clothing and a hyped-up razzamatazz which would increasingly characterise the game. He had also drawn attention to cricket's ability to bring in enormous sums through the sale of media rights, and that turned out to be the biggest change of all.

Nowhere was that lesson learned more effectively than in India, with its population of billions and an enthusiasm for cricket which seemingly knew no bounds. The BCCI, led by a series of entrepreneurial figures who made Packer look like a shrinking violet, not only made media deals which transformed their organisation, but used that wealth to exert ever-increasing power within the ICC. Between 1987 and 1997 there was a fundamental shift, evidenced in specific issues like the hosting rights for the 1996 World Cup and election to the chairmanship, but reflecting a clear transfer of power from England and its traditional allies to India. That change was cemented in 2005 with the relocation of the ICC's headquarters from Lord's to Dubai; the ostensible reason was the tax advantage offered by the emirate's government, but it also brought the organisation closer to its new powerbase in the subcontinent, a symbol of the new, post-colonial order.

As all this was happening, the ICC was further transformed by the appointment in 1993 of its first full-time chief executive, the Australian David Richards. Under Richards and even more under his successor, fellow Australian Malcolm Speed, who took over in 2001, the Council morphed from a talking shop with a part-time secretariat into a fully professional global governing body, steadily extending its reach into more and more aspects of the game. Here, inevitably, there was a contradiction and a potential source of conflict: the Dubai-based managers had their own agendas, but the national boards, especially India and its allies, were keen to retain control over policy, and above all over the money. Some things did not change: the ICC's gatekeeping function, ensuring that a small number of members, the Test-playing nations, retained their exclusive status and their political control, was as strong as ever, even if it was now the BCCI which was calling the shots rather than MCC. But the style was completely different: MCC had ruled with the gloved hand of imperial diplomacy, while the techniques of post-imperial global corporatism were a good deal less subtle. The changed media environment, too, and the size of the financial stakes, ensured that whereas the political battles of the Imperial Cricket Conference had largely taken place behind closed doors, with a bland press release their only public face, those of the International Cricket Council were often played out before the glare of a media pack which was hungry for sensation and not afraid to speak its mind.

The gradual extension of the ICC's reach had many benefits for international cricket. The Imperial Conference had already been interesting itself in possible modifications of the Laws as early as the 1920s, but MCC retained the final word on changes – as indeed, it still does. The introduction of different formats, however, and the establishment of global competitions such as the World Cups, created room for regulations and playing conditions which the ICC itself could set, and it was not slow in doing so. Features of the modern game, like power plays and fielding restrictions, do not appear in the Laws but are enshrined in the ICC's Playing Conditions. The Code of Conduct for players – and officials – which was introduced by Colin Cowdrey in 1991 has now been incorporated into the Laws, and match referees, brought in to enforce that Code, have become an unquestioned part of the international scene. The use of neutral umpires, too, while it did not eliminate controversy over bias in decision-making, had a beneficial effect, and the same might be said of the use of technology to resolve doubtful decisions and remove as many umpiring errors as possible. The approval of venues for international matches, the monitoring of the standard of pitches and of potentially illegal bowling actions, the promotion of women's cricket following the ICC's amalgamation with the International Women's Cricket Council in 2005, and the fostering of the game in countries where it is a new or minority sport through its Global Development Programme, all show the ICC as a modern, global governing body. Even the crisis around an epidemic of match fixing in the 1980s and 1990s was eventually dealt with, and the ICC's Anti-Corruption Unit keeps a steady eye on the ever-present threat of illegal gambling and its subversion of the game.

Yet that positive image is still undermined by the structural failings in governance which Lord Woolf identified and which the response to his proposals further demonstrated. The power of a small number of members to defy the rest remains as strong as ever, and international cricket now faces a new challenge in the lucrative franchise leagues which, spearheaded by the BCCI's Indian Premier League, occupy increasing chunks of the calendar and could, if they are not held in check, squeeze the traditional contests between national teams out altogether. Such a development was foreshadowed, approvingly, by the BCCI's I.S. Bindra in 2005, and his claim that a franchise league 'can be bigger than international cricket' has in part been borne out by much that has happened since. It is not inconceivable, if current trends continue, that the ICC itself will be consigned to the margins of the world game. Were that to be the case, those administrators who so consistently failed to see its fundamental weaknesses and so resolutely pursued their own interests at the expense of the game as a whole would bear the greatest responsibility for its demise.

PART I

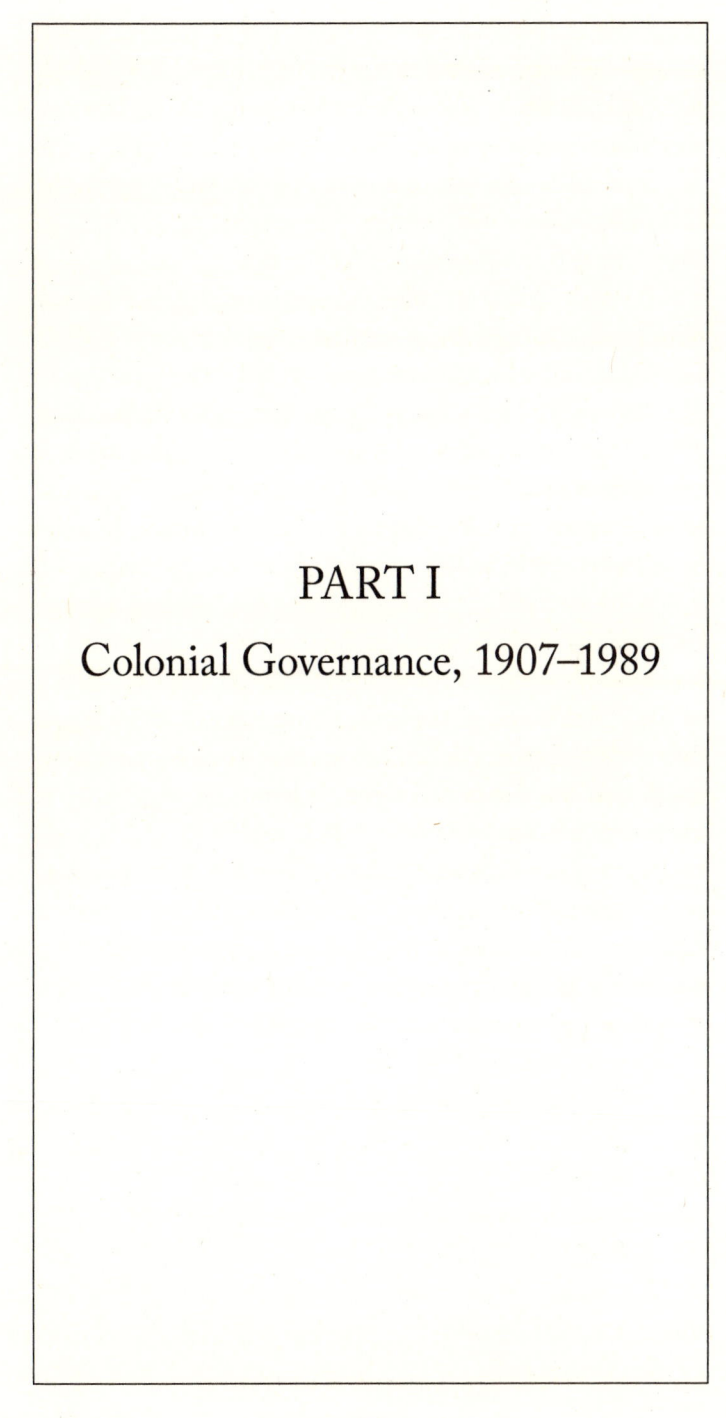

Colonial Governance, 1907–1989

Chapter 2

The Imperial Dream

THE CLUE was in the name. When representatives of England, Australia and South Africa assembled at Lord's on 15 June 1909, with a second meeting on 20 July, the most important issue facing them was a proposal for triangular Test tournaments between the three countries, with the aim of tightening the bonds of Empire. It was, moreover, to become a conference, rather than the Board of Control which had initially been envisaged by its instigator, the 43-year-old mining magnate, Imperialist politician and cricket administrator Abe Bailey. It had taken rather longer to reach this historic moment than Bailey himself had hoped, but the context of the occasion would have far-reaching consequences, determining the future shape of world cricket in ways its participants could not have imagined. The new body's scope would be firmly limited to countries within the Empire, and it would be a relatively informal conference with vaguely defined powers.

The dream had begun with Bailey, who had watched the progress of the South African team on its tour of England in the summer of 1907, and who then conceived the notion of a triangular series involving England, Australia and South Africa. The germ of Bailey's idea existed as early as August, when it was reported in the London *Daily News*, but he formally introduced it with a letter, written on board the *Walmer Castle* on 30 November as he was returning to South Africa, to Francis Lacey, the secretary of MCC. He envisaged, he wrote, 'a triangular or imperial cricket contest' and the choice of the term *imperial* was clearly not incidental, since 'inter-rivalry within the Empire cannot but fail [sic] to draw together in closer friendly interest all those many thousands of our kinsmen who regard cricket as their national sport; while, secondly, it would probably give direct stimulus to amateurism.' The first step, Bailey suggested, 'would be to form an Imperial Cricket Board, to formulate the necessary rules and regulations'.

Bailey's project flowed naturally out of his political convictions: having long been an associate of Cecil Rhodes and involved in the planning of the 1895/96 Jameson Raid which attempted to overthrow the Afrikaner-controlled South African Republic, he was one of 59 participants in that coup to be subsequently tried in Pretoria, receiving a sentence of five months' imprisonment. He subsequently served on the British side in the Second South African War, and immediately after the Treaty of Vereeniging brought that war to an end in May 1902 he was elected unopposed to the Legislative Assembly of the Cape Colony, succeeding no less a figure than Cecil Rhodes himself as the pro-imperialist Progressive Party's member for Barkly West. By early 1908 Bailey had become the Progressive member for Krugersdorp in the newly established Transvaal parliament, and the party's senior whip. Earlier in his career, in March 1894, he had played two Currie Cup matches for Transvaal, taking 3-28 and 4-51 against Natal at Newlands, and four years later, as the war clouds were gathering, he had brought his own Transvaal XI to Durban to take on Natal. In the aftermath of the war British policy was to bring the four colonies into a single union; two – Transvaal and the Orange Free State – had been Afrikaner republics and were now to be self-governing British colonies, alongside the Cape Colony and Natal. But international teams from the four colonies had been playing cricket as South Africa since 1889 and rugby union since 1891, and it was evident that sport could be a powerful unifying influence. For men like Bailey, it was equally important that South Africa should become an integral part of the British Empire, and as president of the South African Cricket Association he saw an opportunity to reinforce the point through his 'imperial tournament'.

The proposal fell upon receptive ground in England where, on 10 December 1907, Lacey promptly put it before the secretaries of the first-class counties at their annual meeting at Lord's. It was claimed by the promoters of the scheme, he was reported as saying, 'that if it were carried out it would be an important factor in keeping alive those currents of friendship which move between the countries mentioned, and he felt certain that they ought, if necessary, to make some sacrifice to carry the scheme into operation'. The latter observation was a shrewd one: a triangular competition would self-evidently disrupt the Championship programme and distract public attention from it, and Lacey attempted to head off objections of this kind by appealing to the county administrators' better natures.

An article in the following day's *Lancashire Evening Post* indicated that not everyone would be as enthusiastic about the idea as the MCC secretary. 'Another step in the invasion of the domain of sport by the Imperial idea,' it began, going on to observe that 'the counties will have to consider how the scheme will affect them, for after all they have to consider themselves first' and adding that 'it is just possible that in seeking after fresh contests people are forgetting that the backbone of first-class cricket is, and must be, the inter-county matches.' But this reservation may have also reflected a certain scepticism about the Imperial project itself: immediately after its discussion of Bailey's plan the *Post* announced the award of the Nobel Prize for Literature to Rudyard Kipling, commenting that while the prize was fully deserved:

'There is only a touch of regret among many that in later years the author has used his pen on behalf of a somewhat tinsel Imperialism, the Imperialism that glitters and fades, rather than for the greater objects of Imperialism, which have been left to more practical and not less earnest minds to advance.'

The paper left unstated its view about whether Bailey's proposal for an Imperial cricket tournament was part of 'a somewhat tinsel Imperialism' or whether he was one of the 'more practical and not less earnest minds'.

The scheme was, of course, notable for what it excluded as much as for what it envisaged. In 1907 only three countries had played what were already being called Test matches, but cricket was being played at a good level in other parts of the Empire as well. Indeed, Ernest Wynyard, whom Bailey had nominated as his representative in England, had toured New Zealand, the West Indies and North America with MCC teams in the previous three years, while an observer at the counties' meeting on 10 December was none other than K.S. Ranjitsinhji, the former England Test cricketer who had recently been installed by the British as Jam Sahib of Nawanagar. Although there was as yet no first-class competition in India, the game had been enthusiastically adopted by most communities, and there were regular inter-communal tournaments in Bombay (now Mumbai) and elsewhere. Furthermore, the meeting heard of plans for a tour the following season by the Philadelphians, while the Gentlemen of Philadelphia, who had already had full tours of England in 1897 and 1903, were acknowledged as one of the finest first-class teams anywhere. Yet they were excluded when cricket was viewed through the narrow prism of Bailey's Imperial project.

Bailey was able to marshal influential support for his proposal. C.B. Fry, one of the most influential of cricket writers as well as being among the greatest players of his day, declared himself in favour; his arguments, however, were practical rather than ideological. Only at the very end of his article in the March 1908 issue of his *Magazine* did he declare that 'Cricket is the one game common to our race everywhere, and alone of all games holds the British imagination,' adding that the proposed tournament was 'the one and only medium for the realisation of the ideal of a Pan-Britannic Olympia'. In January Dr Leander Starr Jameson, the Prime Minister of the Cape Colony, who had instigated that 1895 raid upon the Transvaal which led ultimately to the Second South African War, had declared that he welcomed the scheme 'not only as promoting healthy rivalry in the great national game, but also in its broader significance, which no doubt actuated the mind of the author of the proposal – namely, a popular agency for drawing closer the ties which united the scattered peoples of the Empire, contributing as it must do to influences which served to make them conscious of the national and manly characteristics which they possessed in common.' These sentiments were soon echoed by the Earl of Selborne, the High Commissioner for Southern Africa and Governor of Transvaal and Orange River, who deemed the project both as 'a splendid thing from the point of view of sport' and as having 'a real political value': 'Foreigners may not understand it, but I am quite sure that every time a team of Springboks or cricketers is brought together, representing the whole of South Africa ... the sense of South African unity is increased, and this without distinction between Boers and British. There is no doubt that the Boers followed with intense interest the Springboks' triumphs.'

The political value of the scheme, however, was not restricted to South Africa: 'The more the reality of the Empire is brought home to its people in any shape or form the more the idea becomes part of their natural being, and as there are more people interested in sport than in politics, art, literature, or business, there is a larger number who are touched by the influence of such a contest.'

One could scarcely imagine a more transparent avowal of the ideological intentions of the proposal's supporters, or of the close interconnection of sport and politics.

The MCC committee had referred the scheme to the Advisory Committee of the Counties and on 27 January they supported it in principle, although *The Sportsman* reported that 'the opinions as to how the same might be carried through were very divergent'. The resolution which was passed declared that the counties 'are prepared, subject to the consideration of a detailed scheme, to assist MCC if MCC see fit to invite elevens from Australia and South Africa in 1909 for the purposes of an Imperial Cricket Contest'. Welcoming this decision, Bailey stated that he was 'of opinion that the committee had been influenced by the Imperial aspect of the case' but added that it must be practicable in the view of 'the level-headed businessmen who formed the meeting'.

Meanwhile, lively public debate continued. J. Astley Cooper, who had long been a proponent of a 'Pan-Britannic Games' (which would ultimately come about as the 1930 Empire Games), while believing 'in sport as a healthy federating force for the Empire', described Bailey's scheme as 'too complicated, too artificial, and will ultimately, if it is ever attempted, break down of its own weight'. He would prefer a challenge system, whereby the principle of the Ashes would be extended to allow any Test-playing country to challenge the current holders of the Imperial championship. To this the formidable Lord Harris replied that all the MCC was doing was asking Australia and South Africa whether they wished to take part in a triangular tournament, 'and if they would not like to there was an end of it'. But Cooper insisted that his concern was that 'other communities of the Empire' might emerge at Test level and then be entitled to take part in a tournament which would thus become too unwieldy: 'It would be a simpler plan,' he observed, 'but just as Imperial in its effects, if now that Australia had defeated

England, the South Africans should try their fortune at the Antipodes for the rescue of the "Ashes," and so on.'

On 6 March 1908 MCC unveiled its detailed proposals, which included three-match series of three-day Tests between the three participating countries, running from 31 May 1909 to 23 August. The tours by Australia and South Africa would involve matches against all the first-class counties and MCC. Cables were promptly sent to the Australian and South African authorities inviting them to take part, with South Africa cabling its acceptance by return. Overjoyed, Bailey told Reuters that South Africa appreciated the spirit in which his proposal had been accepted by MCC and the counties, adding that they no doubt realised 'the great importance from an Imperial point of view of such contests'. It was, he said, necessary to convene an Imperial Cricket Conference, where 'all details as to the future carrying out of the game shall be thoroughly thrashed out'.

Even in England, not everyone shared Bailey's views. Commenting on the 'frigid reception' which MCC's draft rules had received, the *Observer* coupled its dissent with a rather unfair attack upon the South African himself: 'It needed no millionaire Maecenas, to whom the glories of cricket were suddenly unfolded, to preach the imperialism of the greatest of all games. The very nature of cricket is imperial; and the best side of its imperialism is not seen when England and Australia are engaged in six-day trials of endurance ... but in that real cricket of the counties, when two more or less indigenous sides are striving in chivalrous sport for the honour of their shires.' Bailey was, of course, no newcomer to the game, but the *Observer*'s Little Englandism was a genuine challenge to the imperialism which he so enthusiastically espoused.

In Australia, too, there were doubts about the whole idea, although there was plenty of support for the imperial concept there and Australians had fought in large numbers on the British side in South Africa. Already towards the end of December 1907 the former Test cricketer Frank Iredale had cabled the *Daily Mail* to declare that 'the possibility is remote of the Australian Cricket Board of Control agreeing to Mr Abe Bailey's proposal', and when MCC's detailed plans became available at the beginning of March the Sydney *Daily Telegraph* commented that 'it is known ... that a majority of the delegates [to the Australian Board] consider the scheme financially impracticable'. The board held a special meeting in Melbourne on 29 May 1908 to consider MCC cables as well as letters from Bailey himself and its own representative in England, the 31-year-old medical graduate and first-class cricketer Dr Leslie Poidevin. Iredale led the charge, moving 'that a Cable be sent to the Marylebone Club Stating that Australia declines to accept proposed Triangular Scheme'. The motion was seconded by the former Australian captain Joe Darling, who went on to propose that should MCC not immediately invite Australia to send a team to England for a bilateral series the board should ask whether such a visit would be welcome. At the same time, the board rebuffed a separate approach from the South Africans regarding an Australian visit to the Union in 1909, Iredale and Darling again combining to move that 'they must first return Australia's visit before any further matches can be played by Australia in South Africa'.

The board cabled MCC the same day, officially declining the invitation to take part. No reasons were given, and a furious debate ensued. Interestingly, at least one newspaper juxtaposed this news with the financial outcome of the recent MCC tour of Australia, for which the states would have to contribute a levy of almost £2,600 to cover the tourists' guaranteed £10,000 and noted that '[p]ossibly these figures will gave pause to those cricketers who think Imperially, especially when it is known that three matches during this tour caused a loss'. That money was at the heart of the Australian position is confirmed by an article in the Melbourne *Herald* of 5 June, in which a columnist calling himself 'Old Cricketer' discussed the board's decision to reject the proposal for a tournament in 1909. 'Although money matters are not the only, or even the chief, cause of the Board's present decision,' he wrote, 'the financial side of the question contains its genuine problems. Australian cricketers prefer to make their own financial arrangements, and they may decide that the triangular prospect is "not good enough". Under such circumstances, the Board would be compelled either to guarantee our men, or seek guarantee from Marylebone, as the London Club did from the Board. Another alternative would be the selection of players who would be prepared to represent Australia, and either accept any financial risk involved in so doing or accept such terms as the Board of Control could offer.'

But other factors undoubtedly played a part as well: when a Reuters correspondent interviewed several members of the Australian team, the view that South Africa should prove itself in Australia before being admitted to a triangular contest was also seen as an issue, while according to a letter from Monty Noble, perhaps the most sympathetic of the Australian players, it was the question of the Tests lasting only three days rather than being played to a finish which most influenced the Australian position.

Australia's refusal triggered an internal debate in England, some taking the view that if Australia were not prepared to take part in a triangular tournament, they should not be invited to tour England on their own. Others – including the MCC committee – favoured such an invitation. The Advisory Committee met on 3 July, and Fry's motion that the counties support the triangular contest was carried by 14 votes to 3. And when Dr Russell Bencraft proposed that MCC should impress on the Australian board 'that the Counties are so strongly in favour of the Triangular Contest that MCC would not be in a position to invite any Colonial Eleven in 1909, except for that purpose', his amendment too was carried, by 11 votes to 3. Not everyone was happy with this, and the minutes proved so contentious that a further meeting was held on 29 July, where a debate worthy of a Savoy opera ensued about who had said what during the earlier discussion. It was unclear whether a formal invitation had already been issued by MCC for Australia to tour in 1909 irrespective of any triangular tournament, although it was quite evident that the Australian board's rejection of the latter proposal had effectively ended the possibility of it taking place that season. 'That,' the chairman, Lord Harris, declared, 'has all passed away; there is no chance of that now.' And after a tortuous discussion the meeting agreed that the invitation to the Australians should be renewed.

This was a reverse for Bailey, but he was far from beaten. *The Sportsman* revealed on 7 September that he now planned to invite the Australians to visit South Africa on their way back from their 1909 tour of England, and to hold his triangular tournament there. That scheme, too, came to nothing, but by the end of 1908 it had at least been agreed that in the course of the following summer a meeting of representatives of the three countries would be held to agree on the future basis of international cricket. In his annual report in December 1908 the Australian board's secretary, William McElhone, noted that its decision to reject the idea of a triangular tournament had 'caused considerable feeling in England and South Africa and at one time it had appeared as if such a decision would result in the visits of Australian Teams to England being seriously prejudiced'. He continued: 'In the end, however, mainly through the able manner in which the facts were placed before the English public by our Representative Dr Poidevin, England admitted that the Board's decision was a just one.'

Perhaps arising from Bailey's proposal for a triangular competition, MCC had also begun to consider the need to regulate international cricket and had also drawn up draft 'Rules for Imperial Cricket.' The Australian board examined these at its meeting on 29 May 1908, and agreed that 'the word "Imperial" be interpreted "International Cricket Matches between Nations".' (It went without saying that the nations in question were still England, Australia and South Africa.) The proposed rules only addressed the issue of player eligibility, suggesting that 'A Cricketer who has played in a Representative Match for a Country can never play for any other Country', adding that except where this first restriction applied a player should always be allowed to represent his country of birth, and that in other cases there should be a residence requirement of 'not less than 4 Consecutive years'. The Australian board found the first of these rules too restrictive, proposing the addition of 'Provided that any Cricketer shall always be eligible to play for the Country of his birth after two years continuous and subsequent residence', and further argued that 'continuous' in the third rule should be replaced by 'previous', again relaxing MCC's proposed restriction.

This was one of the topics on the agenda when, on 15 June 1909, the representatives duly assembled at Lord's: the Earl of Chesterfield (president of MCC), Lord Harris and Lord Hawke for England; Dr Poidevin for Australia (since his fellow delegate, P.A. McAlister, was currently batting in the second Test outside); and H.D.G. Leveson Gower and G.W. Hillyard for South Africa. It was agreed that Test matches were to be defined as between the three countries represented, and that any player should be allowed to represent the country of his birth; there was no immediate agreement on the proposal banning players from turning out for more than one country. Setting a pattern which would persist for more than a century, a decision on this was deferred, along with payments for amateurs and professionals and rules for the appointment of umpires, where England had recently violated the principle that the visiting team should be consulted about the home board's nominations. The concept of a triangular tournament was accepted in principle, although it was acknowledged that existing international commitments meant that the earliest such a contest could take place would be in the 1912 English season.

When the representatives met again on 20 July it was clear that a good deal of negotiation had taken place in the intervening weeks. There was now a schedule of tours through to 1916/17, and there were detailed regulations, including the division of the takings, for the proposed imperial tournament. The contentious issues from the first meeting had been resolved with compromises: a player could not transfer from one Test country to another 'without the consent of each of the contracting parties' and a four-year residence qualification was established for those who had not previously played Tests, while it was agreed that '[t]he umpires in Test matches shall be selected by a committee equally representative of each country'. There was discussion, too, of the arrangements for the series, including such crucial issues as the distribution of complimentary tickets for the participating countries. Whatever had been agreed at Lord's, however, Australian doubts about the triangular scheme lingered: on the eve of their team's return after their tour the manager, Frank Laver, told reporters that his players regarded it 'as an experiment to be tried once in England, and once only'. He thought it was unlikely that such a contest could be held in Australia or South Africa, because of the countries' comparatively small populations. McElhone was able to state in his annual report that as a result of the conference 'the suggestions now before you are such as may result in the Scheme being acceptable to Australia'.

The eligibility rules continued to give trouble. When the Conference again assembled on 16 June 1910 the South Africans sought the removal of the clause about the contracting parties' consent to a player's transfer from one country to another. This was referred to the constituent bodies, and when the Australian board discussed the matter on 17 October it was resolved that 'the Clause be adhered to'. The awkwardness of the Conference's status became clear during the South African tour of Australia in 1910/11. The Australian board conferred directly with SACA representatives during the Sydney Test in early March to discuss possible dates for an Australian return visit 'and the proposed alterations in the schedule' suggested at the 16 June meeting. On behalf of the South Africans, R.P. Fitzgerald read a long letter from his board stating that 1913/14 was the earliest point at which the Australians could be received, and it was agreed that 'the Secretary of the Imperial Conference be informed as to the views of the South African Association ... and the reasons for the position taken up', with the suggestion that the Conference should be convened when Australia and South Africa were both in England in 1912, 'or earlier if necessary'. Once the South Africans had withdrawn from the meeting the Australians determined that 'this Board is prepared to send a team to South Africa at a date to be mutually agreed upon during or after the triangular contest in 1912'. Bilateral discussions remained crucial, then, although the existence of the Imperial Conference was now a complicating factor.

In fact, the Conference met twice in 1911, at Lord's on 30 June, where the dates of the matches in the 1912 triangular tournament were agreed, and at The Oval on 11 September, where some amendments were made to touring programmes in England. The first meeting had referred such matters as playing times and the distribution of gate money to the Board of Control for Test Matches at Home, effectively an MCC committee, while the second brought forward the starting date of the match at The Oval between England and Australia by three days 'to enable the game to be continued, if necessary, beyond three days without a Sunday intervening'. This, it would seem, was a concession to the Australian view that a deciding match should be played to a finish. When the Conference met again on 30 April 1912, it was to appoint the umpires for the forthcoming tournament along with many other minutiae, including a requirement for the umpires to confer with the captains regarding the choice of balls and to inform them when a new ball was being taken.

On the eve of the tournament a lavish volume appeared, edited by Pelham Warner and entitled *Imperial Cricket*. In his preface Lord Hawke described the series as 'the outward and visible sign of the climax of Imperial Cricket' – the echo of the Christian Catechism was doubtless not coincidental – adding that 'the spirit of the game is exactly the same as the spirit of all that is best in our great Empire'. Abe Bailey contributed a chapter, observing that, 'If the strengthening of the bonds of Union within the Empire is one of the many outcomes of this great Tournament, I am hopeful that contemporary cricketers, and those who are to come, will agree that the Triangular Tests of 1912 were not held in vain.'

There is, however, a marked contrast between the conception of Warner's book and the operation of the Imperial Conference. Whereas the former's 20 chapters take in such cricketing outposts as Ceylon (known as Sri Lanka since 1972), Egypt, the Sudan, British Malaya, and Samoa and the Islands of the South Seas (Tasmania, curiously, was given a chapter to itself), there was, of course, no sign of such inclusiveness among the gatekeepers of the Conference and its three constituent boards. Playing standards were, it is true, a legitimate concern, but the development of world cricket would have taken a radically different course had the Conference been more like the Federation of International Football Associations (FIFA), which by 1912 had 20 members, including Luxembourg, South Africa, Argentina and Chile.

And when play finally began on 27 May 1912, the doubts about the tournament's competitiveness were soon realised. South Africa lost their first two matches by an innings: Australia ran up 448 against them at Old Trafford, and then despite a fine 127 from Aubrey Faulkner the South Africans were dismissed for 265, collapsing to an ignominious 95 all out following on, and the match was over in two days. They started even worse against England at Lord's and were bowled out for just 53, Frank Foster claiming 5-16 and Sid Barnes 5-25. England replied with 337, and with Barnes taking a further six wickets for 85 runs the South Africans could only manage 217 at their second attempt, losing by an innings and 62 runs. The first encounter between England and Australia, at Lord's towards the end of June, was ruined by rain: even England's declaration at 310/7 was not enough to breathe some life into the match, Australia making 282/7 with Charlie Macartney very unfortunate to be out for 99.

Barnes was again South Africa's nemesis when the second round of matches began at Headingley: he took 6-52 and 4-63 and England, with 242 and 238, comfortably beat the South Africans' 147 and 159. At Old Trafford a week later, the Australians posted 390 in reply to South Africa's 263, and when the latter were dismissed for 173 Syd Gregory's side were left with just 47 to make, which they did without losing a wicket. The weather was once more the victor when England and Australia met again, this time at Old Trafford where 92 from Rhodes took the hosts to 202, but Australia were 14 without loss when play ended on day two, and the final day was completely washed out.

The last day was again lost when Australia and South Africa met for the third time, but the South Africans had put up a much better performance, half-centuries by Dave Nourse and Gordon White seeing them to 329, by a distance their highest total of the tournament, and they then dismissed Australia for 219. But they still had no answer to England's Sid Barnes, and he took 5-28 and 8-29 as South Africa were bowled out for 95 and 93, England's first-innings total of 176 meaning that they only needed 13 for another ten-wicket win. The two rain-affected draws between England and Australia made their final encounter at The Oval the tournament decider, and it ended in a comprehensive victory for England. Jack Hobbs and Wilfred Rhodes put on 107 for the first wicket after Fry won the toss, and then Frank Woolley made 62 to see his side to 245. Woolley then combined with Barnes to bowl the Australians out for 111, Charlie Kelleway's 43 the only significant contribution, and although Gerry Hazlitt claimed a career-best 7-25, England extended their lead to the tune of 175, leaving Australia with an unlikely 310 to win. Woolley picked up another five wickets to finish with match figures of 10-49, and with Harry Dean taking 4-19 the visitors were all out for a miserable 65.

A further meeting of the Conference took place at Lord's on 16 July, during the second match between Australia and South Africa. The main business was the confirmation of the touring schedule through to South Afica's proposed visit to England in 1917. Australia would visit South Africa in 1915/16, but there were no plans for a repetition of the South Africans' 1910/11 tour of Australia. No statement was made, but the Australian board had sent a cable reading 'Opinion Board against continuation Triangular Contest', and it was inferred that the Conference had no intention, either, of repeating the experiment; the meeting had, *The Sportsman* concluded, 'practically killed any suggestion of another Triangular Tournament'. More disturbingly, it had failed to reach a decision on 'an equitable reckoning' of the current event, should England and Australia finish level, preferring to wait until the necessity arose. In the event, of course, England's victory at The Oval settled the issue, but the Conference's reluctance to commit itself in advance may have been a straw in the wind. In Australia, the board secretary Sydney Smith's annual report was both damning and quietly triumphant. 'The Triangular Scheme,' he wrote, 'proved, as was anticipated, a failure, and as it cannot possibly be carried out in Australia or Africa, will doubtless be not heard of again for many years to come.' More ominously for the future operation of the Conference, MCC had raised doubts about whether it would be prepared to assume 'the same amount of responsibility in financing teams to Overseas Dominions as in the past' and it was agreed that in future independent bilateral arrangements would be made with the other boards.

The original purpose for its creation having been accomplished, however unsatisfactorily, the Conference did not meet again before the outbreak of war, next convening on 6 June 1921. The Australian board actually met on 11 November 1918, the very day of the Armistice, taking the opportunity to state that it 'rejoices at the prospect of an early peace, and joins in the general feeling of thankfulness and pride in the glorious triumph achieved by the Empire and her Allies'. The response of the world's cricketers to the 'Call of Empire', the board added, had 'upheld the best traditions of the national game', and it looked forward to a speedy resumption of the international programme. An 'Australian Imperial Forces' team in fact toured England in the summer of 1919, taking in a visit to South Africa on their way home, and by the time the Conference met in 1921 MCC had visited Australia and a full tour to England by the Australians was taking place. The playing conditions for such tours continued to be arranged bilaterally, without any reference to the Imperial Conference.

There was, however, some widening of the Conference's role once it met. Faced with proposals from the Australian board for changes to the covering of pitches the length of the over (currently eight balls in Australia and six everywhere else) and the follow-on, MCC responded that 'conditions governing imperial cricket are always open to a friendly settlement', adding that this could 'usually be effected at the Imperial Cricket Conference'. While amendments to the Laws remained the responsibility of the Marylebone Club, there was clearly a growing acceptance that the Conference was a suitable forum for the discussion of suggested changes. So the 1921 meeting, in addition to the perennial question of touring schedules, dealt with possible changes to the Laws, the Australians bringing three issues to the table:

the duration of the over; an increase from 150 to 200 in the deficit required for the follow-on; and a ten-minute extension in the time allowed for rolling before the day's play where there had been rain. The meeting was also notable for the fact that Jamaica were permitted to send a representative, their board secretary William Morrison – the first hint of a possible widening of the magic circle of the three Test-playing countries – and he joined England and South Africa in opposing the Australian proposals. It was, however, agreed that Australia would provide the text of its proposed revisions to a further meeting, to be held at The Oval on 15 August, and it was there decided to refer all three questions to a special meeting of MCC. This was duly held on 3 May 1922, and after a long debate on the question of Law 9, relating to the rolling of the pitch, the proposal that the extra ten minutes should be allowed *in Australia only* was carried by the necessary three-quarters majority. The other two measures were subsequently passed as well.

Some matters considered by the Conference were too sensitive even to appear in Smith's report to his board. The minutes of the 1921 meeting reveal that, 'Lord Harris stated that he considered the Imperial Cricket Conference should know that the Australian captain [Warwick Armstrong] had at a recent meeting of the Board of Control announced that a great deal of professional betting took place in England on cricket and that in consequence the Umpires should not be appointed until a few days prior to the Test matches and that the reports of the County Captains on the efficiency of the Umpires were valueless.' Having received an assurance from the Victoria Club, the centre of bookmaking in London, that such allegations were unfounded, Harris informed the Conference that they were unsubstantiated, and Smith and Dr Ramsay Mailer, the Australian representatives, declined to support Armstrong's views. The Conference duly resolved that 'those playing in International contests should not have any authority to interfere in the management off the field or in the appointment of umpires, but their views should be consulted as far as possible'. Confronted for the first time, however implicitly, with the question of corruption in cricket, the administrators firmly looked the other way.

Lurking in the background, however, was another Australian preoccupation: the duration of Test matches played in England. This was currently limited to three days, but so strongly did the Australians feel that this was inadequate, especially when the weather intervened, that during the final Test of the 1921 tour at The Oval, Armstrong had made his disgust at the inevitability of the draw quite clear. Asked about this, Pelham Warner stated that the question of whether the final Test of a series should be played to a finish was now before the ICC. In fact, the Australian representatives did not press the point, Smith simply asking when the Conference reconvened on 15 August, the second day of The Oval Test and the day before Armstrong's protest, 'that the question of playing Test Matches to a finish in England might be further considered'. The can, the first of many, was kicked down the road.

If the invitation to Jamaica to take part in the 1921 meeting was a small step, there were other signs that change might be in the air. In February 1922 the chairman of the New Zealand Cricket Council reported that the council had been asked to 'draw up a definite scheme regarding New Zealand and Australian tours of those countries [presumably England and South Africa]', that A.C. MacLaren had accepted an invitation to bring an English team, and that a visit by South Africa was also on the cards. Even more interestingly, the distinguished English cricket writer J.N. Pentelow surveyed the current state of the world game in the 1924 edition of *Ayres' Cricket Companion*, concluding that 'for genuine Test matches, New Zealand cricket is not quite ripe', and noting that 'the West Indies, India and the Argentine, if not Philadelphia, would all be justified in claiming parity of place with New Zealand'. This willingness to look, not just beyond the present circle of three Test-playing countries but also beyond the limits of the Empire, was, unfortunately, not shared by the administrators, although slowly but surely the possibility of admitting more countries of the Empire to Test status was beginning to register on their radar.

Chapter 3

Widening the Circle, 1926–1939

THE MEETING of the Conference at Lord's on 31 May 1926, after a five-year gap which no one seemed to notice, heralded a new phase in the organisation's history. Six governing bodies were represented, with the newly established West Indies Cricket Conference together with India and New Zealand, joining the three original members around the table, apparently at the invitation of Lord Harris. There had until now been no formal constitution, but this expansion meant that greater definition was required and when the second meeting of the summer took place at The Oval on 28 July it was agreed that 'the governing bodies of cricket within the Empire to which cricket teams are sent, or which send teams to England, shall be entitled to send representatives of such bodies to the Imperial Cricket Conference'.

Even this kept things comfortably vague. Who was doing the sending of teams was left unspecified, although it was perhaps intended, or assumed, that the Conference itself would decide which tours would be recognised and therefore which new members might be admitted. And there was no challenge to the fundamental principle that the Conference was an Imperial club; although it was now necessary to loosen the definition of a Test match, such matches were, it was agreed, 'matches played between sides duly selected by recognised governing bodies of cricket, representing countries within the Empire'.

It should, therefore, come as no surprise that when it was decided without dissent that the Conference should appeal to the Australian board to adopt six-ball overs it was 'in order to effect uniformity throughout the Empire'. It is, perhaps, a little more surprising that when the meeting on 31 May was unable to agree on an Australian proposal that Tests in England should be extended to four days, the manager of the Australian team, Sydney Smith, who was also one of his country's representatives at the Conference, insisted that the proposal's English opponents 'have to realise that the Test matches mean more to the British Empire than the mere playing of a game of cricket'. This appeal seems to have fallen upon deaf ears, however, and no decision was taken on the matter on 28 July, although it was noted that some at least had taken the view that if Tests in England were to be extended it would be preferable to play them over five days rather than four.

The Australian board received detailed reports on the 1926 meetings from its representatives, Sydney Smith and Harold Bushby. These provide a good deal more colour than the official minutes. Both, for example, record how Lord Harris, perhaps in retaliation for Armstrong's comments five years earlier, launched an attack on the standard of umpiring in Australia, although he declined to provide any substantiation for his claim that 'the umpires in Australia were most incapable'. Smith replied that 'the umpiring in Australia was quite as good as that in England', and the matter was dropped, Harris acknowledging that the Australian board acted in good faith although 'they had weak material to work with'. Harris also took the lead in pressing Australia to accept the six-ball over for Test matches, attempting to employ the presence of new members in his cause: 'The Test match idea was spreading,' Bushby quoted him as saying, 'and other countries were anxious to have the six-ball over and desired that it should be uniform'. It was in this spirit that the Australian representatives agreed to take the matter back to their board, although one might suspect that they had no intention of giving way.

Now that they had been accepted into the inner sanctum of international cricket, the West Indies representatives lost no time in urging not only England but also Australia to exchange visits. Bushby, however, was interested in casting his net even wider. He had, he reported to his board, talked with members of the cricket community in Philadelphia, who greatly regretted that the Australians had not been able to play there on their way home. It would, the old Philadelphia player Christy Morris had assured him, 'give the game a boost especially as at the present time it appeared to be declining in popularity, there being only four senior teams playing there'. Morris urged that should Australia tour the West Indies, they should also include Argentina in their itinerary, 'as they had a number of fine cricketers in that country, and he thought the financial obligations would be easily met'. But Bushby was a lone voice, and his board refused to arrange any matches in the USA as the team returned to Australia.

The expansion of Test cricket, however, did take place. The West Indies played three Tests in England in 1928, and there were four in the West Indies when England returned the tour early in 1930. Remarkably, that visit was concurrent with an English side touring New Zealand, where they also played four Tests, so that on 11 January 1930 two England teams were engaged on opposite sides of the world, the West Indies starting a match against a side captained by Freddie Calthorpe, while in Christchurch New Zealand were in the second day of their game against Tom Lowry's England. The tourists won the series in New Zealand, where the matches were over three days, 1-0 with three draws, but in the West Indies the series of five-day games was shared one apiece with three draws, with the West Indians securing a first

Test victory, by 289 runs in Georgetown, British Guiana. George Headley became the fifth player to score centuries in both innings of a Test.

With representatives from the far-flung Empire facing long sea journeys in order to attend, it was hardly surprising that there were considerable intervals between the Conference's early meetings, while even as late as the 1950s governing bodies frequently appointed representatives who were already in England, and who sometimes had only a peripheral association with cricket in the country they represented. Henry Leveson Gower, for example, who had toured South Africa in 1905/06 and 1910/11, the second time as captain, represented them at the Conference from 1921 until 1939, while New Zealand's delegation in 1926 included Henry Swan, an MCC committee member and the New Zealand Cricket Council's representative in London. In May 1929, New Zealand was represented by Admiral Earl Jellicoe, who had been the dominion's governor-general from 1920 to 1924.

At that 1929 meeting the establishment of a schedule of tours was again the principal item of business. The whole operation retained a remarkably ad hoc, amateurish atmosphere. When William Findlay, who had succeeded Lacey as secretary of MCC, wrote to the Maharajah of Patiala in December 1928 to invite India to send representatives to the forthcoming meetings, he indicated that Lord Harris was aware of the 'recent' establishment of the Board of Control for Cricket in India (BCCI), although in fact it had been operating for more than a year. India was indeed present at the two meetings which were held in 1929, at Lord's on 14 May and at The Oval on 19 August; the purpose of the now standard double meeting was to allow the governing bodies to consider the decisions of the first conclave and where necessary to suggest amendments. It was strongly emphasised after the May meeting that the 'suggested list of tours by MCC and visits of Colonial sides to this country' was 'at this moment purely provisional', allowing for the countries affected to request changes. That did in fact happen in 1929, South Africa requesting that their next tour of England be postponed from 1933 to 1935, leading to several readjustments to the programme. The West Indies proposed that all five Tests in England's tour in 1929/30 should be played to a finish, but Lord Harris responded that while a five-Test series was acceptable, 'the feeling in England was opposed to matches without a time limit'. New Zealand urged, successfully in this case, that the 1932/33 MCC side might return through Panama and visit New Zealand on the way, and in fact England did play two Tests in the country on their way back from Australia.

The touring schedule was not the only matter discussed. The Conference also declared that 'they were 'glad to learn that efforts were being made in South Africa to establish turf wickets'. 'The hope was expressed,' the statement continued, 'that these efforts would be successful, and that they will be extended in all countries where the climatic and other conditions permit.' There was less encouragement for Ceylon, who wanted to tour England in 1931 but were told that such a visit would be impracticable; an enquiry the following year about the country possibly being elected to membership was similarly rebuffed, the minutes merely noting that it was 'not thought practicable at present'. The indefatigable Harris, meanwhile, informed the meeting in May that the MCC touring party in Australia had found the travelling 'very tiring' and argued that the 'up-country' matches should be dropped in favour of games against 'the Universities and Public Schools on the various State Grounds'; by the following May the Australian representative W.L. Kelly was in a position to insist that the country matches were 'vital from the point of view of cricket in Australia', and the matter was dropped.

The meetings in 1930, on 20 May and 8 September, revealed an expansion in the Conference's agenda. In addition to a tweaking of the qualification rules for Test matches, Kelly wanted sightscreens to be required at all Test venues in England ('impracticable', said Harris), and there was discussion of Law 6 on the size of the wicket and Law 24 (lbw). The amended regulation on eligibility now required that the boards were 'responsible for submitting in good time for the approval of the Imperial Cricket Conference, whose decision shall be final, the names of those cricketers likely to be selected to play in an approaching Test match tour, with their qualifications', which could be either by birth or by residence. In the latter instance, they were further required to specify 'the dates upon which such residence is founded'.

This represented a significant widening in the role of the Conference, which would now have a continuing supervisory function, maintained between meetings. In practice, this role was assumed by the MCC secretary, but it nevertheless implied that the Conference had a greater degree of continuity than it had hitherto achieved. The 1930 meetings also decided that 'on such grounds where the wicket is completely covered in Test matches prior to the start of play such covering may remain until the first ball is bowled', and that when no play was possible on the first day of a four-day match, it would be regarded as a three-day match for the purposes of Law 55. The Conference also addressed its own constitution, unanimously accepting an Australian proposal that the three founding members should be allowed two votes on any motion with the three newcomers having only one; the ogre of inequality was for the first time formally enshrined in the ICC's own rules.

In 1931 the Conference met just once, agreeing in a further adjustment of the qualification rules that 'any player who has once played in a Test Match for any country shall not afterwards be eligible to play in a Test Match against that country without the consent of its Board of Control'. That was the only meeting that year, but in 1932 the Conference came together three times. On 20 June it had to deal with an unusual case, although it is typical of the way in which business was conducted that it was not published at the time. It was just days before the only Test of the Indian tour of England, and the public reports merely stated that the player lists had been accepted. Three years later, when the possibility that the Nawab of Pataudi, who had played three Tests for England, might be selected as captain of India, it emerged that that meeting in June 1932 had ruled that Lall Singh, qualified neither by birth nor residence to play for India, would be permitted to appear in that one Test, and that Test only. The fact had been turned up by Edward Sewell, a cricket writer who had himself played in the very first All-India side, against Lord Hawke's tourists in 1893, and was mentioned in his article in *The Scotsman* about the Pataudi issue. Singh had been born in Kuala Lumpur in 1909, and had had no contact with Indian cricket until he paid his own way to take part in the trial matches for the 1932 tour; he did not, therefore, fall within the Conference's eligibility rules, and Sewell stated that he was granted permission to play in the Test, 'on the plea of the president, and founder, of the Board of Cricket Control for India, Mr R.E. Grant Govan, that he had been brought a long way at no little expense'. The one Test exception, Sewell added, explained the fact that Singh had not been chosen for India in the 1933/34 series against England. 'These matters,' he wrote, 'show that the latest recruits to the Test match arena are very much in the workings of international cricket, if not actually in what is known as "the news".' And it was revealing that the Conference chose to make no reference to the exception at the time.

Or indeed, to another, more controversial issue. England had included the Nawab of Pataudi in their list for the forthcoming tour of Australia, arguing that although he had been born and raised in India, he had been resident in England – apart from a seven-month visit to India in 1931/32 – since May 1926 and was therefore qualified by residence. The matter was discussed at a second meeting of the Conference on 21 July, but Dr Macdonald and R.H. Mallett replied that they had not yet had an opportunity to consult their board. The decision was deferred until 29 July, although the chairman, Viscount Lewisham, pointed out that 'the Conference need not necessarily be influenced by the Australian opinion as it is laid down that any question arising out of these Rules shall be submitted to the ICC and their decision shall be final'. In the event, the Australian board cabled its agreement, provided that Pataudi had not played for India during his visit.

But however troublesome such matters as the number of balls in an over, the rolling and covering of pitches or the eligibility of players may have been, they were as nothing compared to the crisis which threatened to overcome international cricket during the 1932/33 Australian season. The cause was England captain Douglas Jardine's use of what the English called 'leg theory', quickly named 'Bodyline' by the Australian press: the use of fast, short-pitched bowling directed at the batsman's body and accompanied by a packed field behind the wicket on the leg side. Designed mainly as a method to neutralise the phenomenal success of Don Bradman, Australia's leading batsman – although Jardine always denied this – the approach relied upon the quick bowlers Harold Larwood and Bill Voce.

The storm broke when Jardine deployed its full force in the third Test of the 1932/33 series, played at Adelaide. The trouble began when, early in the Australian first innings, Larwood struck the opener Bill Woodfull over the heart, another delivery later knocking the bat from his hands. When, after Woodfull's dismissal, the England manager Pelham Warner went to the Australian dressing room, Woodfull famously replied to his expression of sympathy: 'I don't want to see you, Mr Warner. There are two teams out there. One is trying to play cricket and the other is not.' Matters went from bad to worse on the fourth day, when the Australian wicketkeeper Bert Oldfield, trying to hook, edged a rising ball from Larwood on to his temple, fracturing his skull. The crowd, which had been incensed by the incidents in Australia's first innings, reacted with even greater fury as Woodfull ran on to the field to tend to his injured team-mate. The atmosphere had never been more charged in more than half a century of Test cricket.

That evening, even before the completion of the Test, the Australian board fired off a cable to MCC, accusing Jardine and his team of unsportsmanlike conduct, asserting that 'bodyline bowling assumed such proportions as to menace best interests of game', and adding that this could 'upset friendly relations between Australia and England'. Five days later MCC replied, deploring the Australian cable and denying any unsportsmanlike play. They had, they insisted, the 'fullest confidence' in Jardine, his team and its managers, but they stated that if the Australian board wished to cancel the rest of the tour they would 'consent with great reluctance'. With one side insisting that their opponents' tactics were deliberate and the other deeply outraged, this was surely a moment at which the Imperial Conference could come into its own. Sidney Smith, a former Australian manager and delegate to the Conference, certainly suggested that the subject should be left in abeyance until the Conference could meet, and after the Australian board had sent another cable indicating that it wished the tour to continue and was prepared to leave the issue of the fairness of bodyline bowling until after it was finished, MCC, while demanding that the accusation of unsportsmanlike behaviour should be withdrawn, agreed to refer the larger question to the Imperial Conference. As S.J. Southerton, the editor of *Wisden*, observed: 'Quite obviously, with opinions on this question of "bodyline" bowling differing so sharply, the Imperial Conference must be the most suitable body to deal with the subject, and then when they have come to a decision the MCC can take the necessary action.'

The Imperial Conference, however, was a ponderous body with ill-defined powers, had never before had to deal with such a crisis, and was, after all, effectively controlled, and certainly managed, by one of the parties to the dispute. When the council met at Lord's on 22 May 1933, the only issue on the agenda was the approval of the eligibility of the players in the forthcoming series between England and the West Indies. By this time, of course, the series in Australia had been completed, in a soured atmosphere but without further dramatic incident, England winning 4-1 and Larwood finishing with 33 wickets at an average of 19.51. The war of words, however, continued, the Australian board proposing in a cable of 28 April the adoption of a new law which would give the umpire at the bowler's end the power to judge that a bowler was 'bowling with the intent to intimidate or injure [the batsman], and to call No Ball accordingly'. This proposal had been referred by MCC to a sub-committee, which might perhaps explain the reluctance of the Conference to get involved, but it did not prevent the English press from immediately dismissing the idea as absurd and impracticable. How could an umpire judge a bowler's intent? When MCC replied, on 12 June, it included a robust defence of England's tactics in the recent series, insisting that any implication that the bowling in Australia had involved 'a direct attack by the bowler on the batsman' was 'improper and incorrect', since 'such action on the part of any bowler would be an offence against the spirit of the game and would be immediately condemned'. This, of course, was precisely the accusation which the Australians had made. The MCC response also sought to deflect criticism by complaining about the level of 'thoroughly objectionable' barracking to which the English players had been subjected, adding the threat that 'unless barracking is stopped, or is greatly moderated in Australia, it is difficult to see how the continuance of representative matches can best serve the interest of the game'.

With the aggrieved parties thus shouting at each other, the Imperial Conference showed itself completely unfitted to act; the MCC cable of 12 June, indeed, while regretting that the issue had to be dealt with by correspondence, only envisaged a bilateral meeting between England and Australia as a solution, completely cutting the ICC out of the picture. The appeal of the *Yorkshire Post* on 12 May 1933 that 'ultimately the Imperial Cricket Conference must hold a full dress debate' went unheeded. On 7 July a meeting of the Conference was called for the 31st to consider the Australian board's proposed new law and detailing MCC's objections to it. But the minutes of that meeting blandly record that '[a]t the wish of the Australian Board' the matter was 'deferred for the present'. What lay behind this tactical withdrawal remains unclear; perhaps it was evident to the Australians that they had little chance of getting their proposal through in the face of MCC's opposition and decided that delay was preferable to outright rejection.

At any event, it was not until 25 July 1934 that the Conference substantively addressed the issue. The previous month, though, the first meeting of the summer had begun with an appeal from the chairman, the Earl of Cromer, for the delegates not to 'concern themselves with the cricketing public, but rather with the public outside the cricketing world'. 'A section of the Press,' he continued, 'was inclined to make capital out of Test Match cricket, and it would be a sorry day for cricket if Test Matches were to create a discordant note and bring about a feeling that such matches should be discontinued.' He was sure that all present would devote themselves to the problems that concerned the game 'in the best interests of cricket throughout the Empire'. All present were undoubtedly aware of what the earl was referring to, and whose interests his remarks were designed to serve.

But by the meeting on 25 July, the day after the conclusion of the fourth Test, things had moved on considerably, in part because Nottinghamshire captain Arthur Carr's use of 'leg theory' in the County Championship had forced English officials to confront the reality of bodyline. It also raised its head during the Australian tour that summer, with Voce bowling short-pitched deliveries to a packed leg-side field during Nottinghamshire's match against the tourists, and at times during the Test series. That meeting considered and overwhelmingly rejected the law proposed by Australia, evidently accepting the English argument that it was impracticable, but its carefully worded motion, while dressed up as a restatement of the MCC position, effectively put an end to bodyline tactics: 'That this conference affirms the principles already laid down by MCC that any form of bowling obviously a direct attack by the bowler upon the batsmen would be an offence against the spirit of the game. This conference is of the opinion that the controlling bodies should not permit or countenance that form of bowling.'

This was a little like the theory of a Just War: every bowler and every captain would claim, as MCC had done in 1932/33, that there was no intention on the bowler's part to attack the batsman directly; if batsmen were hit it was pure bad luck, or because their technique was defective. Which combatant in war has ever admitted that their cause was unjust, but insisted they were going to go on fighting anyway? Nevertheless, the mood had shifted significantly, and packed leg-side fields accompanying persistent short-pitched bowling largely disappeared from the game. The Imperial Cricket Conference, however, despite W.C. Bull's claim that 'the majority present showed much sympathy towards Australia in connection with the happenings when the last English team was here', had played no significant part in discrediting 'leg theory'.

That 1934 Conference also again debated – though without, apparently, reaching any conclusion – possible changes to the lbw law. As it then existed, the law permitted a batsman to pad away a ball pitching outside off stump even if it would have hit the stumps, and there was a growing feeling that a change was required to discourage negative play. There was, the minutes recorded, 'no strong desire for change', but MCC subsequently decided to introduce an experimental law for the 1935 English season which would allow a batsman to be dismissed if a ball pitched outside off and would have gone on to hit the stumps, and on the basis of that experience the MCC secretary wrote to all Conference members in January 1936 asking them to endorse the experimental law becoming substantive. By the time MCC met in May 1936, Australia had joined South Africa, New Zealand, the West Indies and India in endorsing the change, an indication that the mechanisms of the Conference could be employed even between sessions.

On some issues the Conference turned procrastination into an art form. In June 1932 the South Africans had raised concerns about rolling the pitch after rain, proposing an adjustment to Law 9 to permit rolling prior to a resumption or at the end of the day. No decision was taken, and when they reverted to the matter in July 1933, they were fobbed off with advice to look at an absorbent roller which was being used during county matches in England; pleading the special circumstances of heavy thunderstorms in South Africa, they were told the following year that a new version of the absorbent roller might meet their needs. A month later R.P. Fitzgerald came back once more, proposing that their suggestion might be used experimentally during the 1935/36 MCC tour, but in June 1937, even though Australia and New Zealand were now interested in the idea, it was again deferred amidst a series of uncertainties: how much rain would be enough to trigger the additional rolling? Who would be consulted in making the decision? Why were the umpires not involved? Not until 16 June 1938 was the measure agreed, with the addition of a 'responsible officer', appointed by the home board, who would supervise its implementation.

In April 1937, concerned about the financial problems facing the English first-class counties, MCC appointed a commission to investigate and bring forward recommendations. The commissioner was William Findlay, an Old Etonian and Oxford Blue who had been the secretary of the Surrey county club from 1906 to 1920, and assistant secretary and then secretary of MCC itself from 1926 until 1936. The other members were Richard Palairet, another Oxford Blue and former Surrey secretary, and Harry Mallett, secretary of the Minor Counties and one of the founders of the West Indies board in 1927. Findlay, E.W. Swanton declared, 'must have acquired more knowledge of the economics as well as the politics of cricket than any man living'. The commission reported in December, arguing that cricket's problems were largely domestic and making a series of proposals ranging from the introduction of eight-ball overs to a special fund from tour income to help the most financially threatened counties. It was quite evident that visits by Australia were the single greatest money-spinner: the profits from Ashes Test series had almost trebled from £15,795 in 1921 to £44,394 in 1934, and the income from the counties' matches against the tourists had also risen significantly over the same period. Other visitors were less profitable: the profits from playing the Australians were double what was earned by playing South Africa, and four times greater than matches against India. When the takings from these touring fixtures were ignored, the average total loss by the counties per year amounted to £26,875. It was, therefore, unquestionable that a sensible international programme was essential to the viability of county cricket.

The commission, however, was also concerned that there might be too much touring. With the addition of the West Indies and India to the international schedule (New Zealand as yet hardly registered) there had by 1937 been official MCC tours in five of the past seven winters, but there was more resistance to what was called in advance of that year's Imperial Conference 'the evil of unofficial cricket tours, which do not give English players a chance to rest'. The immediate cause of anxiety was Lord Tennyson's tour to India, which took a party of 16 players to the subcontinent to play 24 matches over three and a half months, the journalist L.V. Manning proclaiming in the *Daily Sketch* that '[t]he time has come to make a repetition impossible', but there were smaller initiatives as well: Sir Julien Cahn had taken a team to Ceylon and Malaya the previous winter, Sir Theodore Brinckman was planning a tour to Argentina in 1937/38, and H.M. Martineau had organised a pre-season visit to Egypt every April from 1932 to 1936. A different mindset would have seen such enterprises as contributing to the growth of cricket around the world, but that had never been of much interest to the ICC, and only peripherally to MCC. To eliminate the evil, Findlay's commission recommended 'that clubs when making agreements with their professionals shall insert a clause to the effect that no professional shall accept an invitation to tour overseas unless the consent of MCC be obtained after consulting his committee'. By neatly combining the exclusiveness of international cricket with the class distinction between Players and Gentlemen (who were, of course, independent of employer–employee relationships), the commission unconsciously exposed the power structures which governed the game.

The BCCI secretary Anthony de Mello, meanwhile, was battling gamely to gain as much traction as he could for Indian cricket. The Indians had toured England in 1932 and 1936, playing one Test on the first occasion and three on the second, all of three days' duration, and MCC had visited India in 1933/34. At the 1938 Conference he pursued three objectives: an Indian tour to England in 1941, an MCC visit in 1939/40, and a single match with the Australians in Bombay as they sailed back from their current England tour. 'Thanks largely to Mr de Mello's perseverance', the Lahore *Civil & Military Gazette* was able to report on 19 July, 'the MCC visit is now definitely assured', and negotiations were continuing on the other two issues. The Australians eventually declined, pleading that they had already turned down a New Zealand request that they return through the Panama Canal and play in the Dominion on their way to Sydney. On the 1941 tour, De Mello was pinned by a technicality: he was informed that the present discussion was only about the period 1942–47, and therefore there could be no consideration of the 1941 season. The truth was, however, that MCC was hoping to keep that as a fallow year, and when the confirmed schedule for 1942–47 was released after the 1939 Conference, 1941 was still listed as 'not yet settled'. Within two months, of course, Britain and its Empire would be at war, and any schedule would be abandoned.

The Conference's increasing interest in the Laws, meanwhile, had led MCC to propose a tripartite division of regulation: the Laws themselves 'reserved exclusively for the MCC official code', *Rules*, which would apply to every class of cricket administered by a national board, and *Instructions to Umpires*, for *'any particular grade'* of cricket'. When this was debated in June 1938, H.V. Evatt, who was a High Court judge in Australia as well as being one of the board's representatives, was having none of it: constitutionally, he insisted, 'the Australian board was vested by the State Associations with full power to make new Laws or alter or amend existing Laws for cricket in Australia', and 'it was clear that the various Boards of Control must have the power to make By-Laws and Rules to meet their local conditions'. Individual countries were happy to co-operate with MCC in revising the Laws, but there could be no question of their giving up the right to legislate on their own territory. He was supported in these arguments by the South Africans, and Lord Cobham was reduced to urging that any such changes should be reported to MCC, not least because they 'might be extremely valuable when any revision of a Law was under consideration'.

What was to prove to be the final meeting before the outbreak of war was held on 14 June 1939, where the Conference addressed the definition of a first-class match. A note to Law 1 stated that 'a three-days' match between two sides adjudged First-class shall be regarded as a First-class fixture', but since there was no indication of who would do the adjudging, this was clearly inadequate. The discussion centred on matches by touring teams, since that was unequivocally a matter for the Conference, and MCC subsequently proposed that on official tours all matches of three or more days' duration should be regarded as first-class 'unless the Governing Body of the country being visited raises an objection in the case of certain matches'; once again, and almost obsessively, the club deferred to the power of the individual members, the Conference setting a framework which its members were always free to vary at will. In the case of unofficial tours, it further suggested, the acceptance of the touring side as of first-class quality was entirely a matter for the governing body of the team's country of origin. Even in the case of one- and two-day matches, specifically denied first-class status by the note to Law 1, the governing body of the country being visited would have discretion to declare certain matches first-class. The issue was left unresolved, and it would not be until 1947 that a definition of first-class cricket was finally arrived at. Less than two months later, the Empire was again at war.

Chapter 4

From Empire to Commonwealth, 1945–1961

AFTER MORE than five years of war, during which international cricket had come to a complete halt and the domestic game, except in India, had been reduced to friendly matches, the cricket authorities turned their minds to resuming a normal international schedule. Even before that point, the first steps were being taken. India embarked on a short tour to Ceylon in March 1945, while heavy fighting continued in Burma and the western Pacific. At a gala dinner in Colombo K.S. Ranga Rao, the secretary of the BCCI, suggested that the time had come for Ceylon to be given Test status and become a member of the ICC. Its players gave his claim a little support a few days later by drawing with the tourists in a three-day match. Although they were bowled out for 107 in their first innings, Vinoo Mankad taking 8-35, they did better in their second, reaching 225/7. In November it was reported that Ceylon would indeed apply for membership, with Indian support. Elsewhere, others were contemplating a rapid resumption. A hastily organised series of five 'Victory Tests' between an Australian Services side and an England XI attracted large cricket-hungry crowds between May and August 1945, 367,000 people attending across the five games and a record 93,000 turning up for the final match at Lord's to see England win by six wickets and share the series 2-2.

It was, however, notable that the series was never given official Test status, because the Australian board feared that its team, still formally a military unit, would not be strong enough to compete with England. In fact, with the 25-year-old former RAAF pilot Keith Miller contributing 514 runs, the most on either side, the teams were well matched. The early resumption of cricket was enthusiastically embraced by the Australian Prime Minister John Curtin and by his Minister for External Affairs Dr H.V. Evatt, who urged MCC to send a team to his country at the earliest opportunity. By October the club's committee was, despite some reluctance, proposing a visit in 1946/47, with Australia touring England in 1948. The counties had already indicated that they would welcome a visit by India in 1946, while by the end of the year the SACA had proposed a tour to England in 1947.

In the immediate aftermath of the war, all members were represented by British-based delegates when the Imperial Cricket Conference assembled on 15 January 1946. Gubby Allen and Walter Robins spoke for Australia, Arthur Gilligan for New Zealand, Leveson Gower (as usual) and Group Captain A.J. Holmes for South Africa, and Sir Kenneth Fitze for India. Fitze had been a colonial administrator in India and had served as president of the Central India Cricket Association; now he was a political adviser to the Secretary of State for India. All in all, there cannot have been much difference between that meeting of the Conference and a meeting of the MCC committee. The Conference agreed, as always subject to ratification by the member boards, a touring schedule from 1946 to 1950/51. It also endorsed a bilateral agreement between England and Australia whereby the 1946/47 Test series would consist of matches of 30 hours spread over six days, with that time fitted into five days when Australia next toured England; the final Test would still be played to a finish if the outcome of the series was in doubt. The Ceylonese bid for membership was, however, unsuccessful. It was, according to the minutes, 'not supported by any representative'. Ceylon was informed that 'it was not possible at present to increase the number of countries represented' and that from now on any application would need the support of at least two sponsors. Whatever the BCCI may have thought, Fitze evidently failed to offer his backing for the Ceylonese application.

The following meeting, in May 1947, completed an item of business which had been left unfinished at the outbreak of war: the definition of a first-class match. The new rules took over the somewhat circular statement previously a note to Law 1, to the effect that a match of three or more days between 'two sides of eleven players officially adjudged First-class shall be regarded as a First-class fixture', but they firmly closed one door by listing the bodies entitled to make such calls, namely the Conference's six members. They and they alone would be allowed to determine what was a first-class match played anywhere in the world, including in countries which were not members of the Conference. The Conference's own powers were also formalised to the degree that official tours would be only those that were included in the Conference's approved programme. While the detailed schedules and playing conditions for tours continued to be the subject of bilateral negotiation, the touring programme was controlled by the Conference. So when Australia and the West Indies, for example, were negotiating a visit by the latter to the former in the 1951/52 season, the Australian board sought and received approval from the Conference for its inclusion in the programme.

The first major challenge faced by the Conference after the war was the partition of India in 1947. At midnight on 14–15 August of that year, two independent states were created from what had been British India, with the Muslim-majority areas in the north-west and east forming Pakistan.

Despite the resistance of Mahatma Gandhi, who wanted India to become a single, multi-religious state, the pressure for partition, reinforced by inter-communal violence on both sides, proved irresistible. With the British determined to leave as quickly as possible, a plan for the division of territory was hastily cobbled together. The consequences of this rushed process were disastrous, with violence between the Hindu and Muslim communities reaching unprecedented levels and vast population movements, amounting to at least 14 million people fleeing across the newly created borders, causing a huge humanitarian crisis and souring relations between the two new nations.

For the first time in its history, the Imperial Cricket Conference was confronted by one of its members splitting in two. India had been a member since 1926, and its Test teams had always included a minority of players drawn from states which were now part of Pakistan, and Muslims who might now decide to move there from India. The party which had toured England in 1946 included the Lahore-born Abdul Hafeez, who would eventually become Pakistan's first Test captain, and Gul Mohammad. How should a body which had proved itself ill-equipped to deal with international crises off the field handle this situation? Its response could, in fact, scarcely have been more inept. With India on the way to becoming a republic and, in the context of 1947, its continued membership of the Commonwealth therefore in doubt, it was decided at the meeting on 19 July 1948 that the country's ICC membership would be made provisional for two years, after which its status would be reviewed. In the meantime, however, tours and Tests would remain official. For Pakistan the outcome was even worse: rather than regarding both India and Pakistan as heirs of India's long-standing membership, the Conference ruled that Pakistan would have to apply as a new member; it was, the minutes firmly recorded, 'not eligible to be invited to join the Conference until formally proposed and seconded by Member States'. The chairman, the Earl of Gowrie, even suggested that perhaps India and Pakistan might form a combined Test team (perhaps thinking of the way in which Rhodesia played within the South African system, or the combination of colonies which played as the West Indies). The political circumstances of partition made this an unlikely solution, although it should be noted that the Pakistani state of Sind took part in the 1947/48 Ranji Trophy in India.

In the uncertain conditions which prevailed in 1948 it is understandable that the Conference approached the issue with caution. There was, however, another context for its position. Days before the 1948 meeting MCC had announced that it was cancelling its scheduled tour of India in 1949/50, as a 'first step' towards reducing its tours abroad. This was, in fact, a product of a report by the club's Selection and Planning Sub-Committee, which recommended that in future only certain tours, principally those to Australia, should be recognised as official. Reviewing the report in the *Daily Herald*, Charles Bray described it as 'an apologia for English cricket', and his words were echoed by a correspondent writing as 'County Amateur' in the *Dundee Evening Telegraph* – under the headline 'MCC Apologises for English Cricket' – who described the document as 'remarkably naïve' and suggested that 'MCC have no plans to improve except to stop playing the countries [in] official Tests under conditions in which we may lose'. 'It would appear,' he commented, 'India and the West Indies have little chance of getting any more visits from "official" England teams. If teams do [visit] they will be "unofficial" and so there will be no loss of prestige if they are beaten.' It was this announcement by MCC which dominated the English press coverage of the ICC's meeting, with no mention at all of the issues around the membership of India and Pakistan. Findlay, indeed, spoke at the Conference of 'the overload on English cricketers'.

Turning from such controversial matters, the 1948 meeting also addressed a proposal for creating an Imperial Cricket Memorial at Lord's, to mark the sacrifice of cricketers from all over the Empire in the two world wars. The idea had first been conceived by MCC as early as 1946, and they now sought the endorsement of the Imperial Conference. On this, at least, there was no dissension, and over the next few years donations of memorabilia came flooding in, not only from the six member countries but also from Canada, Fiji and elsewhere. The 1952 meeting was informed that Australian Prime Minister R.G. Menzies, a confirmed cricket lover and Empire loyalist, was highly enthusiastic, and on 27 April 1953 the Memorial Gallery was opened by the Duke of Edinburgh. Now rebranded as the MCC Museum, the gallery retains a plaque dedicated 'To the Memory of Cricketers of all Lands who gave their Lives in the cause of Freedom' in the two wars, and it remains one of the more effective initiatives undertaken by the Conference.

The Board of Control for Cricket in Pakistan (BCCP) was formally established on 1 May 1949, by which time a Pakistan side had already played the West Indian team touring India, in Lahore in November 1948, and made a two-match visit to Ceylon in April 1949. By the time the ICC next met, in June 1950, Pakistan had also taken on the Commonwealth XI in Karachi and entertained the Ceylonese on a return visit. There was, however, no proposal before the 1950 meeting to admit Pakistan to membership. On the contrary, the MCC secretary outlined the correspondence between himself and the BCCP, denying the reported claim of the latter's vice-president that '[w]e get the impression that we are not wanted in the world family of cricket' and press commentary along the same critical lines. The Conference duly backed him up and resolved that 'this conference approves the action in December 1948 of MCC acting in its secretarial capacity in apprising Pakistan fully and accurately regarding the rules adopted in 1946 for the admission of new members. In view of the fact that these rules with which Pakistan was fully conversant had not been complied with by the Board, it was not in order for the Conference to consider its eligibility for admission as a new member country.' The Pakistanis, in other words, had only themselves to blame for the fact that they were not being considered for membership.

Pakistani outrage at this refusal by the Conference to consider its case for admission was exacerbated by the fact that at the 1950 meeting India was restored to full membership. The London Declaration by the 1949 Commonwealth Prime Ministers' Conference had ensured that India would remain a member of the Commonwealth despite becoming a republic on 26 January 1950, and there was therefore no longer a question that the BCCI might fall foul of the ICC rules. But there was no immediate prospect at this point of Pakistan's following suit, and it is, furthermore, difficult to see the relevance of the suggestion, made during the Conference discussion, that it should not concern itself with matters 'outside the conduct of international cricket'. There was no indication that the issue of playing standards, which might possibly have been used to hold up Pakistan's admission, was deployed, but any doubts on that score were in any case dispelled when the hosts had the better of a draw in the first of two matches against Nigel Howard's touring MCC side and went on to win by four wickets in the second, Fazal Mahmood taking 6-40 in the first innings and Khan Mohammad 5-88 in the second. After some conciliatory correspondence, India proposed Pakistan's admission at the next meeting, on 28 July 1952, MCC seconded with the proviso that any tours from abroad would take in India, Pakistan and Ceylon (an indication that concern about the load on players remained at the front of the English cricket authorities' minds), and Pakistan joined the club.

This untidy episode was not the only disturbance of the comfortable existence of the Conference delegates in this period. Following the London Declaration, MCC had circulated proposed new rules which would have renamed the ICC the 'British Commonwealth Cricket Conference' and which would have given the body a much firmer constitutional basis than it had previously had. It still gave the three founding members two votes each to the others' one, but it broke new ground by providing for a new category of associate membership open to 'a Governing Body of a Country within the British Commonwealth in which it is evident that First-class cricket is played'. It went without saying, quite literally, that it was to the existing members of the Conference that this would need to be 'evident', and two-thirds of them would need to vote in favour of the election of any new member, whether full or associate. Given the weighting of the votes, this meant that any two founding members held the veto over any proposal. The proposed new rules also required that any candidate for membership should be formally proposed and seconded by two existing members. When the Conference met in June 1950 the name change and the creation of an associate category both quietly disappeared, the meeting having agreed, according to its final statement, 'that it was desirable to stress its original object' which was 'the establishment of a purely cricket body of which the primary function has been and will be to determine official Test Match status of cricket-playing countries in the British Commonwealth on the simple basis of cricket skill'.

There was no mention in the public statement of the fact that Karl Nunes, on behalf of the West Indian board, had raised the matter of Rule 8, which provided that the founding members each had two votes, while the others had only one. Nunes' proposal to give all members the same voting rights was seconded by India, but New Zealand's Arthur Sims, always a trusty voice for the Old Guard, declared that his board was happy with the status quo, and unsurprisingly, Australia and South Africa agreed with him. The proposers, having made their point, retreated, if the statement in the minutes that a motion to retain the present rule was carried without dissent is technically correct. The West Indians raised the matter again two years later but were told that since they had not given proper notice it could not be discussed. They came fully prepared in 1953, proposing that Rule 8 be amended to read: 'All members of the Conference except associate members may exercise two votes each at a meeting of the Conference.' (Since the associate membership category was not established for a further 12 years, it is unclear why the reference to associates was included.) But they had not lobbied very successfully, since the Indian and Pakistani representatives said that they had no instructions from their boards and therefore could not take a position. With New Zealand again leading the resistance and South Africa firmly against, the West Indian delegation withdrew their motion.

On the field, however, the West Indians were laying down a different kind of challenge to the established order. The England team which toured the Caribbean in early 1948 failed to win a single match and lost the four-Test series 2-0. *Wisden* observed in its condescending way that 'the high merit of the West Indies players was a big surprise' and stated that 'it is essential that MCC treat a West Indies tour as seriously as one to Australia'. Worse was to follow. The West Indies side which visited England in 1950 included, in the legendary 'Three Ws' – Clyde Walcott, Everton Weekes and Frank Worrell – three outstanding batters, as well as the combination of the off-spinner Sonny Ramadhin and slow left-armer Alf Valentine, both 20 years old. After losing the first Test at Old Trafford the tourists won the series 3-1, Valentine claiming 33 wickets and Ramadhin 26. The biggest sensation of all was the West Indies' 326-run victory in the second Test at Lord's, marked by Walcott's brilliant 168 not out in the second innings and Valentine's match haul of 11-152. For the growing Caribbean community in London, in a city still recovering from the devastation of the

Blitz, where signs in boarding-house windows announcing 'No Blacks, No Irish' were not uncommon, their team's victory had a significance far beyond the match and the series, and the Calypso musician Aldwyn Roberts ('Lord Kitchener') celebrated with a 'Victory Calypso', with him and Egbert Moore ('Lord Beginner') leading a joyful crowd from St John's Wood to Piccadilly, singing:

> *Cricket lovely Cricket*
> *At Lord's where I saw it ...*
> *With those two little pals of mine*
> *Ramadhin and Valentine.*

Despite these achievements, it would be another six years before the West Indies were favoured with another visit to England.

There is no question that there was a strong financial dimension to MCC's management of the Conference. Findlay informed the June 1950 meeting that 'in future all MCC tours to South Africa, West Indies, New Zealand and India must be self-supporting' and that 'MCC would require all expenses of every kind connected with such a tour be covered'. Two years later he declared from the chair that 'MCC and the English counties were only too anxious to ensure fair treatment between countries but were not prepared to upset the traditional arrangement with Australia with regard to visits with that country'. Here the realpolitik of international cricket was clearly displayed, and it is striking how little has changed — apart, of course, from the balance of power — in 75 years. England and Australia continue to privilege the Ashes over their relations with lesser, less profitable, cricketing nations, although it is now India which has become the dominant force in determining the international schedules, England and Australia having been reduced to the role of willing co-conspirators.

As well as the question of voting rights, not to mention the way in which MCC continued to control the

Conference, there continued to be the matter of its now-anachronistic name. Though not yet quite a dead letter, the idea of the British Empire had been giving way to that of a Commonwealth of Nations since the Balfour Declaration of 1926. Accordingly, in 1955 the BCCI, reverting to the suggestion MCC had made in 1949, gave notice of a proposal to rename the organisation the Commonwealth Cricket Conference. This at any rate, one might have thought, would not be controversial, but when the proposal was discussed at the next meeting, in July 1956, it was once more Arthur Sims of New Zealand who led the resistance, arguing that there was 'no object in changing the name of the Conference unless there was a very good reason for doing so'. The fact that three of the seven members believed that the current name was outmoded evidently did not constitute a very good reason, and with Australia and South Africa backing the New Zealand position, the question was deferred.

The same fate befell a renewed attempt to change the voting system, again proposed by the BCCI. Their motion, supported by Pakistan, read like a manifesto: 'That in consonance with the spirit of the present times and relationship with all cricketing countries that are affiliated and are units of the Imperial Cricket Conference, the BCCI desires that she should be given equal status by being allowed 2 votes along with countries like England, Australia and South Africa. As cricket is essentially a Commonwealth game and since all cricketing nations are governed by the Imperial Cricket Conference, inequality of status for New Zealand, India, Pakistan and the West Indies, which have only 1 vote each, as against Britain, Australia and South Africa having 2 each, goes against the principle of equality and brotherhood. Hence the BCCI feels that all affiliated countries of the Imperial Cricket Conference should be on par with each other by having the same status and uniform representation at the Imperial Cricket Conference from this year onwards.'

It will surprise no one that such appeals to 'equality and brotherhood' left Arthur Sims and his allies unmoved: he referred to the 'friendly relationship that existed between all countries in the Conference which governed cricket with such acumen and success' and opposed the motion. No one, he said, had ever felt 'any difference of station' because of Rule 8. A little more surprising, perhaps, was the position adopted by Karl Nunes of the West Indies, who chose this moment to break ranks and suggest that his board at any rate should be elevated to equality with England, Australia and South Africa. So the Conference remained divided, and the matter was again deferred. Reporting to the Australian board in January 1957, the incoming chairman Bill Dowling stated that he had been 'impressed by the excellent case put forward by Mr Nunes for West Indies to have equal status with England, Australia and South Africa'. He had voted against, following the board's official line, but he felt that the West Indian case 'was worthy of some consideration'. His colleagues, however, evidently disagreed, and after discussion the board held to its view that 'no alteration to Rule 8 should be made at this stage'. Oblivious to the steadily building resentment they were occasioning among three of the four members who had only one vote each, the Australians continued to foster a balance of power which would eventually blow up in their faces.

By the time of the next meeting, in July 1958, a solution to the voting issue had been found. India again proposed that everyone should have the same number of votes, and this time the motion was seconded by B.A. Barnett of Australia. But Brigadier A.H. Coy of South Africa proposed an amendment, that all members should have one vote, but that a new category of foundation member should be established, to include England, Australia and South Africa, and that on certain reserved matters – changes to the rules, election of new members or removal of existing ones – no change would be made without the support of at least two of the foundation members. With the chairman holding a casting vote, this arrangement entrenched the power of the three original members, but at least gave the impression that for most purposes all the Conference's members were equal. Although the arch-conservative Arthur Sims once more gave his view that the existing system was fine, there was no dissent when this alternative proposal, moved by South Africa and seconded by India, was agreed. The Indians had at least achieved most of their objective, although the foundation members arrangement would cause increasing resentment in the years ahead, until it was finally abolished in 1993.

Another BCCI initiative in 1958 was rapidly torpedoed, this time by its own representative. The board had proposed that rather than always meeting at Lord's, the Conference venue might rotate among the members. It was, on the face of it, a relatively painless way of broadening the ICC's appeal. But it went too far for the BCCI's own delegate, the Maharajkumar of Vizianagram, who took the extraordinary step of withdrawing the motion. 'He felt it was appropriate,' the minutes record, 'that meetings of the ICC should be held at Lord's which is regarded as the Headquarters of cricket.' 'Vizzy' was in a bullish mood that year. When the Conference discussed possible restrictions on players writing in newspapers or books about tours in which they took part, he suggested that a ban for life should be imposed. Other boards, fortunately, took a somewhat less draconian view.

At the same time, the game itself was changing. There were growing concerns about the actions of bowlers in several countries, with matters coming to a head during the 1958/59 Ashes tour in Australia, where Ian Meckiff, Gordon Rorke and Keith Slater all came under scrutiny. Others whose bowling was controversial included South Africa's Geoff Griffin and England's Harold Rhodes. The no-ball law was also challenged by bowlers 'dragging', gaining advantage by getting closer to the batter, of which Rorke was perhaps the most notorious exponent, while the use of intimidatory short-pitched bowling was another symptom of a changed atmosphere in the international game. There was also growing criticism of the pace at which the game was played, fewer and fewer overs being bowled in a day's play. This all meant that the Conference on 14 and 15 July 1960 was one of the most momentous for many years, to the extent that Australian captain and *Sydney Sun* columnist Richie Benaud campaigned successfully for Sir Donald Bradman, the new chairman of the Australian board, to be flown to London to represent his board. Benaud got his way, and Bradman and his predecessor Bill Dowling were the Australian representatives. In addition to the issues around bowling and continuing frustrations with a touring schedule under which England gave priority to Australia, and to a lesser extent to South Africa, granting much less frequent tours to the other members, there was the increasingly acute issue of cricket under South Africa's apartheid regime. Nothing could be done about the touring schedules, although even Arthur Sims was moved to protest at the prospect that New Zealand might miss out on its traditional brief visit by MCC following a tour of Australia, and the South African question, triggered by a letter from Dennis Brutus of the South African Sports Association as well as by controversy over the current Springbok tour of England, was firmly struck into the long grass.

The other issues were more intractable, but the media were informed that 'a very happy atmosphere' had prevailed when the Conference discussed dragging and time-wasting. A decision was made to recommend moving to a front-foot definition of a no-ball, but 'not before September 1962', and the current experimental law on time-wasting was supported, with the addition of a power of the umpires to 'direct', rather than merely 'request', that a persistent offender should be removed from the attack. A similar change was recommended regarding the umpires' power to stop persistent short-pitched bowling. The recommendation on dragging once again underlined the perennial weakness of the Conference's powers; it could do no more than recommend 'that member countries consider this problem with a view of the possibility of the adoption of the front foot principle as an experiment'. While attempts were being made by some countries to limit the draggers' advantage by empowering umpires to force bowlers to land their back foot well behind the bowling crease, many felt that more urgent action was required than the Conference had been able to muster.

The discussion of throwing extended into the Conference's second day, and ended with an agreed definition of a throw: 'If the bowler's arm is bent at the elbow, whether the wrist is backward of the elbow or not and is suddenly straightened immediately prior to the instant of delivery, it is illegal.'

The bowler did, nevertheless, have the right 'to use his wrist freely in his delivery action'. In a wide-ranging review of the current laws, the Conference called upon the governing bodies to 'do all in their power to stop the excessive use of the short-pitched ball', recommended the limitation of fielders on the leg side in order to discourage leg-side bowling, and urged each board to consider taking action on damage to the pitch, reducing the width of the bowling crease, adjusting the new ball law to encourage greater use of leg-spinners, changing the lbw law to punish batters who padded the ball away regardless of where it pitched, and modifying the follow-on law. By making recommendations on so many aspects of the Laws the Conference was clearly expanding its role, since the setting of the Laws was the preserve of MCC; this was an implicit recognition that all members had a stake in ensuring that they were as fair and effective as possible. The Conference had moved a considerable distance from the time when its only concern was establishing a schedule of future tours, Benaud later claiming that the 1960 meeting 'did more for the game than had been done in the previous 51 years of the ICC's existence'.

Chapter 5

The South Africa Crisis and Beyond, 1961–1968

ON 15 March 1961 the South African Prime Minister, Hendrik Verwoerd, declared that as from 31 May, the day on which his country would become a republic, it would also withdraw from the British Commonwealth. His decision came after three days of negotiation with other Commonwealth leaders, where South Africa's application to remain within the Commonwealth, despite becoming a republic, had run into considerable trouble from other African leaders, as well as from Canada and India, because of the racially discriminatory apartheid system. There was no actual desire to refuse the request outright, but the sticking point was an insistence that the meeting should issue a statement condemning apartheid and in favour of human rights, to which Verwoerd was not prepared to agree. He had been, he declared, 'amazed and shocked' by the 'hostility and vindictiveness' to which he had been subjected, and it was with great regret that he had decided to walk away. 'The great majority of the people of my country,' he said (meaning of course the majority of the white minority which was the only sector of the population with any political rights) 'will appreciate that, in the circumstances, no other course was open to us.'

As the press immediately recognised, one of the consequences of this momentous decision would be a profound problem for the cricket authorities. The constitution of the Imperial Cricket Conference restricted membership to Commonwealth countries, and South Africa's departure would mean that one of the Conference's founding members – the country, indeed, from which the very conception of the Conference had come – would no longer be eligible. And that, in turn, meant that since the definition of a Test match was a game played between ICC members, South Africa would no longer be able to play Tests at all. Because the Springboks had never played the West Indies, India or Pakistan and were unlikely to do so under the apartheid system, this only affected the schedules of England, Australia and New Zealand. It was, however, a problem for the Conference as a whole, and it was predictable that there would be fundamental differences between the two groups. Asked about this on the day of Verwoerd's announcement, the MCC secretary (and therefore secretary of the ICC) Ronald Aird acknowledged that it would follow that South Africa would no longer be able to play official Test matches – that insertion of 'official' was already an indication of a potential way out of the difficulty – adding that 'maybe the rules will have to be re-examined'. Even at this moment of crisis, then, sympathy for the position of South African cricket was being signalled.

The Conference, after all, had form in this regard: as cultural historian Usha Iyer has pointed out and as we noted in the previous chapter, it had rebuffed approaches from Dennis Brutus, chairman of the South African Sports Association, and other opponents of apartheid, and it maintained relations only with the all-white South African Cricket Association, to which it referred Brutus's 1960 letter on the subject. The two organisations running cricket in the African, coloured and Indian communities, SAACB and SACBOC, were at no point recognised by the Conference, which held that it was SACA which was responsible for internal questions relating to South African cricket, blithely ignoring the realities of life under apartheid. This was entirely consistent with the ICC's historical structure, leaving as much as possible to the governing bodies and restricting its own areas of responsibility. It was inherent in the 1909 decision to constitute the international body as a conference rather than as a board, as Bailey had initially proposed, a chicken which was now coming home to roost.

The situation was exacerbated by the fact that from the outset the SACA had been the only organisation recognised by the Conference as representing the country's cricket, and it had always been racially exclusive, even before the introduction of the Nationalist government's apartheid policies. A decade before the Conference was established, the outstanding fast bowler 'Krom' Hendricks had been excluded from official cricket in Cape Town because of his 'Malay' ethnicity, and the South African Coloured Cricket Board, established in 1902, was simply never on the radar of SACA or its Imperialist allies. Neither were the South African Bantu Cricket Board (formed within the African communities in 1932) nor the South African Indian Cricket Union which followed in 1940, and even when the South African Cricket Board of Control (SACBOC) was set up in 1947 to bring together all the non-white cricketers in the country, SACA continued to be regarded by the ICC as the only national governing body in South Africa. SACBOC hosted a visit by a Kenyan Asian team in November 1956 and in 1958/59 Basil D'Oliveira, who would later play such a crucial part in the story, captained a 'South Africa Non-European Touring Team' on an 18-match tour of East Africa. These tours, however, and SACBOC's domestic competitions took place outside the framework of the Conference's official cricket, and as far as the Conference was concerned SACA remained the only legitimate governing body.

When the Conference met on 19 July 1961, by which time South Africa's membership had officially come to an end, R.E. Foster Bowley, the SACA president, was invited to attend as an observer. He withdrew, however, while the South African issue was discussed. After Muzaffar Husain, on behalf of Pakistan, declared that South Africa would have to agree to play all the other Test countries without regard to colour before he could vote for their return and was backed up by M.A. Chidambaram for India, the chairman, Sir Hubert Ashton, read out a statement provided by Foster Bowley. This stated that although there was no colour bar in the SACA constitution and 'no law prohibiting inter-racial cricket', SACA had not officially promoted such games 'in deference to stated Governmental policy'.

They had considered doing so, but were concerned that this would provoke the government into banning them, thereby preventing the unofficial games between white and non-white teams which were currently taking place. (He thought, apparently, purely of matches between white and non-white *teams*, with no consideration of integrated teams; in the rigid world of apartheid in 1961, that was clearly unimaginable.) South Africa would, Foster Bowley's statement continued, be delighted to tour India, Pakistan and the West Indies, but 'could not invite any of these countries to South Africa because the Government at ministerial level has stated it will not allow non-white teams in South Africa to play against white teams'. SACA would not be prepared to 'take active steps to remedy the existing position, because to do so would be to involve the Association in politics with we fear, disastrous results'.

This carefully worded statement was evidently designed to give the association's allies in the Conference the greatest possible opportunity to back South Africa's return without actually offering any criticism of apartheid which would alienate the Verwoerd government. It implied that SACA supported multi-racial cricket while indicating that the political situation, and the threat of even more draconian legislation, prevented it from doing anything to make it happen. And it invoked the mantra that politics should be kept out of sport, even while it implicitly accepted that South African politics was already deeply ingrained in the way cricket was played in the country. This provided the opening Australia, New Zealand and England needed to throw their weight behind readmission, at least in principle. The Australian delegates had not been authorised by the Australian board to vote in favour of changing the rules but stated that the matter would be further discussed at the Australian board's next meeting. New Zealand and England, represented by Sir Arthur Sims and Gubby Allen, were supportive but not yet prepared to act, Allen stating that South Africa's evident willingness to play against all the Conference members might 'politically... not be possible for the time being'. With India and Pakistan strongly opposed to readmission, the summary of the discussion was bland but nonetheless misleading: 'It was evident,' it read, 'from the views expressed that there was a general desire to help the SACA in the situation which which they found themselves. Nevertheless, before any question of their readmission to the Conference could be considered, it would be necessary to revise the Constitution. Furthermore, it might well be that for other reasons such a proposal might need consideration.' The public statement asserted that it had not been possible to include the question on the Conference agenda, but that there had nevertheless been a long discussion 'in order that delegates might be in a position to report back to their respective Boards the general feelings of the Conference on this issue'.

With New Zealand scheduled to tour South Africa in 1961/62 the matter had some urgency, but in the event that tour went ahead as if nothing had happened, and the Tests, although officially unofficial, were generally treated as if they were as much Test matches as any played under the auspices of the ICC. The Australian board, too, declared that the matches between Australia and South Africa and between New Zealand and South Africa during the latter's 1963/64 tour would count as full internationals, side-stepping the question of Test status. Again, however, they were universally referred to as Tests by the media in both countries, and statistical authorities like *Wisden* incorporated the players' performances without any real question. Defending this decision in his Notes to the 1965 edition, *Wisden*'s editor, Norman Preston, declared that '[w]hatever are one's feelings about apartheid, I do not think discrimination over the status of an international cricket match will help to solve the problem'.

By the time that latter tour took place the ICC had met twice more, on 18 July 1962 and on 17 July 1963, with the lines of battle essentially unchanged. At the 1962 meeting the Australian representative, Harold Bushby, proposed that each country should be allowed to set its own policy regarding matches against South Africa, while J.L. Kerr of New Zealand argued that until the matter could be resolved all Tests between South Africa and other countries should be regarded as official. Pakistan remained steadfastly at the head of the opposing group, although Muzaffar Husain urged all the delegates to express 'a fund of goodwill to the SACA'. Colonel Sir William Worsley, the chairman, closed the debate by asserting that 'it was, of course, open to any member country of the Conference to visit or receive visits from any other Conference [member] if they liked', thus effectively aligning the ICC with the Australian view that relations with South Africa were a question for individual members and ultimately nothing to do with the Conference, as well as conveniently ignoring the fact that South Africa was no longer a member. Even an argument from the West Indies, India and Pakistan that the touring schedule should be revised to give them more opportunities and South Africa fewer was firmly rejected by the other members. The official statement, indeed, asserted that '[e]very representative was sympathetic to the view expressed by MCC that nothing should be done in a revised programme which might be detrimental to the welfare of cricket in South Africa'. It seems improbable that this view was as unanimous as that bland statement makes it appear.

An argument repeatedly employed by South Africa's supporters within and beyond the Conference was that continued exclusion would not only have a detrimental effect on cricket in South Africa, but that it would be, in H.S. Altham's words on behalf of MCC at the 1963 meeting, 'a mortal blow' to the game across the continent of Africa. There had been up to this point little sign that the Conference had much interest in cricket anywhere except in South Africa and Southern Rhodesia – a British colony which took part in the South African domestic competition and whose players were eligible for selection as Springboks – although MCC was organising its first tour to East Africa in 1963/64. Indeed, other plans were afoot which would offer new opportunities to East Africa, Ceylon and other cricket-playing countries which had until now been excluded from any international framework, but the argument that a refusal to shut the door on South Africa would be catastrophic for the future of the game was simple hypocrisy: England, Australia and New Zealand were determined to go on playing against the all-white South Africans, and were perfectly happy to turn a blind eye to the political, legal and social restrictions which afflicted cricketers from the other communities in the country.

The 1963/64 Springbok tour of Australia and New Zealand had gone ahead without any obvious difference in the status of the Tests or the way they were reported, and for the next few years there was no discussion of the South African question at the Conference's meetings. For both the Conference and *Wisden*, it seemed, the less said about the issue the better. Introducing his report on the South

Africans' 1965 England tour, on which the visitors won the series 1-0 with two draws, Norman Preston nailed his colours to the mast: 'If there was any question whether their representative matches should be labelled Tests since their enforced withdrawal from the Imperial Cricket Conference in 1961,' he wrote, 'the excellence of their cricket definitely settled the matter.' It was a view which by their silence the dominant bloc in the Conference enthusiastically endorsed.

Pakistan, meanwhile, had been pursuing another line, which would ultimately have even more far-reaching implications for the ICC. No doubt remembering their own difficult path to recognition, the Conference's newest member took the initiative in proposing an entirely new category of membership, designed for countries where cricket was well established but where there was no immediate prospect of Test status. The Conference had, self-evidently, been exclusive from the outset, but there were many nations around the world – not all of them present or former British territories – where cricket had been played for as long as it had been in some of the Test-playing countries. Canada and the USA, after all, had played the first-ever international match as long ago as 1844, more than 30 years before the first 'Test' between Australia and England. Furthermore, as well as such members of the Commonwealth as Ceylon – who played regular matches against Madras and against other Indian state teams – Kenya, Tanganyika and Uganda, Fiji, and Malaya and Singapore, there was a long history of cricket in Argentina, who had been accorded first-class status up to World War Two, and in Denmark and the Netherlands.

In 1961, at the same ICC meeting at which the South African problem was first discussed, the Pakistanis proposed the creation of a new category of membership for such 'minor' cricketing nations; it seems unlikely that this timing was purely coincidental. With its usual capacity for obfuscation and delay, it would take four years for the Conference to implement the idea, but, in the end, it brought an end of sorts to the imperial conception upon which it had been established.

As he had been requested to do, Muzaffar Husain brought a worked-out proposal for a 'junior section' to the 1962 meeting, but there was concern about the possible costs of such a widening of the Conference's sphere of activity. The Australian board declared bluntly that they could not 'afford to outlay finance in this direction and would not be willing to subscribe towards the administration of any organisation set up to organise or control such matters'. Altham, the MCC representative, suggested it might be better to create zonal organisations, rather than admitting the lesser cricketing nations directly to the Conference. This, of course, ensured that any action would be deferred for at least another year; although the idea was reportedly 'well-received', it was evidently too radical a notion to be adopted immediately. By July 1963 MCC had come on board, now proposing the creation of an associate category, the members of which would be entitled to send a representative to the Conference, to receive the minutes and to raise matters for the agenda but having no vote. The full members would have 'zones of responsibility', arranging tours for the associates in their zone and helping with administration, keeping, in the words of the subsequent *Times* report, 'a fatherly eye' on their offspring. This was too much for Australia and the West Indies, who declared that they were too busy to take on such responsibilities, although New Zealand said that they would be prepared to look after Fiji. The Pakistanis, who had originally come up with the idea, appear now to have had cold feet, arguing that it would be better to establish the zonal organisations without admitting associates to the Conference itself. The inevitable result was that a decision was again deferred.

By the time of the 1964 meeting everybody had had plenty of opportunity to decide on the best way forward, but extraordinarily, the Australians said that their board had not yet considered the proposal and a decision was again put off. This time, however, there was effectively agreement in principle for the MCC proposal that 'countries with a governing body for cricket recognised by the Conference should be eligible for membership; and that the standard of cricket in such a country should decide its category of membership'. With such a step, the old Imperial limitation would disappear, and there was even an unstated implication that a country in the associate category might in future progress to full membership should the standard of cricket in that country, however that might be determined, reach a sufficient level. Finally, on 17 July 1965, the six existing members found enough nerve to take the momentous step, establishing associate membership and changing the organisation's name to the *International* Cricket Conference.

The new membership category grew slowly at first. Ceylon, Fiji and the United States were admitted in 1965, and the following year they were joined by Bermuda, Denmark, East Africa (a combination of Kenya, Tanganyika and Uganda) and the Netherlands. Malaysia were admitted in 1967, and in 1968 there came the further addition of Canada, with Gibraltar and Hong Kong following in 1969. By this time, therefore, the associates outnumbered the full members, but since they did not have a vote, their influence was negligible. Some had wondered whether, now that the Commonwealth requirement had finally been dispensed with, South Africa might apply for membership, but that did not happen. The associate representatives were not slow, however, to make use of their speaking rights, Philip Snow of Fiji asking the 1966 meeting whether the full members might not help the emerging countries through the provision of coaches. This was supported by MCC's Gubby Allen, who proposed the establishment of a fund to pay for such activities, with a minimum annual contribution of £100 per member. When this idea was discussed the following year it was endorsed by MCC and New Zealand and provisionally by Pakistan; Australia, India and the West Indies, though, were 'loath' to support it, 'owing to their constitutions and other financial commitments', and in India's case, foreign exchange requirements. The commitment to growing the game globally was certainly far from universal.

Another attempt along the same lines came from the USA's N.N. Marder, who at the 1966 Conference revived the idea that each full member might be assigned a sphere of influence, within which they would support specific associates. This received more widespread approval, the delegates instructing the secretary to bring a detailed scheme to next year's meeting. This he duly did, with MCC to look after Holland and Denmark, the West Indies taking Bermuda and the USA, New Zealand supporting Fiji, India responsible for Ceylon, and Pakistan for East Africa; Australia was tactfully not given any such responsibility. Ceylon was particularly keen to create greater opportunities to take on full member sides, repeatedly urging that a visit to the island should be included in the schedules of teams touring India, but when they proposed to the 1968 Conference that there might be a triangular tournament between themselves, India and Pakistan they were firmly knocked back by India, who indicated that such an event was out of the question.

The Conference, meanwhile, continued to busy itself with other matters. Even in the crisis atmosphere of 1961 the South African question was preceded by discussion of whether the new ball should be taken after a specified number of overs had been bowled or runs had been scored. Other matters which took precedence were the perennial issue of the lbw law, the follow-on provision, the appointment of Test umpires, and the duration of Tests, where Australia had to apologise for having allowed the final match of the 1960/61 West Indies series to extend beyond the permitted 30 hours. On none of these matters, of course, was any final decision reached. By the following year, though, the Conference was ready to return to the problem of dragging, agreeing after much debate that all members would experiment with a no-ball law based on the position of the front foot.

A more difficult issue was that of throwing which, as we have seen, had first surfaced at the start of the decade with the questionable bowling actions of Geoff Griffin of South Africa, the West Indian Charlie Griffith and the Australians Ian Meckiff and Gordon Rorke, and which had led the ICC to establish a new definition of a throw. Australia had prudently omitted Meckiff and Rorke from their touring party to England in 1961, but two years later Meckiff made an ignominious exit from the game when he was no-balled three times in an over by umpire Colin Egar in the first Test against South Africa in Brisbane, never to bowl again in first-class cricket. The problem, however, persisted, and in 1963 MCC proposed that the 'moratorium' which had been agreed between themselves and the Australian board at the end of 1960, whereby a bowler who allegedly threw in a match between a county side and a touring team would be reported rather than called, should be given more general currency 'for a limited period of say five to seven years'. The Conference rejected the idea, with the West Indian representative opposing not only a general moratorium but the operation of a special playing condition modifying the Laws (this would later become the standard way in which a more activist ICC would adjust the Laws for particular purposes). In 1965 the Conference got around to recommending a slight adjustment to the law and urging all its members to take measures to deal with illegal actions. This did not meet with universal approval. In a syndicated column, the former England batsman Cyril Washbrook observed that the 'slight alteration in the definition of throwing is not going to make the task of umpires any easier', while his one-time captain Norman Yardley was provoked into a remarkable diatribe against the ICC itself. 'The only worthwhile thing that came out of the 1965 Imperial Cricket

Conference was that, at long last, it had the common sense to change its title'. That apart, at a time when the game needed stimulation and evidence of real leadership, it offered nothing. Nothing at all. And it is high time there was a fundamental change.'

The Conference, he continued, needed to be given executive powers; 'At present it merely emits gas, suggests this, recommends that, hopes for the other, refers back to various boards for comment.' The 1965 meeting 'with its wishy-washy lack of decision did more to slap down the image of big cricket than help to build it up'. *Wisden* was more diplomatic: 'No firm decisions were made,' it reported, adding: 'Some changes were proposed to these new rules and although all the countries had had at least two months to study them, one or two Boards of Control said they were not in a position to express an opinion.'

One of the bowlers with a suspect action was England's Harold Rhodes, who was double-jointed, and MCC brought to the 1966 meeting a proposal that 'freak actions' such as his, employing what they called an 'over-extended arm', 'should not be stigmatised as a throw'. Once again deciding to take no decision – 'a very long meeting produced nothing fruitful', *Wisden* observed – the Conference referred the question back to the governing bodies, and MCC promptly introduced an experimental law which permitted Rhodes to bowl. The following year they proposed that this should become universal, but the other members firmly rejected the idea and any possible resumption of Rhodes' Test career was abandoned.

Still the Conference continued to come up against the old problem that it had little power over its members. On imposing a limit of two on the number of fielders on the leg side, the West Indies continued to resist the majority opinion, and when the Australians proposed at the 1964 meeting that the experimental note to this effect should now be incorporated into the Laws, resistance from the West

Indian representatives was enough to defer the decision for another year. By the following year MCC had added its dissent, arguing that not only was such a rule unnecessary in 'the lower levels of cricket', but that it was undesirable that a captain should be forced to set his field in a particular manner. The idea now emerged of restricting the number of fielders behind the wicket only, but even this went too far for the West Indies, and it was not until 1969 that the restriction was added to the Laws.

That 1967 meeting was notable in other respects as well. In addition to a return by the Australian board to its perennial theme of playing the final Test of a series to a finish when the outcome of the series remained in doubt, the delegates finally took heed of the understandable complaints that the Conference was never able to decide anything. T.N. Pearce of the West Indies pointed out that the Conference's public image was very poor and proposed that it 'should be empowered to take certain decisions on the majority support for members'.

Even the traditionalist Gubby Allen was prepared to concede that representatives should be given greater power to negotiate. Ever since its creation in 1909 the Conference had only ever had the power of recommendation, even in arranging tours, but the events of the past decade had evidently convinced even these conservative administrators that in the modern world they needed a decision-making capacity which the global governing bodies of other sports had enjoyed from their establishment. This produced a recommendation that 'representatives should be given more power and flexibility in their negotiations' at the Conference. A year later, however, this radicalism had ebbed somewhat. Although the secretary expressed his 'concern at the poor public image of the Conference', the issue was now confined to creating a timetable which would enable boards to consider proposals in advance of the meeting. From now on, agenda items would have to be submitted by 1 December with the agenda circulated by 31 December for a Conference in early June. It would be a couple of decades until a reconstituted Council would become a truly decision-making body.

Chapter 6

The Tectonic Plates Begin to Shift, 1968–1978

THE STORM which surrounded Basil D'Oliveira and the cancellation of the 1968/69 MCC tour of South Africa was several years in the making. Born in Cape Town and classified as 'Coloured' under the apartheid system, D'Oliveira was an extremely talented cricketer who had grown up in the SACBOC leagues and who, after captaining a SACBOC team in Kenya in 1958, was the professional at the Central Lancashire League club Middleton before joining Worcestershire in 1964. He soon came into the reckoning to play for England as an all-rounder and made his debut against the West Indies at Lord's in 1966. By the start of the 1968 season he had appeared in 14 Tests, making 709 runs at an average of 41.71 and taking 15 wickets at a costly 53.06; that included, however, England's recent, disastrous series in the West Indies. What happened in that summer of 1968 is one of the most thoroughly researched and frequently written about episodes in cricket history, and we now know the extraordinary lengths to which certain MCC administrators went to keep D'Oliveira out of the team to tour South Africa that winter, so as to avoid a confrontation with Johannes Vorster's government. The South Africans had been concerned about the possibility of D'Oliveira's presence in the MCC side from the moment he played for England, and both they and the MCC leadership were keen that the tour should not be jeopardised.

In the event, things could not have worked out worse for the conspirators. Omitted after the first Test of the series against Australia, where he had made a second-innings 87 not out as England went down to a 159-run defeat, D'Oliveira was recalled for the final game at The Oval and made a fine 158 in the first innings to set up England's victory. He was nevertheless omitted from the touring party for South Africa, a decision which provoked a chorus of disbelief and outrage: many were convinced that it had been made to forestall a cancellation of the tour by the Vorster government. But then, when the seamer Tom Cartwright was forced to pull out through injury, there was little choice other than to bring in D'Oliveira as a replacement, and that provoked Vorster into labelling it a political selection and cancelling the tour. The entire episode has rightly been called a Greek tragedy, as every action taken by MCC and the English selectors on the one hand and by SACA and the South African government on the other, led inexorably towards that conclusion. The full extent of the duplicity of the key actors, especially within the leadership of MCC, has only recently come to light, but the initial omission of D'Oliveira caused outrage among the club's membership, and the political movement to break off all sporting ties with South Africa as long as apartheid survived gained considerable strength.

It seems that the D'Oliveira case was too much even for the ICC. After years of looking the other way, at its meeting in July 1970 it finally tackled the issue, at the prompting of England's Cricket Council, and issued a statement: 'The role of South Africa in the cricket world was discussed in some detail. Concern was expressed over the future of the international cricket between member countries of the ICC and South Africa under existing conditions. The Conference noted the position of the Cricket Council in this respect, as made clear in their statement issued in May. The matter will be the subject of deliberation by individual member countries, and if any member wishes to put forward a proposal, it will be circulated for consideration by the 1971 Conference.'

That the Conference should have reached the point of expressing 'concern' – though only, of course, about some of its members' ability to go on playing against the Springboks – was a step in the right direction, although there was still the problem that no actual decision could be made until everyone had had another year to think about the matter. Rather than, for example, setting up a committee to bring forward recommendations, the delegates preferred to leave it to 'any member' to bring forward a proposal; what had shifted the balance was that following the D'Oliveira episode, pressure had built up in England to cease playing the South Africans, and the deadlock within the Conference was beginning to crack.

But still South Africa's friends within the cricket establishment were determined to block decisive action. After a two-day meeting on 19–20 July 1971 the Conference was still unable to agree on categorical, unified action, and issued a statement which was unusually frank about the extent of the division: 'The International Cricket Conference discussed at length the matter raised by West Indies concerning the future cricket relations of member countries with South Africa. The discussion was confined solely on which was best in the interests of cricket. In this context there was universal concern at, and condemnation of, the effect of South African racial policies on the rights of individuals anywhere of any colour, race or creed, to play cricket together.

'There was, however, a difference of viewpoint whether the Conference should make a ruling restricting member countries in their cricket relations with South Africa or whether this was a question solely for the determination of each member. The Conference recorded its earnest hope that there would soon be effective changes in South Africa which would enable that great cricketing country to take its place in international cricket. The Conference welcomed the moves already made by the cricket authorities in South Africa to achieve this result.'

It is not difficult to identify the forces at work in this text. South Africa's critics had achieved a good deal in at last persuading their colleagues to issue a condemnation of apartheid's effects on cricketers' rights, but they were unable to bring them as far as to demand an end to cricketing contacts. Furthermore, the inclusion of that final sentence welcoming SACA's supposed moves to end, or at least reduce, the racial divide within that country's cricket is a clear concession to South Africa's friends in England, Australia and New Zealand, where the insistence on 'keeping politics out of sport' still served as a cover for acceptance of the apartheid system.

For some, keeping the power of the Conference to a minimum was almost equally important. Sir Donald Bradman, chairman of the Australian board, was quick to welcome the decision to uphold 'the principles which Australia has always felt to be correct, that cricket countries should be free to individually decide what they should do'. He declined to indicate how his board might view the proposed South African tour of Australia in 1971/72, or to comment on the Conference's condemnation of the effects of apartheid on cricket. In the event, bringing the Springboks to Australia proved impossible, and even a further Australian visit to the Republic was quietly dropped.

In spite of everything, however, attempts at 'bridge building' between the South African authorities and their friends in world cricket continued, albeit without much encouragement from the South African government. MCC still hoped that it might be possible for the Springboks to tour in 1975, but by the time the Conference met in July 1973 it was apparent that this was unlikely to happen. On the eve of the meeting, England's Cricket Council took a stand and refused to allow the winners of the Gillette Cup, the English one-day competition, to take part in a tournament in South Africa, adding that no English side would be permitted to do so until more progress was made towards multi-racial cricket. The emergence of one-day cricket did, however, offer the Conference a way out of the difficulty presented by a gap in England's schedule: it adopted the idea of a World Cup as a centrepiece of the 1975 season. The idea had first been mooted in 1971, but the following year the Cricket Council suggested a much larger competition which would also have included three-day and five-day formats. Some countries, the West Indies, India and Pakistan among them, preferred a three-day format, and the matter was referred back to the boards for further discussion. That led to the substantive proposal for a one-day 'International Competition' (not yet called a World Cup) to be held in England in 1975, which was unanimously adopted at the 1973 Conference.

But lurking behind the decision was England's continuing hope that relations with South Africa could be resumed. Announcing the World Cup plan at the conclusion of the Conference on 25 July, the MCC and ICC secretary Billy Griffith let the mask drop for a moment, unconsciously revealing the extent to which the ICC was an instrument of MCC: 'In the event of South Africa not being able to fulfil the conditions clearly laid down in May, 1970, with regard to future Test teams [sic] between them *and ourselves* [my italics], the following countries will be invited . . . ' He was speaking on behalf of the ICC, but the conditions he referred to had been laid down by MCC, and by 'ourselves' he clearly meant England. If it went ahead, the tournament would involve 60-over matches, with eight countries taking part: associate members Sri Lanka and East Africa would be invited to join the six official Test-playing countries.

In 1971 the Conference had given greater recognition to the associates by giving them one vote each, but this was balanced by a requirement that for any proposal to be passed it must be supported by two-thirds of the full members and at least one of the foundation members (England and Australia). The problem with this soon emerged. The following year, a proposal to retain Experimental Law 35 relating to a catch on the boundary was defeated despite having the overwhelming support of the associates, because three of the six full members voted against it. The associates did not wish to be in a position to dictate to the full members, they explained, but they did not find the existing arrangement satisfactory. It was agreed that possible amendments could be considered at the following meeting, but the issue disappeared from the agenda and proved much less significant in the long run than the reserved position of the foundation members.

As well as the inclusion of two associates in the inaugural World Cup, further evidence that the Conference saw the event as an opportunity to promote the game more widely came from the decision to devote part of the profits to 'assist the smaller cricketing countries by providing funds for the benefit of cricket in Associate Member Countries, particularly in regard to their coaching programmes'. 10% of any profit would go to the UK as host, 7.5% to each of the participating members, with the balance passing to the ICC 'to be distributed at their discretion between the non-participating Associate Member Countries, the International Coaching Fund and the Reserve Account for the promotion of the next International Competition'. For the first time, the Conference would be putting its money into the development of world cricket. A management committee was established to administer the coaching fund, chaired by the ICC chairman and including one representative from each of the foundation members, one from the remaining full members, three from the associates, and the ICC secretary. It was recommended that each full member should contribute £250 a year to the fund and each associate £50; small beer, one might think, and it was strange that the associates were expected to contribute to a fund designed to help them, but it was a significant step towards the Conference assuming some responsibility for developing the game outside its traditional strongholds.

Within South Africa, meanwhile, the situation continued to evolve, despite the restrictions of apartheid. Attempting to divide and continue to rule, SACA had begun to support the efforts of SAACB, the organisation for cricket in the African community, but SACBOC, representing the rest of non-white cricket, followed its own path. At its 1972 meeting the Conference took an 'unminuted decision' – itself an extraordinary measure – to invite representatives of the three governing bodies in South Africa, SACA, SAACB and SACBOC, to attend the following year as observers, hoping that in the meantime a cricket council would have been formed to unite them. In July 1973 the secretary reported that 'in the absence of unanimity of agreement' he had not issued any invitations, but SACBOC had indicated that they would like to send observers, with a view to applying for membership of the Conference in their own right. Ronald Aird had replied that they could not be accepted as observers, 'but he undertook to introduce any representative of the SACB[O]C to representatives of Member Countries during the period of the Conference'. Any application for membership would be a matter for the Conference itself.

In fact SACBOC did apply for membership in 1974 and again in 1975, but these approaches were predictably rebuffed, a statement being issued on the former occasion expressing its hope 'that there will soon be effective changes in South Africa which will enable a single body truly representative of all cricket in that country to take its place at their Conference'. In 1976 SACBOC split, a minority electing to join SACA and SAACB in a theoretically non-racial South African Cricket Union. Led by SACA's Joe Pamensky and Rashid Varachia, formerly president of SACBOC and the inaugural president of SACU, the new body integrated its local leagues, and slowly black players began to be selected in provincial teams, at least in Western Province and Boland. This gave credibility to SACU's claim to have introduced truly non-racial cricket despite the opposition of the South African government, but the dissenters in SACBOC pointed to the gross inequalities in playing facilities, the influence of a racially segregated school system, and the wider limitations imposed by the economic and legal structures of apartheid.

The South African tour was eventually cancelled, and in June 1975 the eight teams duly assembled. East Africa and Sri Lanka were outclassed, each losing all three matches, although Sri Lanka did compile a respectable 276/4 against Australia and went down by only 52 runs. The final between Australia and the West Indies at Lord's was a great occasion: Clive Lloyd's 102 enabled the West Indies to reach 291/8 in their 60 overs, Gary Gilmour taking 5-48 for Australia, and then Australia were dismissed for 274, Ian Chappell top-scoring with 62 before becoming one of five run-outs in the innings. Keith Boyce, no stranger to English conditions after a decade with Essex, claimed 4-50. The atmosphere was enormously enhanced by a crowd which included many Caribbean immigrants to Britain, who cheered mightily as their team won what proved to be the inaugural World Cup. What had begun as a response to the South African problem had brought a new dimension to the ICC, revealing that it could, like any other global sporting body, organise major international events. It was a shift which would transform the organisation.

Other forces were also at work, moving in the same direction. When the Conference met four days after that World Cup final, Abdul Hafeez Kardar, representing Pakistan, launched a frontal attack on the privileged position of the foundation members, declaring that 'unequal association and partnership did not really work' and calling for a more equal partnership among the members, especially those with Test status. At the same time, he proposed, supported by India, that Sri Lanka should be elevated to full membership. Speaking for England, F.R. Brown protested that tours involving Sri Lanka would not be financially viable and that not enough was known about the standard of cricket on the island. It would be better, he argued, pursuing a familiar theme, for the Conference to 'wait a year or two'. The West Indies supported this view, and although E.W. Miller, Sri Lanka's UK representative, assured the delegates that the Sri Lankan government would guarantee the financial success of any tour to the country, ACB chairman Tim Caldwell insisted that Australia was opposed to any increase in the number of Test-playing nations, observing, in a revealing phrase, that 'it was difficult enough at present to keep their Test players in an amateur standing'. The Conference told Kardar to bring back his proposal in a year's time, although it noted that the other members were 'not … necessarily prepared to accept Sri Lanka as a full Member purely on a recommendation of that country's performances against India and Pakistan in the coming year'.

Undaunted by this rebuff, Kardar did return to the issue in July 1976, although by this time he was also exercised by another issue: the possibility of Bangladesh becoming an associate member. The former Pakistani territory of East Pakistan had fought a brief but bitter war in 1971 before becoming the independent nation of Bangladesh, and a separate cricket board had been established the following year. In an apparent spirit of reconciliation, Kardar argued that having seceded from an ICC member Bangladesh should automatically become an associate member in its own right, but this did not impress the chairman, who ruled that the Conference must have the opportunity to judge whether 'the seceding country had an organisation properly run as a governing body for cricket and that cricket was firmly established and organised within the country'. This was, he pointed out, the procedure which had been followed in the case of Pakistan itself after the partition of India – although this took no account of the difference between the admission of Pakistan as a full member with Test status and the rather less far-reaching issue of whether Bangladesh should become an associate. Still, he ruled that although he was sympathetic to Bangladesh's claims, their election must wait a year until a formal proposal had been submitted. Another can had been kicked down the road.

Kardar was not any more successful in his advocacy of the upgrading of Sri Lanka's membership. The Australians were still opposed, on the grounds of the increasingly difficult financial pressures of the tour programme, and the West Indies now expressed concern that if Sri Lanka became a Test-playing nation it could lead to Jamaica, Barbados and other Caribbean nations deciding to go it alone. This 'could open the door to the proliferation of Test-cricketing countries'. This fear occasioned an apparently bizarre intervention by J.J. Warr, the ACB's British-based representative and one of its two delegates to this Conference, whose experience of Australia consisted of a tour with MCC in 1950/51: 'Not only was it in West Indies that breakaway situations could occur,' he observed; 'it was not impossible in Australia.' Perhaps Warr was thinking back to the bitter controversy around Sid Barnes in 1952, which had led to an attempt by New South Wales (NSW) to give themselves and Victoria complete control of the Australian board and even led the former to threaten secession. Or perhaps it was merely a joke; Warr's presence in the Australian delegation apparently owed much to his reputation as a witty after-dinner speaker. Whatever he may have intended, the opposition carried the day. When Pakistan and India formally moved that Sri Lanka become a full member, the motion was lost by four votes to two.

It was not only the issues of South Africa and of Sri Lanka's membership which divided the Conference along political lines. When Israel was proposed for associate membership in 1974, Pakistan made its opposition clear,

A.H. Kardar having pre-emptively written to express his board's objections. Although his line of attack was to deny that cricket in Israel met the ICC's criteria of the game being fully established with a competent organisation, it is likely that global politics was the underlying reason; although documentation was presented to the meeting showing that the Israeli association had been established in 1966 and that there were 21 teams playing in four zonal leagues, Kardar continued to oppose their admission. He was to some degree supported by the Bermudian representative, who suggested that cricketers in Israel were immigrants and mostly itinerant, but the American delegate responded that that also applied to his country. A positive report by former England Test cricketer Ken Barrington, who had visited Israel, helped to carry the day, but when a motion for admission, put forward by the UK (so named because the TCCB was still responsible for Ireland and Scotland) and seconded by Australia, was about to be put, Kardar, along with Asaf Ali and Zafar Altaf, walked out in protest. The motion was adopted, with Israel being placed in England's 'sphere of assistance'.

The ICC, meanwhile, were not the only ones who could see the commercial potential of international one-day cricket. In Australia, media baron Kerry Packer had evidently taken note, and before the end of 1975 he had hatched a plot which would revolutionise world cricket even more than the World Cup had done, giving the ICC a humiliating defeat in the process. Packer's primary ambition was to obtain the media rights for Australian cricket for his Nine Network, whisking them away from the Australian Broadcasting Commission (ABC), which had held them since first radio and then television had begun covering major matches. But his attention had been drawn by John Cornell and Austin Robertson, the chief movers in the sports management agency JP Sport, to the dissatisfaction of many of the leading players with the way they were systematically underpaid by the governing bodies. On 16 August 1976, Packer registered a new company called World Series Cricket Pty Ltd, and soon his agents were putting out feelers to players like Ian Chappell, raising the prospect of contracts in the vicinity of $20–30k for 12 weeks' play. For men who normally earned a tiny fraction of that sum, the appeal was obvious. The Australian board, meanwhile, were dismissive of Packer's attempts to wean them away from the ABC when its current three-year contract came to an end, and WSC's negotiations with players around the world began in earnest.

By the time the plan became public, just as the Australian touring team arrived in England in May 1977, no fewer than 35 players had signed with Packer, including 13 of the 17 who were on that tour. There were four from each of England, the West Indies and Pakistan, and five from South Africa. The list included most of the finest players of their generation: Clive Lloyd, Viv Richards, Michael Holding, Andy Roberts, Imran Khan, Graeme Pollock, Mike Procter and Barry Richards. Packer was intending to spend around $2.5 million on a series between Australia and a World XI, which would be played during the 1977/78 Australian season. The Australian board played a straight bat: 'It is the firm policy of the Board that it be the sole promoter of cricket in Australia at international and interstate levels,' the chairman Bob Parish told the press. 'The Board will give consideration to the Channel Nine proposal in due course.' Four days after the story broke, the English Test and County Cricket Board dismissed their captain Tony Greig, who had played an active role in recruiting players for Packer.

With all its members facing an unprecedented challenge, the ICC held a hastily organised meeting in London on 23 June, at which an attempt was made to negotiate with Packer. Taking a leaf out of the Australian board's book the Conference insisted that it was the sole promoter of international cricket, but it was prepared to agree to Packer running a six-week series, half of what he intended, if it did not interfere with the board's schedule. For Packer, however, the bottom line was his desire to take over the exclusive media rights, and when the ICC was not prepared to go further than inviting him to compete with the ABC, the negotiations broke down. Packer did not conceal his anger: had he been given exclusive rights, he told the media, he would have been prepared to walk away and leave the field to the board, but now it was 'every man for himself'. The high-minded rhetoric about paying the oppressed players what they were due disappeared in the heat of the moment; for Packer, it had always been about enhancing his media empire.

Steadily, the lines of battle hardened. Packer had gone ahead and negotiated to use VFL Park, the property of the Australian Rules football authority in Victoria, as his headquarters and main venue in Melbourne, while in Sydney on 25 July the board of the Sydney Cricket Ground Trust announced that its ground, one of the most historic in Australia, would not be available to the Packer circus. The New South Wales government sacked the Trust board the following day. That was also the first day of the ICC's regular annual meeting at Lord's, after which secretary Jack Bailey announced that the meeting had 'disapproved' of any matches arranged by Packer and that they would not be regarded as first-class. More fatefully, the Conference had also decided that as from 1 October 1977 any players under contract to Packer would not be eligible to play for their countries in official matches. Packer stated that this ruling was 'regrettable although predictable', and a week later announced that he was instituting proceedings in the UK High Court to restrain the ICC and TCCB from banning his players from international cricket. He was also seeking an injunction against the Australian agent David Lord to prevent him from trying to persuade Packer players to withdraw, while Tony Greig, Mike Procter and John Snow would also ask the court to overturn their bans.

The first skirmish took place in the High Court on 3 August, and the following day Mr Justice Slynn, having heard that the ICC and TCCB were not intending to take any further action until the legal cases had been concluded, declined to issue interim injunctions against those bodies, although he did grant a seven-day injunction to restrain Lord from 'wrongfully inducing players to break their contracts with Packer'. Extending his campaign against the cricket authorities, Packer now announced that he was also taking legal action in Australia, JP Sport suing the chairman and secretary of the ACB and its delegate to the ICC meeting in July; it was seeking a declaration that the board had contravened a section of the Trade Practices Act, an injunction restraining the defendants or their servants or agents from 'engaging in conduct that hinders or prevents the supply of services by third persons to a plaintiff company', and an interim injunction to prevent the defendants from implementing 'a certain resolution'.

The main hearing in the UK High Court, which ran from 26 September to 7 November, laid bare many of the problems which had long afflicted cricket: the supercilious arrogance of the governing bodies, the simmering grievances of the players, the determination of the Packer camp to break the status quo. Opening for the complainants, Robert Alexander QC described the TCCB and ICC decision as 'a 19th-century lock-out', adding that it was 'illogical, dictatorial, penal and challenges an elementary liberty'. It quickly became clear that Alexander's strategy was to lay heavy emphasis upon the miserable way in which players had been treated by the cricket authorities in the past, and to present Packer as a saviour of the game. His first witness, the deposed England captain Tony Greig, made this case strongly in a day and a half of evidence, stating that he had earned just £7,000 in the previous season and suggesting that the recent increase in the match fee for a Test from £210 to £1,000 was a direct result of Packer's challenge. By contrast, he would earn $30k for playing in Packer's circus and a further $10k as captain of the Rest of the World XI. He also expressed resentment of the TCCB rule which only allowed players' wives to be with their husbands on tour for 21 nights; Alan Knott, he stated, had almost pulled out of the tour of India because of this. John Snow was, if anything, an even more effective critic of the *ancien regime*, testifying that he had had to take unemployment relief during the winter, and referring to 12 years in which he and other players had been forced to assume the role of Oliver Twist.

Packer himself was in the witness box for the best part of three days, making no secret of the fact that his primary purpose was, and had always been, to force the Australian authorities into giving him exclusive broadcasting rights. He had offered the ACB $2.5 million for a five-year contract and had been rebuffed. If the ban on his players continued, he threatened to bring the circus to England to compete with the TCCB's schedule. He had, he said, gone into his meeting with the authorities with two preconditions: that there should be no victimisation of the players and that he should be given exclusive rights to show Tests played in England on his Australian network. But the authorities had rejected the second of these demands, and therefore there could be no further negotiation. He was, he said, astonished by the 'frightening' alacrity with which the players he approached had accepted his offer. In deciding to set up World Series Cricket he had applied three tests: was it good for the public, was it good for television, and was it good for the players? He concluded that it passed all three. The ICC and the TCCB, he argued, were 'carrying the can' for the Australian board, and the case was being fought 'exclusively for Australia's benefit'.

As a string of Packer's contracted players passed through the witness box, stressing the miserable conditions under which they had pursued their careers until now, the defendants suddenly shifted their ground, claiming on 6

October that they were employers' associations under the 1974 Trade Union and Labour Relations Act, a status which might lend greater legitimacy to their action against Packer's players. Alexander was scornful: if they were employers' associations, he said, they would have the power to alter the rules 'to allow only left-handed batsmen, with one eye or one arm, to play, which would be defeating the purpose of being an employers' association'. But Michael Kempster QC, representing the defendants, was equally tough in some of his language: the Packer circus was 'essentially parasitic in its nature': 'Its raw materials are, and can only be, the outstanding players whose reputations have been established, and whose skills have been and are being nurtured, in playing conventional cricket games for and against teams including players of lesser attainment.'

He was, however, prepared to acknowledge that Packer's initiative 'had had a number of beneficial effects', including the raising of players' incomes and the attraction of potential sponsors to the game. Despite the 'disparaging and offensive remarks' Packer had made about the ICC and the TCCB, Kempster added, those bodies did not begrudge him this acknowledgement.

Kempster proceeded to call a dozen witnesses for the defence, starting with the ACB treasurer Ray Steele, who gave the opinion that Packer had been 'mad' to reject the ICC's offer on 23 June, and that the ICC had been mad to offer it. Cross-examined by Alexander, he found it 'eminently reasonable' that the Packer players should be treated as outcasts by the cricket establishment. Not all Kempster's witnesses were equally helpful. Peter Short, from the West Indian board, expressed sympathy with the players, especially Procter (whose career had been overshadowed by the isolation of South Africa), and stated that his board was supporting the ban 'in the interests of presenting a united front'. When the Yorkshire and England batsman Geoffrey Boycott testified, it emerged that Greig had attempted to warn him off, which earned the former England captain a stern warning from Mr Justice Slade. Boycott himself enlivened the hearing with some folksy humour, but he was the only player who openly sided with the authorities. Closing for the complainants, Andrew Morritt QC argued that the administration of cricket was a 'sort of system that can only properly be described as feudal' and asked why a cricketer should not be free to choose for himself whether to play for a private promoter or not.

After two and a half weeks of deliberation, Mr Justice Slade delivered his judgement on 27 November, and it was a scarifying defeat for the cricket authorities. He accepted Morritt's contention that players ought to be able to choose whether to play for a private promoter or not and endorsed Kempster's acknowledgement of the benefits Packer's initiative had brought to the game. He found for the plaintiffs on every point, and imposed the costs of the actions, amounting to about £250,000, upon the ICC and the TCCB. Unsurprisingly, the authorities decided in February 1978 not to risk increasing that bill by appealing the judgement, but by that time Packer's circus had rolled around Australia, drawing reasonable crowds but losing out to the official Tests against Australia when they were in direct competition. But Packer was prepared for the long haul, and over the two seasons of World Series Cricket the crowds grew, especially once NSW premier Neville Wran had pushed successfully for WSC matches to be played at the Sydney Cricket Ground.

With its leading state bodies in New South Wales and Victoria suffering substantial financial losses and its official Test team suffering humiliating defeats, the Australian board capitulated at the end of May 1979. It abandoned its long-standing support of the ABC and gave Packer the exclusive broadcasting rights which had always been his real goal. Furthermore, his newly formed company PBL Marketing was given a ten-year contract to promote and market the game. Beyond the more elaborate television coverage, the gimmickry of which did not appeal to the more traditional cricket enthusiast, with the floodlights and the coloured clothing, Packer's intervention had taught the authorities an important lesson: that cricket had much greater commercial potential than they had ever dreamed of, and that by working with, rather than fighting, those commercial interests they could gain access to vast resources. That was the greatest revolution of all, and although it took some time for them to act upon this lesson, it shaped the future of the ICC as well as of cricket as a whole.

The amateurism which had long prevailed in the Conference and its constituent governing bodies had finally caught up with them. In 1974, when the possibility of sponsorship of Test matches had been raised, the minutes declared that: 'Generally, it was agreed that total sponsorship was undesirable, it being felt that matches at international level should be seen to be self-supporting and proud of being so.'

And even in July 1978, after the ICC's comprehensive defeat by Packer, a report from a marketing sub-committee chaired by former England Test cricketer Raman Subba Row received short shrift, the ACB's Ray Steele objecting that instead of merely offering a 'pool of ideas' the committee was proposing 'an overall international marketing concept'. Steele continued: 'Australia had always considered the ICC to be primarily a forum at which ideas could be exchanged and information pooled, acting always with the consent and approval of members except where specific tasks were delegated from time to time. Australia could not support any change in the role of the ICC to the extent that had been put forward.'

The lessons of the scarifying Packer experience had evidently not been learned, even in Australia, and the ICC continued to bury its head in the sand. Elsewhere, it would soon emerge, due note had been taken, and the Conference would face greater threats even than those which had been posed by Kerry Packer.

There were, moreover, other signs of radical change. As the ICC was preparing to negotiate with Packer in June 1977 the Commonwealth heads of government were meeting at the Gleneagles Hotel in the Scottish Highlands. There they reached an agreement which would define the relationship between sport in South Africa and its Commonwealth counterparts until the collapse of apartheid in 1990. Apartheid in sport, the agreement declared, was 'an abomination', and 'sporting contacts between their nationals and the nationals of countries practising apartheid in sport tend to encourage the belief (however unwarranted) that they are prepared to condone this abhorrent policy'. It was 'the urgent duty of each of their Governments vigorously to combat the evil of apartheid by withholding any form of support for, and by taking every practical step to discourage contact or competition by their nationals with sporting organisations, teams or sportsmen from South Africa or from any other country where sports are organised on the basis of race, colour or ethnic origin'.

The Gleneagles Agreement was a huge victory for the international critics of apartheid, and it quickly became the indispensable point of reference every time sporting links with South Africa came under discussion. Even so, some administrators in cricket and rugby union persistently argued that tours should continue or be resumed. In cricket, the merger in 1976 of the all-white SACA and SACBOC in the South African Cricket Union and the introduction of some multi-racial cricket gave the proponents of continuing contacts ammunition for their arguments, although the existence of a rival South African Cricket Board, led by the voluble Hassan Howa, showed that for many among the non-white majority there could be no accommodation with the apartheid system which remained as strong as ever in most areas of South African life. When the matter was discussed at the ICC meeting in July 1978, it was agreed not to readmit South Africa to international cricket, but to send a delegation 'to study multi-racial cricket in the country'. This, too, was vigorously opposed by a minority of members, the West Indies, India, Pakistan and four associates voting against the proposal.

Amidst these upheavals, the Conference found time to consider other intractable problems. The front-foot law had dealt with drag, illegal actions had for a time been eliminated, but the lbw law and limitation of the leg-side field remained troublesome issues. By the middle of the decade a new problem loomed: the increased use of fast, short-pitched bowling, often with an allegedly intimidatory intention. This was widely condemned, but those Test-playing countries with batteries of effective quick bowlers, notably Australia and the West Indies, were resistant to any regulation beyond that in the Experimental Law 46, which declared that '[t]he persistent bowling of fast short-pitched balls is unfair if in the opinion of the umpire at the bowler's end it constitutes a systematic attempt at intimidation'. In 1976 the Conference unanimously condemned 'dangerous and intimidatory bowling', and the following year it recommended that a bowler should be limited to two bouncers per over in Tests, and no more than three in any two consecutive overs, 'countries introducing this experiment by mutual agreement'. Once again, the old doctrine that playing conditions were a matter for bilateral arrangement seemed to have prevailed, but the 1978 Conference went further, deciding that the limit should be tightened to one bouncer per over, on an experimental basis 'until member countries had the chance of trying it out in their domestic programmes'. Slowly, the Conference was moving towards becoming a governing body in the full sense of the term.

Chapter 7

Platitudes and Procrastinations, 1979–1989

THE ICC delegation which travelled to South Africa in February 1979 was led by Charles Palmer, that year's MCC president. One-time captain of Leicestershire and that county's long-serving chairman, Palmer had toured South Africa in 1948/49 and had (uniquely) been player-manager on the highly controversial 1953/54 tour of the West Indies. He was joined by representatives from Australia, New Zealand, Bermuda and the USA on a tour of the Republic, and their report was tabled at the next meeting of the Conference in July. Its contents were never published but there were strong indications that it favoured an early return of South Africa to the international fold. Interviewing the newly appointed Sports Minister in Margaret Thatcher's British government, Hector Monro, in May, the *Guardian* journalist Richard Yallop had referred to 'strong rumours that sections of the ICC are pressing for South Africa's readmission', and Monro, while stating that 'we have to tread warily', commented favourably on 'the progress South Africa has made towards multi-racial sport'.

This was echoed in the ICC statement following its meeting, which noted that the delegation had 'recorded their commendation of the progress made by the South

African Cricket Union to establish non-racial, or normal, cricket in South Africa'. When Rashid Varachia, the chairman of the SACU, managed to get hold of a copy of the report itself, it was found to declare that '[t]here is no hindrance to any non-white cricketer playing at the very highest level of the game in South Africa for any other reason than cricket ability'. This was either deliberately duplicitous or remarkably naïve, since it ignored the huge disadvantages experienced by non-white players in facilities and coaching, not to mention all the other legal and economic limitations imposed on them by the apartheid system. As Basil D'Oliveira memorably asked, 'How can you play cricket with the white man on Saturday and Sunday and be a black man again on Monday?'

But as *The Guardian*'s John Rodda observed in October 1979, in the same article in which he quoted D'Oliveira: 'Cricket and, more dangerously, rugby football are not part of democratic international institutions, and they can move in ways which are dangerous to the whole fabric of international sport.'

The Gleneagles Agreement addressed the manifestation of apartheid in sport and not the system itself, and there were many in Britain, Australia and New Zealand who were insistent that sport should keep well away from the wider political issues. The existence of the non-racial SACU gave them ammunition for that argument, although Hassan Howa's SACB continued to claim, in a memorandum submitted in June 1979, that no normality was possible as long as the legal, political and economic reality of apartheid persisted. To the SACU, the document argued, non-racialism meant 'the mere physical presence of cricketers of different races and colours on the cricket field', while the SACB held that 'only a non-racial society can create the conditions in which true non-racial organisations can exist and grow: cricket cannot exist in a vacuum. The present cricket situation in South Africa is indeed the product of historical, social, economic and political factors which have shaped society over its entire history.'

The Conference remained split down the middle, no doubt explaining the decision not to publish the report of Palmer's delegation, and even the existence of the pro-South African governments of Margaret Thatcher in Britain and Robert Muldoon in New Zealand (Malcolm Fraser in Australia was a much more critical voice) could not help SACU end its isolation.

With the World Cup scheduled to be held again in 1979, the ICC broke new ground by organising an 'ICC Trophy' for its associate members, serving as a qualifying tournament for the World Cup. Teams from 14 associates, augmented by non-member Wales, took part in the competition, played in the English Midlands between 22 May and 21 June; only Gibraltar, Hong Kong and West Africa were absent. The tournament overlapped with the World Cup: the full members warmed up while the associates were playing their group phase, and the World Cup group matches and semi-finals were played between the ICC Trophy semi-finals on 6 June and the final. Bermuda and Denmark went through their group matches unbeaten, while Sri Lanka came out on top of their hard-fought group, level on points with Wales and the USA, but with a superior run rate. Canada joined the three pool winners in the semi-finals and eased into the final with a four-wicket victory over Bermuda, while Sri Lanka were untroubled in beating Denmark by 208 runs. Half-centuries by Sunil Jayasinghe and Duleep Mendis enabled Sri Lanka to reach 324/8 in the final, played at New Road, Worcester, and although John Vaughan made 80 not out for Canada they could only manage 264/5 in reply. The tournament, though, demonstrated that many of the associate nations had players of genuine quality. The Sri Lankans were undoubtedly the strongest side, with Roy Dias and Mendis making more than 200 runs, but those who took ten or more wickets came from Bermuda, Singapore and

Bangladesh, as well as the two Danes, Ole Mortensen, who went on to a successful county career with Derbyshire, and Carsten Morild. Sri Lanka and Canada both now proceeded to the World Cup tournament.

Even before that final was played, Sri Lanka had dispelled any doubts about the qualification system by beating India by 47 runs in a World Cup group match at Old Trafford. Put in to bat, they reached 238/5, thanks to half-centuries by Sunil Wettimuny, Dias and Mendis, and then Tony Opatha, Stanley de Silva and Somachandra de Silva combined to dismiss the Indians for 191. India, despite the presence of stars like Sunil Gavaskar, Kapil Dev, Dilip Vengsarkar and Bishan Bedi, lost all three group matches, as did Canada in the other group. Australia also failed to make the semi-finals, in which England beat New Zealand by nine runs in a thriller at Old Trafford and the West Indies accounted for Pakistan at The Oval. The West Indians were much too strong for England in their second Lord's final. Viv Richards hit a superb 138, Collis King smashed a 66-ball 86 to get his side to 286/9, and then Joel Garner took 5-38 as England collapsed to 194 all out. As a celebration of world cricket, despite some miserable English weather, the 1979 tournaments had been a great success.

With the door to a South African return to official international cricket as firmly closed as it had ever been, the SACU and its allies abroad turned to the organisation of unofficial tours. The Englishman Derrick Robins had pioneered this approach a decade earlier, arranging four tours between 1972/73 and 1975/76; mainly comprising English county players, these sides had included a sprinkling of cricketers from elsewhere, and the 1973/74 tour had broken new ground by including the former West Indian Test bowler John Shepherd and Pakistan's Younis Ahmed, thus testing the Vorster government's willingness to tolerate a certain measure of multi-racial international cricket. There was even a positive response from the South African side, with two non-white players included in the President's XI which took on the tourists at Newlands, and when an International Wanderers team visited in March and April 1976, they always faced multi-racial opponents, except for their opening game against an African XI at Soweto. But after the Soweto uprising later that year and the international condemnation which it aroused, even these unofficial overtures had been abandoned.

South African observers, though, continued to come to London for ICC meetings, and they kept the idea of unofficial tours alive when they talked to the British press. A statement to this effect by Geoff Dakin, chairman of the Transvaal association, in 1980 provoked the TCCB into sending a letter to English players warning them that they would be banned if they went on such a tour. Several English players, among them the Test opening pair of Geoff Boycott and Geoff Cook, played in South Africa in the northern winters without any action being taken against them, but it was a different matter when, in March 1982, a 'South African Breweries English' team made an eight-match tour of the Republic. Led by Graham Gooch and including such England stalwarts as Boycott, Dennis Amiss, Derek Underwood, Bob Woolmer and Alan Knott, the side took on South Africa in three four-day matches and three 50-over games, losing the former series 1-0 with two draws and the latter 3-0. With India and Pakistan threatening to cancel their England tours in the summer of 1982, the TCCB responded by banning all members of the party from Test cricket for three years, and although there was talk at first of legal action, it was soon clear that the players had little sympathy from their county colleagues and the idea was dropped. The tour was reported to have made a loss of around £335,000..

The South Africans did not ease off in their attempts to persuade the ICC to readmit them. When the Conference met on 21 July 1982, SACU sent its president, Joe Pamensky,

Dakin, and the former Test captain Ali Bacher to London to seek an unofficial session at which they might be allowed to state their case. The three, described by *The Guardian*'s Matthew Engel as 'large, thick-set men who are inclined to wear jackets on even the warmest English summer's day' who were thought by 'more than one person at Trent Bridge last week ... [as] the personal representatives of some Brooklyn Godfather', were rebuffed by the Conference, in part no doubt because of the anger of the members from the so-called 'New' Commonwealth at the rebel tour and the rumours of further such initiatives. But although there was no meeting with the SACU representatives, the Conference did resolve that 'every encouragement should be given to the continued development of multi-racial cricket in South Africa', and, somewhat cryptically, that 'there should be no political interference in team selection and no sanctions against cricket as a result of actions taken by other sporting bodies'. There was also a lukewarm acknowledgement of the TCCB's experimental rule mandating 96 overs in a day's Test play. The conference noted that 'there could be problems in tropical countries with a short dusk'; a cynic might think that the most relevant tropical countries were in the West Indies, where the home side relied heavily upon a four-man pace attack. 'Playing conditions between contestants,' the Conference nevertheless opined, 'should be framed to aim to achieve a similar target.' It was perhaps not surprising that the *Cricketer* editorial referred to the 'usual mixture of platitudes and procrastinations'.

On the field, though, the ICC was pressing ahead with its programme of global tournaments. The associates' tournament was now separated from the World Cup, its second edition taking place in England in 1982. Sixteen countries took part this time: Gibraltar and Hong Kong were there, along with Kenya, who had left the East African combination in 1981 and now competed in their own right, West Africa (members since 1976), and Zimbabwe, who had been admitted in 1981, a year after the country achieved independence. Sri Lanka had finally become a full member in 1981, and therefore qualified automatically for the next World Cup. With years of first-class experience in South African domestic cricket behind them, the Zimbabweans were much too strong for most of their opposition, topping their eight-team group undefeated, and they were joined in the semi-finals by surprise packet Papua New Guinea, who beat Hong Kong, Israel and Canada on their way to second place in the group. In the other pool Bermuda also went through unbeaten, finishing ahead of Bangladesh. Zimbabwe then beat Bangladesh by eight wickets to reach the final, where they met Bermuda, victors by six wickets over Papua New Guinea. Bermuda posted 231/8 in the final, played at Grace Road, Leicester, but with Andy Pycroft making 82 and Craig Hodgson 57 not out, Zimbabwe chased that down for the loss of five wickets with five and a half overs to spare.

Eight teams contested the World Cup the following year, and with Sri Lanka now among the automatic participants there was only room for ICC Trophy winners Zimbabwe. They caused a sensation on the opening day of the tournament with a 13-run victory over Australia: put into bat, they reached 239/6 thanks to Duncan Fletcher's 69 not out, and the all-rounder then took 4-42 as the Australians were held to 226/7 in reply. That was as far as success went for the Zimbabweans, who lost their five remaining matches, mostly by wide margins. India broke the West Indies' stranglehold on the trophy, despite being dismissed for 183 in the final; with Madan Lal taking 3-31 and Mohinder Amarnath 3-12 in seven overs, they dismissed the holders for a paltry 140, Viv Richards top-scoring with 33.

As far as the South African saga was concerned, the threat of punishment did not deter others from following where Gooch and Co. had led. In the closing months of 1982, a team called 'Arosa Sri Lanka', named from the initials of its organiser Tony Opatha, had undertaken a 14-match tour; most of the leading Sri Lankan players had, however, declined to take part, and those who did were banned from first-class cricket for life by the Sri Lankan board. Soon after the Sri Lankans departed, they were succeeded by a West Indies side, which represented a much more severe threat to cricket's international order. Led by Lawrence Rowe and including such big names as Alvin Kallicharran, Sylvester Clarke, Collis King and David Murray, the West Indians were much more serious opposition and gave a much greater propaganda victory to SACU. The players were, however, banned for life from representative cricket and from domestic cricket in the Caribbean, ending their international careers. They marked their double-edged freedom by undertaking another tour the following season. And then, after a gap in 1984/85, former Australian captain Kim Hughes led a strong side on an extended tour, playing 27 matches in three months. Hughes' players, too, were banned from representative and state cricket by the Australian board, prompting a vengeful attack from Hughes, who claimed that '[t]he politics of cricket are stifling the game in this country' and remarked that 'cricket isn't the "beat" of South African blacks'. The Australians returned the following season for what proved to be the last of the rebel tours, a visit which was notable for the inclusion of the left-arm spinner Omar Henry in the South African side for the last two games of the five-match 'Test' series. Already an international for his adopted country of Scotland, he would, after the end of apartheid, become the first non-white player to appear for South Africa in an official international match.

Summing up the whole episode in 1990, the journalist Ted Corbett concluded that '[i]t is fair to say that all these tours began in sordid secrecy, continued in silent, grudging misery and ended in tears'. They did give South African cricket enthusiasts some 'international' cricket to watch, and the effect of the West Indian visits in a country so utterly unused to seeing black and white players competing on level terms should not, perhaps, be underestimated. But the unrelieved whiteness of the South African team, despite all the arguments that black players were just not good enough, served to underline the fundamental, crushing inequalities of the apartheid system, and it is hard to disagree with Corbett's judgement that if the tours achieved anything, 'It was to strengthen the feeling that the best cricket could do for the cause of removing apartheid – to which it was always willing to pay devout, but often insincere, lip service – was to leave South Africa in complete isolation.'

The firmness with which the national boards dealt with their own rebels relieved the ICC from the responsibility of having to take any action beyond 'disapproving' of the tours. The 1983 meeting again refused to meet a SACU delegation but struck a careful balance by refusing the application from Hassan Howa's SACB to be admitted as associate members. Since neither the SACU nor the SACB was fully representative, ICC (and MCC) secretary Jack Bailey said afterwards, neither could become a member of the Conference. A trickier issue was the demand by the West Indies that its side scheduled to tour England the following year should not have to face county sides which included players who had taken part in rebel tours, a demand backed up by a threat to cancel the tour. The Conference left the matter for the two boards to resolve, while reminding the West Indies board 'that it was 'a signatory to an agreement under which all Test countries said they would put no pressure on others over the selection of teams'. Matthew Engel suggested in *The Guardian* that the ICC strategy resembled the advice given to airline passengers just before a crash: 'They put their heads in their hands and prayed the crash would not be too horrific.'

It was not as if there were not plenty of other issues for the Conference to be indecisive about. A proposal, inspired by recent disputes over umpiring, to create an ICC umpires' panel was rejected, the Conference preferring, as

Bailey put it, to emphasise 'that it would be better to go in for education of umpires and perhaps pay them better and organise seminars and meetings'. They did manage to agree that there should be a standard code of conduct for players in Tests; all countries except Pakistan had established their own codes, but a committee was appointed to draft an agreed version which would apply to everyone. The 1984 meeting would also consider a proposal to count wides and no-balls against the bowler. The by now annual review agreed to two more changes, a ban on underarm bowling (a somewhat belated response to the infamous incident in 1981 when Trevor Chappell bowled an underarm delivery to New Zealand's Brian McKechnie to win an ODI for Australia), and a requirement that a runner should have to wear the same equipment as the batsman he was assisting. A proposal from the TCCB to restrict the number of bouncers was turned down.

It was rejected again the following year, although the proposal to count wides and no-balls against the bowler was ratified. The most significant decision of the 1984 Conference, however, was to award the 1987 World Cup to India and Pakistan, whose joint bid won majority support against an offer from England to host the tournament for the fourth time in a row. With the benefit of hindsight, it is clear that this was a crucial turning point for the organisation. The joint bid promised each participating country £75k plus expenses, with the prospect of a further £50k apiece if the tournament made a profit. In that event the 18 associates would also receive £360k among them; since the associates held nine votes to the full members' seven, this was a very important incentive. The 1983 tournament had made a profit of £1.1m, so the likelihood of a lucrative pay day was real enough. It was not just the growing power of money which was reflected here. As Engel observed, 'Many countries felt that a World Cup should be just that and not given to England as an imperial right.' It would not have been surprising had the assembled delegates heard the rumble of Abe Bailey and Lord Hawke rotating in their graves. On South Africa, Engel added, 'everyone agreed to do nothing; and nothing is likely to be done until apartheid is abolished, or they have signed up every cricketer in the world'. England did, however, signal that they would consider themselves free to pick the South African rebels for their scheduled tour of the West Indies in 1985/86, after their three-year bans had expired.

In another far-reaching move, the Conference had created a new membership category, affiliate membership being intended for countries where cricket was officially organised but not yet at a level to justify associate status. The first to be admitted was Italy, prompting Engel to observe condescendingly that '[e]ven if their association only involves a few dotty expats, it is nice to sense the global nature of the game'. Allocating the World Cup to India and Pakistan, he added, was part of the same process.

By the time the Conference met again, in July 1985, it was apparent that the old guard's grip on the global game was not going to be surrendered lightly. The *Sydney Morning Herald* reported that 'some of the game's leading administrators are most apprehensive' about the World Cup being held on the subcontinent, and David Richards, executive director of the ACB, was among those appointed to a management committee to oversee the organisation. Furthermore, all the full members were invited to send an umpire to officiate alongside two each from India and Pakistan, a clear if unstated signal that the local umpires were not altogether trusted. Once again, no agreement could be reached on excessive short-pitched bowling, where Australia and the West Indies, the main culprits, resolutely opposed any action, or on slow over rates, although the Test-playing countries undertook 'as far as practicable' to encourage a minimum of 15 overs an hour.

It was hardly surprising, then, that the Conference's inability to take strong action on key issues should continue to attract unfavourable comment. Writing in the *Leicester Mercury* after the 1986 meeting, Leicestershire secretary-manager Mike Turner dubbed the Conference the second-most 'expensive and wasteful meeting place in the world' after the EEC headquarters in Brussels, adding that 'the world's cricket rulers again failed to get to grips with any of the game's vital problems'. 'A blind eye,' he wrote, 'was turned on all the major issues such as intimidatory bowling, over rates and South Africa.' The one real decision that emerged from the meeting was that matches in the next World Cup, to be held in India and Pakistan the following winter, should be reduced to 50 overs a side in place of the current 60; this was an expedient to enable the games to be played in one day in sub-continental conditions, but it would turn out to permanently define the ODI format. There was general agreement that something needed to be done about persistent short-pitched bowling, but the Conference was unable to take any action beyond writing to first-class umpires emphasising that they would have strong backing for a strict interpretation of the law. As so often, it was left to the umpires to solve a problem the administrators were unable or unwilling to tackle.

The World Cup might have moved elsewhere, but the ICC Trophy was played in the English Midlands for the third time in the summer of 1986. This time 16 countries took part, with Singapore, West Africa and Switzerland (who had only been admitted the year before) the absentees. Last-minute defections meant that the groups were of unequal size, and the larger of the two, with nine teams, turned into a spirited three-way contest between the Netherlands, Bermuda and the USA for two semi-final places. The Dutch had a comprehensive ten-wicket victory over the Americans but lost to Bermuda by 30 runs in their final group game; Bermuda had earlier been beaten by three wickets by the USA, so it all came down to run rate. The Netherlands thus topped the group, with Bermuda taking the second semi-final spot at the expense of the USA.

In the other group Zimbabwe again went through undefeated and Denmark, whose only defeat was by the Zimbabweans, joined them in the semi-finals. A superb unbeaten 127 from Guyana-born Rupert Gomes saw the Dutch to a five-wicket win over Denmark, while Zimbabwe chased down Bermuda's 201/7 without losing a wicket, Grant Paterson making 123 not out. The Zimbabweans posted 243/9 in the final, which was played at Lord's for the first time, and with the medium-pacer Iain Butchart claiming 4-33, the Dutch were dismissed for 218. Canada's Paul Prashad, another Guyanan, was the leading run-scorer in the tournament with 533 runs at an average of 88.83, closely followed by Steve Atkinson of the Netherlands with 508, while the latter's team-mate Ron Elferink took the most wickets with 23, one more than the indefatigable Ole Mortensen of Denmark.

Zimbabwe had qualified for the next World Cup, but soon there were doubts about whether that would ever take place. In November, the West Indian board gave notice of its intention to move that all players with South African links should be banned for life from international cricket, and Zimbabwe signalled their willingness to second the motion. That was a big enough menace to the future of the game, but then the Indian government, led by Rajiv Gandhi, threatened to refuse visas to any player who had played in South Africa. Either of these developments was enough by itself to cast a shadow over the World Cup. The chairman of MCC (and therefore of the ICC) for that year was the former England captain Colin Cowdrey, who embarked upon a furious round of diplomacy to try to head off these twin crises. His solution to the former was to convene a special meeting of the Conference, a measure which was opposed as potentially 'disruptive' by the ACB and by the TCCB, whose chief executive, Alan Smith, said that '[w]e don't feel it is something to be rushed'. That was a statement which might have been applied to any issue the ICC had faced throughout the near 80 years of its existence. But England also insisted that it would brook no interference, from politicians or anyone else, in the selection of its teams, and as Mike Turner pointed out in the *Leicester Mercury*, of England's 345 registered first-class cricketers, more than a third had played in South Africa, 70 of them during the 1986/87 winter. It was an issue which could not be ignored.

In the end, Cowdrey got his way, and the special meeting took place at Lord's on 26 June. N.K.P. Salve, the chair of the World Cup organising committee, said optimistically before it began: 'Cricket is a game of gentlemen and we play cricket at our meetings.' The meeting lasted three hours and defused the potential threat to the Cup by kicking the bomb down the road. Rather than insisting on a vote which could potentially have split world cricket in two, the West Indians moved an amendment to their own motion, by which a working party would be established to make recommendations on the ICC's role and methods of operation to a further meeting of Conference in a year's time. As Matthew Engel and Mike Selvey put it in *The Guardian*, '[t]he end of cricketing civilisation as we know it was put off for at least another year'. The ICC's new secretary, Lt. Col. John Stephenson, said that the meeting had been 'very united and very responsible', while another military gentleman, Pakistan's Lt. Gen. Safdar Butt, remarked: 'I always knew the whole thing could be discussed in a civilised manner.' Sam Ramsamy, the secretary of SANROC, probably assessed the situation correctly when he suggested that the West Indians had made a tactical withdrawal because they knew that England and Australia, the foundation members, would use their power of veto to block the motion.

The regular meeting that year was held in August, and finally the delegates managed to agree on a measure to deal with slow over rates. Unusually, it was revealed that a proposal to require 15 overs an hour, or 90 in a full day's Test play, was carried by six votes to one, with the West Indies the predictable dissenters. Two other English motions, to restrict the number of bouncers and to limit bowlers to a 30-yard run-up, were defeated; according to one of the English representatives, they were so astonished by their success with over rates that they did not press the other matters hard enough. Five three-day matches played by Fiji on their 1947/48 tour of New Zealand were retrospectively declared first-class, but otherwise the usual strategy of deferral prevailed. That was the fate of Zimbabwe's application for full member status, of the question of players' links with South Africa (still under consideration by the select committee), possible revisions to the Conference's constitution, and the issue of multiple eligibility to play Test cricket. The last point had arisen with the case of Kenyan-born Dipak Patel, who had qualified by residence to play for both England and New Zealand, had been given a special dispensation back in February and appeared in both Tests and ODIs for New Zealand, and who was in their World Cup squad. With increasing mobility, it was perhaps time to revisit the rules, but that, like the other matters, would have to wait another year.

Chaired by Raman Subba Row, the review committee evidently recognised that the time had come to weaken the relationship between MCC and the Conference, and on 10 April 1987 Stephenson wrote to the members referring to a 'recognised need for continuity in the Chairmanship of the Conference during what may be a period of change'. The committee's elegant solution was that Cowdrey, a known and comparatively trusted as well as safe pair of hands, should 'serve as Chairman of ICC for a further period of at least one year after his retirement as President of MCC on the 30th Sept. 1987, if this proposal met with the approval of ICC members'. This had the advantage of postponing any ugliness over the election of a chairman by at least 12 months and ensuring that it would be Cowdrey who would preside over the World Cup in India. A power struggle was, perhaps, inevitable, but at least it could be delayed for as long as possible.

The Indian government, anxious not to wreck such a prestigious event, did not carry out its threat to refuse visas, and the first World Cup to take place outside England got under way at Hyderabad in Pakistan on 8 October 1987, where the home side squeezed past Sri Lanka by just 15 runs, thanks to Javed Miandad's 103 and a varied attack spearheaded by Imran Khan and Wasim Akram. That was as good as it got for the Sri Lankans, who like qualifiers Zimbabwe did not win a single game. In a thrilling encounter in Madras the following day Australia beat India by a single run, Craig McDermott taking 4-56 and two run-outs contributing to the hosts being all out for 269 off the penultimate ball after Geoff Marsh had made 110 in the Australian total of 270/6. India won the return game by 56 runs, and otherwise the two carried all before them, easing into the semi-finals; there they met Pakistan and England, the top two from the other group. McDermott was again the key in Australia's semi-final against Pakistan, his 5-44 seeing his side to an 18-run victory, while 115 from Graham Gooch set up a 35-run victory for England over India. Both the hosts were therefore out of the final, but it turned out to be another thriller. Australia made 253/5, David Boon top-scoring with 75, and at 135/2 England appeared well placed to take the Cup for the first time. But then Mike Gatting tried to reverse-sweep Allan Border – reversal was not, after all, invented in the T20 format – and was caught, and gradually the Australians took control, holding on to win by seven runs.

The day after the final the select committee on South Africa met in Calcutta, and was reported to have 'produced a resolution which they hope will solve the problem'. Their report would go to the following year's Conference, and it was intended to keep it under wraps until then. Stephenson told a disbelieving press corps that he had been told to keep his mouth shut about its contents. There were, however, already rumours that two countries were 'not too happy', and given the composition of the committee – representatives of the seven Test-playing countries, plus Zimbabwe, Canada and Gibraltar – it was not too difficult to guess that they might be England and Australia. The latter, it was understood, had suggested a compromise solution whereby the home nation would determine who was eligible to appear in any series, which would mean that the West Indies would be able to bar England's South African contingent when England toured the Caribbean, but would have to play against them in England. As the July showdown grew closer, there were signs that England and Australia would press for yet another deferral of a decision, rather than being put in the position to having to veto an outcome which the majority desired. And so it proved: the West Indies and Sri Lanka proposed an amended version of the Australian compromise, which upheld the right of countries to select the team they wanted but acknowledged the power of governments to withhold visas if they so desired. The whole issue was referred to a special meeting, to be held at Lord's on 23 January 1988. There were, however, warnings that no further can-kicking would then be tolerated.

At the same time, the foundation members' veto power was coming under increased scrutiny, and a separate working party had recommended that it should be abolished from January 1990. Stephenson described the present constitution as 'a mine-field inappropriate to present-day cricket', and the South African question had highlighted how the ill-defined areas in which the veto existed was potentially a gold mine for the lawyers as well as a land mine for the organisation. Nor was that the only legal peril. Players facing a possible life ban from international cricket if South Africa's sharpest critics got their way were hinting at legal action, and the governing bodies concerned were still deeply scarred by their Packer experience a decade before. *Wisden* editor Graeme

Wright observed resoundingly that '[t]he TCCB would be advised to seek the best counsel available if it is to be privy to any restriction of an Englishman's freedom'.

On other issues, too, procrastination remained the order of the day. No action could be agreed, as usual, on the restriction of short-pitched bowling, or on defining the weight of bats. A sub-committee was set up to consider England's desire for an internationally standard residence qualification, in line with its seven-year period rather than the four years in force elsewhere, and a 'high profile' committee was agreed to consider the creation of an international panel of umpires. There had been complaints about biased home umpires for as long as international cricket had existed, and an ugly confrontation between England captain Mike Gatting and Pakistani umpire Shakoor Rana in Faisalabad in December 1987 had turned into a major incident and had brought matters to a head. Neutral umpires had been successfully used in the 1987 World Cup, and it was increasingly clear that an ICC panel was the way ahead. There were many sensitivities to be overcome, but at least the Conference had finally taken the first step. It did, too, manage to suggest an experimental law to enforce the 15-overs-an-hour rule, and suggested another precluding a substitute from keeping wicket. But it was prepared to do no more than offer Zimbabwe 'encouragement' for their bid to become a full, Test-playing member.

Before the Conference could meet in January 1988, the damage being caused by the festering sore that was the South African issue was further underlined by the cancellation of two possible England tours. First, Rajiv Gandhi, with the World Cup safely out of the way, made good on his threat to refuse visas to those who had played in South Africa, and barred seven members of the England squad. The TCCB had no alternative but to cancel the tour. And when they tried to substitute a visit to New Zealand, where England would play a tri-series with Pakistan, the Pakistanis pulled out, and the idea fell through. The long-feared disruption of the international programme was beginning to occur with a vengeance.

Even before the Conference could convene, the ICC was hauled into the courts by the right-wing Freedom Association. A magistrate in London had issued a summons against the ICC secretary John Stephenson under Section 21 of the Theft Act 1968, alleging that he was blackmailing players not to go to South Africa. On the very morning of 23 January this was overturned in the High Court, which described the action as 'an abuse of the process of the court', a 'criminal sledgehammer to deal with a problem which is entirely civil'. That afternoon Norris McWhirter, the Freedom Association chairman, withdrew an application for an injunction, on behalf of the Rhodesian-born players Neal Radford and Kevin Curran, both of whom were playing in South Africa, to stop the enforcement of any ban.

The resolution, or more accurately agreement, which was reached after a day and a half of discussion, ran to 800 words and nearly three pages. It defined 'sporting contact' as 'active participation in cricket or in any other sport in South Africa (except only in the case of another sport than cricket when participation was for private recreational purposes) or outside South Africa against a team a majority of which comprises South Africans', and imposed a sliding scale of penalties, from three years' suspension for juniors aged from 16 to under-19, through four years for individuals over 19 and five years for participating in a tour, with an additional two years for a second offence. Countries retained the right to impose their own, longer bans, but the starting date for the new international system would be 1 April 1989. Importantly, it did not apply retrospectively, although there was a question about the position of players like Graham Gooch, who were on a separate, United Nations blacklist; in fact, the UN committee concerned responded to the settlement by removing all cricketers from that list. There were appeal mechanisms for those who were on the ICC register of banned players.

Reactions to the agreement were predictable. The chairman, Lord Bramall, described the atmosphere as 'very hard but co-operative' and as 'amazingly polite and cordial'; the ICC had, he added, 'faced up to certain realities'. Pamensky said it was 'very punitive and very disappointing' and threatened more rebel tours. Among the players, Clive Rice accused the ICC of acting like Pontius Pilate, while Eddie Barlow predicted the creation of a separate professional circuit among those who would now turn their backs on Test cricket. Turning back the clock to the heady imperial days of Sir Abe Bailey and Lord Harris, Peter Deeley in the British *Daily Telegraph* appealed on behalf of Britain's 'kith and kin' and proclaimed that 'for the sake of a political gesture cricket has sold its virtue'. SACU promptly invited a group including former Australian captain Ian Johnson to visit South Africa, and he rewarded them with a glowing report in the Melbourne *Age*, praising the 'superb job' which had been done in the townships, claiming that cricket in South Africa was now entirely non-racial, and calling for the readmission of the country to the ranks of Test-playing nations. A defiant Mike Gatting went ahead and organised another tour, taking a 16-man party on a 16-match tour in early 1990 which was eventually cut back to seven games; despite the claims of enormous progress, the only non-white player they faced in those matches was Omar Henry.

Before that could take place, however, the ICC held its regular meeting in July 1989, and Pamensky and Bacher were ritually outraged by its refusal to hear them state their case. They would, they said, have invited the Conference to send another fact-finding delegation to South Africa to see what SACU had achieved in dismantling racial barriers in cricket. Another attempt by England and New Zealand to restrict short-pitched bowling was rejected, reportedly on the votes of the associates, but some progress was made on the issue of neutral umpires, with a proposal to create an international panel, with effect from late 1991, referred back to the governing bodies. There were reportedly problems relating to costs, which provide a young Gideon Haigh to observe: 'Visiting umpires cannot just be billeted with local cricket followers, you will understand: only Lear jets, limousines and five-star accommodation will do to ensure the vigilance of our globe-trotting officials.'

It was another disappointing outcome, but deferral and delay had long been the Conference's stock in trade.

The solution to the nearly 30-year agony of cricket's relationship with South Africa in fact came, quite unexpectedly, on the day Gatting's men were losing a five-day match at the Wanderers in Johannesburg, by seven wickets and inside three days. On that day, 11 February 1990, F.W. de Klerk's government released Nelson Mandela after 27 years' imprisonment, and the final dismantlement of apartheid was set in train. On 30 March SACU announced the end of its policy of organising rebel tours, which were, it said, 'counter productive to [its] medium- and long-term aims' in the present political climate, and over the next year prolonged negotiations led to the merger, in June 1991, of SACU and SACB into the United Cricket Board. Finally, South African cricket had a single, non-racial governing body, and the way was clear for its readmission; the following month South Africa again became a member of the organisation which it had helped to found 82 years before.

Sir Abe Bailey (1864-1940), proposer of the Imperial Cricket Conference

Sir Francis Lacey (1859-1946), MCC secretary 1898-1926

Bill Woodfull ducks under a Harold Larwood bouncer, Brisbane, 1933

Imperial Cricket Council, 1960

The eight participating teams in the first Men's World Cup, 1975

ICC President Jagmonath Dalmiya and CEO David Richards at the annual conference, July 2000

The Anti-Corruption Unit meets in London, 10 February 2001

Malcolm Speed, ICC CEO 2001-08

Darrell Hair removes the bails after Pakistan refuse to take the field, Fourth Test, The Oval, August 2006

ICC CEO Malcolm Speed and Jamaica police chief Mark Shields at a press conference following the death of Bob Woolmer, 22 March 2007

Australia celebrate after winning the 2007 Men's World Cup final in near-total darkness

Shashank Manohar and Giles Clarke on the first day of the India-England Test, Mohali, December 2008

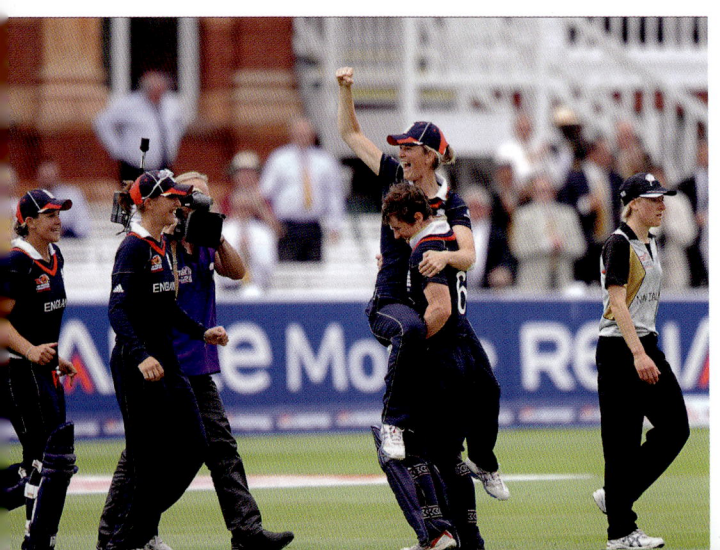

England celebrate a wicket against New Zealand at Lord's during the 2009 Women's World Cup

On 1 August 2009, Brian Murgatroyd (Media and Communications Manager) and Ian Higgins (Head of Legal), meet Narayanaswami Srinivasan and Ratnakar Shetty of the BCCI following an emergency session to discuss the BCCI's refusal to sign on to WADA.

Meeting of the Chief Executives' Committee, Johannesburg, 1 October 2009

Sharad Pawar and Haroon Lorgat with the Men's World Cup, January 2011

The ICC Executive Board, 10 October 2011

Ben Stokes apologises to the New Zealand fielders as the ball runs off his bat for four overthrows in a chaotic end to the 2019 Men's World Cup final.

PART II

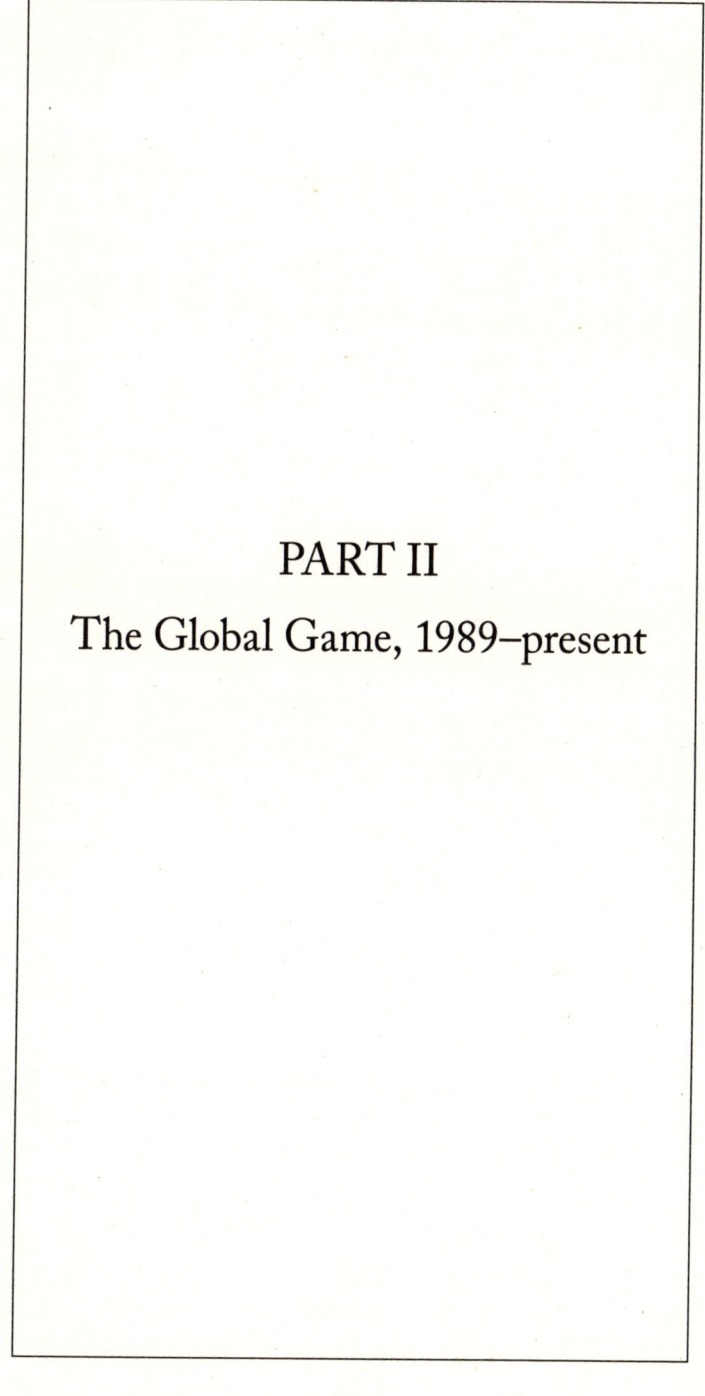

The Global Game, 1989–present

Chapter 8

A Governing Body Fit for Purpose?

ON 12 July 1989 the International Cricket Conference took the fateful step of turning itself into the International Cricket Council. In itself, the alteration of the name brought few immediate transformations. The most significant was the election of the Council's own chairman, an office until now held automatically by the chairman of MCC. But by choosing Colin Cowdrey, who had held the post under the previous system when he was MCC chairman in 1986/87, the delegates opted for a well-known, safe pair of hands, and the facts that he was English and that MCC secretary John Stephenson retained the secretaryship of the ICC as well, ensured that the accustomed structure largely survived. England and Australia retained their veto as foundation members, and while they were outnumbered by countries which increasingly resented their historical stranglehold, and who had been outraged and embittered by the long-running South African issue, it took a little time before the majority was able to mount a successful challenge.

By 1992, the forces for change were ready to show their hand. Pakistan and the West Indies proposed the abolition of the foundation member veto, and although England and Australia were able to forestall an immediate decision, they were induced to accept that the rule should in principle be abandoned. As Mike Selvey observed: 'Although it had never been applied, its potential had undoubtedly wrecked many votes in the past, and in an increasingly democratic world this power to nullify majority votes was regarded as anachronistic by the other member countries.' As if to reinforce the point, Zimbabwe was elected to full membership at the same meeting, despite English objections that the country lacked the cricket infrastructure to justify a place at the table. Six potential opponents were now ranged against the two foundation members and their traditional ally New Zealand, and a key test would be the decision about who should host the next World Cup, for which England was regarded as the leading but by no means automatic candidate. The 1992 meeting deferred a decision – some things about the ICC definitely remained unchanged – but soon afterwards the BCCI confirmed that they would now throw their hat into the ring, joining England and South Africa in the contest.

The meeting which took place in February 1993 was described by TCCB chief executive Alan Smith as 'a shambles', 'fractious and unpleasant', and the worst he had ever attended. England had regarded hosting the 1996 World Cup as theirs by right, but India, Pakistan and Sri Lanka came with a joint bid which was carefully pitched to secure maximum support. At stake were 37 votes, and in addition to a simple majority, a successful bid would need a two-thirds majority of the nine Test-playing countries as well as the support of at least one of the two foundation members. The subcontinental bid guaranteed the 20 associate members £100k each from the tournament profits (as against the £65k offered by England). The TCCB were one full member short of the six they needed for that two-thirds majority, and Zimbabwe, perhaps remembering England's opposition to their candidacy back in July, sided with India, Pakistan and Sri Lanka. An English or Australian veto would have produced stalemate, and rather than deferring the decision to the annual meeting in the European summer, when nothing would perhaps have changed, the TCCB withdrew its bid, in exchange for a promise that they would be allocated the 1999 tournament and with future events rotated amongst the full members. It was a major victory for the BCCI and their allies, and one which would shape the ICC's future for decades to come. And so it was seen at the time: writing in the 1994 *Wisden*, Jack Bailey lamented the decision as 'an outward and visible sign . . . that the playing of cricket as a game, so long the chief preoccupation of those gathered round the tables of the MCC Committee room at Lord's, and pursued invariably with an attitude of quiet and civilised deference, had been overtaken'. The religious language was again not coincidental, but the delusion that the ICC's preoccupations had not been deeply political from the outset was indeed striking. Gone was the 'attitude of quiet and civilised deference', the hallmark of a world in which gentlemen, and most especially colonial gentlemen, knew their place. Col. Stephenson, the soon-to-be-ex secretary, described the English capitulation as 'a most magnanimous, gentlemanly and wonderful gesture made for the good of international cricket'. In fact, the TCCB simply did not have the votes and to use the veto would have split the game irrevocably into two camps, with England and Australia clearly in the minority.

The veto was finally abolished that July, although it was agreed that for 'important' decisions (conveniently undefined) a three-quarters majority would be required rather than the two-thirds which had prevailed until now. As a further indication that MCC's grip on the Council was loosening, Clyde Walcott was elected chairman in succession to Colin Cowdrey, while the new CEO, Australian David Richards, took over the administrative leadership from the MCC secretary. In an interview soon after the meeting Richards defined a threefold task for himself: to administer the game through the code of conduct, match referees' reports and the like; a commercial aspect involving 'ways and means of improving the finances of international cricket without intruding on the territory of individual countries'; and the development of the world game, harnessing the potential of television in taking cricket to new audiences. 'Cricket,' Richards said, 'has to be expansionist.' The appointment of a full-time chief executive was the clearest evidence to date that the change from Conference to Council was not merely cosmetic: the organisation would from now on be much more proactive in leading, governing and promoting the game, although Richards was undoubtedly aware that his actions would be constrained by the power of the ICC's more influential members.

The ill-feeling generated by the battle over the World Cup persisted, and broke into the open again in 1996, when Walcott's term as chairman was due to finish. The contenders to succeed him were Malcolm Gray of Australia, Krish Mackerdhuj of South Africa, and the BCCI's Jagmohan Dalmiya. Dalmiya had majority support, with the associate delegates again firmly behind him, but England and Australia insisted that a successful candidate must also have the votes of at least six of the nine full members, and Dalmiya fell just short of that number. For Australia, a strong reason for opposing him was their ongoing dispute over the $150k guarantee from the World Cup, which PILCOM – the tournament organising committee headed by Dalmiya – was refusing to pay either Australia or the West Indies because of their refusal to play in Sri Lanka. Nor had the situation been eased by I.S. Bindra's recent outburst against the Australian umpire Darrell Hair, whom he accused of biased umpiring at India's expense. In the first round of voting, Dalmiya had 16 votes, Gray 15 and Mackerdhuj nine; Dalmiya, however, was supported by only three full members, with four backing Gray and two voting for Mackherdhuj. When Dalmiya and Gray went head-to-head in a second round Zimbabwe switched their vote to

Dalmiya, while the South Africans abstained. The Indian chairman won the popular vote 25-13, but with both men supported by only four full members there was stalemate, and it was agreed to extend Walcott's term by a year.

There could be no doubt that the present structure of the Council had become unworkable, and the meeting set up a rules committee chaired by the New Zealand board chairman, Sir John Anderson, to undertake the delicate task of negotiating constitutional change. The old guard were clearly unhappy about the role of the 22 associates, whose combined votes outnumbered the double votes of the nine full members and had come very close to electing Dalmiya. As Tim Lamb, chief executive of the newly constituted England and Wales Cricket Board put it, 'The ICC reached its nadir when Argentina had the casting vote on how many bouncers could be bowled in a Test match over.' Anderson's solution was to create a new executive board, comprising delegates of all the full members and three elected representatives of the associates. He further proposed splitting the Council into administrative and cricket wings and rationalising the committee structure into three powerful committees: cricket, development and finance. The issue of the chairmanship would be resolved by a rotation system, under which Dalmiya would have a two-year term, followed by Gray and Mackerdhuj. Dalmiya, meanwhile, was threatening legal action should he not be elected to the chairmanship in June.

Anderson's proposals were considered and adopted at a meeting in Kuala Lumpur in March 1997, held during the ICC Trophy tournament. It was also decided to establish a limited liability company, to give the Council a more secure financial status. The changes came into effect at the annual meeting in June 1998, when journalist Christopher Martin-Jenkins welcomed the ICC's transformation into 'a new body ... which is not only democratic but also, it is hoped, visionary'. With incorporation, he believed, it would be run 'less as a collection of often hostile factions loosely bound together at Lord's and more as a global business'. It is questionable whether concentrating more power in the hands of the full members at the expense of the associates was a truly democratic move, and Martin-Jenkins was certainly over-optimistic in his expectation that the new structure would succeed in harmonising the 'often hostile factions'. Nor did he explain how a more visionary ICC would also become more of a global business.

In some respects, though, Anderson's reforms did change things for the better. As chairmen of the cricket and development committees respectively, Clyde Walcott and Ali Bacher were soon tackling their tasks with renewed energy. In July 1997 Bacher, 'that insatiable dynamo' in Martin-Jenkins' words, was announcing that one-day tournaments would be held at Florida's Disneyworld in 1998 and the two subsequent years, a first step, he hoped, in breaking into the potentially lucrative American market.

While all this was happening, the ICC was moving to turn itself into a significant commercial operation, comparable with the International Olympic Committee and FIFA. In 1993 it had established a wholly owned subsidiary, ICC Development (International) Ltd, registered in the British Virgin Islands and based in Monaco, to manage ICC events, the commercial rights associated with them, and the development programme. In August 1997 the ICC itself was incorporated as a limited liability company, again registered in the British Virgin Islands. Nothing could more clearly mark the seismic shift which had taken place within the organisation since the power base began to drift away from the old bufferdom of MCC, and a crucial psychological step was taken in March 2005, when the board decided by an 11-1 majority to move the ICC's operations away from Lord's and to Dubai in the United Arab Emirates. There were no prizes for guessing which member had opposed the move; the ECB had been campaigning vainly against it for some months. One press comment at the time was headlined 'ICC Moves

Closer to the Money', and as well as the tax advantages offered by the Emiratis the decision clearly demonstrated the way in which the centre of the cricket universe had shifted away from the traditional 'headquarters' in St John's Wood.

The ICC's attempts to maximise its revenue from major events could create considerable problems. Before the 2002 Champions Trophy and the following year's World Cup, players were confronted with a new contract, which would prevent them from fulfilling their obligations to their own individual sponsors where these conflicted with the $550 million. exclusive rights agreement the ICC had reached with the Global Cricket Corporation (GCC). The deal ran until the 2007 World Cup, and the contract would bar players from giving endorsements in conflict with the ICC's sponsors during a tournament and 30 days either side of it. The most immediately affected were the leading Indians, including Sachin Tendulkar, Sourav Ganguly and Virender Sehwag, and at one point it looked as if the BCCI would be forced to send a second-string team to the Champions Trophy. The players' organisation, FICA, supported the players' stand, chairman Tim May complaining that neither the ICC nor the national boards had consulted them before writing the contracts, and talking about 'ambush sponsors'. It was another issue which clearly highlighted the world in which the ICC was operating and which it had helped to create. The leading cricketers were now among the biggest sporting stars on the planet, able to command massive sums in their own right, especially in the subcontinent, and willing to wield their power to get their own way when their commercial interests were at stake, and they felt they were being taken for granted.

In the end a compromise was worked out, whereby the 30-day period of sponsorship purdah after the Champions Trophy was reduced to 17 days. Some key ICC sponsors, however, were unhappy, and made it clear that they would not accept such concessions in future. It was estimated that some $280 million of the $550 million in the deal came from companies with commercial interests in India, so when LG and Hero Honda flexed their muscles, the ICC had little alternative but to listen.

Gray indicated in September that he was in favour of consulting with players' organisations to avoid such confrontations in future. 'Not every country believes in it,' he said, but he saw recognition of the players' representatives as preferable to trying to negotiate with individuals. The ICC's formal proposal, however, attempted to require that the players' representatives must have played Test cricket during the previous ten years, and this was categorically rejected by FICA. The players, FICA insisted, must be free to elect their representatives without restriction. Meeting just after the Champions Trophy was over, the board set up a World Cup Contracts Committee, chaired by Gray and including Dalmiya and ACB chairman Bob Merriman, to consult with the boards, the players and GCC. But they were not prepared to include a FICA representative in that committee, and five boards were also opposed to including a player representative on the Cricket Committee. Management resistance to a stronger player voice in governing cricket remained strong, not least in the BCCI, although the players were given a greater role in the committee dealing with playing conditions and the code of conduct, and a player was to be included in the inspection team which would visit Zimbabwe to assess security in advance of the World Cup.

The dispute over contracts, however, lingered on. In January 2003 BCCI president N.K.P. Salve and a group of former cricketers challenged the World Cup contracts in the Delhi High Court, claiming that 'even though 80% of ICC funds are generated in India, unreasonable demands are made in the contracts'. The court ordered the government not to release foreign exchange to the ICC's India-based sponsors should India be excluded from the World Cup, but the ICC response was to threaten to withhold the BCCI's share of the tournament surplus, estimated at up to $9 million. A compromise quickly emerged, whereby the BCCI agreed to cover any compensation claims by ICC sponsors arising from conflict with the players' own sponsorship deals, but even that did not bring an end to what *Cricinfo* termed 'unsavoury brinkmanship'.

Dalmiya declared that '[t]he ICC can't claim money against us if no one claims against ICC', but GCC did receive approaches from sponsors seeking compensation for the forfeited matches and the contractual conflict, and by June 2003 it emerged that the claims against the ICC could amount to $30 million. Outgoing ICC chairman Gray did not mince his words. The contracts dispute, he said, 'was a problem that was entwined with greed, bad management, lack of communication, nationalism and parochialism'. He did, however, acknowledge that the ICC should have realised that some boards had failed to communicate adequately with their players about the contracts. Dalmiya deployed a thesaurus-full of adjectives, describing the GCC claim as 'frivolous and fictitious', and that of their Indian subsidiary, World Sports Nimbus, as 'baseless, flimsy and exaggerated'. The dispute continued to escalate, Dalmiya threatening in September to sue the ICC unless his board received $6.5 million by 1 November. Meeting in Barbados on that day, the ICC board agreed to release the payments on condition that the countries undertook to repay anything subsequently needed to meet GCC's claims. Even this did not satisfy Dalmiya, who announced that the reports of the meeting had been inaccurate; the new chairman Ehsan Mani, he claimed, had been 'grossly misquoted', and all that was required was a 'personal indemnity' from the boards in question. There the matter rested until April 2004, when Dalmiya stated that almost the entire disputed sum had been released. The BCCI's stance, he added, had been entirely vindicated.

One of the most remarkable reversals in the ICC's history came as the millennium ended. For the first 90 years of its existence, the organisation had prided itself on its exclusiveness, with election to membership, initially bringing with it the right to play Test cricket, highly prized and reluctantly given. That had begun to shift with the creation of associate status and was eroded a little more by the addition of the affiliate category. But even then, only seven affiliates – Italy, Switzerland, the Bahamas, France, Nepal, Japan and the UAE – were admitted between 1984 and 1989. That number almost quadrupled during the 1990s, and by 1999 there were 26 affiliate members. Then, suddenly, the policy changed, and 28 more were elected in the next three years alone, ranging from Afghanistan and the Czech Republic to Costa Rica and Finland, not forgetting the Cook Islands and St Helena. The global sweep continued for several more years, taking in Iran and China, the Isle of Man and the Falklands, Mozambique and Myanmar: by 2008 there were 69 affiliates, and with ten full members and 20 associates, the ICC numbered almost 100 members. Most, of course, had virtually no membership rights beyond recognition, but that was not the point. The ICC had set out to become a truly global organisation, and it received its reward in 2010 when cricket was recognised as a sport by the International Olympic Committee. That, after all, had been the objective of this determined membership drive.

At the same time, all was not well with some existing members. Long-simmering concerns about the state of cricket in Zimbabwe erupted in early 2004, when national captain Heath Streak was replaced and 14 other players joined him in a rebellion against the board. Since soon after independence in 1980 there had been tensions around the pace of Africanisation of what had until then been, at least at the highest levels, an almost exclusively white game. This could not, of course, be isolated from the wider context around the regime of Robert Mugabe, which was highlighted at the 2003 World Cup when Andy Flower and Henry Olonga wore black armbands in protest against 'the death of democracy in Zimbabwe'. When Streak confronted the board over the players' grievances, he was replaced by the 20-year-old Tatenda Taibu.

A series of disastrous Test performances by an inexperienced, largely black team forced the ICC to act. In June 2004, Zimbabwe chairman Peter Chingoka faced a group comprising ICC chair Mani, Dalmiya, Ray Mali of South Africa and Bob Merriman of Australia, and agreed – probably under considerable duress – that Zimbabwe would cease playing Test cricket for a time. Briefly restored to the Test circuit in 2005, a further series of poor performances followed, and in January 2006 Mugabe replaced the entire Board of Zimbabwe Cricket with an interim committee. Such overt government interference in cricket would have led to the immediate suspension of an associate member, but Zimbabwe had powerful allies on the ICC board, and all that happened was that the Test suspension was renewed for another year, again 'voluntarily'.

On-field embarrassments were accompanied by allegations of financial irregularities, which led to the ICC commissioning a report by accountants KPMG South Africa and KPMG Zimbabwe. Their report, submitted in March 2008, concluded that financial records and statements and supporting documents for the 2005 financial year had been falsified, and that significant sums of money could not be accounted for. After consulting with ZC chair Peter Chingoka and other Zimbabwean officials the ICC Audit Committee, chaired by the New Zealand banker Sir John Anderson, recommended that the matter be referred to the Ethics Officer. When the board met, this was opposed not only by Chingoka, who claimed that the audit committee was part of a conspiracy against him and ZC, but also by Norman Arendse (South Africa), Inderjit Bindra (India) and Naseem Ashraf (Pakistan). After a heated debate, Arendse's motion merely to note the report, adding that it 'did not point to any criminal wrong-doing or personal financial gain', and taking account of ZC's intention, assisted by CSA, to 'address irregularities', was carried. CEO Speed, nearing the end of his contract, was reportedly so enraged by this that he refused to attend the subsequent press conference. For ZC's allies this was the final straw. At an informal meeting held during the launch of the new Indian Premier League in Bangalore – which Speed also declined to attend – he was placed on gardening leave until the termination of his contract on 5 July.

Anxious to bring the Zimbabweans back into the fold, in July 2008 the board appointed a 'Task Team' to visit the country and report on the state of the game there. This group, led by Julian Hunte (West Indies) subsequently made 35 recommendations, covering governance, domestic structures, selection procedures, development, the future of the national team, and relations with stakeholders. It was clear that against the background of extreme poverty and political upheaval, Zimbabwe Cricket faced enormous problems, and it took a further three years before the national men's side was deemed ready to return to the Test fold, having in the meantime been allowed to field a team in the otherwise associates-only Intercontinental Cup.

The financial problems, however, continued. Faced with increasing debts under treasurer Ozias Bvute – a surplus of $10 million in 2004 had been converted over eight years to net liabilities of over $14 million – Zimbabwe Cricket took out a series of loans with the Harare-based Metbank, on whose board Bvute himself sat, along with ZC chairman Peter Chingoka and vice-chairman Wilson Manase. The interest rate on these loans was in excess of 20%. When this came to light in December 2011 the ICC agreed to lend ZC $6 million, on condition that it be used to pay off the existing debt to Metbank; instead, various smaller debts to other banks were paid off, while the bulk of the loan was placed in an interest-free Metbank account until a $3 million repayment was made in May 2012. The underlying problem was therefore left unaddressed, and in February 2014 the Zimbabwean board was forced to request a further $3 million loan from the ICC to enable it to pay its players and officials; incredibly, the ICC agreed to this, although it did demand that ZC move its main accounts away from Metbank. For all its high-sounding rhetoric about the integrity of the game, it did not appear that the organisation was able or willing to tackle serious financial mismanagement in one of its full members. When Peter Chingoka died in 2019, ICC chief executive Manu Sawhney paid tribute to his role as 'an important leader in cricket in Zimbabwe', noting that he was 'a respected member of the ICC Board'.

Nor was Zimbabwe the only ICC member with serious internal issues. After breaking away from the East African combination in 1981 Kenya had become one of the leading associates, beating the West Indies in the 1996 World Cup and twice beating India in triangular ODI series before reaching the semi-finals of the 2003 World Cup – admittedly with a little assistance from New Zealand's decision to forfeit their scheduled match in Nairobi because of security concerns. Their success during this period was built on the performances of Maurice Odumbe and Steve Tikolo, two of the finest players ever to emerge from outside the Test-playing countries, and the all-rounder Thomas Odoyo. On the strength of these successes the Kenyan Cricket Association applied for full membership of the ICC, and the ICC had agreed to give them $500k a year until 2006 to help them prepare. Following the 2003 World Cup the board brought forward consideration of their application to 2005, but by that time the precarious nature of Kenyan cricket had become apparent. In March 2004 Odumbe was accused of associating with a known bookmaker, and seven months later he received a five-year suspension, while by the beginning of the following year the KCA had imploded. National team players went on strike over their low salaries, the ICC was investigating wider allegations of corruption in Kenyan cricket, and the Kenyan government stepped in to disband the KCA, freezing its bank accounts.

The association battled on, but in June 2007, soon after its men's side had played in the World Cup for which, as permanent holders of ODI status, they had qualified automatically, it was again disbanded by the government and replaced by a new organisation, Cricket Kenya (CK). Then, in December 2009, CK chief executive Tom Tikolo resigned over allegations that $10,000 he had claimed for a youth tournament in the West Indies the previous year had gone missing. Further disputes with players followed as the board tried to rebuild the team, and with the domestic game ailing, on-field performances fell away. After having come so close to gaining full member status a decade earlier, the Kenyans lost their ODI status at the 2014 World Cup qualifier and joined the also-rans of the associate game.

Even greater organisational problems have dogged the development of cricket in the United States. With its long history of international cricket dating back to 1844 and its comparatively large immigrant, cricket-playing population, the USA was already a target for development as early as 2003, when global development manager Andrew Eade revealed that a scheme to make the USA co-hosts of the 2007 World Cup was under consideration. 'The ICC has been looking at the option of fast-tracking cricket development in the USA', Eade said, adding that the Council believed that with almost 8,000 players 'cricket has a lot of potential in the US.' A programme called Project USA was established with an ICC-appointed chief executive, but the relationship with the USA Cricket Association (USACA) was uncomfortable from the start. USACA, led by its controversial president Gladstone Dainty, refused to sign a memorandum of understanding with the ICC, and even though USACA had received a premature payment of $50k, Project USA was suspended in February 2005. With continuing dissension over delayed board elections, the

ICC was forced to remove the Americans from the second edition of its first-class Intercontinental Cup competition in 2005 because the USACA board and the Council of League Presidents were unable to agree on the selection of a team. Later that year, USACA's membership was suspended over elections to the board, and following a brief rehabilitation the association was again suspended in March 2007, returning to the fold once more in April 2008.

The Americans' on-field performances, too, were often disappointing, but in 2008 the former BCCI chairman I.S. Bindra became the ICC's 'principal adviser', and his eye had fallen on the USA and China as significant potential markets for promoting global events. For Bindra, global development was less about encouraging the playing of the game and more about expanding television audiences. With a rapidly growing immigrant population from India, already numbering over a million by 2000, half a million Jamaicans and significant groups from elsewhere in the subcontinent and the Caribbean, the USA could offer a huge potential market, and although cricket was in its infancy in China – its national association only joined the ACC and the ICC in 2004 – the sheer size of the country's population meant that if the sport ever took off there it, too, would substantially increase the value of the ICC's media rights contracts. The latter initiative would be at best a long-term project, and has to date borne almost no fruit, but if only the internal, political bickering could be brought to an end the expansion of cricket in the USA might have some prospect of success. Unfortunately, the dissension proved close to ineradicable, and in 2017 the ICC was forced to expel USACA completely and take the lead in setting up an entirely new organisation, USA Cricket, which was admitted as an associate in 2019. Even that, however, appears to have made little difference to the endemic squabbling, and despite the creation of an extremely promising franchise league, Major League Cricket, the USA remains firmly on the list of the ICC's problem children. Although the US co-hosted the 2024 men's T20 World Cup, the ICC was forced to remove USA Cricket's administrative responsibilities, running the American side of the tournament itself.

The transformation of the ICC which began in 1989 involved a fundamental contradiction. On the one hand, while a succession of CEOs, from David Richards through Malcolm Speed and Haroon Lorgat to Dave Richardson and current incumbent Geoff Allardice, have striven to create a modern global sporting body, running events, supporting development of both men's and women's cricket, and managing all aspects of the game, they have been accountable to a board with very different priorities, in which factionalism and self-interest have often trumped any high-sounding declarations of purpose. Malcolm Speed's oft-repeated mantra was that the ICC must achieve three key things: 'respect, influence and an appropriate level of control'. This was not, however, to everyone's liking, and Speed's seven-year tenure of the post was marked by recurrent conflicts, most often with the succession of BCCI consiglieri whose objective was to ensure that the ICC impinged as little as possible upon their power. The old governance model, under which the Imperial or International Conference could discuss but the most powerful members decided, was in fundamental conflict with the corporate approach embodied by Speed and the other modernisers; neither gave much credence to a more democratic model by which power might reside in the collective of members acting together. Speed's struggles with the BCCI and their allies are documented in his 2011 memoir *Sticky Wicket*, which gives a rare and detailed, if not altogether impartial, insight into the political machinations which eventually led to his somewhat acrimonious ousting in April 2008.

The subsequent battle over the appointment of his successor, described by Gideon Haigh in the 2012 *Wisden*, illustrated precisely the dysfunction at the organisation's heart. The current chairman, South African Ray Mali, and the BCCI's Sharad Pawar were keen to appoint I.S. Bindra, a former chair of the Indian board, but there was fairly widespread agreement that the strongest candidate was the South African Haroon Lorgat, and after a good deal of unpleasant politicking and political manoeuvring it was Lorgat who was appointed. His four-year term as chief executive was scarcely more peaceful than Speed's, although he was a much less abrasive character who tried to achieve the ICC's goals through diplomacy rather than through confrontation. The ICC's internal dynamics made this no easy task, nor did external forces always work in his favour.

On 3 March 2009 there was a terrorist attack on the Sri Lankan team and match officials in Lahore, in which six policemen and two civilians were killed, and six of the Sri Lankan players, one of their coaches and umpire Ahsan Raza wounded. Umpires Simon Taufel and Steve Davis, who were also in the officials' vehicle, criticised the conduct of the Pakistani police, and Lorgat won few friends outside Pakistan when he told them to 'settle down and be more rational'. Referee Chris Broad also upset the PCB with his criticisms of the security arrangements, leading them to lodge a formal complaint about his comments. But it was obvious that the situation could not be ignored: the Champions Trophy tournament, which was to have been held in Pakistan, was moved to South Africa, and in mid-April the board decided to move Pakistan's matches in the 2011 World Cup to other venues. The board also asked Anti-Corruption Unit (ACU) chief Paul Condon to lead a group reviewing members' security arrangements. In full defence mode, the PCB attacked that 'hasty' change and called for it to be reversed, but they really did not have a leg to stand on. In a Pakistani court they also challenged the organisers' decision to move their secretariat from Lahore to Mumbai, but at a meeting between the parties on 15 June India pulled back from their hardline stance, and it was agreed that Pakistan would remain a host, retaining its fees and membership of the organising committee. Final decisions about match venues and the site of the secretariat would be taken by the ICC's commercial arm. This was not good enough for the PCB, which vowed to continue its legal action; in the end reason prevailed and the matter was settled out of court, the PCB retaining its hosting fee and receiving an undisclosed additional sum in compensation.

Money, and the media rights deals which supplied it, was at the heart of most of the ICC's discord. The $550 million rights deal, struck in 2000, of which the ICC had been so protective, covered all aspects of partnership and sponsorship, but the Council's commercial department had been observing the BCCI's much more sophisticated marketing strategy, and in 2006 the global broadcasting rights for ICC events were sold separately for the first time. The package was for the eight-year period from 2007 to 2015, and the contract was awarded to the Singapore-based ESPN Star Sports for a reported $1.1 billion. While some of this wealth was used to finance the ICC's growing operations, not least a global development strategy, the balance would be distributed to the members, and the creation of an equitable formula for this would become one of the most persistent sources of dissension over the next two decades.

So, too, would the increasing need to satisfy the demands of the media companies who provided it. Following the early exit of India and Pakistan from the 2007 World Cup there were moves to ensure that there would be no repetition, and in October 2010 the board decided that the 2015 World Cup would be restricted to ten teams, further deciding the following April that the ten in question would be the full members. Any possibility of an associate qualifying for the ICC's most prestigious tournament would thus be removed. This almost complete abandonment of one of the Council's central strategies – the associates were compensated with the prospect of a 16-team T20 Cup – led to widespread condemnation, and even the most hawkish of the full members were forced to acknowledge that they had gone too far. In June 2011 the board delayed the introduction of a ten-team tournament until 2019 and conceded that there would have to be some form of qualification process. The controversy had, however, revealed the extent to which commercial considerations had taken over the ICC's decision-making processes, and the political forces which were increasingly at work, different from those which had dominated the first century of its existence, but in many ways even more inimical to the ICC's credibility as a global governing body.

Chapter 9

Lord Woolf, the Gang of Three and Beyond

THE FURORE over the 2015 World Cup had persuaded the ICC's leadership that a review of the organisation was now essential, and a commitment to institute such a review was included in the Strategic Plan 2011–15. In October 2011 Lord Woolf of Barnes, a former Lord Chief Justice in the UK and a highly experienced examiner of controversial organisations, was appointed to lead the review, assisted by PricewaterhouseCoopers, a respected international professional services company, and by Mukul Mudgal, a former Chief Justice of Punjab. Its task was 'to ensure that the ICC is a recognised leader in the field of the governance of sports organisations'. The review team conducted 60 interviews, received submissions from governing bodies, cricketers' associations, journalists and other interested parties in 38 countries, and submitted its report on 1 February 2012.

From its opening words the report made clear the review team's conclusion that in its present form the ICC left much to be desired: 'Cricket is a great game. It deserves to have governance, including management and ethics, worthy of the sport. This is not the position at the present time.'

The report would not, it continued, 'identify the causes and who is responsible for this', although even a cursory reading of the 50 pages of analysis and recommendations which followed left little doubt about who and what was to blame. One keynote was the insistence that board members must owe their 'fiduciary duty first and foremost to the ICC' with the clear implication that a central problem at present was that some at least of the board owed their loyalties elsewhere: 'It is essential for the good of cricket that the ICC acts in the interests of cricket as a whole, rather than the interests of individual members (or a minority of members).'

Anyone who had followed the debates and actions of the Council over the previous decade would have no difficulty in joining those dots. 'The game is too big and globally important,' the report averred, 'to permit continuation of Full Member Boards using the ICC as a "club".'

This fundamental principle led to recommendations for a complete overhaul of the board's composition and function. The review proposed the creation of a new role of independent chairman, because rotating the presidency of the Council, and with it the chairmanship, around the full members did not necessarily produce 'the best choice for the Chairman'. A transparent selection process should lead to the appointment of a chairman based on an appropriate set of skills, and while the role of president would continue, it would be primarily ambassadorial. As far as membership of the board was concerned, representation of the full members should continue, but it did not follow that each full member should have the right to nominate one director, especially if they tended to serve the interests of their own board rather than those of the ICC as a whole. In time, a smaller board, which should also include independent directors, could see some of its members elected to represent groups of governing bodies, as with the associate members at present.

This rethinking of the way in which the board was composed was linked in the review team's mind with ethical considerations. The Council had met the challenge of on-field corruption – match fixing and the like – by establishing an Anti-Corruption and Security Unit, while off-field issues were covered by the appointment of an Ethics Officer to administer an ICC Code of Ethics. But the report questioned whether the latter measures were truly effective and expressed concern about potential conflicts of interest. This brought the discussion back to the 'fiduciary duties' of the directors, and the problem that board members tended to put the interests of the governing body they represented above those of the ICC as a whole. Conflicts of interest were in this sense built into the very structures of the Council, and only a fundamental change of attitude, whereby the Code of Ethics became 'a key part of the ICC's "DNA"', could bring about the change that was required.

Between the lines of almost every paragraph of the report lay the implication that the current system gave undue power to a small minority, who could use their financial and political clout to exclude or bully the rest. Considering the exclusivity of the ten full members, the review team called for greater transparency in the criteria covering the election to full membership and went so far as to propose the decoupling of full membership from Test-playing status. The full membership category should be opened up, based on 'objective criteria taking account of performance in ICC events and ratings (both men's and women's cricket) and other balanced scorecard measures around the wider development of the game'. One disincentive in the election of new full members, the report noted, was the current financial distribution model, which allocated the lion's share of ICC income equally among the full members: expanding the category would therefore lead to a decrease in each board's share.

This led to a discussion of one of the most burning issues of all: the way in which the ICC used its money. The report was quite clear: 'We believe there is an inherent conflict between the consequences of the ICC's objective to increase the commercial revenues from ICC events to maximise distribution to members and its objective to develop the global game.'

The current financial models allocated 6% of gross revenue from ICC-run events to the Global Development Programme and then distributed the balance in the proportion of 75% to the ten full members and 25% to the associates and affiliates, who at that time numbered 95. The review team concluded that fundamental reform was needed, with the distribution model 'revised so that amounts distributed to members are on a needs basis as opposed to an automatic entitlement'. Furthermore, 'The ICC should develop a clear funding strategy to ensure an appropriate allocation of revenue between distribution to Members, funding of development of global cricket and targeted assistance to Members.'

The challenge to the comfortable existence of the full members could scarcely have been clearer. With the ICC's television rights deal for 2007–15 reportedly worth $1.1 billion, even the 7.5% distribution to each full member was a considerable sum, although for the BCCI, and to a lesser extent for the ECB and ACB, it was outweighed by their own sale of TV rights for international and domestic cricket. And it was seen as an entitlement. As the focus of cricket administration had shifted towards income generation, built on the Packer-taught lesson that cricket as a commodity was worth big money, the greed of the biggest players had grown correspondingly, and the suggestion that the profits might be shared 'on a needs basis' came very close to heresy. When Lord Woolf insisted that his recommendations were an indissoluble package this was what he meant: a fairer, more policy-driven distribution of funding was inextricably linked to a resolution of the conflict between the interests of cricket as a whole and those of a small number of powerful full members, which in turn required a complete rethinking of the structure and function of the board and its committees.

This was a much more far-reaching review than the key full members had anticipated, and the review group was careful to ensure that it did not leak before all board members received it simultaneously. The reaction was not long delayed. Even before its release, the report's detractors attempted to prevent its publication, and within a fortnight the chairman of the BCCI, Narayanaswami Srinivasan, revealed that his board's working party had rejected the report, although he did not specify which recommendations were unacceptable. Since the entire document was implicitly directed towards ending the BCCI's stranglehold on the organisation, this decision did not come as a complete surprise. An initial reaction from the ECB was also unfavourable. James Sutherland, the chief executive of the Australian board, on the other hand, said that 'it would be silly' for the report to be rejected out of hand. In early March the ICC Chief Executives' Committee decided that the report needed to be considered by all member boards before a definitive response could be reached by the board, and two days before the board met on 15 April 2012, the Federation of International Cricketers' Associations threw their weight behind Woolf's recommendations: 'As Lord Woolf has observed the current ICC Board structure lacks independence, it lacks the perception of being independent, it lacks the ability to elect a pertinent spread of skills around the Board table, and it even lacks the ability to elect Board members to its own committees. The ICC Board needs relevant expertise and integrity to deal with issues that can and may confront our game. It needs to act in the interests of the wider game, not the interests of a minority.'

One recommendation which aligned with the way in which the ICC was already thinking was for a separation of the roles of chairman and president, the latter to be purely ceremonial, and this at least could be agreed when the board met in April. Decisions on the rest, however, were deferred until the next meeting in June. As cricket's leaders gathered for their annual conference in that month, television commentator and former England captain Tony Greig delivered the annual Cowdrey Spirit of Cricket lecture, in which he defended his role in the World Series Cricket episode and reflected on the revolution it had initiated. The game was, he contended, 'in reasonably good shape', and although there were problems, 'I think most of the problems can generally be addressed if India invokes and adheres to the spirit of cricket. Mahatma Gandhi said, "A nation's culture resides in the hearts and in the soul of its people." As cricket certainly resides in the hearts and soul of Indian people, I am optimistic India will lead cricket by acting in the best interests of all countries rather than just for India.'

Greig acknowledged that under English and Australian control, self-interest had dominated the ICC, 'and countries such as India and New Zealand were undoubtedly discriminated against'. Because the game was now dependent on the money generated by India's television deals, its power within the ICC had become disproportionate: 'India's apparent indifference towards Test cricket and its response towards some of the key issues – the international calendar and the mix of the different types of cricket; its attitude to the earlier ICC corruption inquiries; its indifference to the urgency to introduce anti-doping rules; the rumoured corruption hanging over the IPL; its attitude to the Decision Review System; and its role in the lack of due process in stopping former Australian Prime Minister John Howard being appointed vice-president of the ICC – are all examples of disappointing decisions. But many of the problems with the ICC could be resolved if India invoked the spirit of cricket and didn't try and influence its allies in how to vote.'

The situation could only be resolved, Greig concluded, 'by India accepting that the spirit of cricket is more important than generating billions of dollars; it's more important than turning out multi-millionaire players; and it's more important than getting square with Australia and England for their bully-boy tactics towards India over the years'. Echoing Woolf, he concluded by calling on ICC members to 'put the game's interests before their own interests' and urging that India 'embraces the spirit of cricket and governs in the best interests of world cricket, not just for India and its business partners'.

Greig's words fell on deaf ears. The executive board pushed ahead with the creation of a new paid post of chairman and the corresponding reduction in the powers of the president, but Lord Woolf's other recommendations were simply kicked into the long grass. They were, delegates were informed, 'part of talks between various boards themselves and at Executive Board level'. The little people, the 90% of ICC members who were mere associates and affiliates, were to have no say in these momentous decisions; they did, it was true, have three representatives on the board, but their views could simply be ignored. New Zealander Alan Isaac would be the last president selected by rotation among the full members, and when his term came to an end in June 2014 he would be succeeded by a less powerful president, the real power residing with the newly established chairman. Ominously, the word was that the main contenders were likely to be the BCCI's Srinivasan and the ECB's Giles Clarke, neither of whom was seen as a proponent of Woolf's recommended reforms. By stifling debate on his report the ICC missed its one great opportunity to transform itself into a global governing body worthy of the name; Greig's remark that the Woolf proposals were like asking the United States, Russia, China, France and Britain to give up their veto on the United Nations Security Council was only too accurate, and time would show that, far from ruling in the interests of the game as a whole, the BCCI was intent on exercising even greater power and accumulating even more wealth than it already had.

Even the introduction of the chairmanship, however, carried with it dangers for the enemies of good governance.

In October 2013 it was reported that at a meeting in London Clarke and Srinivasan had agreed that the chairman should be a convenor rather than the head of an executive office. They had concluded, one source confided, that 'there is no role for the chairman in the ICC. It is just an additional layer of bureaucracy which they believe is not necessary.' It was understood that this attempt to weaken the position of the chairman even before it had been filled sprang from a desire to protect the power of the Finance and Commercial Affairs Committee (F&CA), chaired by Clarke, and the importance of that would soon become evident.

By 9 January 2014 the great powers of international cricket had prepared their considered riposte to Lord Woolf's audacity, and it essentially confirmed everything the review team had written about what was wrong with the ICC's structure. A working party of the F&CA, dominated by the BCCI, CA and the ECB, proposed a series of changes, all of which were designed to concentrate power and money in the hands of those three members. A central demand was the creation of a new executive committee, which would become 'the sole recommendation committee . . . on all constitutional, personnel, integrity, ethics, development and nominations matters'. India, Australia and England would have permanent membership of the committee with a fourth member elected by the other seven full members, and the big three would rotate the chairmanship around themselves. The ICC chairman, supposedly created to give the board a degree of independent leadership, would now be rotated among the same three countries, as would the chairmanship of the F&CA committee. The IDI would be replaced by a new body, ICC Business Co., which would handle the next round of media rights negotiations.

The underlying logic of the working party's claims was straightforward: since the ICC's income was overwhelmingly generated through television rights, and that rights sale was dependent on the appeal of cricket in India, Australia and

England, and especially India, those three countries were entitled to an overwhelming share of the power and the profits. Woolf's notion that the ICC existed to promote cricket as a global game was simply ignored; money, and the markets which generated it, should be the only consideration. Realpolitik had trumped woolly idealism, and the gang of three made it quite clear that they were prepared to back up their demands with the raw power of the international schedule, as the BCCI had done when it threatened to pull out of its South African tour. No 'lesser' full member could afford to call that bluff, and the system which would now be instituted would make the ICC constitution of the 1960s and 1970s seem positively democratic. There was no room for democracy, or even fairness, in the globalising corporatism which would now prevail. There would, for instance, be a promotion and relegation system introduced into Test cricket, but India, Australia and England would be exempt from relegation no matter how abysmal their performances on the field might be; the justification for this was that it was 'solely to protect ICC income due to the importance of those markets and teams to prospective ICC media rights buyers'.

The document opened with a resounding statement of principle: '. . . for cricket to survive and thrive into the twenty-first century and beyond, ICC members have to be or become self-sufficient with sustainable investment and growth in their domestic markets'.

A situation had developed, it continued, 'where most members look to the ICC to be told what type of cricket to play and expect the ICC to solve any financial problems that they may encounter'. At the time, these statements were largely interpreted as being critical of the 'lesser' Test-playing countries, but the language made clear that it was aimed at the associates and affiliates as well. And the authors followed up with a breathtaking piece of hypocrisy: the structural changes proposed were intended to ensure that 'the ICC reverts to being a member-driven organisation;

an organisation of the members and for the members. As part of this process, the leading countries of India, England and Australia have agreed that they will provide greater leadership at and of the ICC.'

The power grab, then, was to be seen as an act of generosity, the big three stepping in to save the organisation from the unnamed forces which had led it away from its members. But the rest of the document made it clear that in this new era it would be 'of and for' some members rather than others; in an Orwellian echo, if all members were to be equal, some were to be decidedly more equal than others.

It was, naturally, on the financial issues that the new proposals centred. The current funding model, the working party argued, did not recognise the contribution of individual members, thus creating 'a distorted distribution model that undermines self-sufficiency'. India was responsible, they claimed, for generating more than 80% of the ICC's income, with the other members contributing between 1% and 5%. 'If ICC funds were entirely allocated on the basis of where they come from, all members bar two would suffer a seriously damaging reduction in their income.' In their generosity the BCCI, ECB and CA were not minded to insist on such a reform, but neither were they any longer prepared to accept a system by which all full members received an equal share. The distribution must be weighted towards those who brought in the money, through a new formula based on the notion of a 'contribution cost'. Under such a system the BCCI would take a mere 21% of revenue, compared with the 4.2% they were entitled to under the current system. The blow would be softened by the creation of a Test Cricket Fund to support Test-playing countries outside the ruling triumvirate and to prevent 'no Test cricket being played – or inappropriately little Test cricket' on 'uneconomical tours'.

In an interview with *Cricinfo*'s Daniel Brettig, Wally Edwards, the CA chairman who had played a crucial part in developing the new proposals, gave a revealing insight into the thinking which had led to this coup. The dysfunctionality of the ICC, he said, was largely due to there being 'a very unhappy India in the room, very unhappy with pretty well everything that was happening'. Management was isolated from the board, he believed, and that needed to be corrected in order to make the ICC 'a better business': '[w]hat we're driving at is to make cricket work better and make the competition side of it work better'. For Edwards the threat of India walking away was a powerful motivating force: 'There was a very real chance that India would have gone on an IPL voyage and left world cricket behind.' It was necessary, therefore, to accommodate as many as possible of the BCCI's concerns, and CA and the ECB were willing to take the lead in giving them the power – and share of the revenue – they desired. Edwards denied that the creation of the executive committee would shift power into the hands of the big three. Whatever that committee recommended 'the board then in the end has to approve it. So there's no entrenched power at all, because the board can overrule anything.' The likelihood of that scenario was revealed that June by BCCI secretary Sanjay Patel, who acknowledged that 'we told them that if India is not getting its proper due and importance than India might be forced to form a second ICC of its own'. But a revealing detail emerged four years later, when a tribunal hearing a case about a breach of the Future Tours Programme learned that the ECB and CA had told the PCB that they would not sign the new FTP agreement unless the PCB agreed to support their coup; they were prepared to use standover tactics in order to gain an effective monopoly of power.

Edwards' argument, of course, ignored Lord Woolf's analysis, which suggested that the existing arrangements already gave a minority of board members excessive power, particularly since they were accustomed to acting in the interests of their own boards, rather than of the ICC or world cricket as a whole. Indeed, the F&CA committee's proposals served to legitimise and reinforce that power, placing it firmly in the hands of three members on the basis that they created the wealth in the first place. And it was a power they were absolutely prepared to use. When the venues for the next cycle of major events was released in January 2015, it was India and England who were the principal beneficiaries. India would host the 2016 T20 World Cup, but England were given no fewer than three major tournaments: the Champions Trophy and Women's World Cup in 2017 and the biggest prize of all, the 2019 50-over World Cup.

Much of this was due to the influence of BCCI chair Srinivasan, who became the ICC's first chairman in June 2014 when the restructuring agreed in 2012 came into effect; this, surely, was the antithesis of what Woolf had proposed. Srinivasan's conflicts of interest were legion: as well as serving first as secretary and then as president of the BCCI, his company India Cements was the owner of the IPL franchise team the Chennai Super Kings, the BCCI's rules having been amended to allow board members to own stakes in IPL teams. In 2013, however, his son-in-law, CSK team boss Gurunath Meiyappan, was implicated in a major IPL spot-fixing scandal, and he was indicted following a report in February 2014 by a committee led by retired judge Mukul Mudgal, who had also advised Lord Woolf. In March the Supreme Court demanded that Srinivasan himself step down as BCCI president, stating that it was 'nauseating' that he should retain the post despite having been censured by several courts. This, it seemed, was no obstacle to his becoming ICC chairman four months later, and it was not until November 2016 that he was replaced in that post by Shashank Manohar, who had also taken over as president of the BCCI; it was a fair reflection of the real state of affairs that the change in the ICC chairmanship was announced following the BCCI's annual general meeting.

Manohar was perhaps the one top Indian cricket administrator who was prepared to look beyond the narrow interests of the BCCI, and he soon set about undoing some of the damage which had been done by the Srinivasan regime. The resource system put in place by the gang of three's 2014 coup was so obviously unbalanced that it was ultimately unsustainable, and it was Manohar who instigated the pushback. He established a five-man working group, which after a year of extensive consultations put its proposals to the board in February 2017. A new draft constitution was agreed in principle although India and Sri Lanka voted against, and Zimbabwe abstained. Adopted at the 2017 annual conference, this constitution made significant changes: it abolished the affiliates membership category; it provided for one (female) independent board member; it gave all board members' votes the same weight, eliminating the built-in advantage of the full members; it created the new position of deputy chair, elected from within the board; and it established a membership committee to monitor the status of all members, with scope for progression from associate to full membership.

The sticking point, however, was always going to be the proposed new revenue distribution model, which clawed back some of the financial gains which the BCCI had been able to obtain for itself and its closest allies in the 2014 changes. BCCI representative Vikram Limaye's stated grounds for opposition at this stage were essentially procedural: he had only been assigned his role within the BCCI by the Supreme Court of India on 30 January, on the eve of the ICC board meeting, and he had therefore had no time to review the documents. A BCCI statement went a little further: there was, it claimed, 'no scientific basis behind the percentage distribution allocation that was being proposed other than "good faith and equity"'. This was precisely the ground in which Manohar had chosen to stand. 'I want the ICC,' he said, 'to be reasonable and fair in our approach to all 105 members and the revised constitution and financial model does that.' The principle of change, he added, was agreed, 'and not for debate'.

The day before the board's meeting, moreover, the Chief Executives' Committee had agreed to radical changes in the playing structures for men's international cricket. It proposed the introduction of a nine-team Test championship and a 13-team ODI league, with possible changes as well to the qualification system for T20 World Cups as well. Although the details were not yet spelled out, these proposals also envisaged the addition of two more Test-playing countries although they, like Zimbabwe, would be excluded from the Test championship.

The distribution of revenue proposed by Manohar's working party soon emerged, and it was immediately evident why the BCCI was so unhappy. On the new model its share would be between 10% and 11.3%, as against the 17.6–18% it would have received under the model adopted in 2014. The ECB's share would fall from 5.8–6% to 4.8–5%, while CA's would remain more or less constant.

The working party continued to develop its proposals, operating on principles of 'equity, good conscience, common sense and simplicity, enabling every member to grow, revenue generated by members, greater transparency, and recognition of interdependency amongst members, that cricket-playing nations need each other and the stronger nations there are, the better for the sport'. It was reported that India and Sri Lanka had opposed the changes in February, and when the revised constitution came to the board in April it was passed by 12 votes to two; the modified revenue distribution arrangements, however, had only one dissenter. The BCCI would now receive an estimated $293 million over the next eight years, the ECB $143 million, Zimbabwe $94 million, and the remaining seven full members $132 million each, with the associate pot set at $280 million. One proposal, however, disappeared between February and April: the idea that full members should be subject to a five-yearly review of their performance was quietly dropped. Oversight of the associates was necessary and universally agreed; but applying such measures to the ICC's elite was obviously a step too far.

In June 2017, shortly after changing the membership conditions to make it possible, the board admitted Afghanistan and Ireland to full membership. Both had dominated the associates' scene for some time, and the rise of Afghanistan had been a project to which the ICC had devoted considerable time and energy. There were, of course, some continuing difficulties: the country remained in a state of civil war, and there were strong forces militating against the development there of the women's game. But the success of both in the Intercontinental Cup as well as in shorter formats, and their measures to introduce appropriate domestic structures, fully justified their elevation. At the same time, it was a decision which reinforced the ICC's reputation for never granting anything without taking something away. The World Test Championship, which was about to be given a new form, would include only nine participants, and Zimbabwe, a full member since 1992, would be excluded, joining Ireland and Afghanistan in what was effectively a second division of Test cricket, with few opportunities to take on the more established countries. Although international cricket was admittedly disrupted by the Covid-19 pandemic in 2020/21, it was a significant fact that between 2018 and August 2024 the two newest Test countries had played a total of nine Tests each – although a scheduled one-off match against Australia had twice been cancelled.

The elevation of Afghanistan and Ireland was part of a compromise agreement which was hammered out between the ICC and the BCCI between the meeting in April and the following one in June. With India continuing to object to its reduced share and reportedly threatening to withdraw from ICC tournaments if it did not get its way, a new allocation was worked out which increased the BCCI share to $405 million, an increase of $112 million on what had been overwhelmingly agreed in April. Each of the full members except Zimbabwe would receive $4 million less, while the associate members' share was reduced by a thumping $40 million, which would now be used to fund the new full members, Afghanistan and Ireland. With other adjustments, including a reduction of $16 million in the events budget, the books could be made to balance and the BCCI could be persuaded to accept this model.

Manohar and Dave Richardson, who had succeeded Lorgat in 2012, made a strong team, but when the CEO stepped down in April 2019 Manohar replaced him with Manu Sawhney, the former managing director of ESPN Star Sports whose most recent post had been as CEO of the Singapore Sports Hub, a job he left in controversial circumstances. In his two years running the ICC he made some powerful enemies, falling out with the BCCI, CA and the ECB over the inclusion of an additional major ICC event in the next edition of the Future Tours Programme and over holding an open bidding process for the hosting of the next cycle of ICC events, both of which were opposed by the BCCI and its allies. Those issues were central to the hard-fought chairmanship election between Singapore's Imran Khwaja, the acting chairman following Manohar's sudden resignation in July 2020, and New Zealander Greg Barclay, which Barclay won with the support of the BCCI, CA and the ECB, although he was at pains after his election to deny that the concept of the 'big three' was relevant any longer. Suddenly, though, Sawhney was the subject of complaints about his management style and allegations of bullying and following a review by PricewaterhouseCoopers he was suspended in March 2021 after a process which he described as 'a premeditated witch-hunt'. Four months later he was sacked, former director of cricket Geoff Allardice taking over, and the board abandoned its planned open bidding process. Sawhney was the third CEO in 13 years to be forced out after falling foul of the BCCI and its allies.

As the sale of media rights proved ever more lucrative, the BCCI's demands for a greater share – notwithstanding its own massive rights income, not least from the IPL – continued. With Jay Shah, secretary of the BCCI and son of the Indian Home Affairs Minister Amit Shah, elected chairman of the FCA, it was perhaps inevitable that those demands would be gratified, and the 2023 annual meeting duly received and agreed to proposals for a revised resource distribution model. With the rights for 2024–27, now limited to four years and split up on a regional basis, yielding some $3 billion, a 50 per cent increase on the previous *eight*-year cycle, the new model gave India 38.5 per cent of revenue, estimated at $230 million a year. This significant increase, balanced by reductions in other members' share, was generated by a new formula, recommended by Shah's committee, which starts with all full members notionally allocated an equal share of 8.3%, but with the actual allocation based on three other criteria (or 'component weightings'): an historical component which benefits the full members with the exception of Zimbabwe, Ireland and Afghanistan; performance in men's and women's global events over the past 16 years; and crucially, each member's 'contribution to the ICC's commercial revenue'. The last carries the most weight, echoing the BCCI's repeated claim that since they are the biggest revenue earner thanks to the massive support for cricket in India, they should also receive the lion's share of the revenue.

The outcome from this formula was that England and Australia, who had given themselves a virtual monopoly on lucrative major events during their period of domination in 2014–17, received the largest share after India, with 6.89% and 6.25% respectively, while the remaining full members got between 5.75% (Pakistan) and 2.80% (Afghanistan). But with the substantial increase in rights income, the proponents of this manifestly unbalanced model were able to point out that even Afghanistan could look forward to around $16.82 million a year, and the system was accepted by the annual meeting in July 2023. Even the reduction in the share given to the 94 associate members to 11.19% of the total, it was claimed, would result in constant or perhaps even marginally increased allocations, and protests that this was a ludicrously skewed model fell upon deaf ears. In advance of the board's final decision there was pushback from some of the less advantaged full members and from the associates: Vanuatu CEO Tim Cutler, for example, told Reuters that 'cricket will not grow beyond its current corners of the world … if the allocation of the game's global funds aren't more equally allocated with a view to actually growing the game', while former PCB and ICC chairman Ehsan Mani declared that India's massive share 'makes no sense' for the welfare of cricket globally. Pakistan's protests yielded a minor adjustment in its favour, but there was no relief for the associates, who lack the political clout of a full member like Pakistan. The biblical principle that *to those that have shall be given* remained in force, and if the heady days of the gang of three had not quite returned in full, the ostensible rationality of the FCA's formula was sufficient for its proponents to get their way.

By the autumn of 2024 the BCCI's hostile takeover of the ICC was effectively complete. Having organised, in his capacity as BCCI secretary, a 2023 men's World Cup which was designed as a triumphalist paean for Prime Minister Narendra Modi and the BJP's nationalist agenda – marred somewhat by an Australian victory in the final which left Modi visibly fuming – and seized the limelight when India won the T20 World Cup the following June, Shah was ready to make a bid for power. He was reportedly very active in ensuring that the three associate representatives elected to the board were supportive, and with the incentive of a $15 million fund to support Test cricket, first mooted as long ago as 2014 but never implemented, he was able to command sufficient votes to inform chairman Greg

Barclay that he intended to run against him, and that he was certain to win. Barclay bowed to the inevitable, although noting in a speech to a symposium at Lord's in July that the ICC was 'not fit for purpose', and on 27 August Shah was elected unopposed. Once the 'MCC foreign desk', the ICC appears now to have become the instrument of an overtly nationalist Indian political party and its corporatist ambitions. The vultures have indeed come home to roost over world cricket's Tower of Silence.

Chapter 10

Events, Dear Boy, Events

AS THE ICC began on its new path in 1989 there were only two men's international competitions, the quadrennial 50-over World Cup and the ICC Trophy, the latter serving as a qualifier for the former. But over the next 35 years the world changed radically, and the Council's appetite for major global events, designed in large part to increase the value of their sale of television rights, became seemingly insatiable. In part, of course, this was due to the emergence of the T20 format, for which the first World Cup was held in South Africa in 2007, three more following in the next five years. By this time there was also the 50-over Champions Trophy, initially a biennial event, the original purpose of which was to generate money for global development. This meant that over the next 13 years there was only one – 2008 – in which there was no global men's event. And on top of this the ICC decided, after much soul-searching and several cancellations, to introduce a World Test Championship from 2019, so that now there are world titles across all three formats.

The first World Cup of the new era, and the fifth in all, was jointly hosted in February–March 1992 by Australia and New Zealand, who had beaten off a bid by India and Pakistan to host the event for a second successive time. The schedule was revised at the last minute to include South Africa, who had been readmitted to the fold following the establishment in June 1991 of the United Cricket Board, so that it was a nine-team tournament, including qualifier Zimbabwe. South Africa began by hammering Australia at the SCG; ironically, it was Kepler Wessels, who had played for Australia during his country's isolation and had now returned to the Springbok side, who saw them to victory with an unbeaten 81. They finished third overall, but their semi-final against England ended in farce. England had made 252/6 in 45 overs, their innings cut short because of a slow South African over rate. With the Springboks on 232/6 they needed 22 from 13 balls, but then the weather intervened, and the umpires decided to take the players from the field.

A new system had been introduced for this tournament to deal with rain-affected matches, which required the score to be adjusted on the basis of the least productive overs in the innings of the side batting first. Since South Africa had bowled two maidens, the target therefore remained the same, though with two overs deducted because of the interruption, South Africa had just one ball to score them. To make matters worse, the crowd was initially told that one over had come off, leaving 22 to make from seven deliveries, and the reaction when this was corrected was predictable. And worse still, according to the competition rules the match should have been completed on a reserve day, but this had been overruled by the host broadcaster, Packer's Channel Nine. The Springboks could have been forgiven for feeling hard done by, but they accepted the ludicrous defeat with good grace. Pakistan, having seen off New Zealand in their semi-final, beat England by 22 runs in a hard-fought final.

Now expanded to 12 teams, the 1996 World Cup in India, Pakistan and Sri Lanka got off to an unpromising start when Australia and the West Indies, who were in Sri Lanka's group, refused to travel to the island following a Tamil Tiger bombing in Colombo a month before the tournament was scheduled to start. Having declared Sri Lanka safe, the ICC awarded the points to the hosts, thereby virtually ensuring their progress to the quarter-finals. In the event, they beat India, Zimbabwe and Kenya on the field, and went through undefeated. The major upset of the competition was Kenya's victory over the West Indies, who collapsed to 93 all out in pursuit of their opponents' total of 166, the fourth time an associate had beaten a full member in an ODI; nevertheless, the West Indians went into the last eight, along with India and Australia. There was more controversy in the semi-final at Calcutta, where Sri Lanka, having posted 251/8, had reduced India to 120/8 when rioting by the crowd led the umpires to abandon the match, referee Clive Lloyd awarding it to the Sri Lankans. The other semi-final was a thriller, with the West Indies failing by just five runs to chase down Australia's relatively modest 207/8. The final, played in Lahore, was a triumph for Sri Lanka's Aravinda de Silva, who took 3-42 as his side held Australia to 241/7 and then made an unbeaten 107 to see them to a seven-wicket victory.

The successful ECB bid to host the 1999 tournament provided for matches to be played in Ireland, Scotland and the Netherlands as well as 17 venues in England and Wales, so for the first time, World Cup games would be played at grounds in associate countries. Another innovation was the introduction of a 'Super Six', the top three sides from each of the two initial groups playing three further matches against teams from the other group while carrying forward their results against their fellow qualifiers from their group. Having lost to both Pakistan and New Zealand in the first phase Australia started the Super Six on zero points, but victories over India, surprise qualifier Zimbabwe (who had stunned India in a group match) and South Africa saw them into the semi-finals. Their win against South Africa had come with only two deliveries to spare, but the sides' rematch in the semi-final was even closer. After a shaky start, a fifth-wicket stand of 90 between Steve Waugh and Michael Bevan enabled Australia to reach 213, but when Shane Warne took three wickets to help reduce the Proteas to 61/4 it seemed that the Australians might be taking control. Then Jacques Kallis and Jonty Rhodes put on 84 for the fifth wicket, and with Shaun Pollock and Lance Klusener chipping in, South Africa needed 38 off the last five overs with four wickets in hand. Damien Fleming bowled Pollock, and Klusener and Mark Boucher were left needing 18 off the last two. Glenn McGrath yorked Boucher, and two balls later Steve Elworthy was run out trying to keep Klusener on strike. Off the next delivery Paul Reiffel could only fend a big hit from Klusener over the rope for six, and the final pair required nine off Fleming's final over. Back-to-back boundaries from Klusener levelled the scores, and after a possible run-out off the third delivery, a throw from Steve Waugh to Fleming to keeper Adam Gilchrist beat a desperately lunging Donald and brought the match to a chaotic end, the tie sufficient to take Australia into the final. It was, some thought, the greatest ODI ever played, but the final was an anti-climax, Pakistan collapsing to 132 all out and Australia cruising to an eight-wicket victory.

The difficulties about security in Sri Lanka which had arisen during the 1996 World Cup paled into insignificance when the 2003 event was played. There were again multiple hosts, with most games to be scheduled for South Africa but with six to take place in Zimbabwe and two in Kenya. There had been concerns for months about the security situation in Zimbabwe, where the disputed re-election of Robert Mugabe had led to protracted unrest. An ICC delegation later that year concluded that Zimbabwe was 'a safe and secure country', but anxiety about security continued, and the British government was applying pressure for England to boycott their match there because of its criticisms of the Mugabe regime. In January 2003 the ECB management committee confirmed that England would play, chief executive Tim Lamb declaring that '[w]e are fully aware of what is happening in Zimbabwe and we do not in any way condone the policies and actions of the political regime in that country', but repeating the old mantra that politics must not be allowed to interfere with sport.

In the end, England did forfeit that match, and as a result Zimbabwe, with wins over qualifiers Namibia and the Netherlands and a no-result against Pakistan, went through to the Super Six. Kenya, too, benefited from a walkover against New Zealand, who refused to play in Nairobi because of their security concerns, and by beating Canada, Bangladesh and Sri Lanka finished second in their group. Kenya then beat Zimbabwe in the Super Six phase and, astonishingly, reached the semi-finals, where they proved no match for India and lost by 91 runs. Australia then overpowered India in the final, thanks to an unbeaten 140 from Ricky Ponting, but the tournament was overshadowed by the security problems, the disputes over players' contracts, and by Shane Warne's failing of a drug test on the eve of Australia's opening match. Bad feeling continued. Towards the end of the year England captain Nasser Hussain was scathing about what he called 'a poorly run tournament', stating that by its handling of the Zimbabwe question the ICC had 'let us down, and it had let cricket down'.

The ICC now took the prospects of the qualifiers in hand, establishing a High Performance Programme to help them prepare for the World Cup and initiating a World Cricket League tournament as part of their warm-up. In most cases, this proactive policy made little difference: the only victories Kenya and the Netherlands achieved in the 2007 event were against fellow qualifiers Canada and Scotland, who, like Bermuda, went through the group phase without a win. But the revelation was Ireland who, after tying with Zimbabwe in their opening match, caused one of the greatest sensations in World Cup history by beating Pakistan by three wickets in a rain-affected game. That took them into the Super Eight, where they secured another full member scalp by dismissing Bangladesh for 169 and winning by 74 runs. The Tigers had earlier caused a shock of their own by beating India, who also lost to Sri Lanka and thus, like Pakistan, missed out on the Super Eight.

Astonishing as these on-field events were, they were overshadowed by the death of Pakistan coach Bob Woolmer the day after his side had succumbed to Ireland. The news that he had been found dead in his hotel room broke as Australia were playing the Netherlands in another group match, and it proved a nightmare for the ICC. Although the early indications were that Woolmer had died of a heart attack, within a few days a pathologist concluded that he had been strangled. The Jamaican Deputy Police Commissioner Mark Shields opened an investigation, and rumours swirled that it had to do with discord within the Pakistani camp, or with match fixing. The media pack demanded quick answers, and there were accusations that the Pakistan captain Inzamam-ul-Haq, assistant coach Mushtaq Ali and team manager Talat Ali might have been in some way involved. Lord McLaurin, the former chairman of the ECB, chose this moment to launch a stinging attack on the ICC and its inability to deal with the corruption in the game: 'When you have a terrible situation like we are now facing, one's got to look at the whole of the operation; the directorship; the way it's run; the calibre of the people that are doing it,' he argued.

Rumours continued to proliferate, with the ICC understandably unable to bring the focus back to the continuing tournament. CEO Malcolm Speed did his best, urging that 'what we must all do now is to show how resolute the game is by proving ourselves strong enough to move on from what has happened'. He added, rather optimistically, that a 'great World Cup' would be 'something that will help to put the smile back on the face of our great sport'. With the police investigation, reinforced by detectives from Scotland Yard, continuing, this had the air of whistling in the dark; Inzamam even suggested that had any country other than

Pakistan been involved the competition would have been cancelled.

With India and Pakistan both eliminated, the tournament was in any case rather less of a draw. Such victories could have been seen as evidence of greater competitiveness, which was one of the ICC's declared goals, but it proved much more significant that the defeats were instrumental in both India and Pakistan missing out on the Super Eight. The elimination of India was a financial catastrophe for the organisers and for the holders of the television rights, one which would eventually have far-reaching consequences. For many, the rest of the tournament was an anti-climax, even with Ireland's subsequent victory over Bangladesh, and this feeling was in no way dispelled by a farcical conclusion to the final. Rain reduced the match to 38 overs a side before the start, and with Adam Gilchrist hammering a 104-ball 149 with 13 fours and eight sixes, Australia set Sri Lanka a massive 282 for victory. Despite a second-wicket stand of 117 between Sanath Jayasuriya and Kumar Sangakkara, Sri Lanka were well behind the rate at 148/3 in the 25th over when a further interruption shaved off another two overs, the new target 269 from 36. The light was now failing, and after 33 overs the Sri Lankan batsmen opted to leave the field, Australia apparently winning. But after another delay, and in near-total darkness, the umpires brought the players back for the final three overs, Australia won by 55 runs, and the presentations took place to a chorus of boos for the ICC officials. It was, *Cricinfo*'s commentator observed, 'almost as if cricket was determined to show the world that it couldn't organise a whatsit in a brewery'.

It was not as if the tournament had not already been plagued by controversy. Quite apart from Woolmer's death and the early exit of India and Pakistan, there had been widespread criticism of high ticket prices, especially in countries where many cricket fans had limited financial resources, and the restrictions on signs, musical instruments and outside food and drink (the latter further adding to the cost of attendance) also drew plenty of negative comment. The ICC and the local organisers blamed each other, but the fact was that the tournament had done little to repair cricket's increasingly tarnished image. Other issues were thrown in as the pile-on continued: the presence of the six qualifiers had led to mismatches and lowered the standard; it had all lasted too long; and India, naturally, complained about a format which had seen them go out after losing two matches. Rather than celebrating Ireland's extraordinary achievement, media attention concentrated on the many things which had gone wrong, and it did not come as a surprise when the ICC decided that for the next World Cup in 2011 the number of participants would be cut to 14 and the number of matches from 51 to 49 – scarcely a substantial gain in exchange for the reduced opportunities offered to the associates.

But in October 2010 the board took a much more radical step, further cutting the number of teams in the 2015 event to ten. That tournament, it was decided, would involve an each-play-all round robin, so that there could be no question of any of the major Test-playing countries making an early exit. The lesson from the West Indies in 2007 had been learned, and India, Australia and their allies were taking no chances that the commercial value of their premier competition would again be undermined by a success of an uppity associate. There was an outcry from those who saw this narrowing of the window to the global stage as a betrayal of the ICC's claims to govern in the interests of the whole game, but worse was to follow. When the decision was reviewed six months later it became even more draconian, the board now deciding that not only would there be a ten-team World Cup, but the ten would be the ten full members. The window, in other words, was now bricked up and concreted over. In an attempt at compensation, ICC CEO Haroon Lorgat announced that the World T20 Cup would be expanded from 12 teams to 16. But the 50-over tournament, billed by the ICC as 'the Cup that Counts', would be an all-full-member affair.

An intense round of lobbying before the board next met, in June 2011, persuaded even its more intransigent members that this time they had gone too far. There would, after all, be 14 teams in the 2015 World Cup, although the 2019 event would be cut to ten. And even that victory came at a cost: as soon as it had been agreed, a further proposal was tabled to cut the T20 Cup back to 12. The justification for this was the additional cost of a larger 50-over event, but it was reported at the time that at least one board member had made it clear to associates' representatives at the annual conference that it was motivated more by revenge. 'You'll get your 14-team World Cup,' he allegedly said, 'but you'll pay for it!' Neither on the field nor off it was it acceptable for the smaller nations to challenge the hegemony of those who ruled the game.

The attack on the Sri Lankan team in Lahore in March 2009, which had caused eight deaths and the wounding of six Sri Lankan players and one of the umpires, led to Pakistan being stripped of its position as a co-host of the 2011 World Cup, which had gone to a four-country subcontinental bid despite the fact that, unlike the proposal from Australia and New Zealand, it had not been submitted on time. An unseemly spat ensued, the PCB threatening to take legal action and the ICC taking the improbable position that Pakistan were still co-hosts but just would not be allowed to host any matches. Various alternatives were proposed. That Australia and New Zealand, now scheduled to run the 2015 tournament, should swap with the subcontinental countries, or that Pakistan's matches might be played in the UAE. But in the end those matches were reallocated to the other three hosting countries. Although there was a threat by the extremist Hindu party Shiv Sena to boycott the final if Pakistan reached it and there were allegations that the final which did take place, in which India beat Sri Lanka by six wickets, had been fixed, the tournament generally was a success, the highlights including a tied group match between England and India and Ireland's improbable victory over England, Kevin O'Brien's record-breaking 63-ball knock of 113 enabling his side to chase down their opponents' 327/8 and win by three wickets with five balls to spare.

After so much heated discussion of the format for the 2015 World Cup, the last to include 14 teams before the competition was cut to ten, the tournament itself passed off relatively quietly. The biggest surprise, perhaps, was that England again failed to get through the group phase, losing four of their first five games and beating only Scotland and Afghanistan as Bangladesh finished ahead of them in the group table. There were few surprises in the other pool, Ireland being pipped for fourth spot on net run rate by the West Indies despite having beaten them by four wickets in their group match. This time the top eight sides went into a knockout phase, with South Africa and India joining the two host countries in the semi-finals. In a rain-affected match in Auckland, New Zealand beat South Africa by four wickets, while Australia posted a 95-run victory over India in Sydney to produce a final clash between the host countries. The Australian attack proved too strong for the Black Caps, dismissing them for just 183, and Steve Smith and captain Michael Clarke steered their side to a seven-wicket victory in 33.1 overs to give Australia their fifth World Cup, and their fourth in their last five attempts.

The gang of three's monopoly on major events continued with the 2019 World Cup, which took place in England and ended thrillingly but controversially in victory for the hosts. It was the first of the new-look ten-team tournaments, designed to satisfy the demands of the television companies, with a round-robin phase in which each country played all the others. It was also an entirely full member competition, Afghanistan and the

West Indies having won through a qualifier in Zimbabwe which was marred by a couple of bizarre umpiring errors, the combined effect of which was to deny Scotland the chance of squeezing past their rivals and into the World Cup. The new format did little to shorten the tournament, which comprised 48 matches played over 46 days. Three months before the squads assembled, a terrorist attack on an Indian army convoy in Kashmir led to calls by the BCCI for Pakistan to be banned from the tournament, but for once the ICC resisted the BCCI's demands, and Pakistan took a full part in the competition, even meeting (and losing to) India in a round-robin match in Manchester.

In the semi-finals England cruised past Australia and New Zealand won a much closer encounter with India. The final produced one of the most extraordinary sequences of events in cricket's long history. Electing to bat first, New Zealand made 241/8. A fifth-wicket stand of 110 between Ben Stokes and Jos Buttler enabled England to recover from a shaky 86/4, but then four wickets fell for the addition of 11 runs, and with one over left 15 were still needed. Stokes hit Trent Boult for six, and then collected six more when a return from Martin Guptill was deflected from Stokes's bat and went for four overthrows. That reduced the requirement to three, but when Adil Rashid was run out trying to get Stokes back on strike it was two off the final delivery with the last pair together. Stokes drove a full toss to long-on and completed the single which tied the scores, but Jimmy Neesham's return to the bowler beat Mark Wood's desperate dive and the match went to a Super Over, the first-ever tie in a World Cup final. Those four overthrows had made all the difference although some, including the distinguished former umpire Simon Taufel, argued that the decision to award six runs in total had been wrong; the overthrows should count from the moment the ball was thrown, and at that point the English batters had not yet crossed for their second run.

The drama was, however, far from over. Buttler and Stokes collected 15 off Boult's over, setting Neesham and Guptill 16 to make for a sensational New Zealand victory. Jofra Archer opened with a wide, and then Neesham added a six to a succession of twos to leave his side needing three from the final two deliveries. He could only manage a single off the penultimate delivery, bringing Guptill on strike with two required. A single would not be enough, since the tournament rules specified that in the event of a tied Super Over the trophy would go to the side that had hit more boundaries across the entire match, and England led comfortably on that count, 26 to 17. Guptill clipped Archer's final delivery off his pads out to midwicket and they took the single, but as in the climax of the match itself, Jason Roy's return ensured that there was no time to complete the second and Buttler removed the bails with Guptill well short. England had won the World Cup, but many felt that New Zealand had been unfortunate not to get at least a share of the trophy.

The 2023 50-over World Cup in India was the last ten-team event before the ICC reverted to a 14-team format. The decision to abolish the Super League appeared increasingly short-sighted as the success of the Netherlands in the qualifier in Zimbabwe, in which they had beaten the West Indies to reach the World Cup in India, was in large part due to their Super League campaign, and at a press conference towards the end of that tournament ICC chairman Greg Barclay began to walk the decision back; soon afterwards Geoff Allardice acknowledged that the loss of 'context' as a result of the return to bilateral ODI cricket probably meant that beyond the 2024–27 cycle it might be necessary to return to the idea in some form. Against this trend, however, in advance of the World Cup, MCC's World Cricket Committee and various assorted pundits were calling for the abandonment of the ODI format altogether, citing declining interest among the general public and the media.

The tournament which followed provided enough spectacular cricket to suggest that claims of the demise of the ODI had been premature. Glenn Maxwell was a revelation, his 40-ball century against the Netherlands, the fastest in ODI World Cup history, was followed by an even more remarkable 201 not out from 128 deliveries against Afghanistan, which rescued his side from a desperate 91/7 as they chased a total of 291/5 and saw them to an unlikely three-wicket victory. Although they were so comprehensively Maxwelled, both Afghanistan and the Netherlands had their moments of glory: the Afghans beat a disappointing England, Pakistan and Sri Lanka to give themselves an outside but ultimately fruitless crack at making the semi-finals, while the Dutch repeated their T20 success against South Africa the previous year, and then beat Bangladesh into the bargain.

Hosts India, meanwhile, were carrying all before them, going undefeated through the round-robin phase and then posting 397/4 against New Zealand in the semi-final to win by 70 runs. In Virat Kohli they had the outstanding batter of the tournament, Maxwell not excepted, and with an outstanding, balanced attack they seemed an unbeatable outfit. Their opponents in the final were Australia, who had dismissed South Africa for 212 in the other semi-final and won by three wickets with 16 deliveries to spare. Although it could not compete with the 2019 final for excitement, this one was dramatic in its own way. After Pat Cummins had put India in, the Australian attack never let their opponents take control, and with Mitchell Starc taking three wickets and Josh Hazlewood and Cummins himself two apiece, the hosts were all out for a comparatively modest 240. At 47/3 Australia were in early trouble, but this time it was Travis Head who took the bowling by the scruff of the neck, dominating a partnership of 192 with Marnus Labuschagne and making a 120-ball 137 before falling with just two runs required. Maxwell, appropriately enough, came in to finish the job, and a stunned India had missed out on a title which had almost seemed to be theirs by right.

The year before the 1999 World Cup the ICC had introduced its new Champions Trophy into the international calendar. The first such tournament, played as a knockout competition to keep it short and snappy, took place in Bangladesh in October and November 1998, and was won by South Africa. Although it was designed to raise funds for global development, it was restricted to nine full members. Bizarrely, the hosts were ineligible to take part, since they were still an associate. More disturbing still was the fact that although the ICC had initially announced that the draw would be based on the seedings for the World Cup the following year, when the Bangladeshis issued the schedule sources close to the board noted that in the final version 'ICC's business interest has been given maximum preference'. It was, however, successful enough for the experiment to be repeated two years later, when 11 teams, including hosts Kenya and soon-to-be-promoted Bangladesh, gathered in Nairobi. This time it was India and New Zealand who reached the final, Sourav Ganguly's 117 out of an Indian total of 264/6 matched by an unbeaten 102 from Chris Cairns which saw the Kiwis to their first-ever global title with a four-wicket victory and just two deliveries to spare. Both as a cricket event and as a money-spinner the Champions Trophy had proved a success, raising more than £10 million, and it was now established as a biennial feature of the international programme.

Three more Champions Trophy tournaments took place between 2002 and 2006, hosted by Sri Lanka, England and India as the ICC decided to switch away from holding them in associate countries. The 2002 tournament had been scheduled to take place in India, but it was switched to Sri Lanka after the Indian government refused to grant the organisers exemption from tax. This time the knockout framework gave way to four pools of three, Kenya and the

Netherlands joining the ten full members as holders of permanent ODI status and ICC Trophy winners respectively. Neither of these sides won a game, India and Sri Lanka won the semi-finals against South Africa and Australia, and the trophy was shared after the hosts posted 244/5 and the Indian reply was rained off two overs in. This format was retained in England two years later, with the USA making their debut in a global tournament after winning a Six Nations Challenge in the UAE earlier in the year. This time it was England and the West Indies who reached the final, the latter winning a hard-fought match by two wickets. The competition was not universally popular. It could, *Wisden* editor Matthew Engel suggested in the 2004 edition, be viewed either as a showcase for the game or as 'an abscess – yet another build-up of stinking pus on the fixture list', although he was content the following year to limit himself to describing England's effort as 'a turkey of a tournament'.

For the 2006 event the Indian government did grant a tax exemption. In view of the consistent lack of success of the associates in the previous editions, it was perhaps not surprising that it was now decided to restrict participation to the ten full members, a preliminary round reducing the number of teams to eight and two groups then leading to semi-finals. It was notable, however, that none of the subcontinental sides made it into the last four, Australia beating New Zealand and the West Indies defeating South Africa to reach the final. This was a one-sided affair, as the West Indies were dismissed for 138 and the Australians needed only 28.1 overs to complete an eight-wicket victory. The pitches had been an issue throughout, the final being the eighth match in which the side batting first had been dismissed for under 200.

Under Pawar and Lalit Modi, as we have seen, the BCCI began to flex its muscles ever more strongly. In January 2006 it indicated that after the Champions Trophy tournament it was hosting later in the year it would refuse to take part in future, commenting that 'it did not support the ICC fundraising concept which it believed reduced its own earning potential'. Under this regime India was, it appeared, no longer committed to global development, certainly not at the expense of its own desire to rake in the rupees. This, together with India's attempts to subvert the Future Tours Programme, led Speed to write to Niranjan Shah, the BCCI secretary, in forthright terms: 'The President and I,' he stated, 'are both very concerned that BCCI is moving ahead and taking what appear to be unilateral decisions that are contrary to ICC policy as agreed by the ICC members including the BCCI.' Despite India's threat of a Unilateral Declaration of Independence, five full members and the UAE promptly put forward initial bids to host the 2008 Champions Trophy, with or without the Indians. It was awarded to Pakistan, but security concerns in that country led first to its postponement by a year, and then, after the Lahore attack, to its relocation to South Africa, where it was eventually held in September–October 2009. Now reduced to the eight leading full members, it was won by Australia, who beat New Zealand by six wickets in the final.

The 2013 Champions Trophy in England was a fairly low-key affair, India adding this title to the World Cup they had claimed two years earlier. Although this event was supposedly the last, the ICC decided in January 2014 that England would host another, in 2017. This was definitely to be the final one... until in November 2021 it was announced that Pakistan would be allocated such a tournament in 2025. Locked in a dispute with the ICC over financial and governance issues, the BCCI missed the deadline for submitting its squad for the 2017 tournament and had to be given an ultimatum by the organisers before finally providing its list. Despite losing to Sri Lanka in a group game the Indians progressed via a semi-final victory over Bangladesh to the final, where they met Pakistan. The Pakistanis posted

338/4, Fakhar Zaman making 114 from 106 deliveries, and with Mohammad Amir removing Rohit Sharma and Virat Kohli inside the first three overs India were soon in deep trouble. It took a rapid 76 from Hardik Pandya to give their reply any substance, and they were dismissed for 158 in 30.3 overs. If that had been the end of the Champions Trophy story it would have been an anti-climactic one.

The ICC inaugurated its T20 World Cup in 2007, two years after the first T20 international had been played and a mere four years after the shorter format had been invented. Lasting three and a half hours or so and accompanied by raucous music, fireworks and, at times, go-go dancers, T20 lent itself to the aggressive marketing which increasingly appealed to cricket administrators, and it was intended to bring the game to a wider audience for whom Test matches, and even ODIs, were insufficiently interesting. The ICC, moreover, believed that it was a more suitable format for the development of the game outside its traditional heartlands. The subtleties of five-day cricket were appreciated by a limited audience even in those countries where they had been developed, and it could not be expected, this argument ran, that the longer formats would ever have mass appeal, or be played successfully, outside the charmed circle of the existing Test-playing countries. (The rise of Afghanistan suggested that this was, at best, an exaggeration, but it soon became a mantra, and a fundamental plank of ICC policy.) So there was a certain kind of logic in the argument that the T20 World Cup should have more participants and wider qualification pathways than its 50-over companion.

The inaugural T20 tournament was played in South Africa and the final, in which India defended 157/5 to beat Pakistan by five runs with two deliveries remaining, was thrilling enough to confirm that the format was here to stay – and to persuade the Indians that it had commercial potential. Any lingering doubts were dispelled on the opening night of the next event, in England in 2009, when the Netherlands sensationally beat England by four wickets at Lord's with an overthrow off the final ball. The Dutch were subsequently demolished by Pakistan, who went on to win the cup with an eight-wicket victory over Sri Lanka, but the notion that the so-called minnows could cause upsets against their betters – which was, of course, already established in the ODI format – continued to feed the idea that they were better adapted to the shortest form of the game. In fact, as the full-time players began to evolve into T20 specialists they developed unorthodox strokes and greater variation in bowling, not to mention hitherto unimagined feats in the field, which put them in another class from most of their associate brethren, and in the first four editions of the T20 Cup there were only two wins for associates against full members, the Netherlands' victory over England, and Ireland beating Bangladesh in the same tournament.

Held in the West Indies the following year, the third World T20 tournament was won by England, who comfortably beat Australia in the final; in 2012 the West Indies won the fourth, beating hosts Sri Lanka. Both tournaments featured 12 teams, the ten full members plus two associates, which were Afghanistan and Ireland in both cases. Originally planned as a 16-team event, the 2012 veersion was cut back to 12 as compensation (some might say revenge) for the delayed introduction of the ten-team World Cup. The 2014 tournament in Bangladesh finally saw an expansion, nominally at least, to 16 teams. 'Nominally', because with a not untypical smoke-and-mirrors ploy the tournament was split into two phases, the first of which was really another qualifier. Eight teams took part in this: Bangladesh, Zimbabwe and the six associates who had qualified through a tough 16-team tournament in the UAE the previous year. With only two places available in the tournament proper, aka the Super 10, the expectation was that it would be the two full members who went through, but although Bangladesh, despite losing to Hong Kong, topped their group on net run rate, the Netherlands upset the applecart by finishing on top of the other, notwithstanding a defeat by Zimbabwe. They achieved this with a sensational run chase against Ireland, in which they needed only 13.5 overs to overhaul a total of 189/4. Stephan Myburgh led the way with a 23-ball 63, and then Tom Cooper made 45 from 15 deliveries and Wesley Barresi 40 not out from 20 to pull off an astonishing victory. The Dutch were brought back to earth in their first Super 10 game, when they were bowled out for 39 by Sri Lanka, but they collected another notable scalp before they were done, England dismissed for just 88 as they chased the Netherlands' rather modest 133/5. Sri Lanka won a rain-affected semi-final against the West Indies and India beat South Africa to set up a rematch of the 2011 World Cup final; this time it was the Sri Lankans who prevailed despite Virat Kohli's 58-ball 77, a rapid half-century by Kumar Sangakkara propelling them to victory.

With the power bloc of India, England and Australia now firmly in charge, it was India who hosted the 2016 World T20 Cup, the tournament again divided into a separate eight-team 'first phase' and a Super 10. This time it was Afghanistan, soon to be elevated to full membership, who defied the odds, reaching the main competition at the expense of Zimbabwe, whom they beat by 59 runs. Bangladesh made sure of the other spot; their group in Dharamshala was badly affected by the weather – their match against Ireland and the Netherlands against Oman were both abandoned – and despite a 12-run victory over Ireland in a match cut to six overs a side, the Dutch were unable to qualify after losing to Bangladesh by eight runs on the opening day. Chris Gayle set the Super 10 alight from the outset with a 47-ball century, the quickest to date in T20 internationals, to take the West Indies past England, and although they suffered a setback in their final group match against Afghanistan, who defended a paltry 123/7 and won by six runs, the West Indians joined England, New Zealand

and India in the semi-finals. England beat New Zealand and the West Indies beat the hosts, so the final saw England and the West Indies again lock horns. England made 155/9 thanks to a half-century from Joe Root and seemed well in control when they reduced their opponents to 107/6 with 27 deliveries remaining. Marlon Samuels made a 66-ball 85 not out, but with 19 needed off the final over it was Carlos Brathwaite who smashed Ben Stokes for four consecutive sixes to pull off an extraordinary win with two deliveries to spare.

The next T20 World Cup was planned for Australia in October–November 2020, but by that time the world had been engulfed in the most severe pandemic since the influenza outbreak a century before. With millions dying all over the globe and travel restrictions in place everywhere, international sport came to a standstill, and there were no ICC events for almost two years. The action resumed in Oman and the UAE in October 2021, but not before a complicated double-shuffle which made a kind of sense but which was nevertheless hard to follow. Initially stating that the 2020 Cup would go ahead as scheduled, the Council was forced a month later to say that the health risks were too great. With Australia's international borders closed the ICC's hand was forced, and it was eventually decided that the next T20 tournament, in 2021, would be hosted by India, with Australia taking over the 2022 spot. In the event the pandemic in India was so severe that the BCCI agreed to move its tournament to Oman and the UAE, although the ICC took the line that India would formally remain the hosts. So Oman shared the preliminary phase with the Emiratis, while the main tournament, aka the Super 12, was played in Abu Dhabi, Sharjah and Dubai, the first time any major global tournament had taken place entirely outside the full member countries.

The Netherlands had won the qualifier in 2019, months before the outbreak of the pandemic, but now they had a nightmare run, losing all three of their group matches. Scotland had the opposite experience, winning all three to top the other group and move into the tournament proper ahead of Bangladesh. Sri Lanka dominated Group A; Namibia caused a real shock, beating Ireland as well as the Dutch to advance to the Super 12. But once that began, the favourites asserted themselves, England, Australia, Pakistan and New Zealand reaching the semi-finals; not for the first time, the Indians were underwhelming, losing to Pakistan by ten wickets in their opening game and then to New Zealand by eight wickets, leaving them with too much to do in their remaining games. New Zealand beat England and Australia inflicted a first defeat on Pakistan, both by five wickets with one over to go, and although Kane Williamson lit up the final with 85 from just 48 deliveries a 50-ball 77 not out by Mitchell Marsh was enough to see the Australians home.

Australia, then, were the defending champions when they hosted the other delayed T20 Cup just a year later, in October–November 2022. This time there were two global qualifiers, and for the last time – at least for now – the four teams which came through that process, plus the sides that had finished in ninth to 12th place in India, contested a first phase which was effectively separate from the tournament proper. The Dutch did much better this time, beating Namibia and the UAE to join Sri Lanka from their group in the Super 12, while from the other it was Zimbabwe and Ireland who went through, at the expense of Scotland and a disappointing West Indies. In a hard-fought Super 12 group New Zealand and England (who finished ahead of Australia on net run rate) reached the semi-finals, and in the other India and Pakistan finished clear of the rest.

There were a further four places on offer at the next tournament, to be held in the Caribbean and United States in 2024 and expanded to 20 teams, and the Netherlands caused another upset by beating first Zimbabwe and then South Africa to finish fourth in their group and book their spot in the Caribbean. An unbroken opening stand of 170 between Jos Buttler and Alex Hales, both of whom had a strike rate of well over 150, enabled England to beat India by ten wickets in a surprisingly one-sided semi-final, while in the other Pakistan posted a seven-wicket victory over the Black Caps. In a relatively low-scoring final Pakistan's 137/8 was not enough to deny England the distinction of being the first holders of the two men's World Cups at the same time, as Ben Stokes steered them to victory with a 49-ball 52 not out.

The 2024 men's T20 World Cup highlighted many of the contradictions in the ICC's policy-making. On the one hand, the expansion to 20 teams was a welcome move, and it yielded some notable results. But in the ICC's drive to promote cricket in the United States 16 of the 40 first-phase matches were scheduled to be played there, with very variable results. The most successful of the three venues was the Grand Prairie Stadium in Texas, which produced decent pitches and large, enthusiastic crowds, but the drop-in square at the purpose-built Nassau County International Stadium near New York was initially so poor that the ICC was forced to issue an apologetic statement. Persistent heavy rain caused the abandonment of three of the four games allocated to the ground in Lauderhill, Florida, and the weather also created problems in the Caribbean, partly because the demands of the IPL had forced the World Cup to be held outside the usual West Indies season, with much greater risk of rain. The programme, too, was distorted by a determination to feature high-profile matches such as India–Pakistan (played in New York, where the largest crowd could be expected) and to hold as many games as possible at peak viewing times in the subcontinent. Not for the first time, there were complaints about prohibitively high ticket prices.

As for the cricket itself, while some of the qualifiers were outclassed – Oman, Papua New Guinea and Nepal went through the group phase without a win, but then, so did full member Ireland – and there were a few mismatches, the USA caused a sensation by tying with Pakistan and going on to win in the Super Over, thus qualifying for the Super Eight. There was another tie between Namibia and Oman, the former winning the Super Over, while Scotland had raced to 90 without loss in ten overs against England before rain brought proceedings to an end. Canada also caused an upset by beating Ireland, but the revelation was Afghanistan, who reached the semi-finals of a major global tournament for the first time, before collapsing to 56 all out against South Africa and losing by nine wickets. India then beat the Proteas by just seven runs in a tense final. Overall, the expanded format could be said to have been a success, although the limited opportunity for the leading associates to hone their skills in regular encounters with the full members, especially evident in the batting, remains a running sore which the ICC seems unable or unwilling to address.

Chapter 11

The Future Tours Programme

THE AGREEMENT of a schedule of future tours was from the outset a central, and initially virtually the only, function of the Imperial Cricket Conference. Even in this, of course, it had an essentially secretarial rather than a determinative role: proposals might be discussed at the Conference, but they then had to be referred back to the constituent governing bodies for ratification before they could be codified and released to the public at large. Gradually, though, the powers of the Conference grew, so that when two members were considering a bilateral arrangement, the agreement of the Conference had to obtained before it could become official. As the number of full members increased, new playing formats introduced and the quadrennial World Cup needing to be incorporated, this system became more cumbersome, but the spine of the future tours list remained the Test tours and attendant ODI series which were exchanged between the members.

The establishment of an agreed schedule was, of course, not without its difficulties. England and Australia were reluctant to accept full tours by what they perceived as 'lesser' (and less profitable) opponents, and we have seen how England in particular was keen to reduce the demands upon its leading players by restricting its tours to the West Indies or to the subcontinent. Series between England

and Australia for the Ashes, standardised as two tours in each direction in every eight-year cycle, were the still point around which everything else had to turn. England hosted a Test series every summer, India, Pakistan, New Zealand and South Africa taking it in turns to fill the gaps between Australian tours until, in 1965, the practice was introduced of two three-match Test series against different opponents being played instead of one five-Test series. But persuading the Australian board to accept a visit was more difficult. In the 25 years from 1945 to 1970 the West Indies toured Australia just three times and India twice, while apart from a one-off Test in 1964 Pakistan had to wait until 1972/73 before they were granted a tour. New Zealand were treated even worse. Apart from a single Test against a sub-strength side in Wellington in 1946, Australia's nearest cricket neighbour could not persuade them to meet on the field until 1973/74, when a three-Test series was played.

All this cricket was, course, bilateral, and there were no rankings or other mechanism to indicate who were currently the strongest teams. Not until the introduction of the World Cup in 1975 was there any real competition in the modern sense, and long after that Test cricket continued on its traditional path. At the same time, ODIs began to proliferate. In the 1980 calendar year 22 ODIs were played; by 1985 the number had grown to 65, and it stayed at that level for the next decade. But by 2000 it had blown out to 133. It was, of course, true that Sri Lanka, Zimbabwe and Bangladesh had been elevated to full membership over that period, but even so the increased pressure on players was considerable. At first, ODI series were incorporated into Test tours, but once the lucrative possibilities of sponsored tournaments played in offshore venues like Sharjah became apparent, the lure of extra revenue proved too great for boards to resist.

It was increasingly evident that measures needed to be taken to control the mushrooming expansion, and the notion of future tours shifted from being merely a list of agreed tours to an ICC-supervised schedule which protected Test cricket from the encroachment of the one-day format and would ensure that everyone got a share of the action. It would also bring the institution of a World Test Championship a step closer. *Wisden* editor Matthew Engel had been campaigning for a Test championship since 1995, arguing that 'Test cricket, crucially, depends on context', something sadly lacking in bilateral series of varying length and quality.

In 2000, the board was finally able to sign off on a ten-year Future Tours Programme which committed all ten full members to play each other at least twice, home and away, within that period, with a World Test Championship starting in the summer of 2001. It was not, of course, imposed by the ICC; it was the result of long negotiations with and between the constituent boards, and it was not restrictive, in the sense that countries were free to play each other more often if they wished. But it struck a balance between Tests and ODIs, and it provided both a rational framework for bilateral cricket and some guarantee for the smaller full members, dependent on tours by the bigger nations, especially India, for much of their income. Almost straight away, problems began to emerge. In September 2001, immediately after the 9/11 attacks in the US, New Zealand postponed a tour of Pakistan, scheduled to begin later that month, with India following suit soon afterwards, generating losses of potential income amounting to an estimated US$17 million. What, the PCB could legitimately ask, was the point of an FTP if its terms were unenforceable?

In September 2001 Malcolm Speed acknowledged the problem, indicating that the following month's executive board meeting would consider introducing sanctions for non-compliance with the FTP, possibly of the order of a $2 million financial penalty plus a sum equivalent to the budgeted gross revenues the home country had expected to gain from the tour. The offending team could also lose points on the World

Test Championship table, which would be awarded to the hosts. The $2 million penalty and the points deduction were duly agreed when the board met in Kuala Lumpur in the middle of October, at the same time accepting that series could be moved to a neutral venue should security concerns make it necessary. Chairman Malcolm Gray stated that the decision 'reflects the priority that world cricket has to give to protecting its calendar of fixtures'; 'We have to be tough,' he added, 'in protecting the integrity of the Future Tours Programme from wilful disruption.'

While it was designed to protect the interests of the smaller full members, not everyone was convinced that it would work that way. In the wake of that board meeting, WICB president Wes Hall revealed that his board stood to lose up to US$300,000 on its forthcoming visit to Sri Lanka, and while visits by Australia, England and India to the Caribbean would be profitable, the FTP meant the WICB 'tacking on' visits by New Zealand, Bangladesh and Sri Lanka, which would probably make a loss. Hall's concerns were borne out when the WICB declared the following May that it had accumulated losses of US$15 million over the previous three years, and Hall himself reinforced the point to Gray and Speed, whom he had invited to Jamaica for the board's annual general meeting. It was not just that too many series under the FTP were loss-makers; the scheduling also tended to place the West Indies' home matches at the start of the hurricane season, and his cause was helped by the fact that it rained continuously throughout the ICC officials' visit.

The FTP was discussed when the executive board met in June 2003, but principally in relation to what could be done about cancelled tours. But the problems continued, and that September, during his dispute with the ICC over the release of the World Cup revenue, Jagmohan Dalmiya complained as well about the FTP schedule, which was, he said, 'too crammed'. The requirement that each country play all the others home and away over a five-year period was 'a punishing schedule', and he suggested that the programme be expanded to a 12- or 14-year term for two cycles. And it was not only the BCCI which was a source of difficulty; with the ECB threatening to pull out of its scheduled tour of Zimbabwe in October 2004 because of the political situation there, Speed and his new chairman, Ehsan Mani, had to acknowledge that the ICC had no power to penalise a team which did not fulfil its touring commitments. Whatever the provisions of the FTP, bilateral series remained a matter for the countries involved, and the ICC was unable to impose any sanction if that contract was violated. That said, it could apply pressure, and as the final ECB decision drew closer, Mani pointed out that bilateral agreements were legally enforceable, and that the England and Wales Cricket Board could find itself in the courts if it failed to honour what was 'a binding commitment ... that political considerations would not be a factor when reviewing playing obligations'.

With the British Foreign Secretary, Jack Straw, subtly pressuring them to pull out of the tour while insisting that the final decision was theirs alone, the ECB deferred the matter for a month, by which time the ICC board had met in Auckland and reaffirmed its commitment to the demands of the FTP, signalling that England could be fined up to US$2 million, and could even face suspension from the ICC, if they did not go ahead with the tour. The ECB argued that Straw's 'advice' was effectively an instruction to withdraw, but that cut no ice with the other full members. The ZCU, however, was contributing to its own misfortunes. Its decision to sack 15 players, including the captain, Heath Streak, had led to a second-string side's dismissal for 35 in an ODI against Sri Lanka in Harare, and the ICC was now considering sanctions against Zimbabwe quite separately from the issue of the England tour. As the ECB continued to dicker, its most recently appointed member, Des Wilson, resigned in protest at their failure to take a moral stand,

and condemned the ICC's 'inflexible, and in my view, malevolent enforcement of its international tours programme with draconian and disproportionate penalties that would devastate the English game'. ECB CEO Tim Lamb was only a shade more diplomatic: England had been blind-sided by the proposal in Auckland to change the ICC's rules in order to permit the imposition of a $2 million penalty, which was much heavier than his board had been led to expect. England now had no alternative but to go ahead with the tour, but their blushes were saved when, in June, following pressure on the ZCU by a high-level ICC board delegation led by Mani, Zimbabwe agreed to suspend temporarily its playing of Tests.

As one problem was resolved, however, another reared its head. Faced with a scheduling problem over South Africa's proposed visit to India in November 2004, Dalmiya again attacked the FTP, claiming that it was the result of an ICC 'blunder in drawing up the schedule'. Here he had a point. The slot allocated for the five scheduled Tests and seven ODIs was insufficient for such a programme, with India supposed to tour Australia immediately before and South Africa hosting England the following month. There was some legitimacy to the view that the schedule was simply too crowded, and by September the ICC was beginning to contemplate a restructuring by which only the top eight full members would play a full programme, with Bangladesh and Zimbabwe playing only home Test series. There had even been a suggestion, Speed admitted to a media conference, to reduce the top tier to six with a group of four below that. But a spokesman noted that '[a] small number of teams drive the economic health of cricket, and if we pushed one of those out into a lower division, we risk cutting cricket off at the knees'.

The proposals were considered by the executive board on 18–19 October, who in a characteristic move agreed only to defer any decision until the following March; 'The Board believes,' its statement announced, 'that each country needs time to consider the implications of change with their own stakeholders.' By the time the board met again in March 2005 a deal had been struck which avoided cutting anyone, even Zimbabwe, off at the knees. From now on countries would have six years to complete the requirements of the FTP but would also have the freedom to operate a four-year cycle for certain exchanges if they wished to do so. This enabled England and Australia, for example, to retain their existing schedule for the Ashes, while playing series against Bangladesh and Zimbabwe on a more extended programme.

With the FTP firmly (if controversially) in place, in 2002 the ICC introduced a rolling, weighted rankings system for teams, to join the men's individual ratings which had been operating since 1987 (and which were expanded to include women in 2008). Designed by David Kendix, the system is based on performances over the previous three years, with results older than 12 months counting for only half the value of more recent ones; on 1 August of each year the earliest 12 months' performances are dropped from the calculation. The mechanics are sufficiently complex to be poorly understood by many fans, and this gave rise, especially in its early years, to nationalist suspicions of bias. When India dropped from fifth to eighth in the ODI rankings in July 2003, for example, Speed and Kendix were forced to explain to outraged Indian media that the reason was that their team's recent matches had largely been against sides which were ranked below them and therefore, since the points awarded for any win took account of the relative strengths of the two teams, wins could yield no benefit, while defeats had a strongly negative effect. India's inconsistency was its great enemy, while other sides had beaten higher-ranked opponents, and thus had risen above India in the table. However convincing these arguments may have been, the grumbles continued when the outcomes were at odds with supporters' intuitive feelings or uncritical loyalty to their team. Gradually, however, the rankings came to be accepted as a reasonable reflection of teams' relative strengths.

Unhappiness with the five-year framework of the FTP, meanwhile, continued to simmer, and the board agreed to hold a 'scheduling summit' at the end of August 2005 to plan the programme for the next 18 months. For the first time this discussion included representatives of the six leading associates, five of whom had been given ODI status (thus joining Kenya) following the ICC Trophy tournament and their qualification for the 2007 World Cup. Speed was able to announce after the subsequent Chief Executives' Committee meeting that plans had been drawn up for a shift from the current five-year FTP to one running for six years, which would now be sent to the members for further consideration. It was beginning to look as if Dalmiya's call for a longer cycle might bear fruit, but the idea was more difficult in practice than it had appeared on paper. Pakistan, for example, who had supported the extension, soon found that it was stymied by the agreements the board had already made with broadcasters and sponsors.

Now firmly entrenched as the real power in the ICC, the BCCI continued to flex its muscles, not least at the expense of the agreed FTP. There were even reports at the beginning of 2006 that the BCCI was in discussions with Cricket Australia about a possible breakaway if the FTP were not changed to allow more matches between India, England and Australia, prompting the ICC to dismiss such suggestions as speculative and to point out that the FTP already allowed countries to arrange additional series against one another if they could find room in the calendar. Stretching the cycle to six years would create more room for such bilateral fixtures. Lalit Modi, who had taken over as BCCI vice-president, denied that India's moves represented a threat to the ICC; it was, he said, 'just fine-tuning'. But when, a couple of weeks later, the BCCI board threatened to withdraw from the Champions Trophy and Modi revealed that Australia had agreed to tour India each year between 2007 and 2009, playing no fewer than 14 ODIs and four Tests across the three visits, it was clear that the BCCI was determined to go its own way whatever the ICC might think. Speed was moved, as noted on page 184, to write in protest to BCCI secretary Niranjan Shah.

The Indians, however, were not the only critics of the FTP; when his team arrived in New Zealand as part of a punishing schedule, West Indies team manager Bennett King blamed their exhaustion on the inflexible demands of the programme, and FICA were becoming increasingly exercised about the effect on players generally. FICA chief executive Tim May alleged that the ICC had ignored its own declared principles in putting together the new six-year FTP, noting that '[m]ore than ever we are seeing the game's top players being forced to retire from the demands of one or the other form of the game as a result of the constant and unrelenting schedule'. The response of Mani and Speed was to threaten to drop FICA as a partner, Speed informing May that the ICC was 'of the preliminary view that a spirit of co-operation between players and administrators would be better served by each individual board dealing with its own players/player representatives'. One was left wondering whether the lessons of the Packer debacle had really been learned, but when the details of the 2006–12 FTP were released, Speed was able to insist that it conformed entirely to the limit of 15 Tests and 30 ODIs in each 12 months, to which FICA had been party. The schedule allocated 76 Tests and between 139 and 157 ODIs to England over the six years and 74 Tests and 173–203 ODIs to India; at the other end of the scale, Zimbabwe were given 39 Tests and 97–111 ODIs and Bangladesh 41 Tests and 105–132 ODIs.

The demands of the FTP, however, remained an issue, and in June 2006 Mani announced that a policy committee was being established to look at the programme's future beyond 2012, including the funding model which was used to pay for it. At present, each country received all income from its home series and paid the costs, apart from international air fares and player fees, of its visitor. But not all series were equally lucrative and not all countries had the resources to cover loss-making tours, so quite apart from the continuing problem of player overload the entire financial basis of the system demanded close enquiry. Speed reinforced his arguments at the ICC's business forum in July 2006, repeating that the new FTP fell within the limits set by the players and claiming that 'the FTP is fundamentally good for the game'. Balancing player workload with public and commercial interest, he said, was a matter for the individual members, not for the ICC, which limited itself to directing that elite players be consulted when that balance was under review. There was, however, to be research conducted into the question of player burnout.

The political situation in Zimbabwe remained an issue for some, and Cricket Australia was reported to be considering pulling out of its tour, scheduled for September 2007. The cricket-loving, conservative Australian Prime Minister, John Howard, even promised that his government would pay any fines CA might incur, prompting a reminder from the ICC that these could amount to a US$2 million fine plus any losses ZC might suffer. In the end Howard went a step further, banning the tour and threatening to prevent the players from leaving the country if necessary. This was, claimed a Zimbabwean Information Minister, 'a racist ploy to kill our local cricket', but it prevented the ICC from penalising CA, since the decision had been made by the politicians. Former UK Sports Minister Kate Hoey came out in sympathy with Howard, calling on the ICC to abandon its 'supine' posture and suspend Zimbabwe as long as Mugabe remained President. That, of course, came to nothing, but at least Cricket Australia, who reaffirmed their commitment to the FTP, were off the hook. Others, however, remained dissatisfied. In advance of the 2007 annual meetings, Cricket

South Africa's new CEO, Gerald Majola, claimed that his country was disadvantaged by the FTP, which he said was dictated by Australia, England and India. His particular grievance was the fact that Australia were always scheduled at home over the Christmas/New Year period, protecting their Boxing Day and New Year Tests, while South Africa and the other less powerful members got 'the scraps of what's left over'.

Overcrowded as the men's international calendar had been, it became even worse with the advent of T20Is after 2005, and especially after the first ICC global tournament in the new format two years later. With three formats and additional World Cups to manage, the pressure on the players became increasingly intolerable, even though some countries started to experiment with selecting different squads, differentiating between 'red ball' and 'white ball' specialists. In 2007 the ICC board limited the number of T20Is that any full member could play in a year to seven, excluding ICC events, but financier Allen Stanford's plan for a US$23 million tournament in the West Indies presented a new challenge. Speed immediately warned that the ICC wished any tournament to be 'wherever possible' consistent with the FTP and the cap on T20Is. The ICC broadcast contract with ESPN Star Sports also needed to be protected. That 'wherever possible' caveat was, of course, significant, but the real threat came not from Stanford (whose financial and legal troubles soon saw him disappear), but from the BCCI's new Indian Premier League.

Although IPL chairman Lalit Modi swore in February 2008 that the BCCI had every intention of honouring the FTP which was, he affirmed, 'the most important for all countries and most definitely for the BCCI', it was obvious to most observers that the league's success would create further difficulties for bilateral cricket. There was already pressure for a window for the IPL to be created in the FTP schedule, and although the Chief Executives' Committee tried to hold the line, pointing out that the programme had been settled until 2012, Speed was forced to admit a few days later that if there was sufficient support from the members that was not immutable. At the same time, he stressed the fundamental importance of the international game, without which the IPL would be impossible: 'International cricketers have been coached and developed by their home countries, states, provinces, counties and clubs. They are in demand by IPL teams because they are international cricketers. Their primary duty is to their country.'

All this was undeniably true, but time would show that it counted for little against the wealth that the IPL franchises had at their disposal. The current generation of administrators, Speed stated in March, would 'not be judged by how much money the game makes out of Twenty20 cricket. It will be judged by how well we integrate Twenty20 into the other forms of the game.' But it was not T20 as such that was the greatest issue, but rather the demands of the franchise leagues. Speed's successor, Haroon Lorgat, soon demonstrated that he might be more accommodating than the Australian had been, indicating that he was open to a renegotiation of the FTP if necessary.

The board agreed in July 2008 that all three formats 'should be protected and promoted', with Test cricket 'the pinnacle of the sport', and set about considering the introduction of a proper, centrally organised World Test Championship, the previous version having been quietly allowed to be replaced by the rankings. It also resolved that the ICC should 'look at ways of taking greater central "ownership" of international cricket outside its events', or at least it should create greater consistency in marketing and promotion. Although still expressed as a pious hope, this represented a huge shift in thinking: a core article of faith had always been that bilateral cricket was a matter for the individual members, with the ICC having as little say as possible, but the challenge of the franchise leagues now forced the board to contemplate ICC 'ownership' of the international game. It was easier to state as an ambition than to achieve. Fifteen years later, the ODI Super League was still largely presented, and seen by the media, as separate bilateral series rather than an organised competition, with plenty of talk of 'dead rubbers' and little understanding of how the league actually worked, but it might be argued that in due course the World Test Championship, and more evidently the Women's Championship, would start to take hold. But the idea of a revived WTC was a step too far for the BCCI and ECB when the board met in January 2009, and it was kicked back to ICC general manager for cricket Dave Richardson for further consultation. India and England were concerned that an ICC-run championship could prejudice their lucrative media deals. In the end it was dropped, WICB chair Julian Hunte indicating in his 2009 annual report that it was the opposition of India and its allies which had been instrumental in killing the idea off. A similar fate awaited a proposal for a new ODI league, which was floated in 2011 but discarded.

When the ICC board approved the draft FTP for 2012–15 in October 2009, it promptly drew the ire of FICA, who protested that it was 'just a continuation of the ad hoc bilateral series that we have seen going on for a hundred years', and did not address the game's changing landscape. The association had an alternative model, which included annual, two-division Test and ODI championships and windows for the IPL and Champions League; there was further support, at least for the WTC, when the MCC cricket committee met with their ICC counterparts the following month. David Morgan, the council president, went some way towards meeting the players' concerns when he trailed the possibility of making the Test and ODI requirement either home or away in each cycle, rather than the present home and away. By July 2010 Lorgat was hopeful that a WTC final might be played in 2012 or 2013, and in September the Chief Executives' Committee proposed a four-year competition with the top four sides playing off for the title, the first such cycle finishing in 2013. It also suggested a parallel ODI league, the first edition of which would be completed in April 2014, coupled with the highly controversial reduction of the 50-over World Cup to ten teams. The CEC's recommendations were approved by the board in October and plans for a first WTC final in 2013 went ahead, but in October 2011 they ran into an obstacle. A revived Champions Trophy tournament would bring in the sort of money Test play-offs would not, and the executive board acknowledged that some members were not prepared to accept this financial hit. It therefore concluded that the introduction of a WTC play-off might have to be deferred until 2017. Tellingly, the board also worried about the prospect of a format which could lead to India missing out on the play-offs, and those concerns only became greater when it emerged in December 2013 that broadcasters and sponsors were challenging the whole concept as it became clear that the 'wrong' teams might qualify.

The fundamental weakness of the FTP was exposed in 2013, when the BCCI took issue with CSA over India's scheduled tour that November. The FTP for 2012–20, agreed in June 2011, included three Tests, seven ODIs and two T20Is in that tour, but the Indians, having arranged an additional visit by the West Indies and a tour to New Zealand, proposed cutting this to two Tests and three ODIs. David Becker, the former head of the ICC's legal department, now advising CSA, argued that the FTP was a legally binding agreement, but the BCCI denied this, insisting that only a signed bilateral agreement had legal force. In the end the Indians got their way, including a decision by CSA to suspend CEO Lorgat from dealings with the BCCI and ICC over his alleged involvement in Becker's intervention, although both Becker and Lorgat insisted that the latter had no part in Becker's statement and had, indeed, tried to prevent it. Not until March 2014 did the investigation conclude that Lorgat had indeed had nothing to do with it, paving the way for him to resume the international aspect of his duties. Not coincidentally, perhaps, CSA had by this time signed up to the restructuring proposals of the gang of three.

That group's original proposals when they launched their putsch in 2014 went even further, arguing for the replacement of the FTP by a series of bilateral agreements, giving full members the right to decide who they would play against and getting rid of 'unviable tours'. In June the board called on members to sign their bilateral agreements by October, expressing satisfaction 'that there was now more certainty around long-term scheduling with a reasonable balance between home and away matches for all ten teams as well as between the three formats'. Whether or not there was really an FTP between 2015–23 remains unclear: when the West Indian players pulled out of a tour of India in October 2014 over a pay dispute with their board, triggering an Indian demand for nearly $42 million in compensation, FICA called for the reinstitution of an FTP, noting that following the takeover by the gang of three there was no longer a binding overall agreement. This view was challenged by the PCB, who in 2018 took the BCCI to an ICC tribunal over a memorandum of understanding the two bodies had signed back in 2014, which provided that they would play six series between 2015 and 2023, four of them in Pakistan; in all, they would include 14 Tests, 30 ODIs and 12 T20Is. The agreement had been a condition of the PCB's support for the takeover by the gang of three. Yet none of this had taken place. The tribunal, however, found that the agreed FTP created a moral obligation rather than a legal one. The FTP, once described by an ICC official as 'a basket of bilateral agreements', was no more than a statement of intention, and only became binding at the point at which the two parties signed a final contract. The elaborate, beautifully colour-coded spreadsheets enshrining the multi-year schedule were, in other words, not worth the paper they were printed on.

Yet the glossy spreadsheets were still produced, and during the negotiations for what was undoubtedly a new FTP for 2023–31, opponents of one major ICC event per year were able to point out that the 2015-23 cycle had contained two fallow years, 2018 and 2022. So perhaps there was an FTP when it was convenient to one's case, and otherwise not. Richardson had spoken of an operative FTP in July 2015, when he was worrying about the growing threat to bilateral series, floating the idea of Test and ODI leagues as a way of giving greater 'context'. And this thinking bore fruit more than two years later, when the FTP for 2018–23 included both. Finally, a real World Test Championship was agreed although its workings were complicated: it excluded Zimbabwe and the two newest full members, Afghanistan and Ireland; series would comprise anywhere from two Tests to five, and each country would play only six of their possible nine opponents, enabling India to avoid confronting Pakistan but also meaning that some programmes looked a good deal tougher than others. At the same time, the ICC launched a new ODI league, including all 12 full members and the Netherlands, who had qualified by winning the WCL Championship. Again, it was not an all-play-all system: there would be three-match series against eight of the possible 12 opponents, and the top eight would qualify directly for the 2023 World Cup.

This did give greater significance to the two longer formats, but at the same time the trend away from Tests and ODIs towards T20Is was continuing apace. FICA calculated that in 2021 71% of all men's international matches played were in the T20 format, although that figure was significantly reduced if one included only games played by the full members. The 113 T20Is played between two full members (which included the 2021 World Cup) amounted to almost 48% of all their internationals in that year. And by this time the IPL and its progeny were competing with increasing determination for their place in the schedules; small wonder that FICA remarked that '… tension is created with many of the best players in the world incentivised to prioritise domestic leagues and forgo international fixtures and/or central contracts. This is further amplified by the workload of domestic leagues being generally half that of international cricket on a time/wage basis – i.e. "twice the pay for half the work".'

This was, and is, a greater threat to the ICC than any it has faced hitherto, far greater than bodyline, greater than corruption in Zimbabwe or government interference in Pakistan or Sri Lanka, greater even than the Packer circus or match fixing. It made the negotiation of the FTP both more difficult and more vital than ever before.

The negotiations over the 2023–31 FTP pointed up the new fault line between the gang of three and the rest, the issue now being the number of ICC events in the eight-year cycle. It was, of course, more a question of money than player overload which motivated the BCCI, supported by the ECB and CA: when, in October 2019, the board out-voted India to include one major men's event in each year of what had now become more a rights cycle than a Future Tours Programme, the BCCI protested that this represented a threat to bilateral cricket and hinted that it might refuse to sign off on the agreed schedule. It was backed by CA CEO Kevin Roberts, who insisted on the need to balance events with the rest of the international schedule, and by ECB chair Colin Graves, who wrote to CEO Sawhney that '[t]he impact of the proposed schedule of ICC events on bilateral cricket is a serious concern for the ECB'. Arun Dhumal, CEO of the BCCI, went further, telling the *Indian Express*: 'We are seriously going to oppose their governance structure, business model and the future tours programme.' In the final analysis, he did not see his board signing the Members' Participation Agreement. With the board floating the idea of a new T20 Champions Cup as part of the eight-event structure, the BCCI's new leadership, led by chairman Sourav Ganguly and secretary Jay Shah, responded with a proposal for a biennial four-team 'Super Series' ODI event involving India, Australia, England and one other top country, which would rotate among the big three and yield them yet more income. This challenge to the ICC's programme (and its rule about non-ICC multi-team events being limited to three participants) was swallowed up by the panic over the pandemic, but it gave a clue to the thinking of the new BCCI regime. The dispute played a significant part in Greg Barclay's victory over Imran Khwaja in a keenly contested election to the chairmanship, and having been elected he quickly stepped back from the eight-event model, which the ICC had already put out to tender for the media rights, declaring himself an agnostic on the ideal number of events. In turn, it seems to have been a key element in the decision to get rid of Manu Sawhney, although in the end the majority view prevailed and the FTP for 2024–31 finally agreed in March 2023 did include one men's event per calendar year.

Parity with the men's game demanded that there should also be a women's FTP, and this was introduced in August 2022, running through to the 2025 World Cup. It involved ten of the 12 full members, with Zimbabwe and Afghanistan excluded, and was centred on the Women's Championship, the ODI competition which was now expanded to include Bangladesh and Ireland. Each country would play eight three-match series in the three-year cycle, four at home and four away, which neatly obviated the need for a meeting between India and Pakistan. The top five from that championship would qualify for the World Cup, along with hosts India, while the bottom four would go into an eight-team qualifier. In addition to 135 ODIs, the schedule included 159 T20Is and seven Tests, with England playing five, Australia four, South Africa three and India two. A window was left in March for a women's IPL. With the proliferation of T20 franchise leagues less rapid in women's cricket than with the men there were fewer scheduling problems, but the FTP represented a considerable step forward for the women's game, and a sign that, at last, it was really being taken seriously.

On the face of it, the elevation of Afghanistan and Ireland to Test status was an expansion of the Future Tours Programme, but with only nine participants in the World Test Championship it actually worked in the opposite direction, confirming the relegation of Zimbabwe to second-class status. Between 2017 and 2022 those three countries played a total of 23 Tests between them, with Zimbabwe playing 14 of them; by contrast, in the same period, England played 78 Tests and Australia 56. The Afghans and Irish were less exercised, perhaps, than the Zimbabweans, who had seen their position as a full member steadily eroded, but as the next edition of the FTP came under discussion there was again talk of creating a second division of Test cricket, involving some of the leading associates. In November 2022 the Zimbabwe chairman, Tavengwa Mukuhlani, was able to persuade the executive board to set up a working group to reconsider the FTP with himself as a member, along with the ECB's Martin Darlow and Martin Snedden of New Zealand. Ireland's Ross McCollum, speaking after the meeting, regretted that the World Test Championship had not been expanded to include all 12 Test-playing members, but acknowledged that a two-tier system was seen as too threatening by some of the countries.

The FTP for 2023–27 went some way towards redressing the imbalance, but not very far. What it did do was strike a fair balance between the three formats, with the 12 full members scheduled to play 173 Tests between them, with 282 ODIs and 327 T20Is. These, it should be remembered, are the minimum requirements of the FTP; nothing prevents countries from arranging additional bilateral fixtures or incidental tournaments if they feel so inclined. The heaviest load was England's, with 43 Tests, 48 ODIs and 51 T20Is, which amounted to 314 playing days over a five-year period, or 63 days per year. Zimbabwe still had the lightest schedule with 20 Tests (up from their 14 in the previous quinquennium), 44 ODIs and 45 T20Is, while Ireland had to make do with 12 Tests but 51 ODIs and 47 T20Is. On top of this, of course, there were the franchise leagues, not to mention the 'normal' domestic competitions across at least two of the formats, in which international players might still make the occasional appearance. Following the annual conference in August 2022, and in advance of the release of the new programme, Barclay acknowledged that there was more pressure than ever on the international calendar but stated that '[i]t's not an issue so much for this organisation, but certainly for members to try and work their way through optimum outcomes is going to be a challenge'. The language of management might have been different, but Barclay's perspective was the one that had plagued the ICC since its foundation: however successfully the organisation might have expanded its role so that it had become a simulacrum of a modern governing body, in the final analysis it was powerless in the face of its more powerful members' determination to create room for their lucrative franchise competitions. Those members also decided to kill the Super League, preferring for financial reasons to revert to bilateral fixtures. A quarter of a century after the introduction of the new-style FTP, it remains the plaything of whichever vested interests are dominant at the time, and there are still no coherent pathways to allow developing cricket nations to join the elite on a regular basis.

Chapter 12

Global Development

IN MID-2012 the ICC published a glossy, lavishly illustrated book entitled *Building a Bigger, Better, Global Game: The story of the ICC Development Programme.* In his foreword, then CEO Haroon Lorgat was unequivocally supportive of what had been achieved: 'Some view the development of cricket beyond traditional places as a romantic notion,' he wrote. 'Many, like me, see it as a necessity without which we cannot and will not achieve full potential.' He went on: 'Our vision makes it incumbent on all of us to spread our Great Sport and indeed, as servants of the game, we have an obligation to do so. Once we embrace the concept of abundance rather than scarcity, we will lose the hesitancy to foster growth.'

In retrospect, these resounding words sound less like a celebration and more like a warning. The resistance to the recommendations of the Woolf Report had already had its effect, and it would soon emerge that 'abundance' was a concept which would apply to only a self-selected few of the ICC's members, while 'scarcity' would be the continuing lot of the rest, and especially of the associates and affiliates the GDP was set up to help. 'Sadly,' Lorgat added, 'challenges with governance, administration and integrity have restricted progress in some key countries.' He may not have been thinking of the gang of three when he wrote those words, but it would soon become clear that *their* vision would put paid to much of the progress which had been achieved over the previous 15 years.

When Ali Bacher began to create the Global Development Programme in 1997 he was not entirely starting from scratch. An Asian Cricket Council had been in existence since 1983, and although it was dominated by the four Test-playing countries, it had from the first included Malaysia and Singapore, and by 1997 it had expanded to include Hong Kong, the UAE, Nepal, Thailand, Brunei, the Maldives, Japan, Papua New Guinea and Fiji. A rather different pattern had developed in Europe, where ad hoc club and national team tournaments had led to the formation of a European Cricket Federation, which in June 1997 transformed itself into the European Cricket Council. An African Cricket Association was established in 1997 as well, but by this time Bacher's development committee was beginning to take the initiative, appointing the Australian Ross Turner as the first global development manager. Five regions were established, each with its own office and a regional development officer, and the full members in the region were given responsibility for fostering the game and helping the associate and affiliate members within their territory.

A key element of this plan was the introduction in 1998 of the Champions Trophy, originally called the ICC Knockout Tournament, the proceeds of which were to help fund the development programme. While that eventually fell victim to the machinations around the FTP, coinciding with a reduced emphasis on funding global development, ICC politics also ensured that half the funding from this source always went at India's insistence to the Asian region, with the rest distributed among the other four regions. The full members, moreover, approached their fostering task with varying degrees of enthusiasm. India had a long history of encouraging cricket across Asia, not only with an eye to the political and commercial advantages of such a policy, but

England and Australia had a reputation for being much less supportive, while the West Indies board's internal problems made it difficult for them to look far beyond the needs of their own constituents. England, India and South Africa, though, did provide facilities for the regional offices, with Nigel Laughton, the first RDO Europe, operating from an office at Lord's.

There were differences, too, in the ways in which the regional development managers went about their task. In Europe, where there were already some grassroots structures in place, a strong tournament system was quickly established. By 1999 there were age-group championships at under-15, under-17 and under-19 levels, and for the under-19s there was even a Division Two tournament, involving Italy, Gibraltar and Germany, alongside the five-team first division. In 2001 there were two divisions for each of the three oldest age groups, while an under-13 category, also with two divisions, had been added. Of the other regions, only Asia was in a position to create anything as elaborate as this, with tournaments at under-15 and under-17 (the latter later morphing into under-16) taking place regularly from 2000 onwards, although the under-15 series was abandoned in 2007. These ACC competitions were divided into three levels. With an under-19 World Cup taking place from 1997/98, moreover, there were regular regional tournaments at that level everywhere, as qualifiers for the global event. Many talented young players got their first taste of international cricket in this way: future Ireland stars Paul Stirling and Andrew Balbirnie were in their country's under-13 side in 2003, while future England captain Eoin Morgan and his Dutch counterpart Pieter Seelaar first encountered one another at the European under-15 championship at Limavady in Ireland in 2001. By the same token, the Afghanistan under-17 team which played in the ACC Challenge tournament in 2004 included Mohammad Nabi, Hamid Hassan, Samiullah Shenwari, Karim Sadiq and Rashid Khan, all of whom would go on to become part of one of the most remarkable stories in the history of world cricket.

A similar policy applied in senior men's cricket. The first European championship had been held in 1996, before the ICC unveiled its global development strategy, with seven associates and an English amateur team taking part. Two years later the participants had grown to ten, and in 2000 the championship was split into two divisions. A third division was added in 2007, and by 2009 there were a total of five divisions involving no fewer than 30 countries. There were three divisions in 2010 in Africa and the Americas with 15 and 13 countries respectively, although no Division One tournament was held after a World Cup qualifying competition in 2004. Eight associates and affiliates played in the tiny East Asia Pacific regional tournament.

The Asian Cricket Council followed a slightly different path but with the same broad objectives: after a decade of running a single ACC Trophy which gradually expanded to 17 participants, it split the 50-over competition into an elite division with ten teams and a challenge division with eight. These regional tournaments served multiple purposes: after all, this was a period in which the ICC proudly proclaimed that every member had a pathway to the 'Cup That Counts', the 50-over World Cup, and in theory even the teams in the lowest regional divisions could reach the global qualifier. There was, moreover, a rather broader pathway into the World Cricket League, with, at its largest, eight divisions. And beyond those opportunities, there was intrinsic value in the best players in the smaller associates and affiliates having the chance to play each other in official tournaments.

There were, however, several difficulties. One was the fact that in Europe and the Middle East in particular, and to some degree in North America, most of the players in the lower divisions were immigrants and expats. In the newer European cricketing nations the game was almost wholly dependent on the enthusiasm of players from the subcontinent. Even in Denmark, where the game had been established for a century, second- and third-generation members of the Pakistani community played an ever-greater part in club cricket and then in the national team. Where earlier emigration from Europe had created a significant diaspora in Test-playing countries, there was a pool of (potential) passport holders who could be drawn upon. The first Croatian teams, for example, had a significant number of Australians, New Zealanders and South Africans, and as the Dutch began to consolidate their position among the leading associates, they recruited more and more players from those countries. Even the Irish side which did so well in the 2007 World Cup had an Australian-born captain and three other key players who had learned their cricket in Australia or South Africa. It was, finally, a question of balance: there was no doubt that expatriates could play a vital role in establishing and growing the game and in enabling the national team to compete successfully, but cricket would only have a long-term future when it began to put down roots outside those expat communities. As a European Cricket Council youth development paper put it in November 1998: 'Fundamental to the expansion of cricket in general and, therefore, underlying this or any development plan, are two factors. Firstly, that cricket must be encouraged and promoted amongst the indigenous populations and secondly, that the future of the sport in Europe depends on the ECC activating cricketers, teachers and parents into coaching and administrating cricket.'

A quarter of a century later, it must be acknowledged that the response to this challenge has at best been patchy, and in very few places has it been successful.

What was true for Europe applied equally to much of the Middle East and to continental North America. In the United Arab Emirates, for example, such domestic cricket as there was depended almost entirely on players flown in from the subcontinent, and they also made up the national side which took part in the competitions organised by the ICC and the ACC. Of 17 players who turned out for the UAE in the 2006 Intercontinental Cup, for example, eight had learned the game in either Pakistan or Sri Lanka and five had played first-class cricket there, while at the 2011 World Cricket League Division Two tournament only five of 13 had been born in the UAE, and four of the other eight had first-class experience in the subcontinent. It was even more exaggerated in other Gulf states: at the ACC Trophy Elite tournament in 2009/10, the Omani squad included eight Pakistani-born players, most of whom had played first-class cricket in their home country, and three Indians, and there was a strong Pakistani presence in Bahrain's teams as well. The United States during the same period relied heavily on players from the Caribbean, with a sprinkling from Pakistan and India, while Canadian squads were also plentifully populated with Indians and Pakistanis.

Alongside the GDP, a High Performance Programme was established in 2001, with the experienced coach Bob Woolmer, a former England Test player, appointed as the first High Performance Manager with a budget of US$1 million to help the four associates (Kenya, Canada, Namibia and the Netherlands) who had qualified for the 2003 World Cup to prepare for that challenge. 'My main aim,' Woolmer said on his appointment, 'is to help these countries set up programmes that allow their players to improve their skill levels … if we are successful in achieving that the model will be there for further countries to emulate, providing a blueprint for the ICC to truly globalise the game.' Initiatives such as the Six Nations Challenge held in Namibia in April 2002, which involved the A teams of Sri Lanka and Zimbabwe as well as the four qualifiers, had only a modest effect on their performances in the World Cup. Kenya did succeed in beating both Sri Lanka and Bangladesh, but the other three struggled.

Nevertheless, Woolmer's visionary approach set a pattern which continued under his successor, Richard Done, and might have led to a long-term transformation of the global game had the HPP not fallen prey to scavenging political forces at the end of the decade. One of Woolmer's key initiatives was the establishment of the first-class Intercontinental Cup, at first featuring three-day matches, which were expanded to four days for the third and subsequent editions. Announcing the introduction of the Cup in March 2004, he stated his position unambiguously: 'The multi-day game is the clear pathway to improving the playing level of these countries,' he said. 'Batsmen will learn to build an innings, spend more time at the crease and thereby increase their confidence and ability. Bowlers too will get fitter and more accurate and learn more skills.'

The ICup, as it became known, had a significant influence on a generation of young cricketers, and it paved the way for the admission of Ireland and Afghanistan to full membership and a form of Test status in 2017. Scotland won the 12-team first edition, played between March and November 2004, beating Canada by an innings and 84 runs in the final.

Richard Done, who took over from Woolmer in September 2005 when the latter became Pakistan's national coach, was similarly a believer in an ambitious campaign to help the leading associates reach the next level. Done had played first-class cricket in Australia, and he had very definite ideas about how this could be achieved. His immediate task was to ready the six qualifiers for the 2007 World Cup and three months into the job he organised a winter training camp in Pretoria, attended by 23 players from the six countries. In addition to honing their own skills, they worked on obtaining Level 2 coaching certificates, so that they could contribute to development back home. 'That drip-down effect,' Done said, 'is a long-term key to developing talent in associate countries.' The Intercontinental Cup, meanwhile, continued to develop, with the zonal structure of the first two editions replaced in 2006 by a global schedule, each of the eight teams playing the others either at home or away. With their side including several experienced county players, notably Niall O'Brien, Eoin Morgan and Paul Stirling, Ireland dominated the competition between 2005 and 2008, winning in three successive editions.

The ICup was not, however, immune to the vagaries of ICC politics. Keen to bring Zimbabwe back to Test cricket, from which they had been suspended in 2005, the ICC decided to include a Zimbabwe XI in the 2009/10 edition of the ICup, and to accommodate them without increasing the size of the league it was necessary to drop one of the associate teams. Furthermore, the results of the 2009 World Cup qualifier, a one-day competition, were used to determine the participants in the four-day ICup, which meant that room had to be found for Afghanistan as well. It was decided to institute an Intercontinental Shield, effectively a second division, with the Cup contested by seven teams and the Shield by four. Using the qualifier standings as the selection criterion, however, meant that Namibia, who had topped the table in the 2007/08 edition before losing to Ireland in the final but who had finished eighth in the qualifier, were consigned to the Shield, along with the UAE, Bermuda and Uganda. Presented as an expansion of multi-day cricket but transparently a device to deal with the ICC's long-running Zimbabwe problem, the Shield was abandoned after just one edition, Namibia having beaten the UAE in the final with Craig Williams scoring a century in each innings, and the Cup reverted to an eight-team competition. Afghanistan, meanwhile, won the Cup at the first attempt, beating Scotland by seven wickets in the final.

As part of the preparation for the World Cup the ICC launched a new 50-over competition featuring Kenya and the five qualifiers from the 2005 ICC Trophy. Division One of a new World Cricket League was played in Nairobi in January and February 2007, and after a week of intensely competitive cricket was won by the hosts, who beat Scotland in the final. The Scots had inflicted Kenya's only defeat of the round-robin phase, although Steve Tikolo's men had had the narrowest of squeaks against Ireland. Chasing an imposing 284/4, to which Will Porterfield had contributed a solid 104 not out and Kevin O'Brien a thumping 125-ball 142, Kenya had squeezed home with an over to spare and their final pair together, thanks to Thomas Odoyo's unbeaten 61 from 36 deliveries. Ireland were generally unfortunate, losing to Scotland by three wickets off the final ball of a high-scoring encounter, failing to defend a total of 308/7 against Canada, and dropping a succession of catches in their final game against the Netherlands before falling short by just six runs as they chased their opponents' 260/7. Coming to Nairobi's high altitude after preparation at sea level in Port Elizabeth did them no favours, but there were few hints here of what would follow in the Caribbean a few weeks later. In the final, a well-balanced Kenyan attack dismissed Scotland for 155, and then David Obuya's 93 saw his side home by eight wickets with a dozen overs to spare.

The World Cricket League turned out to be much more than a one-off preparation for the World Cup qualifiers. Division Two and Three tournaments, involving a further 12 associates, were played in Darwin and Windhoek in the course of 2007, and the UAE, Oman, Namibia and Denmark won through to the qualifier for the next World Cup, which would take place in April 2009. And in May 2008 a second edition of the WCL began with a Division Five tournament in Jersey, with the number of participants in the league now expanded to 30. That would increase to 38 by the time it reached its full extent, although by 2015 it was being cut back, eventually being replaced in 2020 by a new, much more limited, but arguably more sustainable, structure. By that time some 55 associate and affiliate nations had taken part in at least one of the 39 global tournaments which had taken place over 13 years, an unparalleled opportunity for players to test their existing skills and learn new ones. The interlocking system of six-team divisions, with two winning promotion and two being relegated each time, may sometimes have been confusing, but the league did much more than give part-time players invaluable experience: umpires, too, were called upon to raise their game, mentored by colleagues from the ICC's international panel, and facilities in the 20 associate and affiliate countries which hosted tournaments were considerably improved.

One of the league's most remarkable achievements was as a vehicle for the rapid rise of Afghanistan, whose squad arrived in Jersey in May 2008 for their first global tournament, within a year earning themselves ODI and first-class status, and becoming a full member within a decade. It was an extraordinary story against a background of war and political chaos, and one which had significant propaganda value for the ICC.

Captained initially by Nawroz Mangal, the Afghans won the final of that Jersey Division Five tournament by two wickets after bowling their hosts out for 80 in a rain-reduced game, then themselves faltering with the bat, and being rescued by a defiant 29 not out from number nine Hasti Gul Abid. It was a victory in many ways typical of their rise. Their bowling, led by Hamid Hassan, was outstanding, their batting rather less so, but they were driven by an absolute conviction that they would win, and they continued to do so, triumphing in Dar es Salaam and, after some tricky moments, in Buenos Aires in the Division Four and Three tournaments to reach the World Cup qualifier in South Africa. There they fell just short of the World Cup spot they – and the ICC – dreamed of, but by finishing fifth, with wins against Ireland, Namibia and Scotland (twice) along the way, they ensured that they would be among the associates' elite for the coming cycle.

All of this, of course, came at a cost. Until 2009 it was funded in large part by the allocation of US$13 million every two years from the Champions Trophy profits, half of this going to the Asian region and the rest used to support the other four regions, the High Performance Programme, and the costs of the development department. From January 2009, however, the earmarking of the Champions Trophy money ceased, with 6% of the ICC's media and sponsorship income instead being designated for development. This was expected to lead to an approximate doubling of the available funding, half still going to the Asian region. There was still special provision for the ten high performance countries, and a pool of around $2 million was established as a special development projects fund. In July 2008 Lorgat was able to announce that the ICC would go even further, committing US$300 million to global development over the next seven years, calling it 'the biggest investment in global development by any sport outside football'. The system was still heavily weighted towards India's protégés in Asia, but this was in retrospect a time of plenty, when the regional offices had sufficient resources to foster local development, there were regular tournaments at senior men's, women's and youth levels, and many associate and affiliate countries received the support they needed to develop the game. It was, however, not destined to last.

The adoption of the draconian proposals of the F&CA had a dramatic impact on the ICC's development programmes. The World Cricket League reached its apogee in its third iteration, when 38 countries took part across eight divisions, and that structure was retained for the next edition, which began in Samoa in September 2012, long before its predecessor had been completed. With qualification for Division Eight determined in regional tournaments, the Council could indeed proclaim that every country had a pathway to the 'Cup That Counts'. But by the time the fifth edition started, in Essex and Hertfordshire in September

2015, the number of divisions had been cut to six. There was one fewer still when the next, and as it turned out the last, began in South Africa two years later. By this time, of course, the World Cup had been reduced to ten teams, so that the prospect of qualifying via the WCL had been virtually eliminated. The final edition of the WCL Championship, however – the top division which after 2010 was played on a home or away league basis linked to the Intercontinental Cup programme – fed into a new Super League (in which there a place for one associate) and via a qualifier into 'League 2', which would replace the highest echelons of the old WCL. With a Challenge League below that, the total number of associate participants had been reduced to 20, with the compensating factor that one of their number, in this case the Netherlands, would play eight three-match ODI series against full members. In all, between 2007 and 2019 cricketers from 44 countries had had the opportunity of playing in at least one international tournament: 12 from the Asia region, 11 from Europe, nine from Africa, seven from the Americas, and five from East Asia Pacific.

The decision to cut back the WCL was not merely a financial one. As it developed, a significant difficulty had become apparent. In many of the participating countries, especially below top divisions, there was no domestic 50-over competition. Players were therefore not only having to take on strong opponents in unfamiliar conditions but were also asked to adapt to an unfamiliar format. Although the desire to reduce the development budget was doubtless a factor for some board members, therefore, it could also be argued that it was unrealistic to expect amateur club cricketers from many associate and affiliate countries to perform adequately in 50-over cricket. By 2011 the die was cast, and the official policy was that most ICC members should concentrate on the T20 format. The first regional T20 tournaments had been held in Asia in 2007 and in Europe the following year, and by 2011 the 50-over tournaments had been replaced in all five regions by the shorter format. These fed into global qualifiers for the World T20 Cup: the first of these was held in Belfast in 2008, with Ireland and the Netherlands reaching the 2009 tournament, where the Dutch shocked England with their last-ball victory in the opening game. Eventually expanded to 16 teams, the global qualifiers continued until 2022, after which the ICC decided instead to adopt a regional qualifying system, with the result that qualification was much tougher in the stronger regions like Asia and Europe than it was in the Americas and the EAP.

On the face of it, the decision to abandon the WCL in favour of a modified structure made sense. There were legitimate questions about the value of flying teams from, say, Fiji, Saudi Arabia and Suriname to England for a week-long tournament, especially when it transpired that several members of the Surinamese squad were really from Guyana and were ineligible to play for Suriname. Many of those who took part were expats who had learned their cricket in the Indian subcontinent, and many, too, were essentially club cricketers. Concentrating the 50-over effort on the leading 20 countries, eight of them playing ODIs and the remainder matches with List A status, was logical enough. As for the rest, the ICC had been arguing for years that T20 was the format most likely to grow the game in emerging cricket countries, and in 2018 it decided that henceforth all T20 matches between its members would have full international status. This led to a proliferation of bilateral T20 series, the results of which fed into a rankings table which was increasingly used by the ICC as a qualifying benchmark for such regional and global tournaments as it still organised. But the system of regular regional leagues which had taken place in the heyday of the Global Development Programme had, except in the Asia region, largely disappeared.

It was not only the World Cricket League which fell victim to the new financial environment. The Intercontinental Cup had provided invaluable first-class experience for a generation of cricketers for the 13 years of its existence and had paved the way for the admission of Ireland and Afghanistan, admittedly on extremely restricted terms, to Test status in 2018. But in that year the ICC withdrew its financial support, inviting 'expressions of interest' from associates with ODI status for a continuation of a multi-day competition at their own expense. Unsurprisingly, the associates were reluctant to assume this burden given their limited resources, which had been further reduced by the decision to take the full member funding for Ireland and Afghanistan from the associates' pot. It was reported in 2021 that with those two countries and Zimbabwe excluded from the World Test Championship and struggling to arrange the Test matches which they were theoretically entitled to play, there had been some preliminary discussions about a return to a multi-day competition involving them and some of the top associates – effectively a 'Second Division' of Test cricket – but so far those conversations have led nowhere. With the ICC funding model increasingly weighted towards the full members and towards India in particular, it is difficult to see how such a competition could be organised without earmarked funding, as had been the case with the Intercontinental Cup.

The decision to run down the Global Development Programme and effectively end the High Performance Programme had further damaging effects as well. Between 2013 and 2015 the regional offices were significantly reduced, and with them the systems of stimulation and oversight which had been possible during the noughties. The new doctrine was that even the smallest members needed to shoulder a greater share of the financial burden, however unrealistic such an expectation might seem. It was, and remains, an open secret that the annual returns of player and official numbers, competitions, clubs and facilities which the associates are required to submit are often hyperbolic, and in some cases are closer to fiction than to reality. Since these returns influence the funding which members receive from the ICC, this cannot be dismissed as mere window-dressing: it is effectively a form of fraud. Limited as the regions' capacity to police the system may be, several countries have had their membership terminated as a result of persistent infringements (generally unspecified) of the Council's rules. Cuba, which had been admitted in 2002 as part of the rush to join the IOC, was the first to go, in 2013. Tonga followed the next year, and Brunei the year after that. After a gap, Morocco was expelled in 2019, with Zambia dismissed in 2021 and Russia a year later.

One area which has been a constant source of frustration for the leading associates is the failure of the ICC's 'mandatory release' system. The problem came sharply into focus in June 2006, when Ireland were scheduled to play their first-ever full ODI against England, but were forced to take the field without Eoin Morgan and Niall O'Brien, who were picked by their counties, Middlesex and Kent respectively, in matches which included that day. Kent's claim to O'Brien was particularly telling, since the reason he was needed was that the first-string wicketkeeper, Geraint Jones, would be playing for England. England's priority was therefore accepted, but Ireland's counted for nothing. It was a story which would often be repeated over the next 16 years, and even a more stringent declaration of policy by the ICC made little or no difference. The current version, adopted in April 2022, states that '[o]n the basis that participation in any form of International Cricket shall always take priority over participation in any other form of cricket, the release of players who want to play in ICC Events and/or in International Matches for the National Representative Team of a Full Member shall be mandatory'.

The policy goes on to include events such as World Cup global qualifiers, the World Cup Super League and 'All One-Day International and Twenty20 matches against Full Members' in the list covered by the requirement and adds that '[a]ny contractual provisions agreed with a player must be consistent with these requirements'. Yet the English counties, and some other domestic bodies, have continued to thumb their noses at these supposedly stringent rules. The Netherlands were forced to play many of their Super League fixtures against full members without most or all of their county players and were again without half their team when they qualified for the 2023 World Cup at a qualifying tournament in Zimbabwe.

In 2022, before the first Super League had been completed, the ICC board decided that it would not be repeated, giving in to those full members who preferred bilateral series where they could pick and choose their opponents, thus maximising their income; when push came to shove, the need for 'context' was much less important than the desire for profit and the pressures of an overstuffed Future Tours Programme. This capitulation to those who preferred meaningless bilateral series was more illogical in view of the fact that the 2027 and 2031 World Cups were to be expanded to 14 participants, which meant that at least two associate countries would be able to qualify.

Since the full members are notoriously unwilling to agree to ODI fixtures against the associates, it is hard to see how, in the absence of the Super League or some similar framework, countries like the Netherlands, Scotland, Namibia and the USA can be expected to acquire the experience which is undoubtedly necessary if they are to perform to their full potential at the highest global level. This applies equally to the T20 format, where there has never been a structure which systemically pits the top associates against the full members, and where from 2025 the World Cup will include 20 participants. It may not be the case that the system is deliberately set up in this way to minimise the chance of a full member being embarrassed by an associate, but that is likely to continue to be the effect. Combined with the chronic limitations of funding which continue to confront the ICC's associate members, the inequities of the situation should be obvious.

Arguments of principle have never carried much weight in the ICC's debates, but the case for a more consistent and enlightened approach to the emerging cricket countries is overwhelming. Players from the established full member countries generally hone their skills in a variety of formats, often including two-day club cricket, before graduating through the first-class game into the international arena. Increasingly, their 'skill set' takes in both red- and white-ball cricket, and while some specialise in one or other format many are able to excel in all three. Even in the most ambitious associate countries, by contrast, opportunities to play multi-day cricket are extremely limited or, more often, non-existent, and the chance to develop skills by facing and overcoming the challenge of better-prepared opponents in high-pressure situations is for most no less restricted. The difference such chances can make is evident from the progress made by the Netherlands during their Super League campaign in 2021–23. Although they won only three matches (two against Ireland and one against Zimbabwe), the lessons they had learned unquestionably contributed to their T20 World Cup victories over Zimbabwe and South Africa, their defeat of the West Indies in the 50-over World Cup qualifier, and their wins against South Africa and Bangladesh in the World Cup itself.

In July 2023 ICC CEO Geoff Allardice was forced to defend the dropping of the ODI Super League from the new FTP. His answer was less than convincing. 'The impact of the Super League as a qualification vehicle' had worked, he insisted, in view of the Netherlands' performances against full members, but '[a]t the time the FTP was being considered the members didn't have quite the same impact with an expanded World Cup'. This was, to say the least, opaque, but it seemed to mean that the prospect of a 14-team World Cup in 2027 had frightened the horses about how a (presumably expanded) Super League would feed into the qualification process. Would it mean that the weaker full members would be at increased risk of missing out on qualification? Yes, 'getting greater context in the calendar' was an important consideration, but not, apparently, at the expense of the interests of full members. The more successful the Dutch were, however, the greater the pressure, and chairman Greg Barclay hinted that perhaps the Super League would have to make a reappearance in the 2027–31 FTP. In the meantime, the leading associates would have to make do with League 2. The lack of consistent, coherent thinking which characterises the ICC's development policies over the past decade lends a poignant note to those optimistic words of Haroon Lorgat back in 2012.

Chapter 13

Women's Cricket

IN 2005 the International Women's Cricket Council (IWCC) formally merged with the ICC, bringing the management of men's and women's cricket under one overall governing body. Established in 1958, the Council had always been less imperial and more progressive than its male equivalent: the Netherlands was one of its founding members, and its first World Cup was held in 1973, two years before the ICC's inaugural event. Seven more women's World Cup events had taken place by the time of the merger, and the Council now had 11 members, as well as Canada and Japan as affiliates. Despite an almost complete lack of media interest, the national governing bodies in several countries had already brought an independent women's organisation within the men's board to create a unified structure: in England, the Women's Cricket Association amalgamated with the England and Wales Cricket Board in 1998, the Australians following suit five years later. It was a measure of the different cultures in men's and women's cricket that the first chair of the ICC Women's Committee was the Netherlands' Betty Timmer, who had been vice-chair of the IWCC, a situation which would have been unthinkable in the men's game. The merger was described by Sarah Potter in *Wisden* as 'a thrilling shimmy for womankind.'

Even in countries like England, Australia and New Zealand, however, where women's cricket was relatively well established, it lagged far behind in playing numbers, facilities and media attention, and in many ICC members it was scarcely on the radar at all. Cricket was not unique in this regard. While women's tennis had a comparatively high profile, disparities in prize money remained a sore point, and it was really only in the Olympic and Commonwealth Games that performances by women received anything like equal attention to those by men. Outside World Cups, bilateral ODIs between women's teams were sporadic at best, and Tests even more so. India and the West Indies played their first women's Tests in 1976, Pakistan not until 1998. Especially in countries like Pakistan, religious and other cultural factors no doubt played a part in this, but more generally it is true that the women's game long remained low among the priorities of male administrators.

Even before women's cricket came under the purview of the ICC, however, there were signs that it was beginning to expand beyond its traditional centres. A Ugandan team had toured Kenya in January 2001, and in April of the following year there was a triangular East African Women's Championship involving Uganda (the winners), Kenya and Tanzania. A four-team African Women's Championship in 2004 also included Namibia, making their debut on the international stage. In Scotland, where there had been isolated women's international matches in 1932 and 1979, the national team was revived in 2000, even holding ODI status when they played in the European Championship in 2001 and the IWCC Trophy, along with hosts the Netherlands, Ireland, Japan, Pakistan and the West Indies, in 2003. But the fusion at global level brought a quickening of the pace. When the Asian Cricket Council organised a women's tournament in July 2007 there were eight participants, including ICC full members Bangladesh along with China, Hong Kong, Malaysia, Nepal, Singapore, Thailand and the

UAE. And whereas Ehsan Mani noted in welcoming the merger in the ICC's 2005/06 annual report that women's cricket was played in 45 countries, the following year's report could boast that 71 countries now had 'some form of organised women's or girls' cricket'.

The new women's committee moved quickly to establish its role. Within months it had adopted universal playing conditions for women's international cricket and had signed up to the ICC code of conduct. There was discussion of the problem of illegal bowling actions, and of the establishment of women's academies. A central plank of the ICC's strategic plan for 2006–10 was the integration of women's cricket, with a series of ambitious if unquantified goals: raising the profile of the game, increasing participation, widening the reach of competitive cricket, and developing an elite playing environment for the top level. Nor was the vision limited to cricket alone: the plan declared an intention to 'work in partnership with other sports to raise the profile of female participation in sport'. By 2008 individual rankings were introduced for women players, parallel with those for the men, although team rankings were not added until 2015. Two decades on from the merger, it can be said to have been one of the ICC's greatest successes.

The first women's World Cup to be held under ICC auspices was hosted by Australia in 2009; it was played at club grounds in Sydney as well as in Canberra, Bowral and Newcastle, with the final played at the picturesque North Sydney Oval. For the first time parts of the tournament were televised, with ICC partners ESPN Star Sports showing seven of the 25 matches. Eight teams took part, the top six from the previous tournament and qualifiers South Africa and Sri Lanka. With three of the four sides in each group progressing to a Super Six, interest in the first phase centred on teams jockeying for position, since points earned against fellow qualifiers would be carried through. This meant that New Zealand and England, unbeaten in their pool matches, started the Super Six with an advantage, while the gap between the leading women's sides and the rest was underlined by the fact that South Africa and Sri Lanka remained winless and were eliminated. The South Africans, though, did give the West Indies a fright in their opening game: bowled out for 116, Stafanie Taylor taking 4-17, Sunette Loubser's side managed to claim eight West Indian wickets before the runs were knocked off. The Super Six was dominated by the big four, a further gap opening up between them and Pakistan and the West Indies. With one defeat apiece New Zealand and England went straight into the final, while India beat hosts Australia by three wickets to claim third place. The final was a low-scoring affair. After winning the toss New Zealand were dismissed for 166, Nicki Shaw taking 4-34 for England, and an opening stand of 74 by Sarah Taylor and Caroline Atkins got the chase away to a solid start. Off-spinner Lucy Doolan removed them both and finished with 3-23, but England's batting was too strong and they completed a four-wicket victory with 23 deliveries to spare.

The inaugural Women's World T20 tournament was held concurrently with the men's event in June 2009, the same eight countries that had contested the 50-over version taking part. The same four teams again proved the strongest, New Zealand and England winning all their group games and going into the semi-finals along with Australia and India. The final, too, was a rematch of the World Cup final, with Katherine Brunt's 3-6 enabling England to dismiss New Zealand for just 85 and win by six wickets. Less than 12 months later a second T20 event was held in the Caribbean, and this time home advantage enabled the West Indies to finish ahead of England in the group phase; Australia were undefeated in that pool, while in the other, New Zealand again won all their matches and were joined by India in the semi-finals. The final was an all-Antipodean affair, and it turned out to be a thriller: Australia battled their way to 106/8, and at 77/6 with 13 deliveries remaining, New Zealand seemed to be heading for certain defeat. But Sophie Devine took on Rene Farrell's penultimate over, and 14 were needed off the last, bowled by Ellyse Perry. A single and a string of twos by Devine left the New Zealanders needing a four off the final ball to tie the scores, but Devine could only manage a single and Australia had won by three runs. By reaching the semi-finals the West Indies had for the first time broken up the tetropoly of England, Australia, New Zealand and India, a much-needed development in the women's game.

The ICC now decided that the qualifier to be held in Bangladesh would serve multiple functions: a ten-team 50-over tournament, it would determine two qualifiers for the 2012 T20 World Cup as well as four for the 2013 50-over event, and it would, moreover, be used to settle which teams had ODI status for the coming period. It was won by the West Indies, with Pakistan, Sri Lanka and South Africa joining them at the World Cup. With the West Indies and Sri Lanka already qualified for the T20 tournament, Pakistan and South Africa took the remaining two spots for that event. The status quo of four top sides, with four more forming a second string was thus confirmed. There were two more ODI slots available, which were claimed by Bangladesh and Ireland, the latter beating the Netherlands to bring an end to the ODI status which the Dutch had enjoyed since 1984. For the Bangladeshi women this was new territory, and they celebrated by beating Ireland to take fifth place in the tournament; Ayasha Rahman and Sharmin Akter shared a century opening stand and thereafter they never looked back, going on to win by 82 runs.

Having won the qualifier, the West Indies went on to demonstrate that their success on their own turf in 2010 had not been a flash in the pan, beating New Zealand and South Africa – the latter by ten wickets – to top their group at the 2012 T20 World Cup in Sri Lanka. New Zealand joined them in the semi-finals, while England were unbeaten in the other pool and waltzed into the knockout phase along with Australia. England and Australia reached the final with victories over New Zealand and the West Indies respectively, and the two old rivals then produced another outstanding final. The Australians posted 142/4, and at 61/3 at the halfway mark, England, who had only lost one match all year, appeared to be well placed to claim another title, despite the loss of Sarah Taylor just at that point. But Australia kept taking wickets, and with two overs left England needed 23 runs with just two wickets in hand. Ellyse Perry bowled the penultimate over and restricted the scoring to three singles and a four by Holly Colvin, leaving 16 required off the last. It was bowled by Erin Osborne, and nine runs came from her first five deliveries, one of them a no-ball. So that meant England needed seven from the last two, but then Colvin was run out desperately looking for a second to long-off, and six were needed from the final ball. Just a single eventuated, and Australia won by four runs.

It had been a disappointing tournament for India, who lost all three group matches, but worse was to follow at the 50-over World Cup which they hosted in 2013. Although they opened their campaign with a comfortable victory over the West Indies, they lost to England and, sensationally, to Sri Lanka, and finished bottom of their group on net run rate. With only one team from each of the four-team pools failing to go through to the Super Six, this was a humiliating outcome for the hosts. The Sri Lankans had also upset England with a thrilling last-ball one-wicket victory as they chased down England's 238/8, but a heavy defeat at the hands of the West Indies, for whom Stafanie Taylor made a 137-ball 171 in a total of 368/8, meant that they could only finish second on net run rate. The West Indies' 209-run winning margin in that game, however, was enough to put them well ahead of India in the final group table. Australia were again unbeaten in their pool, while South Africa comprehensively beat Pakistan to make sure of a place in the Super Six along with New Zealand. With Taylor continuing in superb form, the West Indies maintained their dramatic improvement into the second phase, where they not only beat South Africa and New Zealand, but also inflicted Australia's only defeat of the tournament, dismissing them for 156 to win by eight runs. That set up a rematch in the final, where the Australians had their revenge with a 114-run victory, Jess Cameron top-scoring with 75 and Ellyse Perry taking 3-19. It really did appear, however, that the West Indies had, at least for the time being, supplanted India in the semi-permanent top four of the women's game.

This was confirmed at the next T20 World Cup, expanded to ten participants and hosted by Bangladesh in March–April 2014. The West Indians again reached the semi-finals, losing only to India in their four group matches but going through along with England, because the Indians lost to Sri Lanka as well as to England. In the other pool it was the turn of South Africa to spring a surprise. Having beaten Pakistan in their opening game they finished the group phase with a five-wicket victory over New Zealand, who had opened their campaign by beating Australia but who ended up third in their group on net run rate. The gap was beginning to close between the top four and the best of the rest. The West Indies pushed Australia all the way in their semi-final, reaching 120/2 with two overs left in pursuit of their opponents' 140/5, but in the end the task proved just too great, and they closed on 132/4. England were much too strong in the other semi-final, bowling South Africa out for 101 and knocking off the runs in 16.5 overs for the loss of just one wicket. So the big two again confronted one another in the final, and this time Australia's bowlers quickly took charge, restricting England to 105/8. With Meg Lanning hitting a 30-ball 44 the Australians needed only 15.1 overs to complete a six-wicket win, their third consecutive victory in the T20 World Cup.

'Context' being the watchword in women's as in men's cricket, in August 2014 the ICC introduced a new Women's Championship, based on three-match ODI series among the top eight national teams. The two-year competition would feed into the 2017 Women's World Cup, with the top four sides qualifying directly and the other four going into a qualifying tournament. It was, according to Dave Richardson, another 'meritocratic pathway', and was welcomed by women's committee chair Clare Connor as 'an exciting new initiative that represents a significant step in the continued development of women's cricket'. Australia dominated the first such competition, losing only three of their 21 matches, with single defeats by England, India and New Zealand in series which they won 2-1. England lost their series against New Zealand away and Australia at home, but still finished second overall, having won one more match than the White Ferns. The West Indies again took fourth spot, although this time their position ahead of India owed more to politics than to success on the field.

The perennial issue of bilateral matches between India and Pakistan, which had bedevilled the men's game for so long, now made its presence felt here. Pakistan were scheduled to host a visit by the Indians between August and October 2016, but by 9 November no agreement had been reached, the BCCI failing to respond directly to the PCB while protesting that it was bound by government policy on contacts between the two countries. The Pakistanis had offered to play the series in the UAE, but when the BCCI still failed to respond the ICC's Event Technical Committee awarded all three matches to Pakistan. A 2-1 series win would have been enough to put India ahead of the West Indies and into fourth place in the table, thus taking them directly into the 2017 World Cup. But their inability to fulfil their fixtures against Pakistan meant that they would now have to go through a qualifier first.

That was held in Sri Lanka in February 2017, and for the first time the six ODI-playing countries were joined by teams who had gone through a regional qualifier first; this meant that a total of 23 women's sides had been involved, with China, Hong Kong, Samoa and Thailand taking part in the 50-over World Cup pathway for the first time. Thailand were the surprise. Since making their international debut in 2007 their women's side had made significant progress, winning five of their six matches in their regional qualifier to finish ahead of Nepal, Hong Kong and China. They could not carry that into the global tournament, however, losing all four of their group games. India, unsurprisingly, went through the tournament undefeated, although the final against South Africa was a last-ball thriller. With all their top eight getting a start the South Africans posted a challenging 244 all out, and although Mona Meshram made 59 and Deepti Sharma 71, the ninth wicket fell off the first ball of the final over with eight still needed. Skipper Harmanpreet Kaur was equal to the occasion, hammering Marcia Letsaolo's penultimate delivery over midwicket for six and then lofting the last safely to long-on to take the two India needed. Sri Lanka and Pakistan joined the finalists at the World Cup, while Bangladesh and Ireland, the other two teams to make the Super Six, retained their ODI status and their place in the Women's Championship.

If 50-over cricket was flourishing, along with T20 internationals, the Test format was in the doldrums. This was already apparent by June 2001, when England took on Australia in a two-match series. Australia had not played a Test since 1998, while England's last such match had been against India the following year. Writing for *Cricinfo*, Rick Eyre documented the infrequent Tests which had been played over the previous decade, noting that '[t]here is no domestic competition at state or county level anywhere in the world that involves matches of more than one day in duration, and this makes the jump from one- or two-day cricket to the four-day game even more difficult when Test time comes around'. It was, inevitably, all a question of money: 'Women's cricket is in a sporting backwater when it comes to corporate sponsorship and financial assistance, and this is a serious inhibiting factor when it comes to international sides meeting one another.'

In the event, both Tests turned out to be one-sided affairs, the Australians winning the first by an innings and 140 runs and the second by nine wickets. England were dismissed for 103 and 101 in the first, their combined total almost surpassed by Michelle Goszko's six-and-a-half-hour innings of 204, while Cathryn Fitzpatrick took 8-62 in the match. Karen Rolton's unbeaten 209 enabled Australia to declare at 383/4 in the second Test, 239 ahead, and although Claire Taylor made a defiant 137 when England batted again, Fitzpatrick added another nine wickets to her tally, including a second five-wicket haul for the series with 5-31 in the first innings. All in all, it could not be said to have been a hugely successful advertisement for the format, despite some fine individual performances.

Between 2005 and 2017 only 16 women's Tests were played, all but four of them in one-off games and all but seven between England and Australia. In that period India played five, South Africa two, and the Netherlands one. New Zealand, Pakistan and the West Indies played their last Test in 2004, Ireland (who took part in just one, against Pakistan) in 2000, and Sri Lanka in 1998. The nadir was probably reached in the solitary Test between the Netherlands and South Africa in Rotterdam in 2007, when the discrepancy between the sides was so great that in the Dutch first innings Violet Wattenberg and Maartje Köster took three hours in adding 63 for the third wicket, Wattenberg taking a total of 380 minutes over her 49. It was a feat of endurance worthy of Trevor Bailey and 'Slasher' Mackay in their 1950s heyday, but as an advertisement for the women's game it left a good deal to be desired. The Netherlands were all out for 108 in their first innings and 50 in their second and lost by 159 runs. In 2018 the ICC finally proposed to pull the plug on women's Tests, despite protests from England and Australia. The women's committee gave in to the seemingly inevitable in April, bowing to the view that they were 'financially unviable'. Connor tellingly made the point that three T20Is could be played in the time needed for a Test, adding that, unlike the longer format, they would be shown on television.

As stand-alone fixtures that is perhaps true, but a hybrid series format had existed since 2013 which gave a one-off Test 'context' by combining it with the shorter formats. When Australia toured England in 2013 they played three ODIs and three T20Is as well as a single Test, and points were accumulated from each match to give a series result. England won the ODIs 2-1 and the T20Is 3-0, and with the Test drawn they took the series by 12-4. The formula was varied a few months later when England travelled to Australia; now the Test carried six points rather than two, so that despite losing both the shorter format series 2-1 England took the series by virtue of a 61-run victory in the Test with which it had begun. Thereafter the Test was generally placed in the middle of the series, between the ODIs and the T20Is, although it reverted to the lead-off spot in the 2023 series in England. Series involving either India or South Africa have since adopted similar patterns, but with no trophy at stake, only that between Australia and India in 2021/22 allocated points for the results. The hybrid series format has, however, kept the longest format alive for four countries at least, and it is possible that other full members, such as New Zealand and Pakistan, might return to the women's Test arena at some point in the future.

In other respects the development of women's cricket continued to make significant strides, CEO David Richardson announcing in 2017 that the World Cup prize fund would be increased from $200,000 in 2013 to $2 million. All matches in that tournament would be shown on television or live-streamed; it was, he claimed, 'a turning point in the history of the game'. There was also significant progress in the emergence of women officials. In 2014 New Zealander Kathy Cross had become the first woman umpire to be appointed to the ICC Associate and Affiliate Panel, soon to be joined by Claire Polosak (Australia), Sue Redfern (England) and Jacqueline Williams (West Indies). And in 2019 G.S. Lakshmi (India) was the first woman to be added to the International Referees' Panel. Importantly, too, women have not been restricted to officiating in women's matches, standing in men's games as well.

As part of its more general expansion of global events, the ICC announced in March 2021 that the 2029 50-over World Cup would be expanded from eight teams to ten and the three T20 World Cups to be held between 2026 and 2030 would comprise 12 participants. At the same time, it announced the introduction of an entirely new tournament, the T20 Champions Cup, equivalent to the men's ODI Champions Trophy, which would take place in 2027 and 2031 with six countries taking part. This would, CEO Manu Sawhney said when making the announcement, not only give more women's teams a chance to play on the global stage; it would also open up the qualifying tournaments to a wider range of countries. 'We have been building momentum around the women's game for the last four years,' he proclaimed, 'investing in global broadcast coverage and marketing to drive fan engagement.'

One of the peculiarities of ICC qualifying events was that some matches, between two teams with ODI status, were classified as ODIs, while the rest were not. To clear up this untidiness, Richardson announced on 9 September 2018 that from now on all matches in World Cup qualifiers and in the Asia Cup would count as ODIs regardless of the current status of the participants. This change was, he said, 'befitting of the events and just reward for the teams that have qualified'. Richardson's statement was interpreted at the time as applying to both men's and women's qualifiers, but it later emerged that this was not the case. While the women's teams of all full members were granted ODI status in April 2021, Thailand's games in the next qualifier would, despite their outstanding performances on the field, be defined as List A matches.

If this came as a blow to the Thais worse was to follow. The next qualifier, in Zimbabwe in November 2021, took place in the shadow of the Covid-19 pandemic. It had originally been supposed to be played in Sri Lanka in July 2020 but had been postponed because at that point the pandemic was at its height. A fortnight before the rescheduled tournament was to begin, Papua New Guinea withdrew, stating that several of their players had contracted the illness, and a few days after it finally started a new Covid variant, labelled Omicron, was detected in southern Africa. By the time the tournament was abandoned on 27 November Thailand had won three of their four group matches, beating Zimbabwe, Bangladesh and the United States and losing only to Pakistan. This had guaranteed them a place in the Super Six, and given them a very good chance of qualifying, if not for one of the three World Cup spots, then at least for one of the two places in the next Women's Championship, along with ODI status for that period. Under the tournament playing conditions, however, the cancellation meant that qualifying would now be based on the ICC's rankings, so that the qualifiers for the World Cup were Bangladesh (whom Thailand had already beaten), Pakistan and the West Indies, while it was Sri Lanka and Ireland who went into the Championship. Thailand, under these rules, had no chance of qualifying for either, since they had never enjoyed ODI status and were therefore excluded from the rankings. Protests at this palpable injustice made no difference; Thailand were effectively being punished for their decision to prioritise the women's game and develop a world-class women's team, and suggestions that they might be given wild card entry to one or other of the competitions they had missed out on went nowhere.

Perhaps in compensation for the twin debacles of the reversed decision regarding the status of matches in women's World Cup qualifiers and the cancellation of the 2021 qualifier, in May 2022 five women's teams – the Netherlands, Papua New Guinea, Scotland, Thailand and the United States – were given ODI status by the ICC, bringing the total number of women's ODI teams to 16. Welcome as this was, approximating the 20 men's teams with the same status, it meant little given the near impossibility of the newcomers actually getting any fixtures with anyone except each other. Of the 28 ODIs these five countries played between May 2022 and August 2024, 16 were against each other; Ireland have arranged three-match series against Scotland and the Netherlands and Zimbabwe have taken on similar events against PNG and Thailand, but otherwise the leading associates have been no more successful in persuading the full members to agree to women's ODIs than they have been with the men. In a rational world the Women's Championship might have been given a second division incorporating the eight ODI countries who did not qualify for the higher league – possibly even with promotion and relegation between the two – but this would have redirected resources away from the full members, and that would obviously have been a step too far.

The board's decision to give full member status to Afghanistan despite the absence of a substantial women's programme came back into focus in August 2021, when the Taliban swept back into power in Kabul, triggering the flight of thousands who had supported the previous, American-instigated regime. Although the earlier Taliban government had been enthusiastic about cricket, encouraging the country's original application for ICC membership, its attitude towards women's sport, along with any other manifestation of an independent role for women, was notorious, and it was widely anticipated that their triumph in the prolonged civil war would bring an abrupt, possibly brutal end to the faltering steps which the ACB had taken towards establishing a national women's team. The first Afghan women's team had existed between 2010 and 2014, but had only taken part in one, unofficial international tournament, in Tajikistan in 2012. Despite continuing opposition to women's participation in sport, a further effort had been made in 2020, when the ACB awarded central contracts to 25 players, who had been training under the leadership of Diana Barakzai and national women's coach Tuba Sangar. But by this time the Taliban were once more in the military ascendant, and any steps in this direction seemed doomed to failure. The ICC criteria for full membership clearly required 'a sustained and sufficient pool of players to support strong and consistent national level selection across the senior men's, U19 *and women's teams*' [my emphasis] and 'satisfactory women's pathways', but a clause which allowed the Council to waive one or more of the criteria in 'exceptional circumstances' had allowed Afghanistan's application to be accepted despite the absence in 2017 of any organised women's cricket in the country, and this could now be invoked again as the prospect of the women's game being allowed to develop disappeared.

Within weeks of the Taliban takeover, the ACB appointed Azizullah Fazli as chairman, and soon afterwards Hamid Shinwari was replaced as CEO by Naseebullah Haqqani, a kinsman of the new interior minister, Sirajuddin Haqqani. The impact of all this on the future of the women's game was obvious. With the Taliban raiding the homes of suspected women athletes, the cricket squad fled into Pakistan, most of them subsequently being granted emergency visas to enter Australia. The ICC duly set up a working group to consider this extremely intractable problem and, after a meeting with a representative of the Afghan government, the group's chairman, Imran Khwaja, sounded positive. The representative, he said, 'was clear in his support for the ICC constitution including in principle for women's cricket in Afghanistan'. By March 2023, however, the outlook was gloomier, the group having reportedly concluded that although the Taliban government had not 'interfered in cricket affairs', there was virtually no prospect of women's cricket as long as the Taliban were in power. This was a situation beyond the control of the ACB, the working party argued, and therefore Afghanistan should not be punished for breaching the regulations regarding full membership. Financial support for an Afghan women's team established outside the country had been canvassed, but this 'could prove counterproductive, even dangerous, for those on the ground in the country'. Asked about the problem after the 2023 annual conference, Geoff Allardice admitted that the ban on women's cricket in Afghanistan 'runs counter to the ICC's stated intentions to run a totally inclusive and diverse organisation'. 'We accepted that we can't influence or change the laws of the country,' he added, 'but we are looking to re-establish a framework that helps support what we can do to get women's cricket back up and running in the country, together with looking at what steps might be taken to perhaps look at coercing the board and maybe those around it to do better in terms of restoring women's cricket, which of course was being played in the country until they had the change of regime.'

Caught between support and coercion, the ICC was of course a prisoner of its century-old doctrine of the internal autonomy of its members, as well as its desire to protect Afghanistan's men's team, long one of its favourite projects. The situation was reminiscent of that around apartheid in the 1960s, with gender now the basis for exclusion rather than race. In an attempt to circumvent the difficulty, the Afghan women refugees wrote to the ICC in July 2024 urging them to establish and support an Afghanistan women's refugee team, to enable them 'to represent all Afghan women who dream of playing cricket but are unable to in Afghanistan'. They would not, therefore, be a full international side, but would have the opportunity to continue their development and to play as a unit.

Meanwhile, in a far-reaching step towards gender parity, the board had agreed in July 2023 that henceforward the financial rewards at men's and women's ICC events – overall prize money and the payment for winning any match – would be the same. The plan had been to achieve this goal by 2030, and chairman Greg Barclay professed himself delighted that it had been possible to bring parity forward by six years. Not all ICC members, he acknowledged, were 'at the same place' regarding pay parity, but for its own events the ICC was able to give substance to its commitment to 'inclusivity and equity'. Geoff Allardice added that '[a]s ICC we can control the things that we can control around our events and one of our major ways of distributing funds to players is through the prize money'. Decoded, this meant that while the ICC could institute parity across its own events, it had no power over the decisions of its members.

By July 2024 the ICC's T20I team rankings included no fewer than 74 countries, 30 of which had played 25 or more matches in the period covered. And if the same sides continued to dominate the rankings and tournaments in both the officially recognised formats, there were signs that, at least at the top, gaps were narrowing; Australia and England remained at the top, but South Africa, India and the West Indies were all more competitive than they had once been, South Africa making history in January 2024 by beating Australia in a T20I. What is ultimately more important is that the 66 ranked countries include plenty where women's sport faces considerable social and political difficulties, and if the Afghanistan story is a reflection of a much wider tragedy, the existence of women's teams in Bahrain, Kuwait and Oman demonstrates that cricket can be an instrument of social change. Even Saudi Arabia sent a women's team to the 2022 Gulf Cricket Council's T20 Championship, although that solitary outing has not yet taken them on to the ICC's rankings. But there is no doubt that the growing prominence of women's cricket has not only changed the sport's landscape, but shown that it can open new horizons for women across the world.

Chapter 14

Umpires, Referees and Technology

ALLEGATIONS OF biased umpiring are as old as the game itself, and there were many claims by touring teams over the years that home umpires were making decisions against them. It was even not unknown for touring captains and managements to object to the appointment of specific umpires. But as international cricket gained a higher profile, with matches shown live on television, so the pressures grew correspondingly, and incidents like Mike Gatting's confrontation with Shakoor Rana in 1987 persuaded many that action needed to be taken. The issue, like most other things in international cricket, also had a cultural dimension. Those in the subcontinent were convinced that the complaints against their umpires were racially motivated, part of the old imperial hangover, and that biased umpiring elsewhere was regarded by officialdom with a much more benign eye. That no doubt explained Imran Khan's initiative to bring in two Indian umpires for a Test against the West Indies in Lahore in 1986, and to fly in two English officials to stand in the series against India in 1989/90.

By this time proposals to introduce neutral umpires were gaining momentum at meetings of the Conference, and in 1992 a first, cautious step was taken with an experimental rule requiring one neutral official in every Test match. The first such appointment was the Englishman Harold

'Dickie' Bird, who stood in the series between Zimbabwe and India, starting in Harare on 19 October 1992. It took ten years before the requirement was extended to both on-field umpires, and again it was an Indian tour which broke new ground, with Asoka de Silva (Sri Lanka) and Daryl Harper (Australia) standing in the first three Tests in the series in the West Indies in April–May 2002, with David Shepherd (England) and Russell Tiffin (Zimbabwe) taking over for the final two. They were members of the ICC's new Elite Panel of umpires, which had taken over from the International Panel first established in 1994 and which would now for the most part supply both umpires for Test matches and one for ODIs; the other official in ODIs would be one of the host country's umpires on the International Panel.

Even more significant than the appointment of neutral umpires was the development of the role of match referee. When Colin Cowdrey, the first independent ICC chairman, introduced a code of conduct for international matches he included a referee as the final judge on disciplinary matters. The first such official was former England captain Mike Smith, who refereed the first two Tests of the 1991/92 series between Australia and India. The path to acceptance of match referees was not entirely smooth. On 28 December 1992 the Australian Peter Burge suspended Pakistan bowler Aaqib Javed for dissent during an ODI against New Zealand in Napier, after he had called umpire Brian Aldridge a cheat, and continued ill-feeling between the teams led Burge to warn both sides that he would take further action under the code of conduct if they did not moderate their behaviour. It helped considerably, though, that the ICC was quickly able to assemble a panel of respected referees who had had distinguished careers in international cricket. In addition to Burge, the first cohort included Pieter van der Merwe and Jackie McGlew (South Africa), Clive Lloyd and Cammie Smith (West Indies), Raman Subba Row (England), Srini Venkataraghavan (India) and Frank Cameron (New

Zealand). Between them they were able to ensure that the code of conduct became an accepted feature of the cricket landscape, and that their own role as arbiters of on-field incidents was increasingly taken for granted. With these two developments, neutral umpires and match referees, the ICC clearly expanded its role in the management of international cricket.

This was not achieved, however, without challenges to its authority, principally from the BCCI. In November 2001, match referee Mike Denness penalised six Indian players for their conduct during the second Test at Port Elizabeth, suspending Virender Sehwag for one match and handing suspended sentences to five others, including the captain, Sachin Tendulkar. Tendulkar appeared on television coverage of the match to have been altering the condition of the ball and Sehwag allegedly charged at one of the umpires, while the other four were reported by the on-field umpires for various disciplinary infringements. BCCI president Jagmohan Dalmiya immediately exploded, accusing Denness of racism, demanding his replacement as referee, and threatening to call off the third Test at Centurion. Terrified of the financial consequences of a cancellation, South Africa backed the BCCI position, while the ICC dug in, refusing to replace Denness for the remaining match. When the USB and BCCI appointed former South African Test player Denis Lindsay, an ICC referee, to take over from Denness, the ICC's response was that the game would no longer be regarded as official. Dalmiya objected that they had no power to withdraw official status, but the ICC rightly saw that what was at stake was 'the right of the ICC, as the world governing body for cricket, to appoint referees and umpires, and for those officials to make decisions which are respected by both players and Boards'. If this were not accepted, it added, 'the sport could descend into anarchy'. There were even fears that this seemingly minor episode could lead to a split in world cricket along racial lines.

The match was duly played, without Sehwag and with Lindsay in charge, South Africa winning by an innings and 73 runs. But the dispute did not go away. With England due to play India in Mohali at the beginning of December, the Indians claimed that Sehwag had served his suspension and was now eligible to play, while the ICC position was that since the Centurion match had been unofficial he had to miss the Mohali Test. After some brinkmanship from Dalmiya the BCCI agreed not to play Sehwag, while the ICC undertook to review Denness's decisions and to reconsider the status of the match at Centurion. As if to demonstrate its confidence in Denness, though, the ICC appointed him as referee for the forthcoming series between Pakistan and the West Indies in Sharjah, and at the same time established a commission, chaired by the South African judge Alby Sachs and also including the former Test cricketers Majid Khan (Pakistan) and Andrew Hilditch (Australia), to investigate the possibility of a right of appeal against a referee's decision, along with the introduction of a code of conduct for referees, and the need for greater consistency in their decision-making. But Dalmiya was still not satisfied: he objected to the ICC's nominees to the commission and complained that none of the ten candidates he had proposed – two of whom, Richie Benaud and Imran Khan, had declined – had been included.

By February 2002 it was evident that the BCCI was simply refusing to co-operate with the commission, Dalmiya insisting that it be expanded to a membership of ten or its deliberations put on hold. He took his demand to a meeting of the Asian Cricket Council in Sharjah later that month, where he received the support of the other full members from the region. The matter was thrashed out at the executive board in March, with the Denness affair now referred to a 'Disputes Resolution Committee', chaired by Michael Beloff QC and including three board members: Peter Chingoka of Zimbabwe, Bob Merriman of Australia and Wes Hall of the West Indies. The board also agreed that in future all disciplinary charges would have to be laid by the umpires – it was an obvious flaw that Denness had charged Tendulkar and Sehwag himself and then judged their cases – and that a match referee would be allowed to explain his decisions at a press conference, as Denness had been unable to do. The only point on which the ICC was able to score even a symbolic victory was that the disputed third Test in South Africa remained unofficial.

At the same time that it was moving to take control of umpiring and refereeing, the ICC was also adjusting to the technological possibilities of improved television coverage. Calling together the leading international umpires for a conference in August 1993, the board invited them to consider ways in which a third umpire might review on-field decisions in Tests and ODIs where appropriate TV facilities were available, an option which they had just approved in principle. This revolutionary use of technology, which would eventually evolve into the DRS system of player reviews, had been pioneered by the South Africans in Durban in 1992, when two cameras were used to enable close run-out decisions to be resolved. The number of cameras was soon expanded to four, and the technology proved useful in determining not only run-outs, but also doubts about whether the ball had touched the boundary rope. By 1995 the umpires were ready to take the system a stage further, recommending that it could also be applied in determining whether a catch had been taken cleanly or not. For traditionalists, all this was an erosion of the power of the on-field umpires to make all the decisions, but others, including many of the leading umpires themselves, saw it as a way of avoiding mistakes and reducing tensions on the field. Discussing the issue in 2003, ICC general manager David Richardson confirmed that technology 'will not be introduced at the expense of the umpire's status as the key decision-maker in relation to the rules and regulations'. For the 2004 Champions Trophy, however, in addition to connecting the on-field umpires' earpieces (now standard equipment) to the output from the stump microphones (ditto), decisions on front-foot no-balls were experimentally transferred to the third umpire. Richardson presented this as beneficial to the standing umpire, who 'will not need to adjust his line of sight from the bowler in delivery stride to the batsman receiving the ball'. And Speed was adamant that umpires' decision-making authority was in no way under threat; 'I do not believe,' he insisted, 'the game or its followers want to see umpires reduced to the role of coat racks.' Surveyed before the tournament, international captains expressed themselves in favour of the use of technology, although Australia's Ricky Ponting and Zimbabwe's Tatenda Taibu had more reservations than the rest.

In this first phase it was up to the on-field umpires to call for assistance in making marginal decisions, but in March 1997 a Colombo-born lawyer named Senaka Weeraratna proposed that the use of technology could be extended to give players the right to challenge decisions with which they disagreed. The mental shift required here should not be underestimated. It had always been a fundamental principle that the umpire's decision was final and absolute, and the notion that it might be overturned through the use of technology *after objection by a player* seemed to go against everything that the game had always stood for. After all, the code of conduct which Cowdrey had introduced imposed clear penalties for player dissent. At the same time it could not be denied that umpires were far from infallible, and even with neutral officials there were obvious cases, increasingly shown up by the improved technology, in which mistakes were made. One of the worst cases was the New Year's Test in Sydney in 2008, in which umpires Steve Bucknor and Mark Benson made a series of glaring errors, most, but not all of them, contributing to India's 122-run defeat. Andrew Symonds admitted that he was wrongly given not out on 30 on the opening day, going on to make an unbeaten 162, and with the Indians set to make 333 to win on the final day, Rahul Dravid was given caught behind for 38 off a Symonds delivery which had struck the knee roll and Sourav Ganguly was out to a slip catch off Brett Lee which was generally believed to have been grounded. The BCCI was furious and instructed the team management to complain to match referee Mike Procter. The match had also seen an on-field incident between Symonds and Harbhajan Singh, which led to the Indian spinner being charged with offensive behaviour. He had, it was claimed, called Symonds, one of whose birth parents was Afro-Caribbean, a 'monkey'; Harbhajan always denied this, but there was no question that the Australian had been subjected to monkey noises by Indian crowds at several venues, and Symonds had suggested that Harbhajan was a contributor to ill-feeling between the sides. The spinner was suspended for three Tests, but he and his team-mates continued to insist that there had been no racist taunt. The BCCI stated that for them 'anti-racial stance is an article of faith as it is for the entire nation which fought the apartheid policies'. Since they had initially tried to claim that the monkey noises from the Indian crowd had been worship of the monkey-God Hanuman, this did not perhaps ring entirely convincingly. Indian manager Chetan Chauhan also complained that Brad Hogg had used the word 'bastard' in sledging Anil Kumble and Mahendra Singh Dhoni, a charge which was subsequently dropped, a decision which Hogg himself described as 'a kind gesture, lovely gesture'.

Amidst rumours that the tour would be called off, the ICC confirmed that Bucknor would stand in the third Test in Perth, but then replaced him the following day with the New Zealander Billy Bowden. This was greeted by the BCCI's chief administrative officer as 'a satisfactory decision', although Malcolm Speed was quick to insist that all the ICC was trying to do was to 'take some tension out of the situation', and that Bucknor would continue to umpire elsewhere. They also flew the chief match referee Ranjan Madugalle in to try to mediate between the captains, while retaining Procter as the match referee. The New Zealand High Court judge John Hansen was appointed to hear the Harbhajan appeal, which was delayed until after the completion of the series. With the player claiming, supported by Sachin Tendulkar, that what he had actually said was *'teri maa ki'*, an admittedly obscene Hindi term referring to one's mother's genitalia, Hansen found the charge of racial abuse unproven, and reduced the sanction to 50% of the player's match fee. But the judge also commented that the ICC had only revealed one of Harbhajan's four previous convictions, a result of database and human errors. Had he known, he stated, of an offence in 2001 which had earned the player a one Test suspended sentence and a fine of 75% of his match fee, he would have taken a different view when determining his sentence. Once again, the ICC had managed to emerge with black marks against its reputation.

The mistakes made by Bucknor and Benson, however, remained irrefutable. In March 2008, prompted by ICC general manager Dave Richardson, the Chief Executives' Committee agreed to try out a review system broadly along the lines suggested by Weeraratna, and commissioned the cricket committee, which under the chairmanship of Sunil Gavaskar had been sceptical about the idea, to establish the guidelines for its implementation. Ironically, in view of subsequent events, Sri Lanka and India tested it during their series which began in Colombo that July. Using slow motion replays, noises from the stump microphones which had now become standard equipment in international cricket, and the 'Hawk-Eye' technology to track the ball up to the point of impact (but not to predict its future trajectory), the third umpire would review a decision should this be requested by either side. The testing continued, and by February 2009 Haroon Lorgat was able to argue that '[t]he referral system has improved the rate of giving correct decisions'; the rate of correct decision-making had risen from 94% to 98% as a result of the reviews. Continuing to tweak its system, the ICC now added 'Hot Spot', a technology which created infra-red images to confirm that the ball had touched bat, glove or pad, to its battery of measures informing a review.

The experiment was sufficiently successful for it to be adopted formally for Tests in November 2009, with nine of the ten full members supporting it; the BCCI stood out against it as the Indian players believed that it had worked against them during that Sri Lanka series. Under the Decision Review System (DRS), players could challenge up to two decisions per Test innings, losing one of these challenges should their request for a review prove unsuccessful. In May 2011 the ICC cricket committee recommended that DRS be used in all Tests, and that it should also be employed in ODI and T20 series with one review per side per innings. The BCCI continued to object to the use of Hawk-Eye, insisting that it would only accept the system when it was 'foolproof', and in 2011 the ICC had to back down from its position that the use of DRS was mandatory, accepting that it would only be implemented where both sides agreed. When an attempt was made to leave the decision to apply DRS to the home board, Srinivasan reportedly threatened that India would pull out of any tour where the system was to be used. Not until 2017 was it finally agreed that it would apply uniformly in all series and tournaments involving the full members.

Reviewing the situation in his 2013 Cowdrey Lecture, Simon Taufel reflected on how television and the introduction of technology had altered the game. 'In today's cricket,' he observed, 'the decision of the umpire is scrutinised by all these cameras including slow motion, ultra motion, hot spot front on, hot spot leg side, hot spot off side, ball tracking and prediction, Snicko, stump audio, the mat and then by up to three commentary experts upstairs in the box.' And while such detailed scrutiny eliminated the most obvious errors and many less obvious ones, it also made every viewer an umpire and put more pressure on players and umpires. The system has continued to be tweaked and improved, introducing the 'umpire's call' to allow for extremely marginal lbw decisions, renewing the number of challenges allowed after 80 overs in Tests, removing the 'soft signal' in cases where there was doubt whether a catch had been cleanly taken, and so on. A decade on from Taufel's lecture it takes an effort to remember how controversial the use of technology to assist the on-field umpires once was, and while there will always be marginal cases where one side feels aggrieved and the armchair umpires bitterly disagree with each other, one effect of DRS has been to demonstrate how extraordinarily good most international umpiring actually is.

Another aspect of the game where technology could make a difference was in calculating the result of rain-affected matches. Traditionally, various methods had been used, none of which was entirely fair. The least satisfactory was the Most Productive Overs method, which had produced a farcical result in the 1992 World Cup semi-final between England and South Africa. Two British statisticians, Frank Duckworth and Tony Lewis, therefore devised a system which took account of the advantage enjoyed by the side batting second in a rain-shortened match and of the state of the game when overs were reduced or the match abandoned. This new system was first tried in an ODI between Zimbabwe and England in January 1997 and was formally adopted by the ICC two years later. Though fairer than its predecessors, D/L, as it became known (later adjusted to DLS to reflect the contribution of a third collaborator, Steven Stern), was not without its own difficulties. In the 2003 World Cup final, when Australia posted 359/2 and India were on 145/3 in 23 overs when rain stopped play, D/L showed them as being only 12 runs behind the par score, which was obviously unrealistic. The following October, therefore, the ICC adopted a revised version of the system, which gave a fairer calculation of the target when the side batting first set an unusually high score. Reservations about the system persisted, but most believed it was better than anything else on offer.

Controversy also surrounded another use of technology, the assessment of bowlers' actions to determine whether their action was legal. Having been called by umpire Darrell Hair seven times in three overs on the first day of the 1995/96 Boxing Day Test in Melbourne and again by Ross Emerson during an ODI ten days later, Sri Lankan spin bowler Muttiah Muralitharan was examined through biomechanical analysis at the Hong Kong University of Science and Technology by Prof. Ravindra Goonetilleke, who declared his action legal. The problem, Goonetilleke argued, was that a congenital defect in Muralitharan's arm prevented him from fully straightening it, creating an 'optical illusion of throwing'. When Emerson nevertheless called him again during Sri Lanka's 1998/99 Australian tour, Muralitharan was referred to Dr Bruce Elliott at the University of Western Australia and to another laboratory at Loughborough University in England, and again cleared. Doubts nevertheless persisted, and in March 2004 match referee Chris Broad reported the bowler with respect to his doosra, a delivery which spun to leg rather than to the off, which he was believed to have recently added to his repertoire. The Sri Lankans rallied to Muralitharan's defence, former captain Arjuna Ranatunga even claiming the charge was racially motivated, but the Sri Lankan board again sent the spinner to Elliott in Perth. With the Sri Lankans doubling down on their criticisms of Broad, the ICC decided to replace him as match referee for Sri Lanka's forthcoming tour of Zimbabwe.

ICC general manager David Richardson had recently announced that research had been commissioned into the whole question of spinners' bowling actions, reviewing the 2000 ruling that spinners should be allowed up to a 5° straightening of the arm during their delivery, with medium pacers allowed 7.5° and pace bowlers 10°. This was, of course, unenforceable in match conditions, and there was increasing evidence that many bowlers exceeded these levels. Elliott ruled that Muralitharan's doosra exceeded the 5° limit but recommended that he should be allowed to bowl pending the outcome of the ICC's research, and there were those who insisted that *any* biometrical analysis took so little account of innate human differences as to be effectively useless. Nevertheless, the ICC ruled that the current levels must apply and warned that Muralitharan would risk suspension if he bowled his doosra in present circumstances. In November 2004 the ICC-commissioned research suggested a 15° limit for all categories of bowlers, arguing that this was the point at which the flexion became visible to the naked eye, and this recommendation was adopted by the board with effect from 1 March 2005. Since then, the actions of numerous bowlers have been reported and assessed, and some have been suspended permanently or quietly disappeared from the game. But there has been no further instance of an international bowler being called for throwing.

The Muralitharan storm was, however, soon followed by another, this time involving the Indian off-spinner Harbhajan Singh. His doosra was reported by Chris Broad and the umpires in December 2004, following the second Test between Bangladesh and India in Chittagong, and a further report was made three months later during the ODI series against Pakistan. Harbhajan himself was insistent that his action was fair, but the ICC referred the case to Marc Portus of the Australian Institute of Sport, a leader in biomechanical analysis, who reported that he was unable to reach a definitive conclusion on Harbhajan's action during the Pakistan match and therefore recommended that the spinner be cleared to bowl. This was immediately confirmed by the ICC.

The problem of suspect actions, especially among spinners, however, remained, and in June 2014 the ICC board decided that a crackdown was necessary. Unfortunately, there had just been a falling out with the UWA Sports Biomechanics Group, which had been the ICC's sole partner in assessing bowling actions for the past four years. Disapproving of some key technical aspects of the ICC code, the group had withdrawn its services in March, and at the same time that it was encouraging umpires to be more proactive in reporting bowlers, the ICC was recognising new testing centres in Brisbane, Chennai, Cardiff, Loughborough and Pretoria. Nearly a dozen international bowlers were reported and suspended over the next few months; some, like Pakistan's Mohammad Hafeez and Malcolm Waller of Zimbabwe, were found to be throwing and banned, while others, such as Saeed Ajmal of Pakistan and Sunil Narine of the West Indies were allowed to resume bowling after undergoing remedial training. There was criticism that nine months out from a World Cup was not the ideal moment to institute such a campaign, but many players welcomed it and Richardson cogently asked whether it would have been better to allow illegal bowling to go unchecked until after the tournament.

While technology was supposed to help ensure that obvious errors by the on-field umpires were largely eliminated, the fact that this was not yet universal was painfully illustrated by a below-the-radar triangular ODI tournament in the Netherlands in August 2004. The Dutch hosted Pakistan, India and Australia, and after beating India in the opening match and having their round-robin game against the Australians rained off without a ball being bowled, Pakistan faced Australia in the final. Australia made 192/7, but Pakistan's reply was stymied by two dismissals, both controversially given out caught behind by umpire David Shepherd, and they were all out for 175. There was considerable unhappiness about Shepherd's umpiring, and when Pakistan's chief selector, Wasim Bari, called for him to retire, describing those decisions as 'like target killing',

Malcolm Speed wrote Bari an admonitory letter, calling his remarks 'inflammatory' and 'out of order'. This letter was duly leaked, and when another, from the ICC corporate affairs manager Brendan McClements, also found its way into the public domain, there were suggestions that the ICC was conspiring to humiliate the Pakistani chairman of selectors. The ICC's embarrassment was complete when it became clear that the code of conduct covered team officials, managers and players but not selectors, and that there was therefore no disciplinary action which could be taken. This was a loophole which Speed quickly moved to close.

A much more serious crisis struck the ICC on 20 August 2006, when on the fourth day of the fourth Test at the Oval between England and Pakistan the on-field umpires, Darrell Hair (Australia) and Billy Doctrove (West Indies), concluded that the Pakistanis had been illegally tampering with the ball. Shortly after lunch, with England on 230/3 in their second innings and still 101 behind Pakistan's first innings total of 504, the umpires awarded five penalty runs to England and offered them an alternative ball. Play continued until tea, when England had reached 298/4, but after the interval the Pakistanis did not return to the field. Hair, Doctrove and the not-out English pair came out twice, briefly returning to the pavilion in between, but there was still no sign of Inzamam-ul-Haq and his team. After intense discussions between Mike Procter, the match referee, ECB chief executive David Morgan and Shaharyar Khan, his Pakistani opposite number, Pakistan did take the field shortly before 4.30pm, but the umpires now ruled that following their earlier refusal to play the match had been awarded to England. Khan subsequently complained to the press that the umpires had taken the original ball-tampering decision unilaterally, suggesting that he did not fully understand the power of the match officials, and blamed Hair and Doctrove for not being willing to continue when his team had completed their protest.

A joint statement issued by the ICC and the two boards the following day confirmed that Pakistan had forfeited the match, and that Procter was now reviewing the alleged ball tampering. Pakistan coach Bob Woolmer and manager Zaheer Abbas were adamant that there had been no improper interference with the ball, and that any reverse swing which Umar Gul and the other bowlers might have been achieving had come through legitimate means. Any damage to the ball had come from the fact that England batter Kevin Pietersen had repeatedly hit it into the stands. The Pakistanis were soon demanding that Hair should not be appointed to umpire them again, but Malcolm Speed insisted that no one had a veto over who stood in any match. On 25 August, five days after the original incident, it emerged that Hair had since sent an e-mail to the Elite Panel manager, Doug Cowie, offering to resign in return for a confidential payment of $500,000. He had, he claimed when the e-mail became public, been in negotiations with Cowie, who had asked him to make a written offer; the ICC denied that any such invitation had been made.

The experienced match referee Ranjan Madugalle was appointed to deal with the charges of ball tampering and bringing the game into disrepute against Inzamam, but the hearing was delayed until 28 September because of illness in his family. At the hearing all four umpires, match referee Procter and Cowie all testified that they believed the state of the ball was consistent with ball tampering, but Geoffrey Boycott and television analyst and former county cricketer Simon Hughes disagreed. Madugalle acquitted Inzamam of the ball-tampering charge but suspended him for four ODIs for bringing the game into disrepute. The Pakistani board continued to complain about Hair, and when the ICC board met on 4 November it decided by a 7-3 majority to ban him from standing in international cricket; it was reported that the charge had been led by the four Asian Test countries, and that Hair had been supported by England,

Australia and New Zealand. It was thus evident that the old divisions within cricket were alive and well. The following February, Hair announced that he was going to sue the ICC for racial discrimination, since no action had been taken against his West Indian fellow umpire, to which the PCB chairman Naseem Ashraf claimed that Hair had been 'removed from the ICC panel of umpires because of his bad umpiring and his poor judgement'; this despite the fact that, immediately before the Oval Test, Hair had been ranked the second-best umpire in the world after his fellow Australian Simon Taufel. Hair dropped his discrimination case on 9 October 2007, and after being restored to the Elite Panel on 12 March 2008 he stood in two Tests between England and New Zealand before finally resigning to take up a coaching role.

Although the Laws of cricket declare absolutely unambiguously that once the umpires have finalised the result of a match it cannot be changed, the ICC board decided in July 2008, under sustained pressure from Pakistan, to alter the result of the Oval Test from an England win to 'match abandoned', converting it into a draw. This naturally upset MCC, the custodian of the Laws, and when the board met again in February 2009 they put forward a legal opinion to the effect that the change of result contravened those Laws. After a long discussion the board finally accepted that for the integrity of the game – and, one might add, of the ICC – the original result must stand. It would be fair to say that no one came out of this unpleasant incident well: there had been persistent rumours about the way in which Pakistan's bowlers obtained reverse swing, which the Pakistanis claimed were racially motivated; Hair and his colleagues were unable to produce conclusive evidence to substantiate the specific charge, despite the presence of a dozen television cameras at the ground; Hair's reputation was damaged both by the incident itself and his e-mail demanding $500k; and the ICC's double reversal over the result showed it to be inconsistent and, not for the first or last time, susceptible to political pressure.

It was not only at the highest level that the Council's decision-making authority could be sorely tested. On 26 February 2010 Nepal were playing the USA in a World Cricket League Division Five match at the Tribhuvan University ground in Kathmandu. It was the final round of the league phase, and these two countries were vying with Singapore for the two promotion spots into Division Four. The outcome was likely to come down to net run rate, and with the USA heading for a comfortable victory the news came through to a crowded University ground that at nearby Bhaktapur Singapore had beaten Jersey by seven wickets, taking just 26 overs to chase down their target of 193. That meant that if the Americans, currently on 150/5 in 32 overs and needing only another 13 for victory, completed their win, they and Singapore would go up on NRR and Nepal would miss out on promotion. This realisation was the cue for bricks and other missiles to start raining on to the outfield from the partisan crowd of more than 12,000, and the umpires were forced to take the players from the field. After a delay of three-quarters of an hour, riot police cleared the ground and the match was able to resume. But four overs were deducted because of the interruption, and the Duckworth-Lewis adjustment actually raised Nepal's NRR above Singapore's regardless of the result. The USA completed the win in just nine more deliveries and topped the league table, but Nepal edged Singapore out by 0.004 of a run.

Singapore were understandably aggrieved, and the ICC announced that a three-man committee, comprising head of the legal department David Becker, general manager of cricket David Richardson, and the general manager of the ACU, Ravi Samani, would investigate whether the Event Technical Committee had dealt with the issue appropriately together with all other aspects of the match. ICC chief executive Haroon Lorgat declared the incident unacceptable, adding that 'we can be thankful that nobody was hurt through the irresponsible actions of spectators'. The investigating group's report came to the board in April, but it was then referred to the development committee on the grounds that since the match in question was part of the World Cricket League, that committee should have an opportunity to comment before the board took a decision. It was not explained why the development committee had not considered the matter before the board meeting. But that delay ensured that Nepal would be able to take part in the Division Four tournament in Italy in August, perpetuating the injustice to Singapore. The report was published in May and concluded that there was 'no evidence to support the claims of SCA' that the outcome should be changed. It did, however, recommend that new mandatory safety standards might include sanctions against a home board should its team benefit from crowd interruptions. The horse had, of course, well and truly bolted before that stable door could be closed, and while Lorgat acknowledged that there had been some thought of promoting Singapore along with the USA and Nepal, 'such temptation would create a dangerous precedent to the integrity of competition and the playing regulations'. It was, perhaps, some consolation to Singapore that they were allowed to host that year's ICC Annual Conference.

The scope and the limitations of the ICC's disciplinary systems were exposed at the end of March 2018, when television coverage of the third Test between South Africa and Australia in Cape Town revealed the tourists' Cameron Bancroft apparently using a small yellow object to change the state of the match ball. When the images were seen on the screens at the ground, coach Darren Lehmann sent substitute Peter Handscomb out to speak to Bancroft, who then put the yellow object down his trousers. The umpires now spoke to Bancroft, and he confirmed after the day's play that he had been charged with attempting to change the condition of the ball. He had, he said, been using 'some tape' and granules from the rough patches on the pitch to change the condition of the ball in the quest for more reverse swing. An emotional captain Steve Smith admitted that the team's 'leadership group' had decided on the illegal move to try to save the series but denied that the coaching staff had been involved. Things now moved quickly. Cricket Australia CEO James Sutherland described it as 'a very sad day for Australian cricket', while Prime Minister Malcolm Turnbull called for Smith to be replaced as captain. Within hours Smith was stood down, and in response to a charge laid by ICC chief executive Dave Richardson he was fined 100% of his match fee and given a one-match suspension, the maximum penalty for the offence. Bancroft, the most junior member of the side who had been given the job of committing it, was fined 75% of his match fee and given three demerit points. Both players continued on the field for the rest of the Test, which Australia lost by 322 runs after being bowled out for 107 in their second innings.

The fall-out from what quickly became known as 'Sandpapergate' continued to dominate the headlines. Cricket Australia had acknowledged that Bancroft's claim to have used adhesive tape was a lie, and that it was actually sandpaper which he had employed in his effort to alter the ball's condition. Sutherland soon announced that Smith and David Warner, identified as the architect of the plan, were suspended from playing international and domestic cricket for 12 months, with Warner banned from captaincy for life and Smith banned for 12 months beyond the period of his playing ban. Bancroft received a nine-month suspension, with a captaincy ban for another 12 months. Wicketkeeper Tim Paine took over the captaincy for the final Test, which South Africa won by an even more thumping 492 runs. Although there had been no suggestion of his complicity in the episode, coach Darren Lehmann, amid a chorus of adverse comment on the Australian 'team culture', announced five days after the story broke that he was stepping down.

Coincidentally, it was at this moment that the ICC announced a full-scale review of its code of conduct. By contrast with its anti-corruption measures, where suspensions for several years and even life bans were accepted weapons, the penalties for disciplinary offences during a match were relatively light. The difference between the treatment of Smith and Bancroft by the match referee (and the fact that Warner was not disciplined by him at all) and the bans handed out by Cricket Australia pointed up these discrepancies, although it should be noted that the latter's charges were for bringing the game into disrepute rather than for the narrower offence of ball tampering. Former players like David Lloyd and Martin Crowe had been calling for umpires to be given the power to suspend players during a match, or even to throw them out altogether, but as the ICC review began, CEO Richardson was unconvinced. 'I can imagine,' he told *Cricinfo*, 'the arguments that will happen if a key bowler or a key batsman is sent off the field for disciplinary reasons. Cricket in a funny way is an individual sport. If your key batsman is sent off incorrectly, and it turns out the umpire misheard him, or if a key bowler is sent off when he wasn't actually tampering with the ball, in the end it could affect the game. I can imagine there would be even more controversy.'

Penalty runs had, of course, been in the Laws since the 18th century, and their scope had been greatly increased in the 2000 revision. The integration of the ICC Code of Conduct into Law 42 had expanded these measures further, but it was arguable that penalty runs and the other punishments available were inadequate in the case of really serious infractions. Despite Richardson's reservations, therefore, the 2017 revision gave umpires the power to suspend a player for more serious violations of the code, either temporarily or, for the most serious offences, for the rest of the match. This new power has yet to be used at the highest level, but its mere existence may be enough to concentrate players' minds.

The establishment of the International Panel of Umpires in 1994, followed in 2002 by Elite Panels of both umpires and referees, was a key element in the expansion of the ICC's role, while the incorporation of technology into decision-making, once so controversial, has tended to confirm the generally high levels achieved by the game's leading officials. In a sport so dominated by power politics and unenlightened self-interest these are notable achievements, and although there will doubtless continue to be occasional crises when tough decisions are made and challenged, this is one area in which the ICC can be seen to be administering the game for the benefit of all.

Chapter 15

Cricket's Dirty Secret: Match Fixing and Corruption

THE MATCH-FIXING scandal which broke in 1998, and which reverberated through cricket for many years afterwards, had been a long time in the making. As in other sports, there had been occasional rumours, but in February 1995 the issue had suddenly become big news. The Australian players Shane Warne and Tim May had reported to the Australian board two approaches they alleged had been made to them by Pakistan captain Salim Malik during the Australian tour of Pakistan the previous October, asking them to bowl badly in the closing stages of the first Test in Karachi and in an ODI in Rawalpindi. When the story broke into the open that February, ICC chief executive David Richards described the allegations as 'very serious', and promised a thorough investigation. Other claims quickly began to accumulate: the Pakistanis were accused of throwing their Tests against South Africa in Johannesburg, which they had lost by 324 runs in January, and against Zimbabwe in Harare, the home side's first-ever Test victory, where the margin was an innings and 64 runs. The Pakistan players were driven to declare publicly that they had taken an oath on the Koran before embarking on that 1994/95 tour not to accept bribes to throw matches. And the former Australian

Test player Dean Jones revealed that in 1992 he had been offered $66,000 to provide inside information to an Indian bookmaker during his side's tour of Sri Lanka. Clearly, the corner of wallpaper which the Warne–May allegations had lifted was potentially concealing a very large area of dry rot in the world game.

Within days, the former Pakistani fast bowler Sarfraz Nawaz, now an adviser to Prime Minister Benazir Bhutto, claimed that an ODI between England and Pakistan in Nottingham in 1992 had been rigged, that there had been match fixing in several other games involving Pakistan, and that the Pakistani secret service had been investigating a 'multi-million rupee betting triangle between Sharjah in the UAE, Bombay and Karachi'. Vice-captain Rashid Latif and batter Basit Ali pulled out of the Zimbabwe tour, citing 'differences' with other members of the squad, and soon afterwards Malik was relieved of the captaincy. Although there were predictable reactions in Pakistan that it was all a colonialist plot, triggered by an inability in Australia and England to accept that former colonies like Pakistan could produce a winning team, and even that the allegations had been trumped up to prevent the country from hosting the World Cup, there were voices willing to admit that there was a problem. Imran Khan warned against any attempt to cover up corruption in Pakistani cricket and even Khalid Mahmood, while dismissing the allegations as 'totally ridiculous', observed that the problem of gambling in cricket could not be separated from the growing commercialisation of the game, which he blamed on the influence of Kerry Packer's circus. The ICC responded by adding a clause prohibiting betting to the code of conduct for players and officials.

The Pakistani board asked retired justice and former attorney-general Fakhruddin Ebrahim to investigate the charges against Malik, and in October 1995 he dismissed the allegations as 'concoctions', stating that the sworn statements made by Warne, May and Mark Waugh could not be believed. He made much of the fact that the ACB had declined to send the three players to Pakistan to give evidence in person to the inquiry. Malik, meanwhile, had been omitted from the side to play Sri Lanka on grounds of 'indiscipline and selfish play', but following Ebrahim's findings he was selected for the party to tour Australia at the end of the year. Bizarrely, the ICC seems never to have taken the matter up, despite David Richards's initial promise of an investigation. As the Pakistanis arrived in Australia Bob Simpson, now coaching the home side, remarked on this omission, suggesting that 'the fairest way would have been for the ICC to have had a hearing in a neutral venue'. But in the end neither the ICC nor either of the authorities directly involved had much interest in pursuing the matter further.

Despite their outraged public statements about the Malik allegations, however, the ACB had a clear interest in playing the issue down. More than three years later it transpired that during a one-day tournament in Sri Lanka in September 1994, shortly before the side's visit to Pakistan, Warne and Waugh had accepted cash payments from an Indian bookmaker identified only as 'John' in exchange for inside information about the team. Initially accepting what appeared to be gifts without strings, the pair had subsequently given information to 'John' about the weather and the condition of the pitch during the 1994/95 England series. The ACB had learned of these contacts soon afterwards and had fined both players, but Graham Halbish, the chief executive, and chairman Alan Crompton subsequently claimed that it was the protection of the sport's good name and the privacy of the players which had led them to sweep the matter under the carpet. Richards and Sir Clyde Walcott were informed by the ACB during a visit to Sydney but were told in strict confidence, and they did not pass this incriminating evidence on to the Pakistanis or to anyone else. The extent of the infiltration of cricket by corrupting influences was to remain the game's dirty little secret.

The murmurings, however, continued, and on 10 September 1998 a three-member PCB committee, chaired by Justice Chaudhry Ejaz Yousuf, found Wasim Akram, Salim Malik and Ijaz Ahmad guilty of fixing three matches in 1994 and recommended further investigation of five other players. The matches in question were an ODI in Christchurch, in which Pakistan had laboured their way to 145/9 in 50 overs and lost by seven wickets, a Sharjah Cup match against India, and the Singer Cup game against Australia in September, in which they had managed 151/9 as they chased their opponents' 179/7. The evidence provided by the inquiry was devastating: Aamer Sohail, for example, had testified that in the Sharjah Cup match he had been offered $120,000 to score less than ten and to run out his opening partner Saeed Anwar. The media reaction was understandably savage, but Richards and other ICC officials declined to comment, while Malcolm Speed, at this point ACB chief executive, who might have been expected to welcome the vindication of the Australian players' allegations, said merely that it was 'an internal matter for the Pakistan Cricket Board'. Even now there was no clear recognition that the integrity of cricket was deeply compromised, although to its credit the Pakistani board did immediately institute a new inquiry under Justice Malik Mohammad Qayyum to investigate further the extent of corruption in the game in their country.

There was no chance that the problem would go away, or that a line could be drawn under the Yousuf findings. It was not as if the problem was in any way new. In March 1996 the former Pakistan Test player Qasim Omar had claimed in an interview on Australian television that back in the 1980s he had been paid by bookmakers to throw his wicket away in a Test in Melbourne, and that he had allowed himself to be bowled by Geoff Lawson. Ten years before these new revelations, in 1986, Qasim had alleged that under Imran Khan there was a culture of drug-taking and sleeping with prostitutes in the Pakistani team, specifically citing the 1984/85 tour to Australia, and for his pains he had received a seven-year ban from the PCB for 'making unsubstantiated claims against the team'. Now a member of the Islamic evangelical organisation, the Tableeghi Jamat, he went much further, claiming that he had acted as an agent for bookmakers, and that four or five team-mates had taken money from him for under-performing.

As early as February 1997 the Indian team manager Sunil Dev had reported to his board his suspicions that some members of the side which had just toured South Africa had been engaged in betting, but no action was taken. Later that year there were public allegations about the subsequent Indian tour to the West Indies, and now the BCCI referred the issue of betting and match fixing to a former Chief Justice, Y.V. Chandrachud, who reported in November that while there was no doubt that there was a great deal of betting on cricket in India, he had been unable to find any evidence that players, officials or journalists had ever been involved in any illicit activity. The BCCI decided not to publish the report, and the ICC continued to leave the whole topic to its member boards to deal with.

But the new revelations at the end of 1998, fuelled by the Qayyum inquiry and including the fact that the ACB and the ICC had covered up the fines meted out to Waugh and Warne in 1995, meant that the problem could no longer be ignored. Gloomily but prophetically, Matthew Engel declared in the 1999 *Wisden* that removing rotten apples was insufficient: 'The poison is in the barrel itself,' he observed, 'and it is likely to seep out again and again in the years ahead.' By the time the ICC finally, in May 2000, held an emergency meeting to discuss the cancer of betting and match fixing, the situation had escalated out of control. On 7 April the police in Delhi had charged the South African captain Hansie Cronje and his team-mates Herschelle Gibbs,

Pieter Strydom and Nicky Boje with match fixing during the recent ODI series against India. Leaked transcripts of what were claimed to be telephone conversations between Cronje and the bookmaker Sanjay Chawla had been published, and although Cronje began in the customary way by denying everything, Ali Bacher describing him as 'a man of enormous integrity and honesty', he soon admitted that he had not been 'entirely honest' in his response. He had, he acknowledged, accepted $10,000–15,000 from bookmakers for weather and pitch information during the triangular series with England and Zimbabwe, but he continued to deny that he had ever been involved in match fixing. He was relieved of the South African captaincy, but it quickly became evident that those admissions were just the tip of an iceberg: Cronje had indeed been guilty over a long period of fixing international matches, and he had used his position as captain to involve team-mates in the corruption.

The ICC emergency meeting at last demonstrated that the world governing body had recognised the need for decisive action. It agreed to establish an authority to investigate and deal with allegations of corruption and to require all international players and officials to declare whether they had been approached to act in a corrupt manner, and it significantly increased the penalties for match fixing, betting and related offences. The Pakistani board also undertook to publish the findings of the Qayyum inquiry, which had reported to the government in October 1999 but the findings of which had not yet been revealed. Two days after the meeting in London, the South African board announced that Justice Edwin King would lead an inquiry into match fixing and corruption in that country.

When Justice King reported in December 2000, he recommended greater supervision of players and raised the possibility of the United Board actually controlling betting on cricket, perhaps through a system of licensed bookmakers. The ICC, meanwhile, had appointed Sir Paul Condon, the recently retired commissioner of London's Metropolitan Police, to head its new Anti-Corruption Unit (ACU), and by April 2001 he had compiled a 70-page report into the whole match-fixing question. This report was published at the beginning of May, following its consideration by the ICC cricket committee, and it concluded that while the most blatant excesses had ceased, there was still 'a small core of players and others who continue to manipulate the results of matches or occurrences within matches for betting purposes'. Condon regretted that his investigations had been impeded by what he called 'a conspiracy of silence'. He was, however, able to establish that match fixing had surfaced in England in the 1970s and had become widespread towards the end of that decade and into the 1980s. He blamed both the more extensive coverage of cricket on television and the relatively low payments which cricketers still received for this growth in corruption and recommended that there should be a comprehensive training and awareness programme for players and officials. Access by bookmakers to players needed to be controlled, and players' use of mobile phones should be restricted. Condon also urged that particular attention should be paid to ODIs played in venues like Sharjah, Canada and Singapore. But he was also critical of the functioning of the ICC itself. 'If the ICC continues as a loose and fragile alliance,' he wrote, 'it is unlikely to succeed as a governing body. It must become a modern, regulatory body with the power to lead and direct international cricket.'

Looking back at the situation as it was in 2001, Speed reflected that '[w]e knew as cricket administrators we could not control the activities of corrupt bookmakers and gamblers', especially those in India and Pakistan. 'Betting on cricket,' he wrote in his memoir, 'is a massive industry in these countries. It is illegal. It is underground. It is not Betfair, William Hill and Tabcorp. It is run from offices and shops in remote parts of the sprawling subcontinent cities. It is illegal in that bookmakers can be arrested and charged with offences. If a shop is closed down, it will start up again in another nearby location. On the other hand, because it is illegal, it is unregulated. Bookmakers do not have to apply for licences and agree to conditions of holding those licences as they do in England, New Zealand and Australia.'

Not everyone was impressed by Condon's initial work. Dalmiya described it as 'merely cosmetic' and complained that it 'does not really throw much light on the issue'. The BCCI, meanwhile, was dealing with problems of its own. Several players, including the former captain Mohammed Azharuddin, had been implicated in the Cronje case, and in July 2000 his house, along with those of Ajay Jadeja, Nayan Mongia and Nikhil Chopra and the coach Kapil Dev, had been raided by the Central Bureau of Investigation. The CBI then claimed that Azharuddin had admitted fixing three matches between 1996 and 1999, although he continued to deny these charges. In December 2000 the BCCI suspended Azharuddin and Ajay Sharma for life and Jadeja for five years, while Manoj Prabhakar and physio Ali Irani were banned from holding any post in Indian cricket for five years. Mongia and Kapil Dev were acquitted. Indian courts subsequently overturned the bans on Jadeja and Azharuddin, in January 2003 and November 2012 respectively.

Despite the attempts by some to discredit Condon's findings, the ACU quickly became an established part of the ICC's structure. Condon himself, once described by journalist Osman Samiuddin as 'the Elliot Ness of international cricket', remained in charge until 2010, when he was succeeded by Ronnie Flanagan, another former London policeman. Some insight into the way his unit worked emerged in February 2004, with the leaking of an exchange of letters between Condon and the PCB regarding allegations that the Pakistan side had 'deliberately underperformed' during ODI tournaments in Morocco and Kenya in 2002. The letters themselves were over a year old, but they showed that even though Condon was able to name the alleged fixer, there was at that point insufficient evidence to allow action to be taken. The leak itself led nowhere, the PCB's new chairman, Shaharyar Khan, pointing out that there had been no conclusive proof and that the matter was therefore closed. The episode illustrated both that the ACU was operating to high standards of proof and that the complete eradication of corruption in cricket was going to be very, very difficult. By June 2004 Naruddin Khawaja, the ACU's regional security manager in Asia, was able to claim that, while bookmaking remained part of cricket, players were 'to a big extent' being kept away from 'corrupt elements seeking to soil the sport to make easy money'. The message was that the price of a clean sport was eternal vigilance.

Nevertheless, the suspicion of illicit contacts between players and bookmakers continued. On the eve of an ODI between India and the West Indies in Nagpur in January 2007, Indian police recorded four telephone conversations between the West Indian all-rounder Marlon Samuels and a bookie named Mukesh Kochchar. The ACU promptly despatched a four-man team to Nagpur to investigate further, with Samuels claiming that he had known Kochchar for six years and had no idea he was a bookmaker, while Kochchar insisted that the player was 'like a son' to him. Samuels was allowed to play in that year's World Cup, but in May the West Indies board's disciplinary committee found him guilty of 'receiving money, or benefit or other reward that could bring him or the game of cricket into disrepute', and the ICC suspended him for two years. Samuels continued to protest his innocence.

On 14 May 2010 two Essex players, Mervyn Westfield and Pakistan international Danish Kaneria, were arrested in connection with alleged spot-fixing during an ECB Pro40 match against Durham in September 2009. Kaneria was never charged, but in January 2012 Westfield pleaded guilty to having taken £6,000 to allow 12 runs to be scored off his first over in the Durham game. He was sentenced to four months in jail, and after losing an appeal served two. The ECB subsequently banned Westfield for five years and Kaneria for life on the grounds that he had been instrumental in corrupting his team-mate; the Pakistan player lodged an appeal, and after this had been dismissed by an independent ECB panel, took the matter to the High Court, where in May 2014 he again lost. The outcome was that he was banned for life from official cricket worldwide.

Welcoming the original conviction of Westfield, ICC CEO Haroon Lorgat had been keen to stress that the ICC 'was not directly involved' in the case, but a much larger issue was brewing which *would* extend all the way into the boardroom. The truth was that the bookmakers and their agents had merely become smarter in their tactics. In August 2010 the English tabloid *News of the World* published an exposé claiming that undercover reporters had videotaped the bookmaker Mazhar Majeed taking money in exchange for information about the specific moments in the fourth Test at Lord's at which the Pakistani newball pair Mohammad Amir and Mohammad Asif would bowl no-balls. The two bowlers subsequently delivered no-balls as agreed, and the paper went ahead with publishing its story. The players, including captain Salman Butt, all declared their innocence, and they were supported by Pakistan board chairman Ijaz Butt. The ICC had clearly learned from their past mistakes, and now acted with considerable decisiveness: the three players were suspended pending further investigation. They appealed, and a hearing in October rejected the appeals by Butt and Amir, Asif having withdrawn his on the grounds that he needed to understand the charges against him. Since the players continued to protest their innocence a tribunal was held in January 2011, the panel comprising Michael Beloff QC, Albie Sachs and Sharad Rao; the following month the ICC banned Butt for ten years (five of which were suspended), Asif for seven (with two suspended) and Amir for five. The consequences of the case were not confined to the ICC's disciplinary system. The Metropolitan Police also took the matter up, and on 1 November 2011 Majeed and Amir, who had pleaded guilty, Asif and Butt were all convicted of conspiracy to cheat at gambling and conspiracy to accept corrupt payments. Two days later, Butt was sentenced to two-and-a-half years' imprisonment, Asif to one year, Amir to six months, and Majeed to two years eight months.

Writing in 2013, the former PCB chairman Shaharyar Khan and the anthropologist Ali Khan praised the ICC tribunal's 'manifestly judicious and fair' report. Its analysis of the evidence against Majeed and the players was 'meticulous and compelling, leaving no doubt that the Tribunal's conclusions have been honest and every consideration that could have aggravated or mitigated the players' guilt has been carefully examined'. The players, the tribunal had found, 'did nothing to stamp out a blight that threatens to take the lustre out of the very game that has given them a generous income and extraordinary status'. The two Khans believed, however, that '[m]uch more has to be done to clean the swamp', adding that while the fixing of match results had perhaps been stamped out, spot-fixing remained a serious threat to the game. They went on to analyse in detail the combination of factors which led to Pakistan languishing 'at the bottom of the ladder in the corruption syndrome': poor education, some players' rapid elevation from extreme poverty to relative luxury, a lack of leadership, and a pervasive culture of corruption which afflicts not just cricket but the whole of Pakistani society.

Another example soon followed. The Pakistani wicketkeeper, Zulqarnain Haider, suddenly disappeared from the squad hotel in Dubai immediately after an ODI against South Africa on 5 November 2010, subsequently turning up in London. There he announced his retirement from cricket, citing threats to himself and his family that he had received from unnamed persons, who were pressing him to co-operate with them. Amidst suggestions that he might seek asylum in the UK he was interviewed by the ACU, but a PCB investigation concluded that it could find 'no clear reason' behind his decision to leave the team and fly to London. In April 2011 he was assured by the Pakistan government that his safety would be guaranteed, and after some hesitation he duly returned. Three days later, police in Sialkot arrested eight bookies who they said had been behind the threats to Haider. The PCB then set up another committee to look into the keeper's reply to a request they had made that he explain his flight, eventually fining him 500,000 rupees (about US$8,500) and putting him on probation for the national team for a year. He was back playing first-class cricket in the Qaid-i-Azam Trophy in October, but he was never selected for Pakistan again, retiring at the end of the 2014/15 season.

As if to prove that nothing in cricket was beyond the reach of the BCCI, it was announced in May 2014 that the ACU would be reviewed by a group comprising CEO Richardson and representatives of the gang of three; part of the thinking, it seemed, was that the unit should in future report to the chair of the executive committee rather than to the CEO. FICA immediately reacted, emphasising the importance of the ACU's independence and pointing out that not only players but also administrators could be subject to anti-corruption investigations. In view of the current situation affecting the IPL and the BCCI, where there were serious allegations of corruption, this was far from being an idle observation. The ICC moved as well to ease the treatment of suspended players, allowing them to return to domestic cricket before the end of their suspension, so that they would be able to resume their international careers as soon as they had served out their term.

Big names continued to be caught. Former Bangladesh captain Mohammad Ashraful was one of nine players charged with spot-fixing in the 2013 Bangladesh Premier League and was banned for eight years, reduced on appeal to five years, two of them suspended. In fact he was allowed to return to domestic cricket in 2016, and to international cricket two years later, although he did not play for his country after 2011. New Zealander Lou Vincent and Sri Lanka's Kaushal Lokuarachchi admitted having failed to report corrupt approaches, but the tribunal acquitted the remaining six, triggering an appeal by the ICC and BCB. The BCB was not the only governing body to act more consistently against offenders. In September 2013, for example, Shanta Sreesanth was banned for life by the BCCI for offences during the 2013 IPL; Thami Tsolekile and three others were suspended for 12 years by CSA on charges arising from the 2015 Ram Slam; and in March 2017 Mohammad Irfan received a one-year suspension from the PCB for failing to report a corrupt approach. In April 2018 former Zimbabwe captain, Heath Streak, was suspended for eight years for facilitating corruption and passing information regarding matches in series involving his country, in the IPL and Afghanistan Premier League.

Spot-fixing in particular was a problem which would not go away. In 2018 the Qatar-based TV channel *Al Jazeera* ran two documentaries alleging that slow over rates in two Tests, one between India and England at Chennai in December 2016 and the other between India and Australia in March 2017, were attributable to fixing organised, and subsequently revealed, by a match-fixer named Aneel Munawar, a man with connections to crime syndicates in India, and that further interviews with him revealed that 15 international matches – six Tests, six ODIs and three World T20 Cup games – played in 2011 and 2012 had been the subject of spot- or (rather longer) 'session'-fixing. Seven of those matches involved English players, five Australians and three Pakistanis. Munawar claimed that he had been involved in match fixing for six or seven years, and that the ICC had known about his activities since 2010. These allegations were dynamite, and there were prompt denials from the countries supposedly involved. But leaked telephone recordings and interviews with police investigators appeared to confirm much of the detail, although *Al Jazeera* was careful not to name players who might be the subject of future criminal prosecutions. Veteran journalist Scyld Berry appeared in the second programme to be persuaded by the accuracy of the claims of fixing. More disturbingly still, it harked back to a match between England and Pakistan at The Oval in September 2010, where a session fix identified in advance by the *Sun* newspaper had played out exactly as predicted in front of an ACU investigator, but where the ICC had dismissed the allegations as unsubstantiated. Munawar's name was known to the ACU from this point, *Al Jazeera* claimed, and yet it appeared to be taken aback by the claims in the first of its reports. After a three-year investigation, however, the ICC's ACU found that the claims about the Chennai and Ranchi Tests were unsubstantiated and improbable, although their report made no mention of the matches identified in the channel's second report. So was Munawar a fantasist and/or was *Al Jazeera* the victim of an elaborate hoax? The channel stood by their report, branding the ICC investigation a 'whitewash'. There was, it stated, a clear conflict of interest in an organisation investigating allegations of corruption in a sport for which it was itself responsible.

Increasingly, too, the poison spread beyond the full members, to teams and competitions which had a lower profile and were therefore more likely to escape notice. The second *Al Jazeera* report drew attention to the increasing significance of Dubai as a centre for the illegal Indian betting industry and the match fixing it spawns, and on 16 October 2019 the ICC suspended the UAE captain Mohammed Naveed, Shaiman Anwar and Qadeer Ahmed Khan, who were accused of plotting to fix matches in the T20 World Cup qualifier at the behest of an Ajman-based bookmaker named Mehardeep Chhayakar; five days later the Emirati board suspended another player, Ashfaq Ahmed, who was also alleged to be implicated in the plot. The following day, as the UAE were losing to Jersey, the wicketkeeper Ghulam Shabber flew to Pakistan, subsequently announcing that he had 'left cricket behind'. On 13 September 2020 Ashfaq and yet another player, Amir Hayat, were formally charged with corruption by the ICC and suspended indefinitely. Naveed and Shaiman were found guilty of two charges on 26 January 2022 and banned from all cricket on 16 March 2021, although Naveed then took his appeal to the Court of Arbitration for Sport. A month later Qadeer received a five-year ban, after acknowledging that although he had never taken any money or bowled an illegal delivery, 'I was wrong on different occasions'. Eight-year bans were handed out to Ashfaq and Hayat in March 2021.

Lesser figures, too, were caught in the ACU net. In August 2019 brothers Irfan Ahmed and Nadeem Ahmed, who had played for Hong Kong, received life suspensions from an ICC tribunal after being found, among other offences, to have fixed particular overs in two of their side's matches in the 2014 World T20 qualifier. Another Hong Kong player, Haseeb Amjad, was suspended for five years on similar charges. Nor was the infection confined to players and coaches, and in July 2021 Sri Lankan performance analyst Sanath Jayasundara was banned for seven years after he had tried to bribe the country's sports minister to influence the selection for a 2019 A team tour. And in May 2023 the West Indian Test batter Devon Thomas was charged with seven offences relating to matches in the Lanka Premier League, the Caribbean Premier League and the Abu Dhabi T20; a year later he received a five-year ban after pleading guilty to the charges, several of which involved failing to report an approach rather than actually fixing a match.

There is no reason to suppose that this endemic corruption has been beaten, or that it can be eliminated any time soon. As the leading players are better paid they are, no doubt, correspondingly less likely to risk their careers by succumbing to corrupt approaches or by failing to report them, while both the continuing surveillance by the ACU and its allies in the national governing bodies, not to mention the police, and the greater awareness of the problem in the media are also disincentives. Hence the greater danger involves less well-known and less well-paid cricketers, especially when they are taking part in minor tournaments which fly below the radar and may be less effectively controlled. This is in addition to all the other threats to cricket which arise from the proliferation of T20 and increasingly T10 leagues, not least in associate countries, some of which may have a more widespread culture of political and administrative corruption. As with liberty, so the price of integrity is indeed eternal vigilance.

Chapter 16

The Olympic Question

ON 13 October 2023 the executive board of the International Olympic Committee (IOC) approved the inclusion of cricket, along with squash, softball, lacrosse and flag football, in the programme of the 2028 Olympic Games in Los Angeles. IOC president Thomas Bach was confident that this exposure would grow the game globally, while ICC president Greg Barclay described the decision as 'a great day for the sport'. It was a decision which had been a long time coming: after its concerted drive to expand its membership to over a hundred countries, the ICC had been recognised as an international federation by the Olympic Committee in February 2010, but it took more than a decade for the Council to overcome its internal divisions over participation in the Games and come to the point of actually pressing its case for inclusion as an Olympic sport. That battle was another reflection of the power struggles within cricket's governing body, with India and England long the principal stand-outs against participation on financial grounds, while pleas from the associates that taking part in the Olympics would open up funding opportunities within their own national structures were largely ignored. Only a reversal of policy by the BCCI and the ECB would ultimately make it possible for the ICC to launch its successful bid for inclusion in the 2028 Games.

Curiously enough, cricket had been part of the modern Olympic movement from the outset, long before the Imperial Cricket Conference became a gleam in Abe Bailey's eye. There was an attempt to include the game in the first modern Olympics, in Athens in 1896, but it was abandoned because of lack of interest. Four years later there were four cricket entrants, Belgium, Great Britain, France and the Netherlands, but the Belgians and the Dutch withdrew and the first and still the only Olympic cricket match took place at the Vélodrome de Vincennes, near Paris, on 19 and 20 August 1900 between the Devon and Somerset Wanderers, representing Britain, and a team from the Union des Sociétés Françaises de Sports Athlétiques, mainly comprising British expatriates. The game was played between teams of 12, the Wanderers being bowled out in their first innings for 117, enough to gain them a lead of 39 when they dismissed their hosts for just 78. Batting again, the visitors declared at 145/5, setting the French 185 for victory, but with the occasional first-class cricketer Montagu Toller taking 7-9, they collapsed to 26 all out. The Wanderers players were awarded silver medals, but at the time it was unclear that this match had been an Olympic contest (Olympian it certainly was not), and it was only in 1912, when the IOC retrospectively determined which events had been part of the earlier Games, that it was formally recognised as part of Olympic history.

Although 26 nations participated in the 1900 Olympics, with events being strung out over more than five months, the narrowness of cricket's reach, restricted to England and a tiny number of Anglophile communities in northern Europe, is striking. Australia had single representatives in the athletics and swimming, but the formation of a national governing body for cricket was still in an early and deeply controversial phase, while India's sole participant was a Calcutta-born Englishman, Norman Pritchard, who won silver medals in the 200 metres and 200 metres hurdles. The

South Africans, of course, were still involved in the bloody and bitter Boer War, and there could be no question of their involvement. Seventy-five Americans took part across ten sports, but the Philadelphians showed no sign of interest in sending a cricket team to Paris. By 1904 the inclusion of cricket had been quietly forgotten, and when the Imperial Cricket Conference was established five years later its basis was entirely antithetical to the globalising ambitions of the Olympic movement. The IOC would, in any case, soon come under the prevailing influence of the United States, where cricket was in the process of being supplanted by baseball. Association football, rugby union and hockey would make occasional appearances in the Olympic programme before and just after World War I, but cricket remained firmly off the IOC's radar.

Cricket had, in a sense, wilfully isolated itself from the Olympic ideal: even rugby union had France as one of its powerhouses, but Empire was so deeply engrained in the ICC's constitution that it excluded the great majority of the world from its remit. Then there was the question of professionalism, an essential feature of the game in England but utterly opposed to the obsession with amateur status which drove IOC presidents Sigfrid Edström of Sweden and the American Avery Brundage. Not until Brundage's retirement in 1972 did the Olympic movement begin to make real compromises with professional sport, leading to an open door policy by the mid-1990s. The introduction of associate membership status in 1965 only slowly expanded the ICC's global reach, and it took the sustained membership drive around the turn of the millennium to bring its numbers up to the point at which it could join the IOC.

That, however, was very different from participating in the Games themselves. A cautious toe had been dipped in the water with the inclusion of cricket in the 1998 Commonwealth Games, held in Kuala Lumpur in September, reportedly because of the enthusiasm for the sport of the Malysian king, Tuanku Ja'afar of Negri Sembilan. This forced decisions to be taken about one of the trickier problems facing the ICC: while the West Indies had long been the international representative in the sport for Britain's colonies in the Caribbean and their independent successor states, each country participated separately in the Commonwealth (or the Olympic) Games. Fragmentation had long been a fear of the West Indies board, but now the issue had to be confronted. In the end, Barbados, Jamaica and Antigua and Barbuda were all among the 16 nations who took part in the Kuala Lumpur tournament. India and Pakistan sent second-string teams, however, on the grounds that their senior players were committed to a five-match bilateral Sahara Cup series in Toronto, part of the wave of offshore fixtures which were all the rage at the time. England also declined to take part, pleading that the tournament took place before the end of the English domestic season. Scotland and Northern Ireland were there, though, along with hosts Malaysia, Canada and Kenya. Another difficulty was that while ICC associate member Ireland covered both Northern Ireland, one of the constituent countries of the United Kingdom, and the Irish Republic, only the former was eligible to take part in the Commonwealth Games.

Australia, New Zealand, South Africa and Sri Lanka all sent strong teams, and they all went unbeaten and largely untroubled through the group phase, although Sri Lanka were given a fright by Zimbabwe, winning by just one wicket as they chased the Zimbabweans' total of 265/7. There was another thriller in the semi-finals, but this time it was the Sri Lankans who suffered a one-wicket defeat: dismissed for 130 by South Africa, for whom Nicky Boje took 4-16 in nine overs of left-arm spin, they reduced the Proteas to 96/9 before Boje and Alan Dawson shared a last-wicket stand which saw them stagger over the line. There was no such excitement in the other semi-final, Australian paceman Damien Fleming and left-arm spinner Brad Young combining to dismiss New Zealand for 58 and a rapid 42 not out by Adam Gilchrist ensuring that Australia cruised into the final in less than 11 overs. The final, in front of a Malaysian record crowd of over 7,500, was worthy of the occasion. South African skipper Shaun Pollock removed Mark Waugh, Ricky Ponting and Gilchrist inside the first ten overs and went on to take 4-19, and although Steve Waugh made an unbeaten 90, his side was dismissed for 183. Andrew Hudson and Mike Rindel gave the Proteas a solid start in reply, Rindel top-scoring with 67, and even a late flurry of wickets by Darren Lehmann, who claimed 3-14, could not prevent a four-wicket victory and Commonwealth gold medals for South Africa.

Here, one might have thought, was a pointer towards a significant way of raising cricket's profile outside the sport's traditional centres of strength. But cricket was not included in the Commonwealth Games programme in Manchester in 2002, or in Melbourne four years later. Although the BCCI flirted with the inclusion of cricket in the 2010 New Delhi Games, it would not be until Birmingham in 2022 that the experiment was repeated, and then only in the form of an eight-team women's T20 tournament. Visiting Pakistan in November 2006, IOC president Jacques Rogge stated bluntly that, although he personally liked the game, cricket was 'unlikely to get entry into the IOC community'. And if there were reservations within the ICC about the wisdom of pursuing the route of other global multi-sport events, how much greater were the issues when it was the Olympics which were involved? For the ECB, the issue was the inevitable clash between the Summer Olympics and the English domestic season, but more generally there was the problem of fitting another major quadrennial event into an already crowded international calendar, one, moreover, in which the all-important media rights would be held by the IOC rather than by the ICC. The problem of the calendar was further exacerbated when, in 2007, a T20 World Cup was added to the schedule. It was increasingly the BCCI which was calling the shots, and the Olympic movement had never made much headway in India; it was inevitable, therefore, as the money-men became more and more powerful, that the Olympics would be seen as a threat rather than an opportunity.

This, however, was an issue on which Cricket Australia was prepared to take a larger view. In 2008 its CEO, James Sutherland, commissioned former CA public affairs manager Richard Pope, who had also served as chief press attaché for the British Olympic team, to produce a report on the value to cricket of taking part in the Olympics. Sutherland presented Pope's report, entitled *Cricket Within the Olympic Program – A Golden Opportunity for the Development of Cricket and the Olympic Movement*, to the ICC Chief Executives' Committee and board that July, with a view to cricket being included in the 2016 Rio Games. Noting the potential benefits to the IOC that would come from a heightened 'Olympic signal' in India, Pope went on to argue that cricket, too, stood to gain more than it would lose: 'The only possible commercial downside of cricket's inclusion in the Olympic programme is the need to create a 17-day window in the FTP, once every four years. Although little cricket is played head-to-head with the Olympic Games currently, an upper limit to this cost to global cricket is US$12 million.

'This cost would be well and truly offset by the benefits Olympic inclusion could create: Direct funding of between US$7 million–28.5 million from the IOC's distribution to international federations part of the Olympic programme; global TV rights uplift; and national government funding of cricket as an Olympic sport.'

Pope also observed that 'the opportunity for women to compete at the Olympic Games could be the platform that transforms the women's game over the next century'. None of this, however, could persuade the ICC board. The ECB was worried about the impact of Olympic participation on their TV rights contract with Sky, as well as objecting to the fact that they would have to play as Great Britain; the BCCI was not prepared to subject itself to the Indian Olympic Association; and the WICB foresaw its possible break-up as its constituent nations would have to compete separately in the Olympics. The IOC was certainly interested, but with India and England opposed the idea had no chance of success. Although David Morgan, then ICC president, was talking optimistically in August 2008 about the possible inclusion of cricket in the 2020 Games, the proposal was quietly shelved. Even an empassioned plea by Adam Gilchrist in his 2009 Cowdrey Lecture, in which he described the Olympic movement as 'one of the most efficient and cost-effective distribution networks for individual sports to spread their wings globally', noting that the subcontinent was the Olympics' weakest link as well as cricket's strongest, cut no ice.

One potential obstacle, even if the other objections could be met, was cricket's adherence to the requirements of the World Anti-Doping Agency (WADA) which demanded that athletes who were part of the programme should give three months' notice of their whereabouts for one hour every day; this was necessary in order to facilitate testing outside competition dates. Indian players objected to this on security grounds – some of them were dealing with specific terrorist threats – and they were supported by the BCCI, which was prepared to block implementation of the system, which had been introduced by the ICC from 1 January 2009. These concerns were by no means confined to India alone, and in August 2009 the ICC set up a working group to try to work out a solution with WADA. With the Indian government pressing for adherence to WADA and the BCCI insisting on talking only through the ICC, the issue remained unresolved until May 2010, when WADA gave the ICC until November to bring its members into line; otherwise, it would be declared non-compliant. In June the board finally agreed, subject to minor amendments to the 'whereabouts' clause.

Despite the BCCI's unwillingness to consider participation in the Olympics, other considerations led to a very different position on the Asian Games, which were due to take place in Guangzhou in 2010. Increasingly preoccupied with 'markets' for cricket, ICC eyes were being cast towards China, and at the Asian Cricket Council Pawar and Dalmiya were involved in a bid to get cricket on to the programme of the Guangzhou Games. ACC CEO Syed Ashraful Huq was able to announce in his Council's 2006/07 report that their efforts had been successful, and the following year, with I.S. Bindra now spearheading a campaign to grow cricket in China, Ashraful Huq presented the case for participation in terms which might have been written by proponents of the Olympic case: 'On top of all the money coming into the game from the ACC and ICC,' he wrote, 'there will be a new source of funding from the Olympic Council of Asia for those teams taking part in the Twenty20 event in Guangzhou': 'The countries that get through to Guangzhou 2010 will receive Olympic-level funding, expose themselves in a new forum and undoubtedly make a name for themselves in the world of cricket where I foresee far more commercial and cricketing interaction on a corporate level with China.'

Picking up on the ICC's overt interest in the Chinese market, Ashraful Huq went even further in an interview with Associated Press, observing that 'China's say could help cricket's chances of making it to [the] Olympics', and arguing that that was a major reason for developing the game there.

Eight countries took part in both men's and women's events in Guangzhou, although India were conspicuously absent. In the men's competition a first phase reduced the number of qualifiers from five to four, who then played in the quarter-finals against Pakistan, Sri Lanka, Bangladesh and Afghanistan. The Afghans sprang a surprise by beating a second-string Pakistan side by 22 runs in one semi-final, while in the other, Bangladesh were too strong for an under-strength Sri Lanka. The final went down to the last over, but Bangladesh had five wickets in hand when they passed the Afghans' 118/8 with three deliveries to spare. In the women's event Pakistan took the gold medal, beating Bangladesh by ten wickets in a one-sided final, Japan taking the bronze medal with a seven-wicket victory over China. Despite India's absence the experiment could be said to have been a reasonable success, and Ashraful Huq was jubilant in his annual report. 'If we are saying that cricket is an Asian game,' he wrote, 'if Asia is the true home of world cricket, then it is appropriately part of the biggest sporting event in Asia.' He was delighted that it had been decided that cricket would also be in the programme for the 2014 Games, to be held in Incheon, South Korea. But still India remained an obstacle.

In June 2013 the ICC executive board received a report from the head of strategic management and support services, Jon Long, which reviewed the pros and cons of cricket's participation in the Olympics. There was no doubt that there were financial arguments in favour: if cricket were included in the 2024 Games, Long estimated, the ICC would receive a dividend from the IOC in the region of US$15–20 million, while there would also be benefits for members through their national Olympic committees, which would be a proportionately greater gain for the perpetually cash-strapped associates and affiliates. An Olympic tournament, he added, would be particularly valuable for the global profile of women's cricket, which the ICC was beginning to see as a priority. On the other hand, the desire to hold a World T20 Cup every two years was a considerable obstacle, and might well have to be sacrificed if cricket were to be included in the Olympics. The loss from reducing the frequency of T20 events would far outweigh any contribution from the IOC; the distribution to members from the 2012 World T20 Cup had been US$85.5 million, while smaller federations had only received US$14 million from the 2012 London Olympics. The potential loss to the ECB was even greater: a Games in the middle of the English season could cost up to US$160 million in lost Test revenue. Nor was England the only full member whose schedule could be disrupted by the intervention of an Olympic tournament. The BCCI remained concerned about 'member autonomy', worrying that it might find itself under the jurisdiction of the Indian Olympic Association, while Long added that a high-profile Olympic T20 event could also disrupt the precarious balance between the three formats which the ICC was struggling to maintain. All in all, Long's report concluded, while cricket had 'the capacity to thrive as a sport with or without the Olympic Games ... [a] judgment on whether or not to pursue inclusion . . . is arguably one of the biggest strategic decisions it will face.'

It was certainly too big for the board to take immediately. Prudently, it referred the report to the associates and affiliates, who probably had the most to gain, and agreed to bring the issue back to the 2014 annual conference. The debate there produced no progress, incoming chair Mustafa Kamal saying on his way home that '[w]e feel that our value will be diluted if we go there. Cricket has a legacy, it has importance.' Since a 100m race took no more than 11 seconds, he asked bizarrely, how could there be room for a cricket tournament at the Olympics? More cogently, he observed that football sent 'B, C or D teams to Olympics', and suggested that such an arrangement would do little for cricket. With the BCCI, ECB and CA running the show following the constitutional restructuring, there was clearly little prospect of a bid to be included at the Games.

One major obstacle was removed in July 2015, when MCC's World Cricket Committee signalled that the ECB was now willing to consider cricket's inclusion in the Games. Changes in personnel at Lord's, with Colin Graves taking over as ECB chairman from Giles Clarke, who had been a leading opponent on any Olympic initiative as well as being one of the architects of the coup by the gang of three, had apparently paved the way for this significant shift in policy, and the MCC committee, chaired by Mike Brearley, took the opportunity to throw its weight behind the idea. 'The Olympics is a fundamental opportunity for cricket, in both the men's and women's game,' it argued, '... and with a global reach such a presence would expose the game positively to new markets. Competing in an Olympic Games would be a huge opportunity for players, a massive boost to developing cricket nations and give much greater exposure for the sport to a new audience.'

The ICC should, it urged, reconsider its position with a view to gaining cricket's inclusion in the 2024 Olympics, to be held in Paris. The committee's case was couched in language the ICC board could understand: 'new markets' was code for greater commercial exposure, and with Rahul Dravid and Sourav Ganguly as members of the World Cricket Committee, along with ICC CEO Dave Richardson, there had to be a chance that this time the executive board might be persuaded to agree. In March 2017 Richardson went a stage further, indicating at a conference in London that a majority of members had 'come to the conclusion that the overall benefit to the game in terms of globalising and growing it, outweigh any negatives'. He was, he said, optimistic that 'the time was right' for a serious bid, perhaps for the 2024 Games.

Two years later, chairman Shashank Manohar was still emphasising the 'logistical problems' associated with Olympic participation: the Games tended to be held in non-cricketing countries with no adequate facilities for the sport, and somehow a tournament would have to be fitted into 15 days. But things were definitely beginning to move, and five months later, following a meeting with ICC CEO Manu Sawhney, Mike Gatting, chair of the MCC World Cricket Committee, revealed that the ICC was working towards inclusion in the 2028 Los Angeles Games. This would, he said, be 'a huge bonus for cricket worldwide, it would be fantastic'. A key factor had been the BCCI's agreement to come under the control of the National Anti-Doping Agency, India's arm of WADA. In October 2020 a questionnaire was sent to all ICC members asking them to specify the permanent and one-off benefits which would accrue to them as a result of inclusion, and by April 2021 the BCCI was signalling that it now accepted that the benefits of Olympic participation through increased exposure outweighed any danger to its own position, although there remained uncertainty about the likely format of any Olympic tournament – T20, the new boy on the block T10, and the ECB's beloved Hundred were all mentioned as candidates.

With England and India now on board there was no internal obstacle to an Olympic bid, and in August 2021 the decision to seek inclusion in the 2028 Los Angeles Games was finally taken. A working group was established, to be chaired by acting ICC chair Imran Khwaja, but he was soon engaged in his bitter and ultimately unsuccessful battle with Greg Barclay for the permanent position, culminating in his replacement as chair of the working group by the ECB's Ian Watmore, who had been a Barclay supporter. Then came the furore over the position of CEO Manu Sawhney, Watmore playing a crucial role in his eventual dismissal, and nobody gave much thought to 'the Olympic stuff'. Almost 90% of cricket fans wanted to see cricket in the Olympics, said Barclay, and with 92% of those fans in South Asia and a further 30 million in the USA, inclusion in the LA Games would be of advantage to both the IOC and the ICC. But by the time the ICC began to give the matter its serious attention it had missed the chance of inclusion in the provisional list of new sports for 2028. With a US$3 million budget for pushing the bid, Watmore began negotiations with the LA organisers, but he too disappeared from the scene after his sudden resignation from the ECB chair. In

November 2021 the communications firm Burson Cohn & Wolfe were brought in to run a PR campaign, which would reportedly focus on 'critical influencers in and around the IOC'.

In July 2023 the BCCI finally agreed to India's participation in the Hangzhou Asian Games in September–October (which had been postponed from 2022 because of the Covid pandemic), although the clash with the men's World Cup meant that in the men's event at Hangzhou it would be a second-string side which took part. The women, however, would be at full strength. Fourteen teams took part in the men's competition, including debutants Cambodia and Mongolia, and despite their depleted squads the Big Five dominated, Afghanistan again winning their semi-final against Pakistan and India cruising past Bangladesh. The final, though, was an anti-climax: the Afghan innings was interrupted by rain at 112/5 after 18.2 overs, and with no further play possible the Indians took the gold medal with a better record in the earlier rounds. The bronze medal match was at least completed, even if reduced to five overs a side; set a DLS target of 65 after Pakistan's innings had closed at 48/1, Bangladesh made it with a boundary off the final ball, winning by six wickets. India also took the women's gold, Smriti Mandhana and Jemimah Rodrigues powering them to 116/7 against Sri Lanka, and medium-pacer Titas Sadhu then taking 3-6 in her four overs to restrict the Sri Lankans to 97/8. Bangladesh again took the bronze, beating Pakistan by five wickets.

As it sought to make cricket attractive to the IOC, the ICC had signalled in January 2023 that it would like to see six-team events for both men and women at Los Angeles, probably comprising the six top-ranked countries on both T20 tables. This would obviously prevent any separate qualifying process and would exclude 90% of ICC members from taking part, but it would meet the IOC's desire to reduce costs by cutting down on athlete numbers.

Showing that it had even greater mastery of management jargon than those in Dubai, the IOC had declared a policy of 'evolving the event-based programme with a key focus on simplifying the venue master plan, and reducing cost and complexity in each sport'. Just 12 cricket teams would need only one venue, and use of the ICC rankings would probably ensure that the most powerful full members were guaranteed a ticket to Los Angeles. To be fair, it would also increase the chances of a really attractive first experience of cricket for Olympic spectators and TV viewers new to the sport. As a further bait for the IOC, the ICC also added BCCI secretary Jay Shah to its Olympic working group, neatly playing into the Olympic Committee's keenness to extend its reach on the subcontinent while giving the BCCI a voice in the final negotiations. And in October the fateful step was taken: cricket would return to the Olympics at the 2028 Los Angeles Games, although only for a small number of the ICC's 105 members.

Chapter 17

Franchises and an Uncertain Future

FRANCHISE CRICKET grew out of frustration, legal battles and, above all, corporate greed. It started with the media executive Subhash Chandra, who in 2004 had unsuccessfully taken the BCCI to court in an attempt to gain the TV rights for Indian cricket. His grievance went back to 2000, when his company Zee TV had submitted the highest bid for the World Cup rights but had lost out to the Global Cricket Corporation (GCC). After further unsuccessful attempts to break into the rights market, Chandra decided to go his own way, follow the Packer route, and set up a franchise-based Indian Cricket League. Others, too, could see what a franchise league could achieve. In an interview with *Cricinfo* in March 2005, I.S. Bindra set it out, arguing that such a league, given the extent of the Indian audience, 'can reach the level of European soccer. It can be bigger than international cricket.' Bindra added that Lalit Modi, his vice-president at the Punjab Cricket Association, had recently developed such a proposal, working with 'a certain TV channel', but it had been short-sightedly vetoed by the BCCI.

He did not name Zee TV, but Chandra began in November 2007 with six teams, based in Chandigarh, Chennai, Delhi, Hyderabad, Kolkata and Mumbai, and the teams were captained by such international stars as Chris Cairns and Craig McMillan (New Zealand), Stuart Law (Australia), Marvan Atapattu (Sri Lanka), Brian Lara (West Indies) and Inzamam-ul-Haq (Pakistan). The reaction of the BCCI was predictable: the competition, and the parallel, four-team international series, were declared unsanctioned, the players were banned from official cricket, and the ICC supported the BCCI stance. The league ran for two seasons, with teams from Ahmedabad, Lahore and Dhaka being added to the mix, but with the players shut out of the official game, it inevitably collapsed.

But the BCCI could see that the idea itself was sound, and on 13 September 2007, even before a ball had been bowled in Chandra's rebel league, Lalit Modi, now BCCI vice-president, who had, after all, been an advocate of such an initiative two-and-a-half years earlier, announced that they would be setting up a franchise league of their own, called the Indian Premier League. Modi justifiably insisted that they had had the idea first – though he did not mention the BCCI veto – and had been working on the project for the past two years. In January 2008 an auction was held to set up the eight franchises, which were based in Bangalore, Chennai, Delhi, Hyderabad, Jaipur, Kolkata, Mohali and Mumbai. The auction yielded the BCCI more than $723 million. Controversially, the Chennai franchise went to former BCCI president, Narayan Srinivasan, after the board's rules had been amended to allow members to own stakes in IPL franchises. The Bangalore franchise was acquired by brewers and distillers United Spirits, while other investors included a raft of mainly Indian capitalists and the occasional media personality. The real estate developer DLF bought the naming rights for the first five years for $25 million, while a ten-year broadcast rights deal yielded just over $1 billion. Firmly based on American models, the league conducted player auctions, with the franchises initially limited by a salary cap of $5 million; the most expensive player in that first auction was Mahendra Singh Dhoni, signed by Srinivasan's Chennai Super Kings for $1.5 million. The first season ran from 18 April to 1 June 2008, involving 59 matches, and was hugely successful, immediately commanding huge crowds and massive television audiences in India and across the world, not least among the widespread Indian diaspora.

Its path has not always been entirely smooth, with some franchises suspended or withdrawing for financial reasons, allegations of corruption and match fixing, and the 2020 season being played in the UAE because of the Covid pandemic. But it has transformed the cricket landscape, spawning other franchise-based T20 leagues around the world. With an expansion to ten teams, the 2022 season comprised 74 matches played between 26 March and 29 May, a 'window' of nine weeks during which the international schedule inevitably came to a standstill. In July 2022 it was confirmed that for 2023–27 there would be a two-and-a-half-month window for the IPL in the international touring calendar (FTP), and with less rigid windows for the Australian Big Bash League and the ECB's Hundred, it was increasingly evident that these theoretically domestic, but in fact global, events posed a major threat to the traditional international programme. It was less apparent that the ICC had any effective answer to the ever-expanding demands of a small number of cashed-up governing bodies.

As early as March 2008, Brian Lara was observing that the advent of the ICL and IPL was changing the face of cricket. Challenged by new commercial forces, he said, national boards 'have to be on their toes and have to mind their Ps and Qs'. The emergence of franchises gave players new options and would force the national governing boards to find ways of paying them better. The franchise leagues would also fill the gap between domestic cricket and the international game, enabling players to make the transition more easily. Four months later, ICC CEO Lorgat set up a working group to prevent the Council's 'marginalisation' by the new competitions. He continued to sound optimistic that the ICC would be able to control the situation, commenting in September 2008 that '[a] private businessman might have different ambitions, but we have to protect the game of cricket'.

Fifteen years on, his words sound very like whistling in the dark. Within weeks of his statement, indeed, England and Sri Lanka postponed the latter's proposed visit to England the following year because a clash with the IPL would have meant selecting a second-string touring party. Nevertheless, the ICC seems to have been slow to appreciate the significance of the viper in their bosom. In January 2009 adviser Bindra and CEO Lorgat urged the USACA to set up a franchise league on IPL lines, with commercial team ownership and plenty of overseas players. It was, Bindra claimed, the obvious way to break into the potentially lucrative American market.

By the time of the 2023 round of annual meetings, the Chief Executives' Committee was ready to tackle at least some of the problems generated by the proliferation of T20 franchise leagues. It focused on the rules surrounding the recruitment of overseas players for such leagues: while the International League T20 (ILT20) allowed as many as nine overseas players on each team's roster, Major League Cricket in the USA was going to permit six and Canada's Global T20 allowed five. The full members were concerned about the implications of this for their own cricket, and were therefore keen to impose limits, but with IPL franchise owners also acquiring teams in other leagues around the world, there were potential conflicts of interest involved in restricting the recruitment of overseas players. There was also the question of players from associate countries who might be hired by teams in competitions organised by other associates. A hard cap which treated all foreign players as alike would make it much less likely that they would gain lucrative contracts and get an opportunity to showcase their skills. The compromise which was eventually agreed was that a limit of four overseas players per franchise would only apply to new leagues, with the existing competitions to conform in due course, according to arrangements which were yet to be worked out. Players from associate countries other than the host would count as locals for the purposes of this cap. Moreover, franchises would be expected to pay a 10% release fee for each player to his (or her) home board, although whether this would be a charge against the league, the team, or to be deducted from the player's own fee was also left undefined. The model for the release fee was the practice of the BCCI, which pays home boards a 10% fee for each overseas player contracted.

Welcome as such regulations may be, they do nothing to address the most fundamental problem, which is that the calendar may soon be swamped by an endless series of franchise leagues, leaving little or no room for the ICC's precious Future Tours Programme, or indeed for the full members' domestic competitions. Delivering the 2023 Cowdrey Lecture, former England captain Andrew Strauss welcomed what he called the 'democratisation' of cricket, arguing the future direction of the game 'will be decided not in the meeting halls of the ICC in Dubai, but rather by the purchasing power of the increasing number of those who choose to follow the game'. 'Those who choose to follow the game', one might think, are the fans, whose engagement with cricket is courted with increasing fervour by the ICC's marketing department, but in truth it is not their choices or their purchasing power which determine cricket's future, but the media companies and the occupants of boardrooms in the subcontinent. Strauss was right to say that the ICC was losing control – indeed, its ability to exercise control has been a problem throughout its history – but it is corporatism which is the cause and the beneficiary of its weakness, not some form of consumer militancy.

And then, of course, there are the players, or at least the best of them. They are the ones who stand to gain most, able to sell their skills to the highest bidder in a way that did not exist before the creation of the IPL. As FICA's annual survey noted in 2022, 40% of the leading men's players were now operating as free agents, moving around from one lucrative franchise contract to the next, with a further 42% combining a national and domestic contract with at least one overseas T20 league. The revolution which Packer started and which the IPL turned into a mass movement threatening to sweep away traditional international cricket shows no sign of letting up, and while not every player can command the almost US$3million paid by the Kolkata Knight Riders for Mitchell Starc in the 2024 IPL auction, or even the nearly $2.5 million. which won Sunrisers Hyderabad the services of Pat Cummins, there is no doubt that many leading cricketers are now in the same earnings league as the richest footballers, and well beyond the resources of national boards to command their loyalty.

Not content with reducing the complexities of cricket to a three-and-a-half-hour T20 format, governing bodies continue to tinker. Perhaps the most controversial experiment is the ECB's much-hyped Hundred competition, which decimalised the over to five balls and had the teams switching ends every two overs instead of the usual one. Opinions differ over the success of the format and the ECB's city-based franchise tournament; there was even disagreement about whether it produced a profit in its first two seasons. There is, however, evidence that it brought in a public which had never attended a cricket match before, and the ECB seems committed to keeping it in the schedule. There is, as yet, no sign of its spreading to other countries. In some ways a more radical initiative still (although keeping a six-ball over) is T10, in which matches comprise just 60 deliveries per team and last for about an hour and a half, roughly the same as a football match. The ICC has sanctioned one T10 tournament, played in Abu Dhabi since 2017, which attracts significant numbers of overseas players, and is now established as part of the rolling franchise league circus. Again, the format divides opinion. Many, especially in relatively new cricket countries, see it as an ideal way of promoting cricket to those with no knowledge of the game, but for others it takes a large stride too far in favour of big-hitting batters, devaluing the taking of wickets and marginalising the bowlers (who are limited to two overs each). It has not yet been accepted officially as an international format, although live-streamed tournaments between national teams, as well as those involving club sides, have been organised by the European Cricket Network, run by the Munich-based Australian Daniel Weston.

There can be little doubt that the phenomenal success of the IPL and the exponential growth of franchise league cricket around the globe pose a serious threat to the game's international ecosystem as it evolved in the 20th century, and even an existential threat to the ICC itself. It is, moreover, clear that administrators in Dubai and in governing bodies across the world have no real idea how to respond. What began as an argument about whether to give the IPL a window in the Future Tours Programme has become a question about whether an FTP is sustainable at all. Debates continue about whether Test cricket has a long-term future, even with the recent ICC decision to establish a Test fund to help support the format, and there are calls for ODIs to be dropped from the international schedule outside four-yearly World Cups. Everyone, it seems, must dance to the tune of T20 and the plutocrats who profit from it.

Alongside all this, of course, there remains the perennial problem of the ICC's own constitution. Lord Woolf's accusation that board members generally acted in the interest of their own governing body rather than those of the sport as a whole still stands, and if anything the blatant misuse of power in favour of a small minority has only grown in the years since his report was so categorically rejected. One result of that abuse has been the crisis of the franchise leagues, and another is the blatantly distorted distribution of revenue which hinders the sport's development and perpetuates the misgovernment by keeping other members dependent on the BCCI. Other global bodies have wrestled with the problem as well, and while their arrangements might be – and indeed, are – legitimately criticised, none is as shameless in its proceedings as the ICC. Rugby union, for example, is governed by World Rugby, formerly the International Rugby Board, which adapted its governance structure in 2015 to give wider representation to its smaller members. Unlike the ICC, it has eight foundation members, who still enjoy considerable power, holding 24 of the 52 seats on the council, which meets annually, and seven out of 12 on the executive board. But this numerical advantage is now tempered by the presence in the council of three representatives each from Argentina, Italy and Japan, and from each of World Rugby's six regional organisations. Moreover, there is a general assembly of all members, which meets every two years and which can make recommendations to the council. One striking difference from the ICC is that while the member unions and regions are entitled to two representatives on the council, they may each appoint or elect a third, female representative; as a result, 18 of the 52 council members are women. It is also significant that World Rugby's by-laws require board members to act in accordance with their fiduciary duties and in the best interests of World Rugby and the global game, explicitly demanding that they recuse themselves from any decision in which they have a conflict of interest.

While some might feel that a further reduction in the influence of the foundation members would be no bad thing, this structure is clearly light years ahead of that which exists in cricket. And the question must be whether anything can now be done to rectify the situation. It may be that the full members missed their chance to stand up to the BCCI when they allowed Woolf's recommendations to slip through their fingers in 2012, and that India's grip on the game has now become so absolute that any resistance is futile. If that is the case, then the prospects for the ICC, if not for cricket as a whole, are indeed bleak. It is more than 12 years since Mike Atherton wrote that the ICC 'masquerades as a governing body but is really just an amalgam of vested interests', and 15 since he argued that '[t]he time has come to disband the ICC as a decision-making body and let the paid executives run the show'. Nothing that has happened in the intervening period has reduced the validity of either of those statements, but by the same token much of what has happened has worked against any step to reform the organisation and to turn it, at long last, into a governing body worthy of the game it runs.

The ICC faces three great challenges – constitutional reform; the introduction of an equitable, development-oriented resource distribution model; and an accommodation of the franchise leagues – and all three demand that the other members find the courage to stand up to the BCCI. They did it to a degree in 2016 under the leadership of Shashank Manohar, but Shashank Manohars are thin on the ground and, it seems, especially so in India. There *are* some justifications for India's hegemony: the massive appetite for cricket which unquestionably exists in the country and in the subcontinent more generally, not to mention the disgraceful domination of the game by England, Australia and their allies for the first 80-odd years of the ICC's existence. Neither of those factors, though, nor the brutality of an unleashed Indian capitalism, can justify cricket's being held to ransom by a small number of nationalist politicians and greedy oligarchs. The fiduciary duty of the ICC board, invoked in vain by Lord Woolf, demands that cricket's wealth be spent in the interests of the game as a whole, and that requires a resource distribution model which is actually the inverse of that adopted in 2023. Those who need it least should receive least, while there should be serious investment in keeping the weaker full members afloat and helping the emerging nations to add to their number. To put it another way, in a world where T20 cricket can pay for itself, significant resources need to be invested in maintaining multi-day cricket, including Tests, as the pinnacle of the game, cricket in its purest and most subtly balanced form.

For that to happen, however, the ICC board must comprise men and women who understand that their primary duty is to the ICC and to the sport it exists to serve, not to the narrow interests of a national governing body which puts them there to protect its corner at all costs. If those currently in charge are too stupid or too venal to see this for themselves, then somehow those who genuinely care about cricket's future must find a way to get the message across, to make it clear that the power they enjoy comes from all of us, that we are all, in modern parlance, stakeholders in the game. Administrators in every governing body from St Helena and Samoa to Australia and England must come to understand that by tolerating the BCCI's excesses and submitting to its bullying they put not only themselves but the ICC and cricket itself in peril. If they don't get their act together soon, the ICC will inevitably become, and ultimately deserve to be, a pimple on the backside of a relentless behemoth, charging into an increasingly lucrative and increasingly barren future.

Acknowledgements

ANY WORK such as this necessarily draws on the knowledge and insights of many people, garnered over many years. In this case that certainly includes my colleagues at Cricket Europe and Emerging Cricket, websites which, while primarily dedicated to coverage of the ICC's associate (and previously affiliate) members, has inevitably drawn us into dealings with and discussion of the wider governance of world cricket. Special mention should be made of John Elder and Tim Cutler, respective founders of the two websites, and of colleagues Barry Chambers, Andrew Nixon, Daniel Beswick and Nick Skinner. And I owe a particular debt to Tim Brooks, who began as co-author of this book and who gracefully withdrew to pursue other writing priorities, agreeing at the same time to be one of the text's first readers.

Thanks are also due to Alan Rees, the MCC librarian, who was enormously helpful during a visit to the Lord's library, and to Richard Hinds, who provided access to relevant material from Cricket Australia's archives.

A different kind of debt is due to the late John Nethercote, an informed and entertaining raconteur of the game, and to his partner, Dr Gail Radford, who kindly passed on to me his large collection of cricket books.

One or more chapters have been read by the aforementioned Tim Brooks, Bertus de Jong, Tristan Lavalette, Shounak Sarkar, Richard Sykes and Simon Taufel; I am grateful for their useful commentary, to which

I have tried to do justice. All the opinions, of course, remain my own.

No book sees the light of day without the commitment and expertise of its publishers, and my sincere thanks are due to Bruce Talbot, Jane Camillin and the team at Pitch Publishing for their support for this project though its successive incarnations.

Last but no means least, to volunteer copy-editor Patti Warn, who has not only read the entire manuscript twice with unfailing attention but also provided moral support and much-needed sustenance throughout the writing process.

Notes On Sources

General

The most important primary source is the minutes and correspondence of the ICC and, for the earlier period, of MCC, which are preserved at Lord's.

Indispensable too, especially where the primary records are unavailable, are the reports on meetings in the annual *Wisden Cricketers' Almanack*, volumes which also include useful contemporary comment by the successive editors and, on key issues, substantive articles.

Newspapers also provide valuable contemporary evidence. There are collections of digitised newspapers at the British Newspaper Archive, and on Trove (Australia) and Papers Past (New Zealand). For the period since 1999, the online archives of *Cricinfo* are indispensable, often providing the most detailed discussion of ICC meetings and their outcomes as well as the wider political issues.

Among wider studies of cricket's social and political history, Stephen Wagg's *Cricket: A Political History of the Global Game, 1947–2017* (Routledge: London 2019) offers valuable insight into the post-war context in the individual countries, as well as perspicacious comment on the ICC itself. Less focused on the ICC but nevertheless relevant is Keith Sandiford and Brian Stoddart's collection of essays, *The Imperial Game: Cricket, Culture and Society* (Manchester/ New York: Manchester UP 1998).

Other general surveys which cover key aspects of the subject include Kersi Meher-Homji, *Cricket Conflicts and Controversies from Pre-Bodyline to Post-Bollyline* (Sydney: New Holland 2012), Peter Wynne-Thomas and Peter Arnold, *Cricket in Conflict* (Feltham: Middlesex: Newnes Books 1984), Ted Corbett, *Cricket on the Run* (London: Stanley Paul 1990), and Guy Fraser-Sampson, *Cricket at the Crossroads: Class, Colour and Controversy from 1967 to 1977* (London: Elliot and Thompson 2011).

I: COLONIAL GOVERNANCE, 1907–1989

Very little has been written on the early history of the Conference, although there are useful insights into the Australian side of the story in Gideon Haigh and David Frith's, *Inside Story: Unlocking Australian Cricket's Archives* (Melbourne: News Custom Publishing 2007), and the South African background is incidentally covered in Richard Parry and André Odendaal, *Swallows and Hawke: English Cricket Tours, the MCC and the Making of South Africa, 1888–1968* (Chichester: Pitch Publishing 2022).

One of the most valuable discussions of this period, and one of the most detailed studies of the workings of the ICC, is Usha Iyer's 2013 doctoral thesis, 'Decolonisation and the Imperial Cricket Conference, 1947–1965: A Study in Transnational Commonwealth History?' (University of Central Lancashire).

The South African story is authoritatively covered by André Odendaal (ed.), *Cricket in Isolation – The Politics of Cricket in South Africa* (Cape Town: A. Odendaal, 1997) and by Brian Crowley, *Cricket Exiles – The Saga of South African Cricket* (Cape Town: Don Nelson 1983). There is also useful discussion of this and other issues relating to the ICC in Jack Williams, *Cricket and Race* (Oxford and New York: Berg 2001).

Apart from Basil D'Oliveira's autobiography, and ultimately a more comprehensive guide to the murky events of 1968, is Peter Oborne's *Basil D'Oliveira: Cricket, Conspiracy: The Untold Story* (London: Little, Brown 2004). Briefer but informative discussions can be found in Ted Corbett, *Cricket on the Run: Twenty-Five Years of Conflict* (London: Stanley Paul 1990).

The conflict between Kerry Packer and the global cricket authorities has been widely analysed and discussed. Two indispensable book-length studies are Henry Blofeld, *The Packer Affair* (London: Collins 1978) and Gideon Haigh, *The Cricket War* (Melbourne: Text Publishing 1993). Also valuable is Eric Beecher, *The Cricket Revolution* (Melbourne: Newspress 1978), which includes a comprehensive timeline up to May 1978. There are useful chapters in Wynne-Thomas and Arnold, *Cricket in Conflict* and Corbett, *Cricket on the Run*.

II: THE GLOBAL GAME, 1989–present

Among his many books which are relevant to our subject, Gideon Haigh's *Sphere of Influence: Writings on cricket and its discontents* (Melbourne: Victory Books 2010) is an indispensable guide to the rise of Indian influence on the ICC and world cricket more generally up to the time of its publication. There are further indispensable insights in his *Uncertain Corridors: Writings on Modern Cricket* (Melbourne: Viking 2013) and elsewhere in his copious writings, including now in his blog Cricket Et Al.

A detailed and judicious, if inevitably partial, account of events between 2001 and 2008 can be found in Malcolm Speed's memoir *Sticky Wicket: Inside Ten Turbulent Years at the Top of World Cricket* (Sydney: HarperSports 2011).

On corruption in cricket, Mike Coward's *Bookies, Rebels and Renaissance – Cricket in the 80s* (Sydney: ABC Books 2004), Brian Radford's *Caught Out: Shocking Revelations of Corruption in International Cricket* (London: John Blake 2011) and, more generally, Mark Peel, *Playing the Game? Cricket's Tarnished Ideals* (Worthing: Pitch Publishing 2018).

Index

Aamer Sohail 272
Aaqib Javed 249
Abdul Hafeez (Kardar) 61, 95-8
Afghan Cricket Board 244-5
Afghanistan 13, 140, 191, 214-5, 219
 full membershiip 164, 210, 225, 243
 rise of 185, 221, 292-3
 women's cricket in 243-6
African Cricket Association 213
African Women's Championship 231
Ahsan Raza 147
Aird, Ronald 74, 94
Al Jazeera 281-3
Aldridge, Brian 249
Alexander, Robert, QC 101-3
Ali Khan 279
Allardice, Geoff 146, 165, 180, 228, 245-6
Allen, Gubby 59, 77, 82, 86
Altham, H.S. 79, 81
Amir Hayat 283
Amiss, Dennis 112
Arendse, Norman 141
Anderson, Sir John 135-6, 141
Archer, Jofra 180
Argentina 39, 43, 80, 135
Armanath, Mohinder 114
Armstrong, Warwick 38-9, 42
Asaf Ali 98
Ashfaq Ahmed 283
Ashraful Haq, Syed 292-3
Ashton, Sir Hubert 76
Asian Cricket Council 145, 213, 215, 217, 231-2
 ACC Challenge 214
 ACC Trophy 215, 217
Asian Games 292-3, 297
Atherton, Michael 307
Atkins, Caroline 233
Atkinson, Steve 120

Attapattu, Marvan 300
Australia 12, 21, 95, 111, 123, 169, 178, 192
Australian Board of Cricket Control (*later* Australian Cricket Board) 27-31, 33, 36, 37, 42, 48, 69, 71, 96-7, 118, 120, 134, 138, 153, 192
 and associate membership 81
 and Bodyline 49-51
 and Kerry Packer 98-105
 and match-fixing 269-73
 and South African question 77-9, 91
Australian Institute of Sport 259
Ayasha Rahman 234
Ayres' Cricket Companion 39-40
Azizullah Fazli 244
Azharuddin, Mohammad 276

Bach, Thomas 285
Bacher, Ali 112-3, 127, 136, 213, 274
Bahamas 140
Bahrain 217
Bailey, (later Sir) Abe 21-3, 27, 34, 75, 118, 127, 286
Bailey, Jack 100, 116-7, 133
Balbirnie, Andrew 214
Bancroft, Cameron 265-7
Bangladesh 96-7, 111, 114, 182
Bangladesh Cricket Board 281
Bangladesh Premier League 280-1
Barclay, Greg 165, 167-8, 180, 209, 211, 229, 246. 285, 296
Barlow, Eddie 127
Barnes, Sid (England) 35-6
Barnes, Sid (Australia) 97
Barnett, B.A. 69
Barresi, Wesley 187
Barrington, Ken 98
Basit Ali 270
Becker, David 205-6, 264-5

Bedi, Bishen 111
Beginner, Lord (Egbert Moore) 67
Beloff, Michael, QC 251, 278
Benaud, Richie 71-2, 251
Benazir Bhutto 270
Bencraft, Dr Russell 29
Benson, Michael 253-5
Bermuda 82, 98, 110, 114, 119-20
Berry, Scyld 282
Bevan, Michael 171
Big Bash League 301
Bilateral series 193, 206-8, 211, 224, 227
Bindra, I.S. 18, 134, 141, 145, 147, 292, 299, 302
Bird, Dickie 248-9
Board of Control for Cricket at Home (England) 33
BCCI 12-13, 16, 18, 44, 55, 58, 60, 68, 70, 134, 137-9, 146-7, 153-4, 157-60, 161-3, 164-5, 179, 183-4, 199-200, 202, 205-6, 208, 237, 251, 254, 299-301, 305-6
 and DRS 155, 256
 and media rights 148, 155, 166, 299
 and the Olympic Games 285, 289, 291-2, 294-5
 corruption and 155, 161, 273, 276, 280, 281
Bodyline 48-52
Boje, Nicky 273-4, 288
Boon, David 123
Border, Alan 123
Boucher, Mark 172
Boult, Trent 179
Bowden, Billy 254
Boyce, Keith 95

314

INDEX

Boycott, Geoffrey 103-4, 112, 262
Bradman, (later Sir) Donald 48, 71, 91
Bramall, Lord 127
Brathwaite, Carlos 188
Bray, Charles 62
Brearley, Mike 295
Brettig, Daniel 159-60
Brinckman, Sir Theodore 55
Broad, Chris 147, 258-9
Brown, F.R. 96
Brundage, Avery 287
Brunei 226
Brunt, Katherine 233
Brutus, Dennis 71, 74
Bucknor, Steve 253-5
Bull, W.C. 52
Burge, Peter 249
Burson Cohn & Wolfe 297
Bushby, Harold 42-3, 78
Butchart, Ian 120
Buttler, Jos 179-80, 190
Bvute, Osias 142

Cahn, Sir Julian 55
Cairns, Chris 182, 300
Caldwell, Tim 96
Calthorpe, Freddie 43
Cameron, Frank 249
Cameron, Jess 236
Canada 80, 82, 110-11, 114, 124, 217, 230
Carr, Arthur 52
Cartwright, Tom 89
Central Bureau of Investigation (India) 276
Ceylon (see also Sri Lanka) 34, 45, 55, 58, 60, 63, 79
Chandra, Subhash 299-300
Chappell, Ian 95, 99
Chappell, Trevor 117
Chandrachud, Y.V. 273
Chaudhry Ejaz Yousuf 272
Chauhan, Chetan 254
Chawla, Sanjay 274
Chennai Super Kings 161, 300-1
Chesterfield, Earl of 31
Chhayakar, Mehardeep 282-3
Chidabaram, M.A. 76
China 140, 145, 292-3
Chingoka, Peter 141-3, 251
Chopra, Nikhil 276
Civil & Military Gazette (Lahore) 55-6
Clarke, Giles 156-7, 294-5
Clarke, Michael 178
Clarke, Sylvester 115
Cobham, Viscount 56
Code of Conduct *See ICC*
Colvin, Holly 235

Commonwealth Games 287-9
Condon, Sir Paul 147, 274-7
Connor, Clare 237, 240
Cook, Geoff 112
Cook Islands 140
Cooper, J Astley 26-7
Cooper, Tom 187
Corbett, Ted 115
Cornell, John 98
Costa Rica 140
Covid-19 pandemic 164, 188-9, 242, 297, 301
Cowdrey, Colin 17, 120-2, 131, 133, 249, 253
Cowdrey Lecture 155, 256-7, 291, 303
Cowie, Doug 262
Coy, Brigadier A.H. 69
Cricinfo 159-60, 175, 238-9. 267
Cricket Australia 157-60, 199, 201, 208, 266-7
and the Olympic Games 290-1
Cricket Council (England) 89, 91-2
Cricket South Africa 201-2, 205, 281
Cricketer, The 113
Croatia 216
Cromer, Earl of 51
Crompton, Alan 271
Cronje, Hansie 273-4, 276
Cross, Kathy 241
Crowe, Martin 267
Cuba 226
Cummins, Pat 181, 304
Curran, Kevin 126
Curtin, John 59
Cutler, Tim 167
Czech Republic 140

Daily Herald (London) 62
Daily Herald (Melbourne) 28-9
Daily Mail (London) 28
Daily News (London) 21
Daily Sketch 55
Daily Telegraph (London) 127
Daily Telegraph (Sydney) 28
Dainty, Gladstone 144
Dakin, Geoff 112-3
Dalmiya, Jagmohan 134-5, 138-9, 141, 195-7, 199, 250-1, 276, 292
Danish Kaneria 277-8
Darling, Joe 28
Darlow, Martin 210
Davis, Steve 147
Dawson, Alan 288
Dean, Harry 36
Deeley, Peter 127
De Klerck, F.W. 128
De Mello, Anthony 55-6

De Silva, Aravinda 171
De Silva, Asoka 249
De Silva, Somachandra 111
De Silva, Stanley 111
Denmark 15, 82, 110-11, 120, 216
Denness, Mike 250-2
Dev, Sunil 273
Devine, Sophie 234
Devon and Somerset Wanderers 286
Dhoni, Mahendra Singh 254, 300-1
Dhumal, Arun 208
Diana Barakzai 244
Dias, Roy 110-11
Doctrove, Billy 261
D'Oliveira, Basil 75, 88-90, 109
Donald, Alan 172
Done, Richard 218-9
Doolan, Lucy 233
Dowling, Bill 69, 71
Dravid, Rahul 254, 295
Dubai 13, 16, 136, 282
Duckworth, Frank 257
Duckworth/Lewis/(Stern) method *See ICC*
Dundee Evening Telegraph 62

Eade, Andrew 144
East Africa 75, 79, 82, 92, 95, 113, 143
East African Women's Championship 231
East Asia Pacific Region 215
Edinburgh, Duke of 63
Edström, Sigfrid 287
Edward VII 14
Edwards, Wally 159-60
Egar, Colin 84
Egypt 34, 55
Ehsan Mani 139, 141, 167, 196-7, 200, 232
Elferink, Ron 120
Elliott, Bruce 258-9
Elworthy, Steve 172
Emerson, Ross 258
Engel, Matthew 113, 116, 117-8, 121, 183, 194, 273
England 12, 21, 43-4, 111, 117, 124, 132, 171, 178-80, 192
and South African question 77, 79
England and Wales Cricket Board 134-5, 153, 157-60, 163, 172-3, 192, 196-7, 204, 208
and the Olympic Games 285, 289, 290-1, 294
merger with WCA 230
ESPN Star Sports 148, 165, 202, 232

European Championship 215
European Cricket Council 213, 216
European Cricket Federation 213
European Cricket Network 305
European Women's Championship 231
Evatt, H.V. 56, 59
Eyre, Rick 238-9

Fakhar Zaman 185
Fakhruddin Ebrahim 270-1
Falkland Islands 140
Farrell, Rene 234
Faulkner, Aubrey 34
Fazal Mahmood 61
Federation of International Cricketers' Associations (FICA) 137-8, 154, 200, 204, 207-8, 280, 304
Findlay, William 44, 54, 62, 67
Fiji 82, 122
Finland 140
Fitze, Sir Kenneth 59-60
Fitzgerald, R.P. 33, 53
Fitzpatrick, Cathryn 239
Flanagan, Ronnie 276
Fleming, Damian 288-9
Fletcher, Duncan 114
Flower, Andy 140-1
Foster, Frank 35
Foster Bowley, R.E. 76
Franchise leagues 18, 203-4, 299-305, 307
France 140
Fraser, Malcolm 110
Freedom Association 126
Fry, C.B. 24-5, 29, 36

Gandhi, Mahatma 61, 155
Gandhi, Rajiv 120, 125
'Gang of Three' *See* ICC
Ganguly, Sourav 137, 182, 209, 254, 295
Garner, Joel 111
Gatting, Mike 123, 125, 127-8, 248, 295-6
Gavaskar, Sunil 111, 255
Gayle, Chris 187
Ghulam Shabber 283
Gibbs, Herschelle 273-4
Gibraltar 82, 110, 113, 124
Gilchrist, Adam 172, 175, 289, 291
Gilligan, Arthur 59
Gilmour, Gary 95
Gleneagles Agreement 106, 109
Global Cricket Corporation 137-9, 299
Global Development Program *See* ICC
Global T20 (Canada) 302

Gomes, Rupert 120
Gooch, Graham 112, 114, 123, 126
Goonetilleke, Ravindra 258
Goszko, Michelle 239
Gowrie, Earl of 62
Grant Govan, R.E. 47
Graves, Colin 208, 294-5
Gray, Malcolm 134-5, 138-9, 195
Gregory, Syd 35
Greig, Tony 99-104, 155
Griffin, Geoff 70, 84
Griffith, Billy 92
Griffith, Charlie 84
Gul Mohammad 61
Guardian, The 108-9, 113, 116, 121
Guptill, Martin 179-80

Haigh, Gideon 128, 146-7
Hair, Darrell 134, 258, 261-4
Halbish, Graham 271
Hales, Alex 190
Hall, Wes 195, 251
Hamid Hassan 214-5, 221
Hamid Shinwari 244
Handscomb, Peter 265
Hansen, John 255
Harper, Daryl 249
Harris, Lord 26, 30, 31, 38, 41-2, 44-6, 127
Haseeb Amjad 283
Hasti Gul Abed 221
Hawke, Lord 31, 34, 47, 118
Hazlewood, Josh 181
Hazlitt, Gerry 36
Head, Travis 181
Headley, George 44
Hendricks, 'Krom' 75
Henry, Omar 115, 127
Hilditch, Andrew 251
Hillyard, G.W. 31
Hobbs, Jack 35-6
Hodgson, Craig 114
Hoey, Kate 201
Hogg, Brad 254
Holding, Michael 99
Holmes, Group Captain A.J. 59
Hong Kong 82, 110, 113-4
Howa, Hassan 106, 109, 116
Howard, John 155, 201
Howard, Nigel 64
Hudson, Andrew 289
Hughes, Kim 115
Hughes, Simon 262
Hundred, The 301, 304
Hunte, Julian 142, 204
Hussain, Nasser 173

Ijaz Ahmad 272
Ijaz Butt 278

Imran Khan 99, 123, 248, 251, 270, 272-3
Imran Khwaja 165, 209, 244-5, 296
India 39, 41, 58, 111, 114, 118, 117, 123, 180-2
and South African question 76-7, 107, 112
media rights in 148, 155, 166, 299
partition of 14, 60-2, 96-7
Indian Cricket League 299-300
Indian Premier League 18, 142, 161, 202-3, 280, 281, 300-2, 304-5
International Cricket Council (Imperial Cricket Conference, etc.)
affiliate membership 118, 140, 153, 158, 162, 212, 293-4
and Bodyline 49-52
and over rates 121
and South African question 74-8, 89-92, 108-10, 124, 126-8, 131
Anti-Corruption Unit 18, 147, 151-2, 264, 274-7, 280, 282-4
Associate membership 15, 65, 80-3, 92-3, 110, 113, 118, 127, 132, 135, 140, 153, 158, 163, 182, 212, 287, 293-4, 302
Associate and Affiliate Umpires Panel 241
Champions' Trophy 137, 147, 161, 169, 182-5, 205, 213, 222, 241, 252-3
Chief Executives' Committee 154, 163, 199, 202-5, 255, 290, 302
Coaching fund 82-3, 93-4
Code of Conduct 17, 117, 133, 138, 232, 249, 253, 261, 267, 270
Code of Ethics 152
Cricket Committee 255-6, 275
Decision Review System (DRS) 255-7
Development Committee 213, 265
Disputes Resolution Committee 251
Duckworth/Lewis/(Stern) system 257-8, 264
Executive Board 135, 151, 156, 177, 194, 197-8, 202-5, 208-9, 251-2, 259-60, 262-4, 265, 290, 293-4, 307-8
Finance and Commercial Affairs Committee 157-61, 166, 222
First-class status 57, 60, 122

INDEX

Foundation Membership 46, 65-6, 69-70, 93, 95, 124, 131-2
Full membership 140, 152-3, 192, 206, 213-4, 227, 302
Funding model 13, 153, 159, 162-7, 200-1, 222, 305-6
Future Tours Program, Men's 160, 165, 184, 192-211, 213, 227-9, 303, 305
Future Tours Program, Women's 209-10
'Gang of Three' 12, 157-61, 178, 206, 212-3, 280, 295
Global Development Manager 213
Global Development Program 17-18, 136, 153, 212-16, 220-26
'Hawke-Eye' 255
High Performance Manager 217-8
High Performance Programme 173, 217-20, 222, 225
'Hot Spot' 256
ICC Business Co. 157
ICC Development (International) Ltd 136, 157
ICC Trophy 110-11, 113-4, 119-20, 135, 169
Imperial Cricket Memorial 63
Intercontinental Cup 142, 218, 224-5
Intercontinental Shield 219
International Referees Panel 241
Intimidatory bowling and 14, 70-2, 107, 119, 122, 124-5
Kerry Packer and 98-106, 124, 200
League 2 223
Mandatory Release System 226-7
Match referees 133, 249-52
Media rights 148, 153, 157-8, 166
'Most Productive Overs' 170, 257
Name of 13-14, 65, 68, 131, 134
Olympic Games and 285-98
Project USA 144
Rankings, individual 198
Rankings, team 198-9, 246
Regional Development Officers 213
Rules of 30-3, 41-2, 46-7, 74-5, 135-6, 162
Six Nations Challenge 217
Slow over rates and 125
Spirit of Cricket 13

Super League 180, 204, 207, 211, 223, 227-8
Technology, use of 17, 252-3
Test cricket and 14
Throwing 70-2, 84-5, 258-60
Triangular cricket tournament 22, 24-37
T20 format 223-4
T20 Champions' Cup, Women's 241
T20 World Cup, Men's 148, 161, 163, 167, 169, 176-7, 185-91, 224, 227
T20 World Cup, Women's 233-4, 236, 241
Umpires' Panels 116-7, 125, 127-8, 249, 262-3, 268
Women's Championship 204, 209, 237, 243
Women's Committee 230, 232, 237, 240
Woolf review 11-12, 150-6, 212
World Cricket League 173, 215, 217, 219-24, 264-5
World Cup, Men's 15, 92, 95, 110-11, 117, 120, 123, 132, 137-9, 140-1, 143, 147, 148-9, 151, 161, 167, 169-82, 193, 215, 297, 305
World Cup, Women's 161, 209, 232-3, 238, 241
World Test Championship 163-4, 194-5, 203-5, 207, 225
International Olympic Committee 136, 226, 285-91, 293-4, 297-8
International League T20 302
International Wanderers 112
International Women's Cricket Council 17, 230
IWCC Trophy 231
Women's World Cup 230
Inzamam-ul-Haq 174-5, 261-2, 300
Iran 140
Irani, Ali 276
Iredale, Frank 28
Ireland 13, 173-4, 186, 216
and the Commonwealth Games 288
full membership 164, 210, 225
Irfan Ahmed 283
Isaac, Alan 156
Isle of Man 140
Israel 97-8, 114
Italy 140
Iyer, Usha 74

Ja'afar, Tuanku 287-8
Jadeja, Ajay 276
Jamaica 38
Jameson, Leander Starr 25
Jameson Raid 22, 25
Japan 140, 230
Jardine, Douglas 48-9
Javed, Miandad 123
Jayasinghe, Sunil 110
Jayasundara, Sanath 283
Jayasuriya, Sanath 175
Jellicoe, Admiral Earl 44
Johnson, Ian 127
Jones, Dean 269-70
Jones, Geraint 226
JP Sport 98-9, 101

Kallicharan, Alvin 115
Kallis, Jacques 172
Kapil Dev 111, 276
Karim Sadiq 214-5
Kaur, Harmanpreet 238
Kelleway, Charlie 36
Kelly, W.L. 45-6
Kempster, Michael, QC 103
Kendix, David 198
Kenya 88, 113, 143-4, 171
Kerr, J.L. 78
Khalid Mahmood 270
Khan Mohammad 64
King, Bennett 200
King, Collis 111, 115
King, Justice Edwin 274-5
Kipling Rudyard 23-4
Kitchener, Lord (Aldwyn Roberts) 67
Klusener, Lance 172
Knott, Alan 102, 112
Kochchar, Mukesh 277
Köster, Maartje 239
Kohli, Virat 181, 185, 187
Kolkata Knight Riders 304
KPMG 141
Kumble, Anil 254

Labuschagne, Marnus 181
Lacey, Francis 22-3, 44
Lakshmi, G.S. 241
Lamb, Tim 135, 172-3, 197
Lancashire Evening Post 23
Lanning, Meg 236
Lara, Brian 300-1
Larwood, Harold 48-9, 50
Laughton, Nigel 214
Laver, Frank 32
Law, Stuart 300
Laws of Cricket 13, 17, 37-8, 46, 52-3, 56, 71-2, 83-6, 93, 107, 117, 119, 263, 267
Lawson, Geoff 272
Lee, Brett 254

Lehmann, Darren 265-6, 289
Leicester Mercury 119, 121
Letsaolo, Marcia 238
Leveson-Gower, H.D.G 31, 44, 59
Lewis, Tony 257
Lewisham, Viscount 48
Limaye, Vikram 162
Lindsay, Denis 250-1
Lloyd, Clive 95, 99, 171, 249
Lloyd, David 267
Lokuarachchi, Kaushal 281
London Declaration 64-5
Long, Jon 293-4
Lord, David 100
Lord's Cricket Ground 13, 16, 21, 70, 136-7, 168
Lorgat, Haroon 146-7, 165, 176-7, 203-6, 212, 222, 229, 255-6, 264-5, 278, 301-2
Loubser, Sunette 233
Lowry, Tom 43

Macartney, Charlie 35
Macdonald, Dr Robbie 48
MacLaren, A.C. 39
Mackerduj, Krish 134-5
Madan Lal 114
Madugalle, Ranjan 255, 262
Mailer, Dr Ramsay 38
Majid Khan 251
Majola, Gerald 201-2
Major League Cricket (USA) 145, 302
Malaya 34, 55
Malaysia 82
Mali, Ray 141, 146-7
Malik Mohammad Qayyum 272-4
Mallett, R.H. 48, 54
Manase, Wilson 142
Mandela, Nelson 128
Mandhana, Smriti 297
Mankad, Vinoo 58
Manning, L.V. 55
Manohar, Shashank 161-3, 165, 295, 307
Marder, N.N. 83
Marsh, Geoff 123
Marsh, Mitchell 189
Martin-Jenkins, Christopher 135-6
Martineau, H.M. 55
Marylebone Cricket Club (MCC) 13, 14, 17, 26-7, 29, 33, 36-7, 53, 54-6, 62-3, 67-8, 131, 133, 168, 263
  and associate membership 81-2
  and Bodyline 49-51
  and South African

question 79, 88-9, 91-2
World Cricket Committee 180, 135, 294-6
Maxwell. Glenn 181-2
May, Tim 137, 200, 269-71
Mazhar Majeed 278-9
McAlister, P.A. 31
McClements, Brandan 261
McCollum, Ross 210
McDermott, Craig 123
McElhone, William 30, 32
McGlew, Jackie 249
McGrath, Glenn 172
McKechnie, Brian 117
McLaurin, Lord 174
McMillan, Craig 300
McWhirter, Norris 126
Meckiff, Ian 70, 84
Meiyappan, Gurunath 161
Mendis, Duleep 110
Menzies, R.G. (later Sir Robert) 63
Merriman, Bob 138, 141, 251
Meshram, Mona 238
Metbank 142-3
Miller, E.W. 96
Miller, Keith 59
Modi, Lalit 183, 199, 202, 299-300
Modi, Narendra 167
Mohammad Amir 185, 278-9
Mohammad Ashraful 280-1
Mohammad Asif 278-9
Mohammad Hafeez 260
Mohammad Irfan 281
Mohammad Nabi 214-5
Mohammad Naveed 282-3
Mongia, Nayan 276
Monro, Hector 108
Morgan, David 204, 261, 291
Morgan, Eoin 214, 219, 226
Morild, Carsten 111
Morocco 226
Morris, Christy 43
Morrison, William (Jamaica) 38
Morritt, Andrew, QC 104
Mortensen, Ole 111, 120
Mozambique 140
Mudgal, Judge Mukul 11, 150, 161
Mugabe, Robert 140, 172, 201
Mukuhlani, Tavengwa 210
Muldoon, Robert 110
Munawar, Aneel 281-2
Muralitharan, Muttiah 258-9
Murray, David 115
Mushtaq Ali 174
Mustafa Kamal 294
Muzaffar Husain 76, 78, 81
Myanmar 140
Myburgh, Stephan 187

Nadeem Ahmed 283
Naruddin Khawaja 277
Naseebullah Haqqani 244
Naseem Ashraf 141, 263
National Anti-Doping Agency (India) 296
Nawroz Mangal 221
Neesham, Jimmy 179-80
Nepal 140, 264-5
Netherlands 15, 82, 119-20, 180-1, 185-6, 189-90, 216, 227-8, 230, 260-1
New Zealand 41, 43, 45, 111, 169, 178, 193
New Zealand Cricket Council 39, 132
  and South African question 78-9
News of the World 278
Noble, Monty 29
Nourse, Dave 35
Nunes, Karl 65, 69

O'Brien, Kevin 178, 220
O'Brien, Niall 219, 226
Observer, The 27
Obuya, David 220
Odoyo, Thomas 143, 220
Odumbe, Maurice 143
'Old Cricketer' 28-9
Oldfield, Bill 49
Olonga, Henry 140-1
Oman 188, 217
One-Day Internationals 193-4, 207-8, 226, 237
  ODI status, women's 242-3
Opatha, Tony 111, 114
Osman Samiuddin 276
Osborne, Erin 235

Packer, Kerry 15-16, 95-106, 124, 170, 200, 208, 270, 299
Paine, Tim 266
Pakistan 60-2, 111, 112, 117, 118
  Terror attack (2009) 147, 177, 184
Pakistan Board of Control 63-4, 68, 131-2, 147-8, 160, 167, 177, 194, 199, 206, 237, 262-3, 270-3
  and associate membership 80-1
  and corruption 270-3, 276-80, 281
  and South African question 76-7, 107
Palairet, Richard 54
Palmer, Charles 108
Pamensky, Joe 94-5, 112-3, 127
Pandya, Hardik 185
Papua New Guinea 114
Parish, Bob 99

INDEX

Pataudi, Nawab of 47-8
Patel, Dipak 122
Patel, Sanjay 160
Paterson, Grant 120
Patiala, Maharajah of 44
Pawar, Sharad 146-7, 183, 292
PBL Marketing 104-5
Pearce, T.N. 86
Pentelow, J.N. 39
Perry, Ellyse 234, 235-6
Philadelphia 24, 39, 43, 287
Pietersen, Kevin 262
PILCOM 134
Poidevin, Dr Leslie 28, 30-1
Pollock, Graeme 99
Pollock, Shaun 172, 289
Polosak, Claire 241
Ponting, Ricky 173, 253, 289
Pope, Richard 290-1
Porterfield, William 220
Portus, Marc 259
Potter, Sarah 230
Prabhakar, Manoj 276
Prashad, Paul 120
Preston, Norman 78, 80
PricewaterhouseCoopers 11, 150, 165
Pritchard, Norman 286
Procter, Mike 99-100, 103, 254, 261-2
Project USA *See* ICC
Pycroft, Andy 114

Qadeer Ahmed Khan 282-3
Qasim Omar 272-3

Radford, Neal 126
Ramadhin, Sonny 66-7
Ramsamy, Sam 121
Ranatunga, Arjuna 258
Ranga Rao, K.S. 58
Ranjitsinhji, K.S. 24
Rao, Sharad 278
Rashid, Adil 179
Rashid Khan 214-5
Rashid Latif 270
Redfern, Sue 241
Reiffel, Paul 172
Rhodes, Cecil 22
Rhodes, Harold 70, 85
Rhodes, Jonty 172
Rhodes, Wilfred 35-6
Rhodesia 62, 79
Rice, Clive 127
Richards, Barry 99
Richards, David 16, 118, 133-4, 146, 269-72
Richards, Viv 99, 111, 114
Richardson, David 146, 165, 204, 207, 237, 240-2, 252, 255, 258, 264-7, 280, 295

Rindel, Mike 289
Roberts, Andy 99
Roberts, Kevin 208
Robertson, Austin 98
Robins, Derrick 111
Robins, Walter 59
Rodda, John 109
Rodriques, Jemima 297
Rogge, Jacques 289
Rolton, Karen 239
Root, Joe 188
Rorke, Gordon 70, 84
Rowe, Lawrence 115
Roy, Jason 180
Russia 226

SANROC 121
Sachs, Alby 251, 278
Sadhu, Titas 297
Saeed Ajmal 260
Saeed Anwar 272
Safdar Butt 121
Salve, N.K.P. 121, 138
Samani, Ravi 264-5
Samiullah Shenwari 214-5
Samoa 34
Samuels, Marlon 188, 277
Sangakkara, Kumar 175, 187
Sarfraz Nawaz 270
Sawhney, Manu 143, 165, 208, 241, 295-6
Scotland 220
Seelaar, Pieter 214
Sehwag, Virender 137, 250-1
Selborne, Earl of 25
Selvey, Mike 121, 132
Sewell, Edward 47
Shah, Amit 166
Shah, Jay 166-8, 209, 298
Shah, Niranjan 184, 200
Shaharyar Khan 261, 277, 279
Shaiman Anwar 282-3
Shakoor Rana 125, 248
Sharjah 193
Sharma, Ajay 276
Sharma, Deepti 238
Sharmin Akter 234
Shaw, Nicki 233
Shields, Mark 174
Shepherd, David 249, 260-1
Shepherd, John 111
Shiv Sena 177
Short, Peter 103
Simpson, Bob 271
Sims, Arthur 65, 68-71, 77
Sind 62
Singapore 110, 119, 264-5
Singh, Harbhajan 254-5, 259

Singh, Lall 47
Sirajuddin Haqqani 244
Slade, Mr Justice 104
Slater, Keith 70
Slynn, Mr Justice 101
Smith, Alan 120, 132
Smith, Cammie 249
Smith, Mike 249
Smith, Steve 178, 266-7
Smith, Sydney 36, 38-9, 42-3, 49
Snedden, Martin 210
Snow, John 100, 102
Snow, Philip 82
South Africa 21, 25, 29-30, 32-3, 36, 44, 53, 65-6, 68-70, 73-80, 88-92, 94-5, 106-7, 108-10, 128, 169-70, 172
  apartheid in 14, 73-6
  isolation of 90-1, 106-7, 118, 123, 127, 131, 132
  rebel tours of 111-12, 114-6, 127
  turf wickets in 45
  withdrawal from Commonwealth 73
South African African Cricket Board 74-5, 94
South African Bantu Cricket Board 75
South African Coloured Cricket Board 75
South African Cricket Association 23, 27, 33, 45, 53, 59, 74-6, 89, 91, 94, 106
South African Cricket Board of Control (SACBOC) 74-5, 88, 94-5, 106
South African Cricket Board 106, 109, 116, 128
South African Cricket Union 94-5, 106, 109, 112-3, 116, 127-8
South African Indian Cricket Union 75
South African Republic 22
South African Sports Association 71, 74
South African War (1899-1902) 14, 22, 25, 286-7
Southerton, S.J. 49
Speed Malcolm 16, 142, 146, 174, 184, 194-5, 198-201, 203, 253-4, 261-2, 272, 275-6
Sportsman, The 26, 30, 36
Sreesanth, Shanta 281
Sri Lanka 15, 92, 95-7, 114, 123, 124
Sri Lanka Board 132, 162
Srinivasan, Narayanaswami 154, 156-7, 161, 256, 300-1
Stanford, Allen 202
Starc, Mitchell 181, 304

319

Steele, Ray 103, 105
Stephenson, John 121-4, 126, 131, 133
Stern, Steven 257
Stirling, Paul 214, 219
Stokes, Ben 179-80, 188, 190
Strauss, Andrew 303
Straw, Jack 196
Streak, Heath 140-1, 196, 281
Strydom, Pieter 273-4
Subba Row, Raman 105, 122, 249
Sudan 34
Sunrisers Hyderabad 304
Suriname 224
Sutherland, James 154, 266, 290
Swan, Henry 44
Swanton, E.W. 54
Switzerland 119, 140
Sydney Morning Herald 118
Symonds, Andrew 253-4

Tableeghi Jamat 273
Taibu, Tatenda 141, 253
Talat Ali 174
Taliban 243-5
Tamil Tigers 170
Tasmania 34
Taufel, Simon 147, 179, 256-7, 263
Taylor, Claire 239
Taylor, Sarah 233, 235
Taylor, Stafanie 233, 235-6
Tendulkar, Sachin 137, 250-2, 255
Tennyson, Lord 55
Test cricket
  Women's 238-9
Test and County Cricket Board (TCCB) 113, 117, 120, 125, 132-3
  and Packer case 101-4
Thailand, women's cricket in 238, 242-3
Thatcher, Margaret 108, 110
Thomas, Devon 283
Tiffin, Russell 249
Tikolo, Steve 143, 220
Tikolo, Tom 144
Timmer, Betty 230
Toller, Montagu 286
Tonga 226
Trade Union and Labour Relations Act (UK) 103
Triangular Tournament *See* ICC
Tsolekile, Thami 281
Tuba Sangar 244
Turnbull, Malcolm 266
Turner, Mike 119, 121
Turner, Ross 213

UAE Cricket Board 283
Uganda 231
Umar Gul 262
Underwood, Derek 112
Union des Sociétés Françaises de Sports Athlétiques 286
United Arab Emirates 136, 140, 177, 188, 216-7
United Cricket Board of South Africa 128, 170, 274
United States 15, 80, 98, 110, 119, 144-6, 190, 217, 264-5
USA Cricket Association 144-5, 302
USA Cricket 145-6

Valentine, Alf 66-7
Van der Merwe, Pieter 249
Vanuatu 167
Varachia, Rachid 94-5, 109
Vaughan, John 110
Vengsarkar, Dilip 111
Venkataraghavan, Srini 249
Vereeniging, Treaty of 22
Verwoerd, Hendrik 73-4, 76
Victoria Club (London) 38
Vincent, Lou 281
Vizianagram, Maharajkumar of 70
Voce, Bill 48, 52
Vorster, Johannes 88-9, 111

Walcott, Clyde 66, 133, 134-5, 136, 271
Wales 110
Waller, Malcolm 260
Warne, Shane 171-2, 173, 269-71, 273
Warner, David 266-7
Warner, Sir Pelham 34, 39, 48
Warr, J.J. 97
Wasim Akram 123, 272
Wasim Bari 260-1
Washbrook. Cyril 84
Watmore, Ian 296
Wattenberg, Violet 239
Waugh, Mark 271, 273, 289
Waugh, Steve 171, 289
Weekes, Everton 66
Weeraratna, Senaka 253, 255
Wessels, Kepler 170
West Africa 110, 113, 119
West Indies 43-4, 45, 62, 66-7, 95, 111, 124, 173-6, 192-3
West Indies Cricket Board 65-6, 97, 116, 131-2, 195, 277
  and associate membership 81
  and Olympic Games 288, 291
  and South African question 90, 107, 120-1

West Indies Cricket Conference 41
Western Australia, University of 258, 260
Westfield, Mervyn 277-8
Weston, Daniel 305
Wettimuny, Sunil 111
Wisden Cricketers' Almanack 49, 66, 78-9, 85, 124-5, 133, 146-7, 183, 194, 230, 273
White, Gordon 35
Williams, Craig 219
Williams, Jacqueline 241
Williamson, Kane 189
Wilson, Des 196-7
Women's Cricket Association 230
Wood Mark 179
Woodfull, Bill 48-9
Woolf, Lord, of Barnes 11-12, 18, 150, 153, 156, 158, 212, 305-7
Woolley, Frank 36
Woolmer, Bob 112, 174-5, 217-8, 262
World Anti Doping Agency 291-2, 296
World Cup, Men's *see* ICC
World Rugby 306
World Series Cricket 99, 104, 155
World Sports Nimbus 139
Worrell, Frank 66
Worsley, Sir William 78
Wran, Neville 104
Wright, Graeme 124-5
Wynyard, Ernest 24

Yallop, Richard 108
Yardley, Norman 84-5
Young, Brad 288-9
Younis, Ahmed 111

Zafar Altaf 98
Zaheer Abbas 262
Zambia 226
Zee TV 299
Zimbabwe 13, 113-4, 120, 122, 124, 132, 140-3, 162, 163, 170, 172-3, 201
Zimbabwe XI 219
Zimbabwe Cricket Union (later Zimbabwe Cricket) 196-7, 201
Zulqarnain Haider 279-80